THE SECRETARY'S SECRET

BY
MICHELLE DOUGLAS

AND

RODEO DADDY

BY
SORAYA LANE

MILLS & BOON

THE SECRETARY'S SECRET

BY
MICHELLE DOUGLAS

First published in Great Britain 2011
by Mills & Boon, an imprint of Harlequin (UK) Limited,
Eton House, 18-24 Paradise Road, Richmond, Surrey TW9 1SR

© Michelle Douglas 2011

ISBN: 978 0 263 88922 2

23-1111

Harlequin (UK) policy is to use papers that are natural, renewable and recyclable products and made from wood grown in sustainable forests. The logging and manufacturing processes conform to the legal environmental regulations of the country of origin.

Printed and bound in Spain
by Blackprint CPI, Barcelona

At the age of eight **Michelle Douglas** was asked what she wanted to be when she grew up. She answered, "A writer." Years later she read an article about romance writing and thought, *Ooh, that'll be fun.* She was right. When she's not writing she can usually be found with her nose buried in a book. She is currently enrolled in an English Masters programme for the sole purpose of indulging her reading and writing habits further. She lives in a leafy suburb of Newcastle, on Australia's east coast, with her own romantic hero—husband Greg, who is the inspiration behind all her happy endings. Michelle would love you to visit her at her website: www.michelle-douglas.com.

To my grandparents, Bunny and Beryl Snaddon,
with love and thanks for all those
wonderful summer holidays!

PROLOGUE

THE intercom on Kit's desk buzzed and instantly her heart hammered up into her throat.

'If you'd come through now, Ms Mercer.'

Kit's toes curled at the rich black-coffee voice. Her heart lurched back into her chest to thump out a loud tattoo. When she leant forward to depress a button, her finger was surprisingly steady given what was happening to the rest of her body. 'Certainly, sir.'

Her finger might be steady but the huskiness of her voice was more Marilyn Monroe than sensible, strait-laced secretary. It should appall her, belying as it did her attempts to match her employer's professional formality, but it didn't. His formality made her lips twitch.

That formality delighted her; energized her.

She seized her shorthand pad and tried to stop herself from racing straight into his office. Cool. Calm. Collected. Her smile widened. No hope of that whatsoever!

Still, she paused at the door to smooth a hand down her skirt. Adjusted her shirt. Undid her top button. Her fingers lingered at her throat, remembering…

Heat rose up through her. Anticipation fired along each and every one of her nerve endings.

She did her best to dispel the images that rose up through her. She didn't want to appear like a trembly, needy teenager in the throes of her first crush. She wanted to look like a woman in control, like a woman who knew what she wanted. She wanted to look seductive.

She bit her lip to rein in a smile. What she wanted was for Alex to take one look at her, grin that sexy grin of his and take her in his arms. Kiss her. To sweep the polished surface of his enormous desk clear and make love to her.

Her legs grew languid, her breasts pushed against the crisp cotton of her shirt. She gulped in a steadying breath. *Stop it!* Alex had indicated how he wanted to play this. And last night had proved just how well she and Alex played together. She smiled again. She couldn't seem to stop smiling. They'd play it Alex's way this morning. Tonight they'd—

No. There'd be plenty of time to think about that later.

She lifted a hand to check her neat, businesslike bun and then, swallowing back her excitement, she pushed through the door, chin held high. 'Good morning, sir.' She made her voice brisk.

'Take a seat, Ms Mercer.' He nodded to her shorthand pad. 'You won't need that.'

She placed it on the desk in front of her then very carefully folded her hands together in her lap and waited for a cue. She loved that oh-so-serious look on his face, couldn't wait until he said something sexy and husky in that masculine burr of his. She couldn't wait to take the pins from her hair, to shake it out till it fell around her shoulders in a newly washed cloud, and to then walk around this enormous desk of his. No, not walk—sashay. She'd sashay slowly around to him like the siren she was starting to think she was.

The siren she'd become in his arms.

Once she was face to face with him she'd slide up to sit on his desk. She'd cross one leg over the other, making sure the action hitched up her skirt to reveal the silky tops of her stockings, held in place by a lacy suspender belt the colour of coffee cream. Then she'd undo the buttons on her blouse, her fingers lingering over each one, until she'd revealed breasts practically spilling out of the tiniest wisp of lace imaginable in matching coffee cream.

And she wanted to watch his face while she did it.

She zeroed in on his face now, holding her breath and waiting for her cue, aching to play out that fantasy. His lips opened, lean and firm, and the breath hitched in her throat. Thick, hot yearning tumbled through her.

This man was all she'd ever dreamed of and more. Last night had revealed that to her in undeniable glory. They'd moved together with an accord that had been more than physical. Last night had been the most wonderful night of her life. When Alex's passion and gentleness and generosity as a lover had touched her soul.

Words emerged from those lean lips of his. Kit relished their black-coffee timbre, savoured their resonance, and drew in deep breaths of his dark malt scent. She'd caught a trace of that scent on her sheets this morning. She'd placed those sheets in the washing machine with a faint sense of regret before she'd left for work. She'd cheered herself with the thought that it'd take more than laundry powder and water to wash those memories away. Of course, there were all those new memories they'd make too and—

'Kit?'

The staccato whip of Alex's voice hauled her out of her thoughts. It hit her then that she'd been so busy relishing and savouring that she hadn't taken in a single word he'd said. 'I'm sorry.' She glanced down the length of her nose at him in as cheeky a fashion as she dared. 'I was a million miles away.'

It took an effort of will to hold back her smile.

He let out a breath and glared. She blinked and sat back with a frown. What on earth had she missed? Had something gone awry with the Dawson deal? The deal Alex had been chasing for the last eight months. The deal that they'd clinched and then in their elation…

He leant forward and his glare intensified. 'Do I have your full attention?'

She swallowed. 'Yes.'

'I was saying that what happened last night was unfortunate and regrettable.'

Each word was clipped out with precision. Short, sharp, unmistakable. Barbs, bayonets, slashing at her. Kit flinched and half lifted an arm as if to ward them off.

No!

His mouth grew straighter, grimmer. 'I'm sure you agree.'

Unfortunate? Regrettable? Her stomach tumbled in sudden confusion. How could he say that? Last night had been wonderful.

'I beg your pardon?' She prayed he wouldn't repeat it. She prayed she'd heard him wrong.

He held her gaze. Unlike her, he didn't flinch. He looked cold, hard…alien. 'This time I believe you heard what I said. And that you understand exactly what I mean.'

The room spun. She gripped the edge of her chair and hung on tight, praying her sense of balance would return and halt this sensation of endless freefall.

A denial sprang to her lips as the room and Alex swam back into her line of sight. *He was wrong!*

She released her iron grip on her chair. 'Let me get this right.' Her hands trembled. Perspiration gathered beneath the collar of her shirt, beneath the underwire of her bra. 'You're saying you wish last night never happened?' The perfectly monitored air-conditioned air chilled the skin at her throat, at her nape, of her bare-but-for-nylons legs. She resisted the urge to chafe her arms. 'That you…*regret* last night?'

'That's exactly what I'm saying.'

She stared into his face—cold, hard, the face of a stranger—and greyness leached in at the edges of her consciousness, swamping her joy, blanketing her in a thick fog that her mind struggled to think through.

The air conditioning chilled a layer of ice around her heart, numbed her brain and robbed her eyes and mouth of all natural moisture. She'd never realized before how much she hated air conditioning.

Beyond Alex, through the floor-to-ceiling plate-glass window, morning light glinted off the white sails of the Sydney Opera House with an absurd gaiety that was reflected in a thousand different points of light in the water of the harbour.

How had she read this man, this situation, so wrong? She lifted her hands to massage her temples. She wasn't some doe-eyed schoolgirl easily seduced.

No hot-blooded woman would deny Alex's all-male magnetism, and last night she had most definitely been hot-blooded.

But not doe-eyed!

A demon of panic clawed at her throat. *This wasn't how it was supposed to end.* He couldn't deny this connection that existed between them.

She dragged her gaze from the sight of the harbour, alive with yachts and ferries, to the man on the other side of the desk. He leaned towards her and she forgot to breathe. What would he do if she leaned across the table too and pressed her lips to his? She'd bet her bottom dollar it'd drive the deep freeze from his eyes.

He jerked back, folded his arms. His face became even

more stony and unreadable. 'It can never happen again.' He must've registered her shock because he added, 'Not that I'm denying it was enjoyable, pleasurable.'

His eyes darkened, as if in memory of the amazing things they'd done together last night, and everything inside her clenched.

'Nevertheless, it cannot happen again.'

'Why not?' The question slipped out of her like the air from a slowly deflating party balloon. She knew it wasn't what he'd wanted her to say. She hitched up her chin. Why shouldn't she ask? It wasn't as if she had anything to lose.

Except a good job.

Well, okay, it was a great job.

And maybe some pride.

She pushed her shoulders back. Who gave two hoots about pride at a time like this? And good jobs were a dime a dozen to someone with her qualifications. 'Why not?' she repeated, louder this time.

'Because you're the best damn secretary I've ever had!' He slammed his hand down on the desk, the force half spinning him in his chair. He glared at the wall to her left. 'And I don't want to ruin a great working relationship by sleeping with you.'

Why were men so afraid to call it making love? She stared at him, willing him to meet her eye, silently urging him to unsay his words and to put this right. When he didn't she said, 'From memory, there wasn't much sleeping involved.'

She cleared her throat and leaned towards him. 'And, for the record, I don't think it was unfortunate and I certainly don't regret it.' *So there.* All his square-jawed, broad-shouldered, tight-buttocked masculinity could take that!

One of his superb shoulders shifted, its power barely disguised by the impeccable cut of his suit. She recalled the feel of the firm flesh of those shoulders beneath her fingertips, the crisp whorls of hair on his chest, and her mouth went dry. She recalled the silky hardness of him and her body's delight at his touch with a clarity that made her insides tremble. She would never forget her soul's delight at a night of lovemaking that had blown her apart and put her back together again both at the same time.

He pushed out of his chair. 'It can't happen again.'

Oh, yes, it could. And so, *so* easily.

He shoved his hands into his pockets and pinned her to the spot with his dark, frigid eyes. 'And it won't happen again, Katherine, because I don't do long-term, I don't do marriage and babies, and I certainly don't do happy families.'

He'd called her Kit last night, not Katherine.

'And if I continue to sleep with you you're going to eventually realize I'm telling you the truth and that you can't change me. Then you'll get hurt and angry, there'll be ugly scenes and recriminations and then you'll up and leave without giving me so much as a week's notice.'

It took a moment for the actuality of his words to sink in. When they did, her jaw slackened. He had to be joking, right? These couldn't be his actual thought processes.

His dark hair glinted almost black to the Opera House's white. She stared at him and her stomach billowed with an inexplicable emptiness as the scales finally fell from her eyes. For the last eleven months she'd been in love with a lump of rock.

Alex Hallam was a lump of rock.

Not something light and porous like limestone either, but something hard and impenetrable.

Like granite.

CHAPTER ONE

'KATHERINE MERCER?'

The receptionist glanced up expectantly as Kit pushed through the door. Kit nodded and tried to find a smile. 'Yes, that's right.'

'Dr Maybury is almost running on time. If you'd take a seat, she shouldn't be too much longer.'

Kit smiled her thanks. The surgery had managed to fit her in for the last appointment of the day and the waiting room was deserted.

She sat. She crossed her legs and bounced her foot. She glanced at her watch. She shifted on her seat, glanced around the waiting room, glanced at her watch again and finally seized a magazine. It wasn't that doctors' surgeries made her nervous. It was just—

The magazine fell open to a celebrity wedding spread with the bride and groom in a variety of cheesy but romantic poses—arms wrapped around each other, staring deep into each other's eyes, feeding each other wedding cake. For a moment all Kit could do was stare. And then she slapped it shut and shoved it back into the magazine rack.

All that giddy happiness.

She closed her eyes and pulled in a breath. It was three months almost to the day since Alex had so brutally ended their... She could hardly call it a relationship, and still there were images—like the ones in that magazine—snatches of conversation, a scent, that could hurtle her back in time and remind her of her stupidity. Remind her of the ridiculous dreams she'd woven about a man who hadn't been worth a single one of them. Reminded her of her appallingly bad judgement.

It was crazy too because she and Alex had hardly spent any time together during these last three months. He'd flown to the Brisbane headquarters of Hallam Enterprises the day after his no-nonsense rejection of her and he'd remained there for six weeks. He'd only been back in Sydney for two days when she'd found herself given the fancy title of Project Manager and moved to another department two floors down.

She'd welcomed that change, but... She uncrossed her right leg to cross her left leg instead. She bounced her left foot. She let out a breath and stared up at the ceiling. Was she becoming too hard to please? Was that it? It was just... The project she was heading up was one that had previously excited her. She should be raring to go, eager, engaged. But she traipsed into her office each day as if she had nothing more interesting to do than filing and data entry.

Why?

She was the one who'd urged Alex to pursue the book deal McBride's Proprietary Press had offered him over four months ago. And she was the one who'd hoped she'd get the chance to head the project up.

Midway through last year, she'd written a profile on Alex for a book titled *Australia's Most Successful Entrepreneurs*. That had led to a whole chapter in another book called *Advice From Australia's CEOs*. Now McBride's were launching a new series called *From Go to Whoa*, and they wanted a book with Alex's name on the cover detailing a land development project from its earliest stages through to the final development. The title they'd floated was *Commercial Land Development: from Scrubland to Shopping Mall*. Kit had already substituted *shopping mall* with *sports resort*.

She should *love* what she was doing.

Her eyes narrowed. Had she lost her zest for life because a man had disappointed her? *Pathetic!*

She slapped her hands down onto her knees and glared at the wall opposite. From now on, whenever thoughts of Alex surfaced she was ousting them out of her head pronto. It was time she started having fun again.

She brightened marginally. At least for the next three weeks she didn't have to worry about running into Alex, didn't have to steel herself for accidental meetings in the corridors at work, there wouldn't even be the risk of catching an unexpected glimpse of him in the distance. A week ago he'd left for a month-long odyssey to Africa. Rumour had it that he was doing some kind of aid work.

Not that he struck her as the aid worker type.

She uncrossed her legs. Re-crossed them. Well, okay, maybe he had three and a half months ago, but not since—

No. She wasn't doing that any more. She was through thinking about Alex, through trying to work him out. 'Enough,' she muttered under her breath. She had more important things to think about.

Like the reason she was sitting in her doctor's waiting room at ten to five on a Friday afternoon.

She gripped her hands together. If this was what she thought it was, then…

She squared her shoulders. She'd get through it. Adjustments would be necessary, but it wouldn't be the end of the world. This could be taken care of.

'Ms Mercer?'

Kit jerked around at the receptionist's voice and tried to smile. Would she have to have a needle? She didn't like needles.

Of course you'll have to have a needle. The doctor will have to take blood.

The receptionist smiled kindly, as if she sensed Kit's nervousness. 'This way; the doctor is ready for you.'

Dr Maybury was middle-aged, kind and unfailingly practical. 'Now, Kit, it's been a while. What seems to be the problem?'

Kit pulled a face. No sense in beating about the bush. 'I'm worried I might have diabetes.' She pulled in a deep breath and quickly detailed her incredible thirst, her endless trips to the bathroom—especially at night. 'The thing is, though, that sometimes there's nothing, just a drop or two. And I'm so tired all the time. And hungry.'

'Dizziness? Nausea?'

'I've felt faint a couple of times.'

'Blurriness of vision?'

Kit shook her head.

'Well, let's not waste any more time.' Dr Maybury handed Kit a cup. 'We'll test your urine.'

Ten minutes later, Dr Maybury turned to her and folded her arms. 'I'm pleased to say you are not diabetic.'

Kit slumped in relief. 'Oh, that is good news! The thought of having to give myself daily insulin injections…' She shuddered.

'Kit, you're not diabetic, but you are pregnant.'

Kit blinked. She shook her head. 'What did you just say?'

The doctor repeated it.

She shook her head again. 'But...' Her chest tightened, her stomach cramped. 'But I can't be! I just had my period.'

'Some women maintain their period throughout their entire pregnancy.'

Kit could only stare. 'Heavens,' she found herself murmuring, 'how unfair is that?'

Dr Maybury smiled and Kit shook herself again. 'No, you don't understand. I can't be pregnant. I haven't had morning sickness and...and my breasts haven't been sore... and...I mean you have to have sex to get pregnant and I haven't had sex in, like, forever!'

She hadn't had sex since that magical night with Alex. Her mouth went dry. 'Except... One night...'

'One night is all it takes.'

'But...but that was three months ago.' She couldn't have been pregnant for three months and not known.

Could she?

She thrust out her arm. 'Please, do a blood test or...or something!'

'I will take blood and send it off to the lab to make a hundred per cent certain. But, Kit, the pregnancy test I just used is roughly ninety-seven per cent accurate. I can do an internal examination to eliminate that final three per cent of doubt if it will put your mind at rest.'

Kit nodded mutely.

After the internal exam and when Kit was dressed again, she forced herself to meet the doctor's eyes. 'Well?'

'There is not a doubt in my mind that you are pregnant. And, like you say, I'd put you at about three months. The results of the blood test will give us a better indication of your due date.'

She could tell the doctor the exact date of conception, only she didn't have the heart to.

'Kit, what do you want to do?'

She couldn't be pregnant. She just couldn't be. Alex, he'd…

She closed her eyes.

'If you'd prefer a termination, we can't leave it too much longer.'

Her eyes flew open.

'Do you want children, Kit?'

'Yes.' The word croaked out of her.

But she'd wanted to do it the right way—married, with a divine husband whom she adored and who adored her in return, and with a mortgage on a cute little house and… and planned. Not like this!

'You're twenty-eight. How much longer did you mean to leave it?'

She didn't have an answer for that. Through the fog of her shock, though, one thing started to become increasingly clear. She swallowed, twisted her hands together. 'I don't want to terminate my pregnancy.'

Her doctor smiled.

The answering smile that rose up through her suddenly froze. 'Oh, but I've been drinking tea first thing in the morning and again at lunchtime and—'

'You don't have to give up caffeine altogether. Are you exceeding more than three cups a day?'

'No.'

'Then that's okay. Alcohol?'

She winced. 'I usually have a glass on Friday and Saturday nights.'

'Any alcoholic binges in the last three months?'

'No.'

'Then there's nothing to worry about.'

'I haven't been taking folate.'

'You can start that today.'

Kit leaned forward. 'You really think my baby is okay?' She couldn't stand the thought that she might have somehow hurt her unborn child.

The doctor patted her hand. 'Kit, you are a healthy young woman. There's absolutely no reason to suppose your baby isn't healthy too.'

She let the doctor's words reassure her. Finally, that smile built up through her again. 'I'm really pregnant?' she whispered.

'You really are.'

'But that's lovely news.'

Alex Hallam wouldn't think it was lovely news.

The doctor laughed. 'Congratulations, Kit.'

Who cared what Alex Hallam thought? She was through thinking about him, remember? She beamed back at the doctor. 'Thank you.'

Pregnant!

Kit left the surgery and turned in the direction of the train station. When she arrived there she couldn't remember a single step of her journey.

Pregnant? A tentative excitement wrestled with her apprehension. One moment joy held sway. In the next, anxiety had gained the upper hand. An unplanned pregnancy? She gulped. It sounded so irresponsible. Irresponsible people shouldn't be allowed to raise children.

She hugged her handbag. No. She hadn't been irresponsible. She and Alex had taken precautions. It was just that sometimes, obviously, accidents happened.

She frowned over that word—*accident*. Her baby wasn't an accident. It was lovely, a miracle.

Alex wouldn't think their baby lovely. He'd definitely think it was an accident, a mistake. She closed her eyes. It was pointless telling herself now that she was through with thinking about Alex. They were having a baby. That changed everything.

Her hand moved to her abdomen, cradled it. She imagined the tiny life inside and her mouth went dry. How on earth would Alex react when she told him the news?

I don't do long-term, I don't do marriage and babies, and I certainly don't do happy families.

Nausea swirled through her. Her eyes stung. Would Alex reject their child as ruthlessly and dispassionately as he had rejected her? Her throat thickened and then closed over completely. When her train arrived she boarded it like an automaton, found a window seat and concentrated on her breathing.

A baby deserved a mother *and* a father. Had she robbed her child of that chance because she'd misjudged Alex so badly? She should pay for that mistake, not her baby. She'd messed everything up and now her baby would pay the price.

The rush and clatter of an oncoming train as it sped past her window made her flinch and then sit up suddenly straighter. What was she doing? She couldn't control how Alex would react, but she could control how she dealt with the news. She had a miracle growing inside her and she wanted this baby with every atom of her being. The weight pressing down on her shoulders melted away. A smile built up inside her.

She was having a baby!

The minute Kit entered her apartment she let out a whoop, shrugged her arms out of her coat and threw it up in the air. She was going to have a baby! And then she danced around the coffee table before falling onto the sofa and grinning at the blank screen of her television, at her sound system, at the magazines scattered on the coffee table.

She was going to be a mother.

Her hands formed a protective cocoon across her abdomen. 'I'm going to be the best mother that ever walked the earth,' she vowed, making the promise out loud to her unborn child.

And Alex *I-don't-do-happy-families* Hallam?

She lifted her chin and pushed all thoughts of Alex aside for a moment. He was out of contact for the next three weeks and she wasn't going to let thoughts of him darken her day or dim her joy. He might not do happy families but she did!

She reached for the phone and dialled her mother's number in Brisbane. Today was for joy. 'Mum, I have some wonderful news.'

'Ooh, do tell, darling.'

She heard her mother's grin down the line. It widened hers. 'Mum, I'm going to have a baby!'

She held the phone away from her ear as her mother squealed her delight. 'Darling, I'm so happy for you! I can't wait to be a grandma. When are you due?'

Kit counted six months off on her fingers. Was that how one did it? She shrugged. 'Some time in March, I think.'

'I'll take holidays,' her mother vowed. 'I want to be there for you.' There was a slight pause. 'And the daddy?'

'He doesn't know yet…and he's not going to be thrilled. I…um…got him all wrong.'

'Oh, darling.'

Kit's eyes filled at the sympathy in her mother's voice. 'Do you really think I have to tell him?' Keeping it from him, would that be so bad?

'Yes, darling, you must.'

Kit knew her mother was right.

'Are you quite sure you got him so wrong?'

'Quote: I don't do long-term. I don't do happy families.

End quote. I don't think he could've made it any plainer, do you?'

Her mother exhaled one indignant breath.

She shook her head at the remembered pain of his words. It didn't matter. Not any more. 'It was a learning experience. The baby and I will be just fine. We'll be better off without him.'

'I'm sure you will be,' her mother agreed, 'but what about him? Will he be better off without you and the baby?'

She snorted. 'Of course not. But, as you and Grandma have always said, you can lead a horse to water...' Still, if Alex did want to be involved...

'I see.' A pause. 'Not all men are like your father, Kitty-Kat.'

She smiled at the childhood nickname. 'I know, Mum. And I will tell him about the baby. Just as soon as he gets back from Africa next month.' And who knew, maybe Alex would surprise her.

'Good. So tell me...'

She had a vision of her mother settling into her favourite armchair, feet tucked beneath her.

'What are your plans? Do you mean to stay in Sydney?'

What was she going to do? Kit wriggled around until she lay on her back. She propped an ankle on the arm of the sofa. She'd never envisaged raising children in the city. She'd always thought...

She gave a sudden laugh as she realized exactly what she was going to do. 'I'm going to go home, Mum. I'm going to raise my child in Tuncurry. It was a wonderful place to grow up.'

'Your grandmother will be thrilled!'

Kit started mentally writing her resignation letter. She'd give two weeks' notice on Monday.

CHAPTER TWO

'GOOD morning, Mr Hallam.'

'Phillip.' Alex inclined his head as he exited the elevator on the top floor of Hallam Enterprises' Sydney office. He told himself that eventually he'd get used to seeing Phillip rather than Kit behind that desk.

'It's good to have you back, sir.'

'Thank you.' Alex walked through to his office. He closed the door behind him and glanced around. Everything was neat, tidy and shining. Outside the window, the harbour sparkled in the early spring sunlight.

Nothing had changed.

Except Kit no longer sat at that desk in the foyer.

It had been almost four months since he and Kit had…

He dragged a hand down his face to try and dispel images that were still far too vivid.

He dropped into his chair. This last month in Africa had provided him with some perspective, given him some distance. It had renewed his determination, had allowed him to gather his strength again. With Kit, he'd made a mistake. He'd paid dearly for that mistake too. He'd made love to her and in the next instant the nightmares about little Chad had started up again. He couldn't go there, couldn't do that again. Not for anyone. Not even for Kit.

He'd learned his lesson and he would never make the same mistake again. Not with Kit. Not with any woman.

He swung in his chair to survey the harbour, a scowl building through him. Reckless. Idiotic. That was what he'd been. He should've taken more care around her. He should've…

He shouldn't have hurt her.

The knowledge that he had pounded at him, lashed him with guilt. Even now. She deserved so much more than anything he could ever offer her. She deserved the best. She would never find the best with him. He didn't do family, forever and commitment. He couldn't do it.

He tried to focus on the scene before him, willed himself to appreciate its beauty. When that didn't work he dragged a hand down his face. It took an effort of will to stop his shoulders from slumping. He'd regret hurting Kit till the day he died, that was something he couldn't change. But no doubt she'd found a way to move on and so had he.

There was just one more test.

He leant across and pressed a button on his intercom. 'Phillip, can you set up a meeting with Kit Mercer for some time tomorrow afternoon.'

There was a hesitation at the other end of the line. 'Sir, Kit resigned. All the details are in a file in your in-box. She finished up at the end of the week before last.'

Alex didn't say anything. He sat back and stared at the intercom. He stared at his in-box. He tried to work out how he felt.

Betrayal. And relief.

The betrayal was nonsense. Kit owed him nothing.

He rubbed the back of his neck. Relief? Maybe she was right. Maybe this was the answer—cut all ties and never clap eyes on each other again.

He leapt up, paced, stopped to track the Manly ferry's

progress into Circular Quay, and remembered Kit telling him how much she loved working for Hallam Enterprises. She'd said it was her dream job. He remembered her smile, the way her eyes had shone…and her gratitude to him. *To him!* His mouth dried. That had been the same day they'd clinched the Dawson deal, and that night they'd made love.

His hands clenched. He recalled how, in their few meetings since then, two faint lines would appear on her forehead whenever she looked at him and how her eyes would dim. He'd taken her dream job, all the satisfaction she found in her work, and had turned it to ashes.

Letting her walk away, never having to see her again, that would be easy. It'd also be incredibly selfish. Kit had loved her job. She shouldn't be made to suffer on his account any more than she already had. He had to make this right!

He swore loud and hard. That was what his trip to Africa had been about—wanting to do something positive rather than negative, helping rather than hurting, making someone's life a bit better rather than a bit worse. He'd needed to feel that he could make a difference in a good way instead of a bad one.

Letting Kit walk away was making a difference in a bad way. He'd done enough damage where she was concerned. He had no intention of adding to the score.

He scattered the contents of his in-box across his desk until he found the file he wanted. He tucked it under his arm. 'Tell Donald he's still in charge,' he shot at Phillip as he strode from his office. He punched the button for the elevator…twice…three times. 'There's something I need to take care of.'

Phillip did his best not to gape. Kit would've stood, hands on hips, and demanded to know where he was going, what time he'd be back and what he expected her to tell all his appointments for the day. Alex shot into the elevator before Phillip could ask him anything so unanswerable.

All of those answers depended on Kit.

Alex double-checked the file that lay open on the car seat beside him, and glanced again at the house opposite. There was no doubt about it, this was the address. This was where Kit now lived.

He frowned. It was a far cry from her stylish one-bedroom flat in French's Forest. That building had been all square blonde brick with a couple of well-trimmed hibiscuses out the front. This wasn't anywhere near as well-ordered. This was…messy.

Paint peeled from weatherboards, and one end of the tiny veranda sagged. What lawn there was needed cutting. Shrubs grew willy-nilly in the front garden. Most of it was obscured, though, by the enormous bottlebrush tree on the front path that was so laden with red blossoms it sagged beneath their weight. It took him a moment to realize the hum came from the bees in that tree rather than his shock.

Kit's talents would be wasted in this two-horse town.

He'd researched Tuncurry on his phone at a roadside restaurant a couple of hours back. Apparently it was a sea-side township purportedly inundated with holidaymakers in the summer, four hours north of Sydney. A glance at his watch told him he'd been on the road for five hours.

Five hours? He hadn't even had the sense to pack an overnight bag. He dragged both hands back through his hair. He didn't even have a plan.

He did know the outcome he wanted, though. For Kit to return to Hallam Enterprises.

He pushed out of the car and straightened his tie. All he had to do was the right thing. He had to make things right for Kit again so she could go back to the job she loved. End of story.

The gate squeaked when he opened it and the wood and wire fence swayed when the gate slammed back into place behind him. The door to the house stood wide open, but nobody appeared at his first knock, or his second.

He hesitated, then opened the screen door. 'Hello?'

The room was empty—unlived in empty. No furniture. No people. He was about to holler another hello when a door at what he guessed was the back of the house thudded closed and a few seconds later Kit came tripping into the room wearing faded jeans, a navy-blue singlet top and with her hair scraped back into a ponytail. He cleared his throat. She swung to him and froze in one of the shafts of sunlight that came streaming in through the front windows.

His stomach hollowed out. Dear Lord, she was lovely. A sense of regret stole through him, giving him the strength to push his shoulders back. 'Hello, Kit.' He took two steps into the room and let the screen door close behind him.

'Alex?'

Two lines creased her forehead. He had an insane urge to walk across and smooth them out.

'What on earth are you doing here? I thought you'd ring or email, but…'

The sound of a truck screeching to a halt outside had her glancing behind him. 'You'll have to excuse me for a minute.' She shook herself, dusted off her hands. 'It sounds as if my new furniture has arrived.'

She moved past him and out to the veranda to wave to the truck. She smelled of soap and fresh cotton and she barely spared him a glance. He surveyed the room in an effort to distract himself from the way her jeans hugged the curve of her hips, at the memory of how his hands had traced those curves and how she'd—

His heart started to pound. He gritted his teeth. He glanced to his left, guessing the hallway that opened off there led to the bedrooms and bathroom. Given the proportions of the outside of the house, he'd guess there would be two bedrooms.

The mundane calculations helped settle his heart rate.

Kit half-turned in the doorway, not quite meeting his eyes, and smiled as if he could be anyone. 'How was Africa?'

'Amazing.' He found himself suddenly eager to tell her all about it. He knew she'd appreciate it, that she'd understand. He opened his mouth to find she'd already swung away to greet a burly man with a clipboard.

'Delivery for Mercer?'

'That'd be me,' Kit said with a smile that held genuine warmth, and Alex's stomach dropped. Kit didn't want to hear about his trip. And there was no conceivable reason on earth why she should be glad to see him.

'Do you need a hand?'

The burly man glanced at Alex, took in the suit and tie and shook his head. 'We'll be right, mate. We do this for a living.' He turned back to Kit. 'Just tell us where you'd like the stuff.'

Bemused, Alex watched as Kit indicated where she wanted the dining table and chairs—in the small part of the L-shaped living room, which he discovered adjoined the kitchen with a door that led out to the back garden.

'I want the dresser there, the sofas here and here, and the entertainment unit against that wall.'

'Rightio. Oh, and the boss was really sorry the delivery was delayed so he sent someone to install those shelves you ordered.'

'That was kind of him. I want them on that wall there.'

She indicated an internal wall and Alex had never felt more like a third wheel in his life.

She turned to look at him again. And again those two lines creased her forehead. 'We'll um…be out the back if you need us.'

'No probs.'

Kit hitched her head in the direction of the back garden and Alex followed. Her back garden wasn't any neater than the front. A row of haphazard azaleas bloomed along the fence to the right. A banksia stood sentinel at the back fence while, to the right, a giant frangipani stood wedged between the back of the house and a garden shed, threatening to push them both over. Some patches of the lawn were more sand than grass.

Kit, however, didn't seem to find anything wrong with the place and she certainly wouldn't care what his opinion of it was either. That much was evident.

'Are you just passing through, Alex, or is there a purpose to your visit?'

Her ponytail bounced as she knelt down in front of a Cape Cod chair, picked up a piece of coarse sandpaper and started sanding.

His stomach started to cramp. He felt ridiculous in his dark suit and tie out here in her garden. He dragged the tie from around his neck and shoved it into his jacket pocket. He undid his top button and ordered himself to take a deep breath. 'There's a reason.'

Her ponytail kept bobbing. She was sanding that chair all wrong. If she weren't careful, she'd pull a muscle. He had to clench his hands to stop from reaching out, hauling her to her feet and turning her to face him.

He couldn't touch her. He'd made so much progress and he had no intention of backsliding now. He just wanted to make things right—do the right thing. Touching her would be a step in the wrong direction.

'Then any time today would be good…'

His teeth clenched when she still didn't turn around. He unclenched them to say, 'I'm waiting for you to spare me a moment of your attention.'

'From memory, when you were offered my full attention you didn't want it.'

Just like that, the old tension wrapped around them. Her hand froze mid-sand as if she couldn't believe she'd uttered the words.

He wanted to swear and swear and swear. He should've had a plan. He should've rehearsed what to say. He should've known better than to trust his instincts when he was anywhere in the vicinity of Kit Mercer.

'You resigned!' The words shot out of him like an accusation. Unrehearsed.

'You always were quick on the uptake.'

Kit had always been sassy, but rarely sarcastic. His hands clenched and this time he did swear. 'Can't we try and keep this civilised?'

Finally she turned and planted herself in the half-sanded chair. 'Why?'

All his frustration bubbled up, threatening to choke him. 'Look, I didn't force you to sleep with me, all right? We were consenting adults and you were as into it as I was. I know I didn't live up to your expectations and I'm sorry. I wish to God it had never happened. But it's done now and I can't undo it.'

Her eyes hardened. 'Fine!'

'What else can I do, other than apologise?'

'Leave?'

The word kicked him in the centre of his gut and he knew then that this woman had left her mark on him for life. He also knew that if he was to save his sanity he had to rip her out of his life completely.

But he should be the one to suffer. Not her.

'I can't accept your resignation, Kit.'

An angry flush stained her cheeks. Her eyes glittered. 'That's your problem, Alex, not mine.'

'You loved your job!'

'So?'

'And you were brilliant at it.'

She blinked.

'Come back to Hallam Enterprises and I will double your salary.'

'No.'

'I'll triple it.' He planted his feet. 'Kit, you're too valuable an employee to give up on without a fight.'

She stared up at him and he could've sworn her bottom lip wobbled. 'Alex—'

'Look, come back. You don't need to relocate and change your whole way of life. If working with me is so difficult for you, I'll relocate instead to our Brisbane office. I will leave Donald in charge of operations in Sydney, I'll triple your salary and you won't have to clap eyes on me again. I promise.'

Her eyes had grown huge. She pressed her hands to her cheeks. 'I thought you'd ring, Alex, or email. I didn't expect you to just turn up like this.'

Her hands shook. Her colour kept flooding and then receding. Should he have given her some warning? He'd been so intent on his mission he hadn't thought what might be best for her.

But he knew how much she'd loved her job. She gained more satisfaction out of her job as project manager than he did running the entire company. She shouldn't feel compelled to leave because of what had happened between them.

Still, he'd been a fool to think that any meeting between them could be anything less than fraught.

He raked both hands back through his hair. In the warm spring sunshine his skin started to prickle beneath his suit jacket. 'Why don't I come back tomorrow at, say, 10:00 a.m.? It'll give you a chance to think over my offer. You're obviously busy here and—'

'No!' She surged to her feet. 'I don't want to drag this out. Alex, I will not be returning to Sydney. I mean to make this place home. I grew up in Tuncurry and I've missed it. This is where I want to live. The lifestyle, the people, the pace, it suits me more than Sydney ever did.'

Didn't she care that her talents would be wasted here?

'Your offer was more than generous—' she hauled in a breath '—and I do appreciate it, but...'

She didn't finish her sentence. She didn't have to. Her shrug said it all. Bile rose up to burn his throat, his tongue. His recklessness, his *weakness*, had made this woman's life worse and there was nothing he could do to make amends. 'What will you do?'

'I'll get a job. I have a lot of contacts here and the tourism industry is thriving. With my qualifications, it'll be a piece of cake.'

She had every right to that confidence. Whoever was lucky enough to employ her would find they had a gem.

'You're sure you won't reconsider?'

She shook her head. And then she went so pale he found himself stepping forward to take her arm. She lifted her hands to ward him off. Stepped away so he couldn't touch her. As if his touch would poison her. Just for a moment he had to rest his hands on his knees.

'Alex, I don't want to raise my children in the city. I want to raise them here.'

He flinched at that word—*children*—and then straightened, but part of him was glad—fiercely glad—that she'd uttered it. It reminded him of the impossible gulf that lay between them.

Her lips twisted and her eyes hardened at whatever she saw reflected in his face. But her colour didn't return. He noted the way she twisted her hands together. To stop them from shaking?

'Alex, I didn't resign from Hallam Enterprises because I found it impossible to work with you. I resigned because I'm pregnant.'

He stared. For a moment it seemed as if time were suspended. And then her last two words hit him in the stomach like blows from a sledgehammer. *I'm pregnant.*

I'm pregnant. I'm pregnant.

No! He fell back. Not… *No!* 'You can't be serious?' The words rasped from a throat that burned like acid.

'I've never been more serious about anything in my life.'

Her hands twisted and twisted. He stared at them and prayed they could save him. 'With…?'

But he couldn't finish the question. He reeled away from her, reeled all the way to the back fence and the banksia tree. He dug his fingers into the hard bark of a branch and held on until the nausea passed. Anger pounded through him then, hot and thick and suffocating. At the edge of his consciousness he could hear Chad's laughter taunting him like it did in his nightmares.

He swung around, strode back to where Kit stood and jabbed a finger at her. 'You expect me to believe it's mine?' The words were harsher than anything that had ever scraped out of his throat before.

She folded her arms, moistened her lips and met his glare head on, although tears filled her eyes and he doubted she could see him properly through them. But she didn't let a single one of them fall. 'Just walk away, Alex,' she whispered. 'Just turn around and walk away and we'll pretend that none of this ever happened.'

His heart pounded in his throat, his pulse raced. He'd come here to make her the offer of a lifetime. Instead, she was extending that offer to him.

He could walk away.

He didn't want to walk. He wanted to run!

CHAPTER THREE

ALEX lurched across to the nearest azalea bush, where he promptly and comprehensively vomited. Kit had to sit again and focus on her breathing to avoid that urge herself. Up to this point, her pregnancy had been remarkably nausea free.

She rubbed at the niggling ache in her back. In her free moments, when she'd tried to picture telling Alex he was going to be a father, she'd expected yelling and shouting, accusations and disbelief, even a hard, angry silence.

Shock—yes.

Vomiting—no.

Had her father vomited when her mother had told him she was pregnant with Kit?

She shook the thought off and deepened the massage to the left side of her back, her fingers doing what they could to shift the pain there and their own nervousness. With Alex, she'd have preferred the shouting and anger. A part of her would have preferred it if he'd taken the out she'd offered him and had walked away without one single backward glance. She flicked a quick glance in his direction.

He still might yet.

She tried to stamp out the sympathy that rose through her at the memory of the white-lipped panic that had sent him wheeling away from her, at the red-faced panic that had sent him hurtling back, at the grey-skinned despair that had sent him staggering across to that azalea bush.

Having an unplanned baby wasn't the end of the world!

Her throat ached. Her eyes stung. Her news had made him vomit. *Vomit!*

I don't do happy families.

He wasn't kidding, was he?

Her temples throbbed. The ache in her back that had been plaguing her since yesterday increased in ferocity. A hot flush wrung her out and then a chill gripped her. She might not be able to stop herself from feeling sorry for Alex, but he was an adult, a grown up. He might not do happy families, but she did. There was no way on God's green that she was going to let him hurt her baby.

Their baby.

No—her baby! Alex didn't want this child. She did with every molecule of her being. She would provide for this baby and give it everything it needed.

A baby needs a father.

She thrust her chin out. She'd coped perfectly well without one.

Really?

She dropped her head to her hands with a groan. She'd ached to have a father who'd wanted her, who'd loved her.

'Kit?'

Alex's face was void of all emotion. It made her catch her breath. How could he hide all that…that *turmoil* away, just like that? She searched his face for a spark of…anything.

She searched in vain.

'You're saying it's mine?'

'Yes.'

'We used protection.'

She didn't want to do this. She wanted to curl up and sleep the afternoon away. She wanted to forget all about Alex Hallam. 'We'd have been better off if I'd been on the Pill.'

'Have you thought everything through? Considered all your options?' He planted his hands on his hips, his eyes narrowed. 'You know you have options, don't you?'

'You're talking about a termination?'

'That's certainly one of your options and—'

That had her surging to her feet. She ignored the pain that cramped her back. 'What a typically male thing to say! You're...' She couldn't find words enough to describe the entirety of his awfulness.

He wanted her to get rid of their beautiful baby?

Oh, that so wasn't going to happen!

'Look, I'm just saying it's an option, that's all. I was just checking that you'd considered *all* your options.'

'Is that so?' She folded her arms. After the heat of her first flush of anger she went cold all over. Chilled-to-the-bone cold. 'But a termination would make your life so much easier, wouldn't it?'

'Only if the child is mine.'

For a moment she couldn't breathe. He doubted it? He thought she would lie about something as important as this? She'd envisaged anger and shock, resentment, when she told Alex the news but not once had it occurred to her that he might not believe her. She'd never given him any reason to think she would lie.

She wrapped her arms about her middle to stop from falling apart. 'I am not terminating my pregnancy.'

He didn't blink. He didn't flinch. 'Fine. But if you claim the child is mine then I demand a paternity test be carried out upon the child's birth.'

She hitched up her chin. 'Alex, you've made it clear

from the start that you're not a family man.' Well, perhaps not exactly from the start. But he had rectified that particular misapprehension on her part with startling speed. 'I don't want anything from you. I assure you I have everything that I need. Frankly, I don't know what you are still doing here.'

His gaze sliced to the path that led around the side of the house—the path that would take him to his car and freedom. She recognized the hunger that flashed across his face before all expression was cut off again.

'I—'

An almighty crash from within the house interrupted whatever he'd been about to say. Kit spun around. One of the deliverymen appeared at the back door. 'I…uh…a wall's fallen down.'

She blinked. 'It's what?' She took off at a run. Her beautiful house!

'Kit, wait, it might not be safe!'

She ignored Alex's shout. It couldn't be any more dangerous than being out in the back garden with him. His footsteps pounded behind her, but he didn't catch up with her until she came to a dead halt at the edge of the living room. He slammed into her and she winced as pain cramped her back again. She coughed at the plaster dust thick in the air.

'Sorry.' He gripped her shoulders to steady her. 'Okay?'

She couldn't answer him. The warmth of his hands had memories sideswiping her, memories that demanded she turn and rest herself in his arms. Crazy! She couldn't talk but she could resist such insane impulses. She managed a nod.

He immediately transferred his attention to the deliverymen. 'Anyone hurt?'

She closed her eyes. She was a hundred different kinds of a fool where this man was concerned.

The deliverymen all assured Alex that they were unhurt and Kit opened her eyes to survey the damage. She waved a hand in front of her face to try and dispel some of the dust. 'What happened?'

Her house. Her beautiful house.

As the dust settled, a great hole appeared in her wall where her brand new shelves should've been. They lay in disarray amidst the clutter and mess on the floor. Alex swore. 'Didn't you look for a supporting beam?'

'Course I did,' a dusty figure muttered. 'Take a look yourself.'

Alex did. He poked and prodded and then swore at whatever he'd discovered. Kit's heart sank. Her budget didn't run to expensive repairs and—

All her thoughts slammed to a halt when he stuck his head through the hole and peered upwards. 'Alex!' The protest squeaked out of her. What if more stuff fell down?

It was only when he backed out again that she noticed the three deliverymen edging towards the door. 'What do you think you're doing?' She'd meant to utter the words in her best scary secretary voice, but it came out as a squeak too.

'Sorry, love, but we've delivered your furniture. There's nothing more we can do here.' With that they turned tail and fled.

'Hold on a minute!'

A firm hand wrapping around her upper arm prevented her from setting off after them. 'It's not their fault, Kit. Let them go.'

She wrenched herself out of his grip and then coughed as dust rose up around them, disturbed by her agitated movements. It settled on the shoulders, the sleeves, the lapels of Alex's finely tailored suit. It settled everywhere, even on his eyelashes. Kit yanked her gaze away. She didn't want to notice how the dust on his eyelashes made the brown of his irises deeper and clearer. She didn't want to notice anything about Alex Hallam.

He went to take her arm, but she evaded him. She didn't want him touching her again either. She didn't want to notice how his touch was imprinted on her soul. As if she were his woman. She wasn't!

She whirled away from him. 'What do you know about any of this anyway?'

He brushed a hand through his hair, shaking plaster dust out of it. He shrugged and sort of grimaced. 'I'm a builder by trade, Kit.'

'No, you're not. You're a multi-millionaire property developer.' She planted her feet. 'Builder my foot,' she muttered under her breath.

'I'm a multi-millionaire property developer *and* a builder by trade.'

She frowned. 'But you have an economics degree.' She'd seen it on the wall of his office.

'Mature-age entry. Part-time attendance. How do you think I funded a tertiary education?'

She stared at him and then shook her head. Had she ever really known him?

All the intimate ways she had known him rose up through her. When he raised an eyebrow she realized she was staring. She pushed the memories away and bit her lip, wished it weren't so hard to catch her breath. 'So...' she waved at the hole in the wall '...you know about all this?'

He nodded.

She bit back a sigh. 'Right then, you'd better tell me the worst.'

He glanced at the wall and then back at her. A frown formed in his eyes. 'The wall stud is rotten with damp. That's why it didn't hold the shelves and, as you can see, when they fell they took a great chunk of plaster with them. Kit, there's a hole in the roof. Looks as if you'll need to find a new place to rent.'

'I'm not renting, Alex.' Kit wanted to sink to the floor amid all the chaos and rest for a bit. 'I've bought this house. It belongs to me.'

Alex pushed his jacket back to plant his hands on his hips. 'How the hell does one buy a house in just three weeks?'

'Private sale.' Her hands rested in the small of her back as she grimaced and stretched. 'We rushed it through.'

The owners had seen her coming a mile off. 'At least tell me you had a building inspection done.'

'The previous owners told me it was fine. The real estate agent said he could vouch for them personally.'

'Did you get anything in writing?'

He knew the answer before she shook her head. How could a woman so savvy and efficient in dealing with demanding clients and difficult staff make such an elementary mistake? His gaze drifted to her waist and his lips thinned.

She rested her hands on her knees and only then did he notice how unwell she looked. Pregnant women, they threw up a lot, right? He grimaced at the reminder of his own behaviour earlier. 'Kit, are you going to be sick?'

'Don't think so,' she mumbled.

She straightened. He noticed the way her hand went to the small of her back as if trying to massage away a pain there. He did a rough calculation. If he were the father, Kit would be nearly four months into her pregnancy. He couldn't remember when Jacqueline had started getting back pain. He was pretty sure it was later than four months. 'Are you sure you're feeling all right?'

'I'm pregnant,' she snapped. 'I don't have some disease!'

He figured he deserved that, but…he really didn't like her colour.

'And it's been a great day,' she continued. 'The father of my child throws up when I tell him the happy news and now I have a hole not only in my wall but, if what you are telling me is true, in my roof too! You know what, Alex? I'm feeling on top of the world right now.'

She had a point. Several, in fact. Rather valid points at that. He couldn't help it. He glanced at her waist again. As far as he could tell, there wasn't any change there at all.

Perhaps this could turn out to be a glorious mistake?

He glanced at the hole in the wall and knew he was grasping at straws. Kit had a hole in her wall *and* she was pregnant.

He was in the middle of a nightmare.

He was going to suffocate. All the plaster dust in the room felt as if it had lodged in his throat. He didn't do kids. He didn't do family. *He wanted out of here.*

He dragged in a hoarse gasp of air and closed his eyes, concentrating on his breathing. Kit had told him he could walk away.

He wanted to run, escape, as fast as he could.

He wanted to stampede for the door. Charge through it and never come back.

He opened his eyes, glanced at the door and then glanced at Kit, who'd backed up to perch on the edge of the nearest sofa, which was still wrapped in the heavy-duty plastic it had arrived in. He frowned as he looked at her more closely. One moment she was pale, the next she was flushed. Before he had time to think better of it, he reached out and rested the back of his hand against her forehead.

She slapped it away. Glared. 'What do you think you're doing?'

She was burning up!

He dragged a hand back through his hair. His retreat was moving further and further out of reach. He could almost feel it slipping through his fingers like water...or plaster dust.

'You're running a temperature.' Hell! He couldn't leave a sick woman to fend for herself. 'Come on. You need a doctor to check you over. I'll take you up to the hospital.'

'Don't be ridiculous!'

By rights, her glare should've withered him to the spot. He sat next to her, he was careful not to touch her. 'You're not feeling well, Kit, and you're running a temperature so you can be excused for making poor judgement calls.'

'Poor judge—'

'But do you really want to take the risk that a high temperature might harm your baby?'

'Oh!'

Her bottom lip wobbled and one of her hands moved to cradle her abdomen. That action told him exactly how much this baby meant to her. For a moment he had to fight the nausea that punched through him again.

'You really think I'm running a temperature?'

'I know it.'

'Okay,' she finally whispered. 'But not the hospital, the medical clinic.'

'Fine.' He would take her to see a doctor. He would bring her home again. He'd book into a hotel overnight. Tomorrow, he and Kit would discuss what needed discussing and then he would walk out of her life for ever.

CHAPTER FOUR

KIT's pallor, the way she bit her bottom lip and her down-turned mouth all struck at Alex's heart, making him forget his own panic. He wished he could make her smile. He'd been able to—once.

He stood and pretended to survey the sofas. 'You know what? The plastic-wrapped look was a smart choice. I think it could really take off.'

She didn't smile.

'I hear babies make a lot of mess. You might want to keep this look for the next three or four years.'

He couldn't believe he'd said the word *babies* without flinching. 'You know, we could plastic-wrap the whole interior of this room. You could just hose it down at the end of every day. It'd save you loads of time.' He was glad he'd made the effort when her lips shifted upwards the tiniest fraction.

He shook himself. Enough of this. 'C'mon, let's get you to the medical clinic.' He reached down and helped her to her feet. He didn't release her arm. 'Are you feeling dizzy or faint?' Should he carry her to the car?

His skin pulled tight with need. It rocked him to find just how much he wanted to touch her, to have her in his arms.

She shook her head. Carefully, as if the action hurt. 'I

just feel as if I have a bad case of the flu without the sore throat and sniffles.'

His chest clenched. The sooner she saw a doctor the sooner she'd get medicine—antibiotics or whatnot—to make her feel better. But when she removed her arm from his grasp all he could think for a moment was how the day had darkened. They were just about to leave when they found the door blocked by two figures.

'Hello, lovey, we're Frank and Doreen from next door.' An elderly couple tripped into the room. 'Hello, Kit dear.'

He blinked. *Lovey?* Him? Nobody...*nobody* had *ever* called him lovey. He rolled his shoulders, cracked his neck.

'Hi, Auntie Doreen.'

Her aunt!

'The boys just told us what happened. We thought we'd pop our heads in to see if there's anything we can do.' Doreen turned to Alex. 'Frank here used to be a welder, you know.'

Frank here looked about seventy in the shade.

'He's handy with his hands.'

And then she winked at him.

Alex swallowed back a smart rejoinder. How on earth did a welder propose to fix a hole in a wall, not to mention another in the roof? Even if he was *handy with his hands*.

Nevertheless, when the older man extended his hand Alex shook it. 'Alex Hallam.' He glanced at Kit. She looked ready to drop. 'I'm sorry, but Kit is running a temperature. We're off to the medical clinic.' He waved a hand at the mess. 'I'll deal with all this later.'

'You run along, lovey, while we see what we can do.'

He didn't want this unconventional pair messing with Kit's house. Things were bad enough already.

'We'll close the door when we leave.'

Kit didn't seem concerned or put out by Doreen's words so he shrugged and edged her towards the door.

Doreen leant across to squeeze Kit's hand as they passed. 'So glad your young man has finally arrived.'

'Oh, but he isn't—'

'Young,' Alex bit out. He continued to shepherd her all the way out of the door and towards his car. They didn't have time for explanations.

Alex accompanied Kit into the doctor's consulting room. She didn't put up a fight, but he had a feeling that had more to do with how unwell she was feeling rather than a sign of her trust in him.

The doctor frowned and pointed to a chair when Alex started pacing up and down. He planted himself in it and tried not to fidget. Then he scowled. The doctor looked as if he was just out of high school! Surely he was too young to know which way was up, let alone—

'Relax, Alex,' Kit groaned.

Relax? How could he relax when she looked like death warmed up? Why hadn't he picked up on that earlier? He could have unknowingly made her worse. He'd walked into her house as if he'd had every right and demanded she come back to work. Without a thought for what she really wanted. All to ease his conscience. As if he knew what would make her happiest. As if he knew what was best for her.

He knew zilch.

He dragged a hand back through his hair. He did know one thing. When a woman told you she was pregnant with your child, you shouldn't throw up. Bad reaction. Wrong reaction. Completely inappropriate.

And completely out of his control.

But…Kit was carrying *his child*?

He slammed a wall down on that thought.

Not his baby, Kit's. And if Kit lost her baby because of anything he'd done—

Bile rose up to burn his throat. He choked it back. He would never forgive himself if that happened. Never.

'Kit, you have a kidney infection. I suspect you've had a urinary tract infection, not all that unusual during pregnancy, which has travelled to your kidneys.'

Alex's head snapped up at the doctor's words. 'How serious is that?' he barked. It sounded bad.

Kit didn't look at him, but her hands shook. He clenched his to fists. 'What he said,' she whispered.

'We've caught it early.'

Her hands cradled her abdomen and Alex couldn't take his eyes from them. Such small, fragile hands.

'Will my baby be okay?'

'Yes. As long as you do everything I say.'

Kit swallowed and nodded. Alex leaned forward to make sure he caught every word the doctor uttered.

'I'm booking you in for an ultrasound on…' he surveyed his computer '…on Thursday. It'll put both you and your regular doctor's minds at rest. I'll also prescribe you a course of antibiotics, and no, they won't harm your baby,' he added before Kit could ask. 'But, until your ultrasound, I want you to have complete bed rest.'

'Oh, but—'

'You can get up to go to the bathroom. You can have a quick shower or tepid bath once a day. But the rest of the time I want you in bed.'

Kit's hands twisted in her lap. 'I…'

The doctor peered at her over the top of his glasses. 'It's better to be safe than sorry, isn't it?'

'Yes, of course. It's just…'

The doctor turned to Alex. 'She'll need someone to stay with her, look after her.'

Alex nodded, ignoring the way his stomach dropped. 'I'll do that.' Thursday? He could stay till Thursday, or even the weekend. Kit wouldn't be sick if she wasn't pregnant. And she wouldn't be pregnant if it wasn't for him.

Thursday or the weekend? It was the least he could do.

He could see that Kit didn't like the idea. In fact, she probably loathed it. Not that he could blame her.

The doctor pointed at Kit. 'You rest. It's important, you hear?'

Kit nodded and swallowed. 'I hear.'

Alex wanted to hit the doctor for frightening her.

The doctor's glare transferred itself to Alex. 'She's to have no stress, no worry. She's not to be upset in any way.'

Alex's hands clenched as fear punched through him then too. 'Right.' No stress, no worry. He could manage that. For Kit. Till Thursday. Or the weekend.

'I don't need you to stay with me, Alex,' Kit said the moment he pulled his car to a halt out the front of her house and turned off the ignition.

He didn't blame her for not wanting him there. In her shoes he wouldn't want him staying over either, but hadn't she heard a word the doctor said? She needed someone to stay with her, look after her. He wasn't leaving until someone trustworthy was here to fill his shoes.

'I'm happy to call one of your friends or a relative—perhaps your aunt Doreen—to stay with you, but I'm not leaving you alone, Kit. You heard what the doctor said,' he added when she opened her mouth to argue.

She closed it again. She looked pale and wrung out, and he grimaced. 'Look, this is the story, Kit. I'm staying in Tuncurry tonight. Now, whether that's on one of your new sofas or in a hotel room is up to you.'

'But—'

'It's getting a bit late to be driving back to Sydney, especially when I'm still jet-lagged from the Africa trip.'

She rested her head against the back of the seat as if it were too hard to hold it up under her own steam. He wanted to reach out and trace the line of her jaw, the curve of her cheek. He clenched his hand. Just get her into bed where she can rest. No stress, no worry.

He swallowed. 'Kit, how does this sound for a plan? You let me crash on your sofa, just for tonight, and tomorrow we can discuss other arrangements?'

She closed her eyes and then finally she nodded. 'Okay.'

He had a feeling she'd agree to just about anything at the moment if it meant she could rest.

He discovered that didn't mean she'd let him carry her into the house, though. He stayed close behind her on the slow trek from the car to the house, in case she needed a hand. They both paused on the threshold. The living room looked like a bombsite, though Frank and Doreen had obviously done their best to sweep the debris into one tidy pile.

Kit picked up a note from the coffee table. 'Doreen has left us a casserole.' She started to turn. 'I should pop over and thank her.'

'I'll do that. You go to bed.'

She didn't look at him. She glanced about the room and her shoulders slumped. One of her small hands inched across her stomach. Alex's chest burned. She looked so lost and alone. He touched her shoulder, but when she glanced up at him with big worry-filled eyes he found himself drawing her into his arms and pressing her head to the hollow of his shoulder. 'It's going to be okay, Kit.'

'You don't know that,' she mumbled, but she didn't draw away.

He stroked her hair in an effort to reassure her, but found himself revelling in her softness, in how good she smelt, instead. 'We'll do everything the doctor says and you and your baby will be fine.'

She stared up at him then, a frown in her eyes.

'If the doctor had been really worried he'd have admitted you to hospital.'

She nodded, but the frown didn't leave her eyes. 'What are you still doing here, Alex?'

'There are things we need to talk about.' Maybe honesty would win him a measure of her trust. 'It doesn't matter how much I might want to leave, I can't until we've thrashed some things out. But that can wait until later in the week. What's important at the moment is for you to get better again.'

He hooked an arm under her knees and lifted her into his arms. Carrying her was easier than arguing with her.

Carrying her was divine.

'Point me in the direction of your bedroom.'

She pointed to the corridor that led off the living room. 'First door on the right.'

The moment he set foot inside it, he wanted to back out again. This bedroom, with its big wooden bed and plaid quilt in pastel shades piled decadently with cushions, was pure Kit. It reminded him of *that night*.

He set her down on her bed and then backed up fast, almost falling over his feet in his haste. 'You need to rest—doctor's orders. Nothing else matters at the moment, Kit. I'll go and serve you up a plate of your aunt's casserole.' Even sick, she looked divine.

'Honorary aunt. Doreen isn't my real aunt.'

Right.

'Alex?'

He turned in the doorway.

Her chin lifted as she met his gaze. 'You're going to leave us, aren't you, me and our baby?'

Her bottom lip wobbled as the words whispered out of her. Each word pierced his flesh.

She bit her lip, maybe in an attempt to get it back under control, and then she pursed her mouth. 'You know, Alex, I can understand you not wanting a future with me. I get that.'

She glanced away, swallowed. Her throat worked. He wanted to close his eyes.

She turned and her gaze met his again, her eyes dark and shadowed. Confusion and turmoil chased themselves across her face. 'But how can you turn your back on our baby?'

A weight slammed into place. He must look like a monster in her eyes.

Maybe he was.

He wanted to tell her to rest but the words wouldn't come.

'You don't care what's best for me. You don't care what's best for our baby. All you care about is what's best for you.'

She spoke almost as if to herself and her words chilled him. He wanted to tell her she was wrong, but…

He shook himself. 'Kit, I'm not abandoning you. I will be staying until the weekend.'

Her lips twisted. 'What good do you think that will do anyone?'

He didn't know how to answer.

She shifted slightly, her eyes suddenly glittering. 'You know what? It might just be simpler if I make you a lump sum payment.'

'What the hell…?'

'For the donation of your sperm. That way, everyone knows exactly where they stand. There'll be no misunderstandings.' She lifted her chin. 'I'm sure you can get those fancy lawyers of yours to draft something up.'

Horror welled through him. She couldn't be serious! He—

No stress, no worry.

He clenched his hands to fists, drew in a ragged breath and swallowed back the denial that shot through him. Her eyelids had started to grow heavy. A sheen of perspiration filmed her face. She continued to glare at him with her chin hitched up like a warrior's, but he knew a discussion like this couldn't be good for her. 'Rest now, Kit. We'll talk later.'

Not that there was much more to say, he realized, his mouth growing sour with the knowledge. He turned away and headed for the kitchen. Food and making sure Kit rested—he'd focus on what he could do.

An hour later, Alex found himself on Frank and Doreen's front veranda, hand raised to knock on their door. He'd made a deal with Kit—she'd try to sleep and he'd come over and thank Frank and Doreen.

He shifted his feet, scowled at the ground and knocked.

'Lovey!' Doreen appeared. 'C'mon in.'

He shook his head and fought the urge to fidget. 'I don't want to leave Kit for too long in case she needs me. I just—'

'Frank! It's Kit's young man, Alex.'

Alex gritted his teeth.

'Come in and have a beer, young man,' Frank offered.

Again, Alex shook his head. 'The doctor has diagnosed Kit with a kidney infection. She should be fine but he's ordered bed rest for the next few days. I don't want to leave her alone for too long.'

Both Frank and Doreen nodded sagely, as if this made perfect sense. As far as Alex was concerned, the longer he remained in Tuncurry, the less sense anything made.

'Kit wanted me to come over and thank you.' He suddenly realized how grudging that sounded, as if he hadn't appreciated what they'd done—their attempts to tidy up, the casserole. 'I mean we wanted to thank you.' But he and Kit, they weren't a *we* and he didn't want to give the wrong impression. 'Just…' He gave up. 'Thank you. It was thoughtful of you.'

Frank eyed him. 'You're a city boy, right, Alex?' When Alex didn't say anything he added, 'You'll find we're more community-minded out here.'

Community? It took an effort to stop his lips from twisting. From where he was standing, that just meant Kit would probably get stuck with looking after Frank and Doreen in a few years' time when they both started losing their faculties.

Still, they had checked up on her today and that had been a nice thing to do. And they'd made sure she had food.

Both Frank and Doreen looked at him expectantly. He cleared his throat. 'It's nice to know Kit has such good neighbours.'

'No doubt we'll all get better acquainted now you're here, lad.'

Alex took a step back. No way! The expectation, the cosy familiarity, the good-spiritedness, it wrapped around him, threatening to suffocate him, to bury him. He took another step back. 'I…uh…should get back to Kit. Goodnight.'

He turned and fled.

There wasn't any comfort in returning to Kit's house, though. He glared at the hole in her wall and then threw himself down on the nearest sofa. White dust rose up all around him.

His curse ground out from between gritted teeth. He couldn't bolt and leave Kit's living room looking like a demolition site.

If the child she was carrying was his…

He leapt up and stomped off to find a broom, a bucket and some cleaning cloths. Tonight he'd be sleeping on plastic because he wasn't taking the wrapping off the sofas until he'd had a chance to vacuum, and he wasn't vacuuming tonight. It'd wake Kit and she needed to rest.

Alex checked on Kit again at midnight. She'd taken her antibiotics, she'd eaten some dinner and then she'd slept. So far, so good. She needed to get well. He wanted her to get well as soon as possible.

So you can leave?

He tried not to scowl.

From the light of the hallway he caught sight of the title of the book on her bedside table—*What To Expect When You're Expecting*. He picked it up and tiptoed back out into the living room. Lowering himself to the sofa that would be his bed for the night, he turned to the page she had bookmarked.

And froze.

Everything went blank.

The bookmark—it was an ultrasound photograph of Kit's child.

Of his child.

He snapped the book shut and rested his head in his hands. A baby. A child.

He lifted his head, darkness surging up to fill the empty places inside him. He wasn't doing that again. He couldn't.

You don't care what's best for our baby. All you care about is what's best for you.

Kit didn't understand. Him getting out of her and the baby's lives—that would be best for her and the baby.

And for you too.

He nodded heavily. And for him too. It didn't stop a part of him from feeling as if it were dying, though.

When he finally fell asleep that night, Alex had a nightmare about Chad. He raced through a darkened mansion, his legs wooden and heavy, his heart pounding faster and faster as he searched for the two-year-old. Chad's laughter, always just out of reach, taunted him and spurred him on. The rooms in the mansion went on and on. He tried calling out Chad's name but his voice wouldn't work. His legs grew heavier and heavier. It took all his energy to push forward. He pulled open the final door, surged through it, to find himself plummeting off the edge of a cliff.

He woke before he slammed into the jagged rocks at the bottom, breathing hard and with Chad's name on his lips. He lay in the dark and tried to catch his breath, his skin damp and clammy with perspiration. He tried telling himself Chad was safe, living somewhere in Buenos Aires with his mother, but that didn't ease the darkness that stole through his soul.

Before he and Kit had made love, he hadn't had a nightmare about Chad in over ten months.

He shoved the thought away. It wasn't Kit's fault she made him feel things he hadn't felt in a long time. It was his fault for giving in to temptation. Biting back a groan, he pushed up into a sitting position. Past experience told him he would get no more sleep tonight. He dragged a hand down his face. That was okay. There was still plenty of cleaning to do.

A sharp rap on the front door just after nine o'clock had Alex falling over his feet to answer it before the noise of another knock could wake Kit.

The woman who stood on the other side raked him up and down with bold, unimpressed eyes. 'I'm Caro,' she said without preamble. 'Kit's best friend.' She didn't stick her hand out. 'Doreen rang me. I take it you're Alex?'

'That's right.'

She folded her arms. 'I've heard all about you.'

He gathered none of it had been complimentary.

'How's Kit?'

'Asleep,' he ground out.

'All night?'

'She was up—'

She brushed past him into the living room. 'She's not supposed to be up!'

He clenched his jaw till he thought his teeth might snap. He unclenched it to say, 'The doctor said she was allowed up to have a quick shower once a day.' He felt like a school-boy hauled up in front of the principal. 'She had breakfast, took her antibiotics and now she's sleeping again.'

'You'd better tell me you prepared her breakfast.'

Who the hell did this woman think she was? He was tempted to shove her back out of the door again. 'Look, I'm worried about her too. I mean to make sure she follows the doctor's orders to the letter.'

'I'm going to pop my head in to check on her.'

'Don't wake her,' he growled.

She tossed him a withering glance before disappearing down the hallway that led to Kit's bedroom.

He scowled after her. She had another thing coming if she thought he was offering her coffee.

Darn it! She was Kit's friend. He stalked into the kitchen and put the jug on to boil.

Caro entered moments later. 'You and me—' she pointed to him '—outside, now.'

He blinked. 'Are you calling me out for a fight? I've got to warn you, Caro, I don't hit women.'

She smiled sweetly. 'It should be a walkover then, shouldn't it?' She glared and held the back door open. 'I want to talk to you and I don't want to disturb Kit while I'm doing it.'

And she was itching to bawl him out. It didn't take a degree in economics and a finely honed ability to read people to figure that one out. He decided it might be safer if Caro didn't have a hot drink in her hand. He preceded her out of the door and into the back garden. Kit's bedroom faced the street. They shouldn't disturb her out here.

'How long before you shoot through again?'

Again? What did she mean, again?

He rolled his shoulders and scowled. If he'd known Kit was pregnant he wouldn't have left for Africa when he had. He'd have…*delayed it for a week?* a sarcastic voice muttered in his head.

He thrust out his jaw, folded his arms. 'I'm not leaving today. I told Kit I'd be here for her and I will be. There are things we need to sort out.'

Caro folded her arms too. 'You can forget it if you mean to offer her money.'

'This is none of your damn business.'

'Kit is my best friend. I love her. Can you say the same?'

For a moment he couldn't utter a single word. The same suffocating shroud that had blanketed him at Frank and Doreen's last night twisted about him now.

'Exactly what I thought,' she snorted. 'You're going to turn tail and run.'

'I am not!' he shot back, stung by the loathing in her voice. He'd wanted to bolt yesterday, but he was still here now, wasn't he? 'And I have to pay child support. It's a legal requirement.' That was only honourable and right.

She stuck out a hip. 'You're a right piece of work, aren't you?'

His jaw dropped.

The next moment Caro's face was wreathed in smiles. 'Hey, honey-bun, you're supposed to be in bed.'

He turned to find Kit in the doorway. She raised an eyebrow in his direction. 'You're still here.'

Had she thought he'd do a runner while she was asleep? He straightened. That was exactly what she'd thought. He forced himself to grin—no stress, the doctor had said. 'Sure I'm still here.' She was still convinced he meant to abandon her.

Isn't that exactly what you mean to do?

He bit back an expletive. He wasn't doing happy families, but he thought about that hole in her wall. Someone had to fix it. He could fix it.

He could make sure Kit had everything she needed and that she was ready for the baby before he sailed off into the sunset.

Kit glanced from Caro to him. He did all he could to keep his expression bland. He tried not to groan when she moistened her lips.

'What's going on out here?'

'Caro and I were just having a chat.' He would not upset her. 'You know the doctor's orders. You want me to carry you back to bed?'

'I'm going, I'm going. May I have a chamomile tea?'

'Coming right up.'

Kit disappeared. Caro grabbed his arm before he reached the back door. 'You mess with my friend and I'll come after you with a meat cleaver.'

He held the door open for her, bowed her inside. 'Chamomile tea for you too?'

'Ooh, lovely.'

She'd pay for that smile. He'd sweeten her tea to within an inch of its life.

But one thing had become increasingly clear—he'd come after himself with a meat cleaver if he hurt Kit any more than he already had.

CHAPTER FIVE

'WERE you giving Alex a hard time?' Kit asked after Alex had delivered their teas and then beat a hasty retreat.

'You bet.' Caro grinned. 'I read him the riot act.'

'Oh, Caro!' But Kit couldn't help laughing as her friend kicked off her shoes and climbed up onto the bed beside her.

Caro grimaced when she took a sip of her tea.

'I thought you liked chamomile.'

'I do.' Caro's lips twitched. 'It's just that first sip, you know? Anyway, tell me how you are feeling.'

'Much, much better. My temperature is back to normal and the awful cramps in my back have become a low level ache...much easier to deal with. And I don't feel as if I've been hit by a bus any more either.' She shuddered. 'I thought I was going to be stuck with that back pain for the next six months.'

'Your colour is good. The antibiotics must've kicked in.'

'I think the doctor is being a panic merchant,' Kit grumbled. She almost felt whole again. 'What am I going to do in bed for another two and a half days?'

'It's better to be safe than sorry.'

Which was what Alex had said when he'd brought her breakfast.

Caro took another sip of her tea. 'You don't think he deserved the riot act?'

'I don't know. I…I can't believe he's still here.' Though he had been sort of sweet last night—reassuring and kind. Somehow he'd managed to defuse her misgivings and her awkwardness, without her even realizing it. She wasn't quite sure how. 'He even vacuumed the living room while I was having breakfast if you can believe it.'

And he hadn't thrown up again. Her lips twisted. At least, not that she knew about.

She glanced at her friend and a different emotion surged through her. She took her and Caro's mugs and set them on the bedside table, and then she took Caro's hand. 'I have something really important to ask you.'

'Shoot.'

'Me getting sick like this, it's made me realize a couple of things. I…' Her stomach knotted and a lump lodged in her throat. Caro squeezed her hands but didn't rush her and Kit loved her all the more for it. 'Caro, if something should ever happen to me… I mean, it probably never will…' She hoped to heaven it never did. 'But…but if I died, would you look after my baby? I don't know who else I trust as much as you. Mum and Grandma would help out, of course, and—'

'Yes.'

Caro didn't hesitate. Kit closed her eyes in relief. 'Thank you.' But a weight pressed down on her. If she'd done this right, her baby would have two parents to rely on rather than one. She'd robbed her child of that and she knew, no matter how much she tried, she would never be able to make that up to her baby. Ever.

Unless Alex had changed his mind and wasn't going to walk away from his child after all. It seemed a slim hope.

A tap on her door brought her crashing back. Alex

stood in the doorway. Her chest clenched. Had he heard what she'd just asked Caro? The pinched white lines around his mouth told her he probably had. She swallowed. But he didn't care, did he? Not about her and not about the baby.

He'd wanted her to terminate her pregnancy!

Her heart burned. Sorrow and anger pulsed through her in equal measure. What did he care what safeguards she put in place to take care of *her* baby? He meant to leave again just as soon as it was humanly possible. She was sure of it. Her best guess was that he'd organise for Doreen and Caro to take it in shifts to look after her for the next couple of days so he could hightail it back to Sydney.

Perhaps she should confront him about that right now? It was just that the doctor had ordered her to rest—no stress, no worry. Yesterday she'd been feeling too fuzzy to take those orders in properly. But today… She swallowed. Today she'd do anything to keep her baby healthy. Fighting with Alex, confronting him about his intentions, had to wait. She raised an eyebrow. 'You wanted something?'

He rubbed his nape. He didn't meet her eyes. 'I wanted to check if Caro was staying for a while. I need to pop out to grab a few things.' His voice was devoid of all emotion.

'Pop away,' Caro said with an airy wave of her hand, not even looking at him.

Alex left without saying another word. Kit pleated the quilt cover with her fingers. 'Do you think he'll be back?' Maybe he'd make that dash for Sydney right now.

'Oh, I'm sure of it.'

She didn't understand Caro's grin but, before she could ask for an explanation, her friend said, 'Snooze or a game of gin rummy?'

'Ooh, go on. Break out the cards.'

* * *

The first thing Kit saw when she woke was the framed photograph of her ultrasound picture on her bedside table. She stared at it for a moment before hauling herself into a sitting position and reaching out to pick it up.

'I thought it might help.'

The second thing she saw was Alex sitting in a dining room chair at the bottom of her bed. Her stomach tightened. She dismissed that as a symptom of her kidney infection. 'Help?'

'I thought it might give you added incentive to follow doctor's orders and stay in bed.'

She had no intention of disobeying the doctor's orders—her baby's welfare was too important for that—but Alex's thoughtfulness touched her all the same. She stared down at the picture, lightly ran her fingers over the glass, following the contours that made up her baby.

'I couldn't make head nor tail of it,' he confessed.

It suddenly seemed wildly important to Kit that he did. 'Head here—' she pointed '—tail there.'

Alex didn't move to get a better look and she remembered then that he didn't want this child. She pressed the photo frame to her chest. She wanted to tell her baby that it didn't matter.

Only it did matter. A lot.

'Why are you sitting guard at the end of my bed?'

'I didn't want you getting up again unless you had to. I'm here to fetch and carry.'

Oh.

'Caro said to ring if you needed anything.'

Caro had gone? How long had Kit been asleep for? She and Caro had played cards for over an hour and then she'd napped. She glanced at the clock. She'd napped for three hours! Caro would've had to leave to collect Davey from pre-school.

'Your friend is a psychopath, by the way. Can I get you something to eat or drink?'

Kit's lips twitched. She settled back more comfortably against her pillows. 'No, thank you.' She still had an almost full bottle of water on the bedside table. 'I know Caro can come across as kind of scary, but she has my best interests at heart.'

'I know,' he said softly. 'I'm glad you have such a good friend.'

She was so surprised she couldn't speak.

He shifted on his chair. He was too big for it. It wasn't the kind of chair made for lounging, but the only other option was to invite him to join her on the bed and no way on God's green was she doing that. The last time they'd been in bed together...

It had been heaven.

Once the thought flitted into her mind, it lodged there—a stubborn, sensual reminder that pecked at her, teased her. All the sensations Alex had created in her with deft fingers and a teasing mouth, with the dark appreciation of his eyes and intakes of breath as she'd explored his body with as much thoroughness as he'd explored hers—exquisite, torturous reminders—they all flooded through her now and her body instantly came alive in some kind of primal response. She recalled with startling accuracy the taste of him, the feel of him against her tongue, her palms...his scent. The way he'd—

'Kit!'

She jerked out of the recollection to find herself leaning towards Alex, breathing hard. Her name had scraped out of his mouth on a half-strangled choke. He was breathing as hard as her.

Oh, dear Lord! She wanted to close her eyes. She'd been

staring at him, practically *undressing* him with her eyes and begging him to—

And his eyes had darkened in response. She swallowed. She'd recognized the answering hunger that had stretched across his face before it had been comprehensively snapped off from her view.

He shot out of his chair and pretended to adjust the blind. She knew he was giving them both time to pull themselves together again, but she couldn't help noticing his hands weren't any steadier than hers.

How could it be like this? How could she want him so badly when she didn't even like him? How could he want her, knowing she was pregnant? She'd seen what the news of her pregnancy had done to him.

But he did want her. She read that too clearly to mistake it for anything else.

He raked a hand back through his hair. 'I picked you up some magazines while I was out.' He spoke to the window, not to her.

'Thank you.' She breathed a sigh of gratitude. Her voice was low, but at least it worked.

He finally turned. 'I thought if you wanted I could haul your television in here and set it up so you at least have something to watch.'

She shook her head. 'That's not necessary.' It'd only mean setting it back up out in the living room when she was well again. She suddenly frowned. Had too much sleep fogged her brain? 'Alex, why are you still here? Don't you have a company to run?'

'The company isn't important.'

She stilled at that, glanced down at the photo frame. Had he changed his mind about having a baby? Yesterday he'd been in shock and denial. But maybe today... 'Are you trying to tell me that you've come around to the idea of being a father?'

'No.' The single word was inflexible. His face had gone impassive, emotionless. It was an expression she was starting to recognize, and loathe.

'Then don't you think it would be better for both of us if you just left?'

He didn't say anything.

'Between them, Caro and Doreen can take perfectly good care of me.'

He dragged a hand down his face then before seizing the chair and pulling it back a foot or so and planting himself in it. He leant forward to rest his elbows on his knees. 'Caro told me that over the course of the next two days Doreen is booked in for a rash of tests at the hospital. It's something to do with late onset diabetes,' he added quickly when she bolted upright, 'and it's nothing serious, but…'

But it meant Doreen wouldn't be available to look after her. Kit settled back again, chewing her lip.

'And Doreen told me that Caro's mother is arriving from England tomorrow and—'

'Oh!' Kit clapped a hand to her forehead. 'Caro is collecting her from Sydney Airport. She's leaving at the crack of dawn to get there in time. I forgot.'

'She was going to change her plans and make other arrangements for her mother, but I told her not to. If you think I did wrong, then I can call her now and—'

'No, no. Caro hasn't seen her mum in over a year.' And while Caro's mother was staying for a month, Kit certainly wasn't going to be responsible for delaying their reunion.

'And we've all been trying to ring your grandmother,' Alex continued, 'but…'

Kit smiled faintly. 'But she's a gadabout who refuses

to carry a mobile phone. If you leave her a message on Tuesday you might hear back by Friday.'

'And your mother lives—'

'In Brisbane,' she finished for him.

She pressed her fingers to her temples. *Think!*

'Kit?'

She glanced up.

'I'm staying in Tuncurry until the weekend.'

'But—'

'It's non-negotiable. There are things we need to discuss, but they can wait until you are well again. It's just as easy for me to stay here and keep an eye on you than it is to book into a motel.'

Easy for who?

'And it's the least I can do.'

She sagged into her pillows, suddenly unutterably weary. 'What do you mean?'

'I know I hurt you, Kit.'

She wanted to look away, but those dark eyes of his held hers and something whispered between them. The memory of soaring together for one unforgettable night and touching the stars. No matter how much she wanted to deny it, this man had touched her soul. In that moment she recognized that she'd touched his too.

It didn't mean they had a future together, though. She saw that just as clearly.

'I hurt you, Kit, and I know I'm disappointing you now.' He rested his head in his hands for a brief moment. 'Knowing me has made your life worse. I can't begin to tell you how sorry I am about that.'

She blinked and then frowned. He looked as if he actually meant that.

'Helping you out for the next two and a half days is the least I can do.'

Two and a half days? When he put it like that, it didn't sound like much. And, frankly, there was no one else available because she had no intention whatsoever of imposing on either Caro or Doreen.

'Don't you think your baby's welfare is more important than anything else at the moment?'

'Yes,' she whispered. She did. With all her heart.

'So do I.'

She blinked and frowned. He did?

'So why don't we just do what the doctor ordered—you rest and I'll be general dogsbody?'

She drew in a breath. What he was proposing, she may not like it, but it made sense. She let out the breath in an unsteady whoosh. 'Okay, Alex.' She nodded. 'It seems to be the best solution. And…um…thank you.'

'No thanks necessary,' he said roughly.

She frowned suddenly, hitched up her chin. 'But you know what? Regardless of what you think, being pregnant, that hasn't made my life worse. Having a baby is wonderful.'

He turned grey. She shrugged. 'I just want you to know that you don't have to feel guilty about that. At least, not on my account.'

If he really did mean to walk away from his child, though, she hoped guilt would plague him every day of his sorry life.

He moved to fiddle with her CD player on the other side of the room. The sound of lapping water and soft squeals and gurgles filled the room.

She stared at him when he turned back around and then at the CD player. 'What on earth is that?'

'It's called *Sounds of the Sea*.' He shrugged and held up the CD case. 'It's supposed to be calming and relaxing.'

He'd bought her a relaxation CD!

'I got it from one of those hippy places when I went shopping earlier.' He rubbed the back of his neck and didn't quite meet her eyes. 'You know the doctor said you needed to relax. I thought the CD…'

'I thought you went shopping for a change of clothes, a toothbrush.'

'I did. And for food—your refrigerator was practically empty!'

'There are plenty of frozen TV dinners.' She shrugged at his stare. 'I don't cook.'

He planted his legs, hands on hips. 'What do you mean, you don't cook?'

She waved her hands in front of her face. 'This is all beside the point. Alex, you're doing my head in!'

One corner of his mouth kinked up. 'I'd appreciate it if you didn't mention that to Caro.'

The silence between them filled with the laughter of dolphins—oddly hypnotic. She shook herself out from under its spell. He might find this amusing, but she'd lost her sense of humour. There was too much at stake for laughing. Her baby…

'I just don't get you at all. You wanted me to terminate my pregnancy—'

'No, I didn't! I—'

'You threw up when I told you I was pregnant but now you're doing everything you can to make sure the baby stays healthy.'

He was silent for a moment. 'You want this baby, Kit. You've already given your heart to it. You love it. I would never take that away from you.'

Her chest clenched. Frustration, remembered joy and then the ensuing crushing desolation, Alex's generosity as a lover and then his callousness the next day, it all rose up through her now. She didn't understand him at all and yet she'd agreed to let him stay in her house.

She was having his baby!

She needed to understand at least some of what had happened between them or...

Or she'd have learned nothing.

'You were the most incredible lover, Alex, generous and thoughtful. You made me feel beautiful and cherished.' And loved, which just went to show how skewed her judgement had been.

He leapt up, going white at her words.

'And then the next day you acted as if what had happened between us meant nothing. No, even less that that, as if what had happened between us was an aberration.' She lifted her hands. 'Why?'

'It wouldn't have been fair to let you think we had a future.'

'But you were so utterly cold, so callous. You didn't even bother trying to let me down gently. What did I do wrong? Please—I don't ever want to make that same mistake again.' She had a baby to think of. Her heart jammed in her throat. What if next time it wasn't just her heart she broke but her child's too? If her judgement about him could be so off, how could she ever trust it again?

'How could you have changed so completely? What was that all about? Was it you? Or did I do something?' She couldn't hold the questions back. Her voice rose as each one burst from her. 'Why?'

Alex's face twisted in an emotion she couldn't identify— anger? Panic? Horror? He thrust an arm towards her stomach. *'Because I didn't want that!'*

The shouted words reverberated in the quiet of her cool, shady bedroom. They pulsed in the air like live things. Her hands crept across her stomach in an attempt to block her unborn baby's ears. In an attempt to protect it from pain and hurt. In an effort to console it. Her knees drew up beneath the covers to form a barrier between him and her.

'You really don't want this baby, do you?' She'd known that before, but now she knew it in a harder, more real way. And it hurt. It died, that part of her that hadn't been able to give up hope. Hope that once he'd recovered from the initial shock he'd come around, perhaps even welcome this baby into his life.

Alex was never going to accept this child.

'I'm sorry.' He'd gone a hideous kind of grey. 'I shouldn't have yelled.'

Perhaps not, but she couldn't really blame him. She'd pushed him. She hadn't meant to, it had just happened. But now she had her answer.

He dragged a hand back through his hair, eyed her uncertainly. 'Time for us to get calm again.'

'I am calm.'

Strangely enough, that was true. She felt icily and preternaturally calm. It didn't stop her from suspecting she may well cry buckets over all this later. 'I'm tired,' she whispered.

'I'll leave you to rest.'

CHAPTER SIX

ON WEDNESDAY evening Kit woke to the smell of something divine coming from the kitchen.

Alex poked his head around her bedroom door as if he had some finely tuned radar that let him know when she was awake. 'How are you feeling?'

'Good, thank you. Actually, really good.' Back-to-normal good. She pushed herself into a sitting position and smiled when her back proved totally pain-free. 'I can't believe how much I'm sleeping, though.'

'Your body needs the rest.' He shuffled his feet, glanced away. 'Dinner will be ready in five if you need to…' He waved towards the bathroom.

'Freshen up?' she supplied.

'Uh, right.'

No sooner had she made it back to bed and settled the covers around her when Alex walked in with a tray. Kit groaned as he set it on her lap. 'This smells heavenly.'

'It's just a beef and potato salad.'

She could tell he was pleased, though. She speared a piece of beef, popped it into her mouth and closed her eyes in bliss as she chewed.

When she opened her eyes she found Alex frozen to the spot, his eyes glued to her mouth. Her stomach, skin, even her ears, all tightened. 'I…um…' She cleared her throat and tried to tamp down on the heat rising through her. She set her fork to her plate before she dropped it, and searched her mind for something to say. 'You're…um… not going to eat out there on your own, are you?'

He snapped back. 'I thought—'

'Bring your plate in here, Alex. Do you know how boring it is being confined to bed?' And then she wondered if that was such a good idea. She didn't really want to spend more time in Alex's company than she had to, did she?

'It's only for one more day.'

'Half a day,' she corrected.

He stood for a moment as if undecided before leaving the room and returning with his plate. He settled himself on his chair.

She should get a nice little tub chair for this room. It was the last thought she was aware of thinking before she returned to her food. She couldn't believe how ravenous she was, and how much better she was feeling. She scraped up the last of the sauce with a piece of lettuce, chewed in avid appreciation and finally set her tray aside. 'That was unbelievably delicious. Though you didn't have to go to any trouble, you know?'

'No trouble.'

She didn't believe that for a moment. 'You could've just tossed a TV dinner into the microwave and I'd have been grateful for that.'

He polished off the last of his food too and set his plate on her dressing table. 'I can't believe you don't cook.'

'It's boring and messy and takes too long.'

'It doesn't have to be any of those things.'

'I do other things. I can crochet. That's nice and domestic.'

'You have a baby on the way. You need to know how to cook.'

Yes, she had a baby on the way. *His baby.* Only he didn't want anything to do with it.

An awkward silence opened up between them, turning her tongue to lead.

Alex cleared his throat. 'Finished?'

'Yes, thank you.'

'Would you like some more?'

'No, thank you.'

Her hands clenched in the quilt when he left with their empty plates. *Why was he still here!*

He returned a short while later with two mugs of steaming tea. He handed her one and settled himself on the seat at the end of her bed again.

'So.' He cleared his throat. He didn't look any more at ease than she did. 'This is where you grew up?'

She took a careful sip and then nodded. 'The house where I grew up is a few blocks closer to the river.'

'And you have lots of friends here, lots of honorary aunts and uncles?'

Was he trying to reassure himself that she had backup for when he did leave? Was that what all this was about? Him staying here looking after her—was it his attempt to assuage a guilty conscience?

No, no, he was too ruthless for that.

She bit her lip. He'd framed her ultrasound photo.

He'd bought her a relaxation CD.

Maybe he had a *seriously* guilty conscience?

'Kit?'

She shook herself, searched and found the thread of their conversation again. 'This was a great place to grow up. Doreen next door used to be the school secretary at my old primary school and what she doesn't know about my old classmates isn't worth knowing.'

He grimaced and she could see how this small-community lifestyle might seem suffocating to him, but she wasn't going to lie about the kind of life she wanted for herself and her baby. 'I barely clapped eyes on my neighbours in Sydney.' Everybody was too busy working long hours, dealing with long commutes into the CBD. 'I like knowing my neighbours' names. I like chatting over the back fence. I like knowing that they're keeping an eye on me and that I can do the same for them.'

She had no regrets about leaving the busy pace of the city behind.

'Auntie Doreen is a good friend of my grandmother's. My grandma used to live across the street.' Which was probably why she'd jumped at the chance to buy this house. The street held good memories for her.

Alex frowned. 'She doesn't live there now, though, does she?'

Her eyes narrowed. 'No, Alex, she doesn't. I'd have sent you to sit on her veranda to wait till she'd returned home from wherever it was she'd been, so it could be her rather than you sitting here talking to me right now.'

'I didn't mean…'

'She moved into a retirement village in Forster five years ago when my mother relocated to Brisbane. She delights in all the activity the village offers. She has a very full social life.' Before he could ask, she added, 'Forster is across the bridge.' Forster and Tuncurry were twin townships separated from each other by the channel of water that fed into Wallis Lake.

Did he really mean to abandon his child? As the question speared into her, an ache stretched behind her eyes, pounding in time to her pulse.

'You look tired again. I should let you get more rest.'

He went to take her mug but she kept hold of it, forcing him to look at her. His fingers felt cool against hers.

Unbidden, images of what he'd done with those fingers rose up through her. She snatched her hand away. She didn't know how he managed to keep hold of the mug or prevent its dregs from spilling over her quilt. All she knew was that she couldn't think when he touched her.

'What the—'

Whatever he saw in her face had him biting back the rest of his words. His jaw had clenched so hard she suspected he wouldn't be able to utter them now anyway.

'I want to ask you something.' She was appalled at her uneven breathiness. She'd wanted to sound cool, calm and in control. Unflappable.

Where Alex was concerned, though, she was highly flappable. And flammable!

His choked out, 'Ask what?' didn't help either. She knew precisely how flammable he could be.

He didn't meet her eyes. The pulse at the base of his jaw jumped and jerked.

She stared down at her hands to find her fingers mechanically pleating the quilt.

Alex reached out and trapped them beneath his hand, stilling them. 'Kit, just tell me what's on your mind.'

He sat back down and just like that some of the tension eased out of her. She pulled in one long, hard breath. 'You said you weren't leaving Tuncurry until we'd sorted out a few things. I want to know what those things are.'

'There'll be time enough for that once you've received the all-clear from the doctor tomorrow.'

She could almost see him replay the doctor's words through his mind. *No stress, no worry.*

She folded her arms. 'Look, I'm going to worry about this until we sort it out. Either you let me stew about it all night or we can talk now.'

For a moment she thought he was going to refuse, get

up and walk away. 'Can we keep this calm?' he finally asked instead.

'We're adults, aren't we?' she countered.

He surveyed her for a long moment. It took a concerted effort not to fidget under those dark inscrutable eyes. 'Okay, Kit.' He nodded. 'Once the child is born I want a paternity test carried out. If the child is mine then I'll arrange for child support payments.'

She kept her voice perfectly polite. 'No.'

He leant forward. 'What do you mean, no? I have every right to demand a paternity test.'

'Really?' Even though she'd steeled herself for this, she was still surprised at how much his distrust hurt. 'Just for argument's sake, let's say that we do get the test done and you discover that the baby is yours, and, believe me, Alex, that is what you'll find out. But once you have incontrovertible proof, what is it going to change? Are you going to want visitation rights? Are you going to be a *real* father to this baby?'

He turned ashen. 'No, but I'll at least make sure that financially you and the baby are taken care of.'

'You can take your blood money and sod off, Alex!' She abandoned all pretence at politeness. 'I can look after this baby on my own—financially and otherwise.'

'It is my duty to provide financial support. It's a legal requirement.'

'It's your duty to be a proper father, but it's obvious that moral requirements don't figure on your radar! So you can take your legal requirements and stuff them up your shirt for all I care.'

She wanted to drop her head to her knees and weep for her unborn child.

'I can't believe you're prepared to turn your back like

that on your own child, Alex. And I can't believe that you could accuse me of lying about this, of—'

'I'm not accusing you of anything!'

'Yes, you are!'

He swore, scrubbed both hands down his face. 'Hell, Kit, this isn't about you.'

'Not about me? How can you—'

'I've been lied to once before.'

The world tilted to one side for a moment before righting itself again. Kit moistened her lips. When she could speak again she asked, 'When? Who…?' Who would do such a thing?

'My ex-wife.'

Her own hurt vanished. Just like that.

His face had gone unreadable, impassive. She suddenly found that she wanted to cry for him too. 'What happened?'

He dropped his head to his hands. For a long moment Kit didn't think he'd answer. Finally, he dragged both hands down his face and straightened. 'Jacqueline and I had been married for fifteen months when she fell pregnant. She told me the baby was mine and I had no reason to doubt her. We'd dated for over a year before we married.'

He'd loved a woman once, enough to marry her? She rubbed at her arms but it couldn't erase the sting that bloomed across her skin.

His mouth tightened. 'It never occurred to me that she'd lie. And God help me, but when I found out she was pregnant I couldn't wait to hold my son. We called him Chad.'

Kit's spine lost all its strength. Her hands crept up to cover her mouth. Before her eyes, Alex aged. His skin lost its colour. The lines around his mouth and eyes grew more pronounced. Shadows took up residence in his eyes. She dragged her hands back down to her lap, gripped them together. 'When did you find out the truth?'

'Not until Chad was two.'

Her mouth went dry. Alex had spent two years, not to mention the nine months of the pregnancy, loving his son—his Chad—and giving his heart to him completely? He didn't have to say that out loud—the evidence was written in every line of his body, in the grief that twisted his mouth and made his shoulders slump.

'Oh, Alex! What happened?'

'She took him away.'

She had to gulp back a sob at the raw pain in his voice.

'She had paternity tests carried out and they proved that I...'

'But you'd raised him. You loved him!' The words burst from her. 'Alex, you must've had rights.'

'She and her lover—Chad's biological father—left before I'd gathered my wits. They fled to South America.'

Kit stared at him. No! This episode in his life—it couldn't end like this. Alex had loved that little boy. That little boy would've loved Alex.

'The legal advice I received wasn't promising. After all, what legal rights did I really have?' His face twisted. 'Oh, I had the money to drag the case through the courts for years, but in the end who would I really be hurting?'

Chad. The knowledge sucked the air out of her lungs. He'd done what was best for the little boy he loved, but it hadn't given him an ounce of comfort. It had left a deep and lasting scar.

'Don't cry for me, Kit.'

It wasn't until he reached across to brush her tears away with the pad of his thumb that she realized she was crying.

'I'm not worth it.'

Wasn't he? Suddenly she wasn't so sure.

'Because the fact is, no matter what I tell myself, I can't go through that again.'

A weight settled in the middle of her chest.

'I once had a son, Kit, and now I don't. So you see, the paternity test, it isn't about you, it's about me. If your child is mine I will do what is legally required, but nothing more.'

CHAPTER SEVEN

ALEX strode out to the dark of the back garden and tried to draw air into his lungs.

He hadn't meant to tell Kit about Chad. He didn't talk about Chad. To anyone.

His gut clenched. He strode down to the back fence to wrap his fingers around the hard bark of the banksia tree until they started to burn and ache. He hadn't realized how much Kit's inability to fathom his previous treatment of her had plagued her, tormented her, had her questioning her own judgement and doubting herself. His mouth filled with acid. This was why he should have been more careful in the first place—resisted the temptation she'd presented, the lure of a life that he knew could never be his. But her sunshine had touched his soul, and for a short time he had been lost.

And she'd paid the price.

He'd wanted—needed—to reassure her that none of this was her fault. The only way to do that was to tell her about Chad. To tell her why he couldn't go through all that again.

Her unborn child—it was a source of joy for her.

For him… For him it was a constant source of torment, reminding him of everything he'd had and then lost, reminding him of the gaping hole at the centre of himself that nothing could fill. In losing Chad he'd lost the best part of himself.

If there'd ever been a best part of himself.

He didn't want another child.

He didn't want to *love* another child.

He'd given Chad everything—his time, his care, all the love in his heart. But it hadn't been enough. Jacqui had still left. He'd still lost the child he loved.

He wasn't going through that a second time.

Losing Chad had proved something that deep down he'd always known but had never wanted to believe—he didn't have what it took to be a family man. He refused to hide from the hard facts now. He could not give Kit what she so badly wanted—a stable and loving family unit.

What was the point in trying when he'd only lose it all again anyway?

Not hiding from the hard facts again? He gave a mirthless laugh. His demand for a paternity test was a lie, a blind, an excuse to hide behind. Kit wasn't lying. Her baby was his. He just didn't want to believe it, that was all. Kit didn't care about his money and she sure as hell didn't see him as a great catch. She'd prefer it if he *wasn't* her baby's father.

He rested his head against the trunk of the tree. Jacqui had taken Chad away from him without a backward glance. There were no guarantees that Kit wouldn't do the same. Eventually.

He would not relive that nightmare. Not for Kit. Not for anyone. If that made him a monster in her eyes, then so be it.

He loosened his grip on the tree to glance around the garden, which was partially illuminated by the light from the kitchen window. His gaze fell on the Cape Cod chair that Kit had been sanding the other day.

Do something useful.

He strode towards it. His mind worked best when his fingers were busy, and tonight he needed his mind to be at its peak.

Because, no matter what he told himself, he couldn't just up and leave when the weekend rolled around. He might not be able to offer Kit emotional support, but he couldn't abandon her with a house threatening to fall down around her ears either. Not when she was expecting a baby. He had to come up with a plan she'd go for and fast.

Because if he didn't, once she received the all clear from her doctor tomorrow he may well find himself very politely thanked and very firmly asked to leave. And who'd make sure she had everything she needed then?

Kit woke early on Thursday morning. She tried to go back to sleep but the nerves leaping and jumping in her stomach wouldn't let her.

Today she'd have her scan. Today she'd find out if her baby was okay.

A tap sounded on her bedroom door and Alex's head poked around its corner. How did he always know when she was awake?

'Good morning.'

She swallowed. He looked fresh and alert and good enough to eat. She pushed up against the pillows, dragged her hands back over her hair, tried to smooth it. 'Morning.'

'How are you feeling?'

'Fine.' Physically in herself, she was. She felt as if she'd never been sick in the first place.

But what if her high temperature had harmed her baby? What then? She knew worrying about that would do her no good, but not worrying was impossible.

Alex's eyes narrowed. 'Breakfast?'

She shook her head. She doubted she'd be able to keep anything down. 'A cup of something hot and herbal would be great, though.' Despite what the doctor had said, she'd given up caffeine the day she'd found out she was pregnant. She'd wanted to give her baby every chance.

Alex appeared with two mugs of…lemongrass tea. The fragrance made her stomach loosen a fraction. She accepted her mug with a lift of the lips that she hoped would pass for a smile. 'You do know that I don't mind if you drink coffee, don't you? You don't need to abstain just because I am.'

'It doesn't seem fair to drink it when you can't. Besides, this lemon stuff is halfway decent.' His nose wrinkled. 'But you can keep that chamomile nonsense to yourself.'

She found herself chuckling, even amidst all the anxiety swirling through her.

'Nervous, huh?'

She didn't know how he'd sensed it. She'd thought she'd done a good job at covering it up. It seemed pointless trying to deny it, though. 'A little.'

He surveyed her for a moment, set his mug on the floor and then leaned towards her. 'Your temperature came down very quickly, Kit. You've had lots of rest, good food and medicine. You're young, strong and the picture of health again. There's no reason to believe that your baby isn't strong and healthy too.'

She nodded. She knew he was right.

'But?' he said softly.

She set her mug on the bedside table as her stomach clenched up again. 'Do you believe in fate, Alex?'

'Not really.'

He didn't pick his mug up again. He remained with elbows on knees, his full attention focused on her. For a moment it made her feel spotlighted—at the centre of his world. She shook herself.

'Why?' he asked.

She swallowed again, found her fingers had started pleating and unpleating the quilt. She gripped them together to still them. 'Maybe I'm not fated to be a mother. I didn't realize I was pregnant for three whole months. I drank caffeine and the occasional glass of wine, and…and I didn't do stuff that I would've done had I known.'

He frowned. 'Kit, you're going to be just fine.'

'Fine?' Her voice rose. 'How on earth can you say that? On Monday I didn't even realize I was sick! Honestly, Alex, what does that say about me and the kind of mother I'm going to make?' Her heart ached. She pressed her palms to her eyes for a moment before dragging them back into her lap. 'It doesn't reflect very well on me, does it? For heaven's sake, I don't even know how to change a nappy! Maybe…' She gulped. 'Maybe I'm not meant to be a mother.'

'What the hell…? No!'

Alex jumped up, knocking over his mug in the process. With a swift curse he tore off his T-shirt and used it to mop up the spill.

As a broad expanse of naked flesh met her gaze, Kit's eyes went wide. She could feel them getting bigger and bigger as the space in her lungs for air became progressively smaller and smaller. Her thought processes slammed to a halt. Alex's shoulders and chest and the sculpted line of his back—tanned, muscled and toned—all beckoned to her. She knew from experience how firm his skin would be to the touch. And how warm.

Her pulse skittered and skipped and skated through her veins.

'Didn't want the rug to stain,' he said, his voice gruff as he glanced up at her.

She sucked her bottom lip into her mouth, felt an answering tug in her womb as he rose to his feet and stood before her in all his half-naked glory. She remembered another time… Her stomach, her lips, her limbs softened.

Oh, dear Lord! She tried to catch her breath. 'I…um… You didn't need to ruin your shirt in the process.'

He lifted one powerful shoulder as he sat again, the T-shirt hanging negligently from his hands. 'I'll throw it in the wash later. It'll be fine.'

The muscular definition of his biceps and the sinewy strength of his forearms had her melting against the bedclothes. He was so tanned. Had he worked beneath a hot African sun without his shirt?

'You're going to be a great mother, Kit.'

That dragged her attention back. His eyes had darkened to coal and they stared at her intensely as if by their very force they could compel her to believe his words.

'What makes you so sure?' she whispered. She wanted to believe him—desperately—but…

'Look at how much effort you're going to in order to provide your baby with the best life you can. You've moved back to this place that you love because you think it's a good place to raise your child. You've bought a house and you're getting it ready for your baby's arrival. You're surrounding your baby with a community of people who will love it almost as much as you will.'

She bit her lip.

'Kit?'

She glanced up into those coal-dark eyes again.

'You love your baby. That's more important than knowing how to change a nappy or abstaining from caffeine or…or anything! You want to be a mother, right?'

She nodded.

'Then you're going to be just fine. You'll learn all the things you need to know about being a mum along the way. You have your family and friends and your baby books to help you. You'll probably make the odd mistake because you're human like the rest of us, but it won't mean you love your baby any less and it won't make you a bad person. It certainly won't make you a bad mother.'

She blinked, considered his words, and then sent him a shaky smile. 'You're right. Thank you. I'm sorry, I just panicked for a bit.'

'Nothing to apologise for.'

He leaned back in his seat. It highlighted the flatness of his stomach and the way the muscles there coiled and flexed beneath his skin. Her gaze drifted downwards and she noted how the waistband of his jeans sat low on his hips. Her mouth and throat went dry.

'There's something I'd like to discuss with you, Kit. I was going to wait until after your doctor's appointment, but that's still hours away.'

She sensed that he wanted to distract her from brooding on her worries about her baby's health. She started to lift her eyes, wanted to thank him again for easing her fears, but his chest and shoulders proved more of a distraction than his words. His chest started to rise and fall with a rhythm that matched hers. Her fingers clenched in the quilt. A pulse pounded at the base of his throat. Firm, lean lips opened. Heat swirled through her.

That magnificent body leapt up. Kit's breath caught and she started to lean towards him—

'I'll be back in a moment.'

The words—hoarse with need—scraped out of his throat and caressed all the hairs on her arms into lifting as if in surrender. He surged out of her room, the muscles in his back rippling, and Kit melted back into her pillows, her mind too fuzzed to work.

He returned a moment later, dragging another shirt on over his head.

Heat of an entirely different variety burned her cheeks, her face, her throat then. She wanted to cover her head with the bedclothes. Instead she buried her face in her lukewarm mug of tea while Alex opened the bedroom window wider to let in the cool morning air and then busied himself with her CD player. *Sounds of the Sea* filtered into the room. He kept his back to her and she wondered if he was having as much trouble getting himself under control as she was.

Eventually she managed to clear her throat. 'You wanted to talk to me about something?'

He turned then, moved his chair another foot or so away from her bed. If he kept doing that he'd end up in the bathroom.

He sat. 'That's right, I did.'

'Well?' she prompted when he didn't continue.

'Kit, do you have a job lined up yet?'

She stared. A job? And then she rolled her eyes. 'You don't need to worry about my finances. I had a very nice nest egg squirreled away before I left Sydney.'

'Enough to cover expensive repairs on your house?'

She bit her lip and glanced away. She could get a bank loan.

When you don't have a job. Ha! Fat chance.

Her stomach clenched and her pulse started to race. She'd better start job-hunting asap because she needed the house ready for when the baby came. She glanced back at Alex. She'd failed in providing her baby with a father. She couldn't fail on this too. Alex had calmed her fears about her ability to be a good mother, but to prove she could be a good parent she had to get this house, and her life, on track fast. Finding a job was the first place to start.

'Kit, I want to barter an exchange of labour with you.'

'A…' She stilled. 'Why?'

'Because I think it would be to both our benefits.'

An exchange of labour?

'I'd really like you to finish that book project for McBride's.'

'Alex—' she lifted her hands and then let them drop again '—there are any number of people at Hallam Enterprises more than capable of finishing that project. Didn't you read my report?'

'It was *your* passion that had that book offer tabled to us in the first place. It was *your* passion that sold me on the deal. It's *your* passion that will make it a success.'

'Your name on the cover will do that—your experience, your expertise.'

'I can't write the thing, though. You're the one who translates all that so-called experience and expertise into a compelling, readable account. That's where your expertise lies. We make a good team, Kit.'

She stilled at his words. A team—her and Alex?

'I want you to finish overseeing the work on the book because you are the best person for the job. With an Internet connection here you can work remotely. You won't need to go into the office.'

'You said a barter of labour. What will you be doing?'

'Fixing your house.'

Her jaw dropped. 'Alex, you've just returned from a month abroad. You can't afford to take more time off work.'

His chin tilted at an arrogant angle. 'It's my company. I can do what I want. Besides, Donald has everything under control in the Sydney office.' He shrugged and the arrogance vanished behind the beginnings of a smile. A wry smile admittedly, but potent for all that. 'He's doing a good job and I am only a phone call away if there's an emergency.'

'But...' Her mind wouldn't work.

'I'll fix the hole in your roof and the hole in your wall. I'll repoint the piers on the southern side of the house and replace the guttering. I'll check for dry rot and—' his lips twisted '—not-so-dry rot. I'll modernise the bathroom and give the whole place a lick of paint, inside and out.'

Her eyes widened as his list grew. Whatever he saw in her face made him leap to his feet and stalk over to the window, hands shoved deep into his pockets.

She moistened her lips. 'It sounds as if I'm getting the better end of that deal.'

'Financially you'd be better off if you stayed on the books at Hallam Enterprises, took the maternity leave you'd be entitled to, and paid a builder to make the repairs.'

She needed a job *and* she needed the house ready for when the baby came. Alex was offering her both in one fell swoop. He didn't want to be a father, but he didn't want to leave her in the lurch. That much was clear.

Maybe the truth of the matter was that Alex couldn't walk away from his child and he just hadn't realized that yet.

She remembered the expression on his face when he'd talked about Chad. He had glowed with love, his face soft with it, before the anguish had taken over. He'd wanted a child once.

She lifted her chin. 'Will you help me decorate the nursery?'

He shuffled his feet, rolled his shoulders. His lips turned down but his chin didn't drop. 'Consider it added to the list.'

'Then, Alex Hallam, we have ourselves a deal.'

'Excellent!'

Just for a moment, his smile bathed her in light.

'Ready for breakfast yet?'

'Yes, please.' Suddenly she found she was ravenous.

The doctor unwrapped the blood pressure monitor from around her arm. 'I'm delighted to say you're as fit as a fiddle.'

To her left she was aware of Alex sagging in his chair. Relief? She wouldn't be privy to that particular emotion until after the scan. She gripped her hands together and prayed her illness hadn't harmed her baby in any way.

'I'd like you to keep taking it easy for a bit, though. Rest when you get tired. You also need to make sure you finish the course of antibiotics.'

She could practically see Alex file those instructions away in case he needed to bring them out and wave them under her nose and recite 'doctor's orders' at her. It made her feel looked after, cared for, as if someone had her back. It was why she hadn't kicked up a fuss when he'd accompanied her into the doctor's consulting room. He'd looked after her so comprehensively these past few days. Besides, this was his baby too. He deserved to know if it was healthy and developing normally.

'Okay, let's do the scan. Jump up onto the table.' The doctor gestured to an examination table.

Alex leapt to his feet, paled. 'I'll…um…wait outside.'

'Alex, no!' Kit grabbed his hand, her stomach twisting and her heart pounding. If the news wasn't good she didn't think she could face it on her own. His mouth whitened. His shoulders clenched, but he didn't shake his hand free from her grip. Eventually he nodded.

'Thank you,' she whispered. She tried to release his

hand, but found that she couldn't. Finally he smiled, just a slight drawing up on the right side of his mouth, but it helped ease some of the tension that had her wrapped up tight.

'C'mon, Kit, up onto the table.'

He helped her up onto it, which was just as well because her legs had turned to putty. He held her hand when the doctor squirted cold gel onto her stomach.

'There's your baby, Kit.'

Kit's gaze shot to the monitor. 'Is it okay? Did my high temperature—'

'Your baby is perfect.'

She closed her eyes and sent up a prayer of thanks.

'Everything looks exactly as it should,' the doctor continued. 'Your temperature came down very quickly. I can't envisage any problems. Look, here's the head…an arm.'

Her body went loose and light as relief, joy and gratitude all flooded through her. She turned to grin up at Alex, to share her joy, but Alex wasn't looking at her, he was staring at the screen. At the picture of their baby. And just for a moment hunger stretched across his face. It thickened her throat. It made her want to throw her arms around him.

And then he went pale. Perspiration beaded his forehead, his top lip.

'Would you like to know the sex of your baby?'

Alex dropped her hand, he backed up and then he bolted from the room. A chill settled over her. She tried to blink the sting from her eyes.

'Kit?' the doctor queried softly.

She stared back at the screen and shook her head. 'I… uh…think I'd like that to be a surprise.'

He nodded and let her stare at the screen for a bit longer.

'You know what the pregnancy books say, don't you?' he finally said.

It took a force of will to focus on the doctor's words rather than the doubts cascading through her mind. 'What's that?'

'A woman becomes a mother the moment she finds out she's pregnant. A man becomes a father only when his child is placed in his arms.'

She moistened her lips. Could he be right?

Her heart burned. She had a feeling it would take a miracle for Alex to embrace fatherhood again.

Then she recalled the hunger that had stretched across his face. Maybe it wasn't a miracle they needed, just some time?

She fastened her jeans again, thanked the doctor and left the consulting room to find Alex pacing in the corridor. Without a word, he took her arm and led her outside to the car. He opened the passenger door for her, but she didn't duck inside. She stood her ground until he met her eyes. 'I'm sorry I put you through that. I'm sorry I asked you to stay when it quite obviously brought back bad memories for you.'

'You have nothing to apologise for, Kit.' His voice was clipped and short. 'I'm just glad that your baby is well.'

It's your baby too! she wanted to shout as he walked around to the driver's side.

She ducked inside the car and waited until he was seated beside her. 'If I'd known the scan would remind you of Chad I wouldn't have asked you to stay.'

He didn't say anything.

'The thing is—' she swallowed '—I wouldn't have thought the memory of Chad's scan would be a bad thing. I'd have thought it'd be a happy memory.'

'There is nothing happy to be had in any of those memories!'

She flinched at his tone, its hardness. 'I…I was afraid that the scan would show something bad. I couldn't face that on my own. Your being there, it helped…thank you.'

The pounding behind Alex's eyes intensified at Kit's simple words. Finding out her baby was well and healthy— it should have been a moment of joy for her. He'd ruined that.

But he hadn't been able to stay in that room a moment longer. His stomach had become a hard ball of anguish that he thought would split him in two. The picture on the screen and the sound of the baby's heartbeat had threatened to tear him apart.

A bead of perspiration detached itself from his nape to trickle all the way down his back.

That's not Kit's fault.

He closed his eyes and dragged in a breath, tried to grab the tatters of his control and shape them back into place around him. He would fix her house; he would make arrangements to pay her child support. He'd fulfil his obligations. And then he'd get the hell out of her life. He didn't have anything more to offer her.

He sent her a sidelong glance. She'd gone pale. The knowledge that he'd robbed her of her joy left a bitter taste in his mouth. He had to clench his hands on the steering wheel to stop from leaning forward and resting his head on it.

He started up the car because there wasn't anything else he could think to do. 'I thought we could do some shopping, do something about the woeful state of your freezer. I figured it was time someone taught you to cook.'

His attempt at levity didn't work.

'I don't much feel like shopping.'

Idiot! Why hadn't he been able to control his reaction to the scan? She'd been ill. She was still recovering. He was supposed to be looking out for her.

He opened his mouth to apologise, to explain, but the words wouldn't come. He revved the car extra hard. He shoved his shoulders back. 'You're right. It's time we got back. I'm expecting a delivery from the hardware store.'

The delivery had already arrived by the time they returned. The wood was neatly stacked in the front garden beneath a tarpaulin. Frank was in the process of stacking all the tools Alex had hired onto the veranda out of the weather.

He strode up to Alex and clapped him on the shoulder. 'Howdy, neighbour.'

The familiarity had him rolling his shoulders. 'Hello, Frank.' It took a concerted effort not to add, *I'm only here temporarily, you know?*

'What did the doctor say, Kitty-Kat?'

Kit lifted her chin and smiled at Frank with an easiness that made his heart burn. She hadn't smiled at him like that since he'd arrived in Tuncurry.

'I got the all-clear. Mother and baby are doing fine.'

'That's grand news, love.'

It was. And Alex had rained on her parade. He didn't deserve her smiles.

Frank gestured to the tools. 'Good to see you haven't wasted any time. What's the plan?'

Alex told him because it was easier than following Kit into the house and dealing with the reproachful silence she'd subjected him to in the car.

He'd deserved it, he knew that, but he didn't know how to put things right. It'd be better for all concerned if she just kept thinking of him as some kind of unfeeling monster.

He battled the scowl building up inside him and told Frank how he meant to replace the joists and wall studs in the living room wall after he'd fixed the broken tiles on the roof, and then how he was going to re-plaster the wall and paint the house.

'If you need a hand…'

Frank's eager face finally burned itself into his brain. Frank wanted to help, was dying to be useful, and Alex didn't have the heart to rain on another person's parade today. 'You wouldn't happen to be handy with a sander by any chance, would you?'

'I would be.'

Alex clapped the older man on the shoulder. 'Then you're hired. A second pair of hands will be a godsend.'

Frank beamed at him and Alex found he could still smile. After a fashion.

CHAPTER EIGHT

KIT and Alex spent the next week working on their individual projects. Because there was so much dust and
noise from the work Alex was doing in the living-dining
area, Kit had set up a temporary office in one corner of
her bedroom—a card table, her laptop and a file that was
over a foot thick that had been couriered from Sydney.

Alex always broke off at lunchtime to make sure she
ate. And that Frank ate too, if the older man was helping
and hadn't already left for one of his tri-weekly swims that
Doreen insisted he keep up. 'Mondays, Wednesdays and
Fridays, lovey. Doctor's orders.'

Kit had the distinct impression that some days Frank
was more of a hindrance than a help. His pleasure at being
of use, though, touched her. So did Alex's patience with
him.

It was a side she hadn't seen to Alex before. As the
multi-millionaire executive in Sydney, Alex had been demanding, dictatorial and, at times, difficult. He paid his
executives top dollar and as a result he expected them to
be on the ball—no excuses. But this Alex, the builder-
tradesman working on her house in Tuncurry, he was more
laid-back, more relaxed. More human.

He made her heart beat harder too.
Nonsense! Don't rhapsodise.

It was just…if Alex could be this good with an eager elderly gentleman, then wouldn't he be great with a child?

The thought hitched her breath, made her stomach churn and her fingers tremble. She pushed away from the card table to pace. She'd been lucky thus far in her pregnancy—she hadn't suffered much from nausea. But whenever she thought of Alex's reaction during her scan, her stomach rebelled and bile rose in her throat.

He had become so *dark*!

She paused in her pacing to pull both hands back through her hair. She couldn't deny it. She wanted a father for her baby. Even a part-time father was better than no father at all. Before she'd found out about Chad, she'd thought Alex the lowest of low lifes. But now she knew he would never hurt their baby the way her father had hurt her.

She remembered all the nights as a child when she'd lain awake yearning for a father, the joy when he'd finally become a part of her life. The devastation when she'd found out how little she'd really meant to him.

Chad had meant the world to Alex. It didn't take a genius to figure that one out. Couldn't this baby mean the world to him too?

She swung away, hands clenched. It wasn't fair that her baby—*their* baby—be forced to suffer because of another's crimes. What was really holding Alex back from embracing fatherhood a second time? Did he think history would repeat itself?

She stumbled. Was that it? Did he think she would take his baby away from him the way his ex-wife had?

She turned to stare at the door. If that were the case… She bit her lip. She had to get him to un-think that as soon as she could.

* * *

Alex glanced around as Kit emerged from the hallway door and carefully closed it behind her. Keeping it closed kept the worst of the dust out of the bedrooms.

Last week, Alex had moved a camp bed and his clothes into the spare bedroom. The nursery. It shared a wall with Kit's bedroom. He wasn't sleeping well. One wall didn't seem like much of a barrier and at night, whenever he closed his eyes, all he could see was Kit's glorious nakedness. It made him ache and burn.

Just like her impersonal politeness made him ache and burn. He missed their easy-going banter, the connection that had once existed between them. Telling himself it was for the best didn't help.

Grinding his teeth together, he ordered himself to focus back on the sanding, but before he could he caught an eyeful of the way her breasts pressed against the cotton of her simple shirtdress and he found he could barely move let alone get back to work. Her curves had become curvier in the last few days and only a saint could deny noticing.

Both he and Kit knew he wasn't a saint.

Kit glanced behind him. 'Ooh, no hole!' She pointed and moved towards it.

'Don't touch. It's still wet.' He'd only just finished plastering it. He glanced back at her, tried to keep his eyes above neck level. 'How's your work coming along?'

Her lips turned down and he could've kicked himself for asking. He didn't want her thinking he was checking up on her or anything.

She wrinkled her nose. 'Slow.'

She thrust out one hip and surveyed him. Her legs went…all the way up. He gulped. She hadn't been wearing that dress at lunchtime. Just as well too. With the memory of that much bare skin on display he'd have made a mess of the wall.

'Wanna go fishing?'

That jerked his eyes back to her face. The beginnings of a smile played around the corners of her mouth. He'd do a lot to turn it into a full-blown smile.

'Fishing?'

She shrugged as if it was no skin off her nose whether he said yes or no, but that smile no longer threatened to come out and play.

He shifted his weight from one leg to the other and then back again. He should stay as far away from this woman as he could. 'I've never been fishing.'

She rolled her eyes. 'That's not what I asked. Would you like to give it a go?'

Did he? He didn't know. The thought of spending the rest of the afternoon skiving off with Kit sounded great. Too great if the truth be told. He should resist it, wrestle her house into shape and then get the hell out of here. 'Where?'

'On the breakwater.'

He stared at her blankly. Her hands flew to her hips. 'Alex Hallam, haven't you explored even the tiniest bit since you've been here? Haven't you had a look at the beaches or the lake or anything?'

He knew where the hardware store and the supermarket were. He didn't need to know anything else. Besides, he'd had too many other things on his mind—like Kit's pregnancy—to play tourist.

Garbage! All you've done is avoid thinking about Kit's pregnancy. In fact, he suspected he'd rather staple gun his hand to the wall than talk about pregnancy and babies.

So he'd concentrated all his efforts on her house instead.

Not on the fact that he was going to become a father.

And not on playing tourist.

In case Kit hadn't noticed, he wasn't precisely in holiday-maker mode.

She shook her head, almost in pity. 'C'mon, all work and no play is making Jill a *very* dull girl.'

She eyed him up and down. It made his skin go tight and hot. Her eyes skittered away and he watched as she swallowed once, twice. 'What you're wearing will do fine, unless you'd rather change into a pair of board shorts.'

He shook his head. She'd said fishing. Not swimming.

'Put that down.' She pointed to the sander. 'You can come and help me haul the fishing rods out of the garden shed. Chop-chop.'

He kicked himself into action. It was only one afternoon.

Alex parked his car and spent a moment just drinking in the view. Finally he turned to Kit. 'I had no idea it would be so beautiful.'

The grin she sent him warmed him as effectively as the sun on the bare flesh of his arms. She settled a floppy canvas hat on her head and gestured in the direction of the breakwater. 'C'mon.'

She insisted on carrying one of the fishing rods—the lightest one—and Alex carried the other rod, the tackle box, a bucket and the net. He couldn't explain the primal urge to take her rod, though, and add it to his load.

Perhaps it was just good manners?

Yeah, right! If he had any manners whatsoever he wouldn't be trying to catch as big an eyeful of those golden legs of hers as he could.

She pointed to their right. 'This is called the Rock Pool. It's where all the local kids learn to swim. It's where I learned to swim.'

A sweep of golden sand and clear water stretched out

from the breakwater to a smaller bank of rocks bordering the channel. Kit told him the channel led into Wallis Lake. The breakwater provided a wave trap and this little bay had been roped off to provide a safe place to swim. Tiny waves lapped at the shore in rhythmic whooshes and the water was so clear he could see the sandy bottom, free from rocks and seaweed. He couldn't think of a prettier place to learn to swim.

To their left, though, stretched mile upon mile of golden sand and the foaming, rolling breakers of a surf beach. The salt in the air and the sound of the breakers intensified the further they walked out on the breakwater. The firmness of the path beneath his feet, the warmth of the spring sun and the sound of seagulls on the breeze eased tension out of his shoulders he hadn't even known was there.

'Is that where you swam as a teenager?' He pointed to the surf beach. He'd bet at sixteen she'd been a golden surfer girl.

She grinned at him and it struck him that she still was.

'Sometimes. But when I was a teenager my friends and I hung out at Forster beach.' She waved her hand to her right, indicating somewhere across the channel. 'It was *way* cooler.'

He laughed at the teenage inflection. He paused to glance back at the bridge that spanned the channel and connected the two townships of Tuncurry and Forster. It was white and wooden and gleamed in the sun.

She nudged his arm and urged him forward again. 'C'mon, I want to see if my favourite rock is taken.'

She had a favourite rock?

It was a huge flat monstrosity about three-quarters of the way along the breakwater that looked as if it would comfortably hold four people with room to spare. She gave a whoop and immediately clambered down to it.

'Heck, Kit!' Alex tried to keep up with her, tried to put a hand under her elbow to steady her. An impossibility given his armful of fishing rod and tackle box. He dropped the bucket. 'Steady on. You're pregnant. You're supposed to take it easy.'

She turned back to look at him, hand on her head to keep her hat in place. 'It doesn't make me an infirm old granny, you know? Now, c'mon, front and centre. I'm going to teach you how to cast off and if you don't get the knack by your third go I'm going to push you in.'

The bark of laughter that shot out of him took him completely by surprise, but Kit's eyes were so bright with pleasure that he didn't try to suppress it.

He managed to cast off successfully on his second go. Kit cast off next and then settled on the rock, feet dangling out over the water several metres below. Alex folded his large frame down to sit beside her. 'What now?'

She sent him a wide-eyed stare. 'Why, we wait to catch a fish, of course.'

But he could sense her laughter bubbling just beneath the surface and it made him grin. It made him feel as if he was on holiday.

It made him feel young.

His grin, or whatever she saw in his face, made Kit's eyes widen. Her eyes dropped to his lips and he recognized the flare of temptation that flitted through them.

If she leaned forward and kissed him, he would kiss her back. Right or wrong, he would cup one hand around the back of her head, slant his lips over hers and explore every millimetre of those delectable lips of hers. Slowly. Thoroughly.

They were both holding fishing rods. How much trouble could one little kiss cause…in public, on a breakwater?

He glanced down at the oyster-encrusted rocks below

and found his answer. It took every ounce of strength he had, but he turned his eyes seaward. 'What are we hoping to catch?'

'Who cares?'

Her voice came out all breathy. Alex's hands tightened on his rod. He kept his gaze doggedly out to sea, but from the corner of his eye he could see the way she swung her legs.

'I am wearing my swimming togs under this dress, you know?'

'What?'

'You seem very disapproving. You think my dress is too short, don't you?'

'No, I—'

He broke off. He could hardly explain the reason he kept staring was because he couldn't help it, because she fascinated him, because he wanted her. *That* wouldn't help either of them.

'Bream,' she said. 'A couple of bream would be nice. Or whiting. They taste great—sweet and juicy. Lots of bones, though. A flathead, maybe? Just try and avoid hooking a grey nurse shark. It'll snap the line.'

'I'll do my best,' he managed.

'It'd be nice if the tailor started to chop.'

He didn't know what that meant. No doubt if he hung around long enough he'd find out. If he stayed.

Sitting here now beside Kit, that was easy to imagine.

'Oh, but it's good to be back.'

He turned to find she'd tilted her face to the sun—pleasure, gratitude and satisfaction all alive in her face. His gut clenched. He tried to remember her in one of her prim dark suits. He could—with remarkable alacrity—but… 'You belong here.'

Not that he'd ever considered her out of place in the city,

but here…she was home. Had he really intended to drag her away? How did a measly job compete with all this?

'What?' she teased. 'On a breakwater, fishing?'

'You bet.'

She adjusted her line…somehow. Alex just let his be and hoped it was doing what it should be. 'It sure beats the rush and bustle of the city, don't you think?'

He didn't answer. She was right, but he didn't answer.

'I was lucky to grow up around here.'

Her child would be too.

'Did you grow up in Sydney?'

'Yes.'

'Whereabouts? North, south, east or west?'

His stomach tightened. He didn't like talking about his childhood. But her question, it was innocent, innocuous. 'In the western suburbs until I was twelve and then Vaucluse.'

She spun on her rock. He shot an arm out to steady her. 'You grew up in Vaucluse—as in on the harbour—and you've never been fishing?'

'Would you eat what came out of the harbour?'

She pursed her lips, then nodded. 'Good point.'

He removed his arm from around her waist. He couldn't stay here in this golden place near this golden woman. Eventually everything he touched turned to ash.

He wouldn't do that to Kit.

In the next instant he nearly fell off the rock. 'Holy crap!' The fishing rod had developed a mind of its own.

Kit started laughing so hard tears filled the creases at the corners of her eyes. 'Reel in! Reel in!' she finally managed to choke out. 'You've hooked a fish, you landlubber.'

'A fish?'

He promptly set about reeling it in.

'Ooh, it's a big one!' Kit gave him instructions—"Play

the line out a bit, don't lose it on the rocks'. Frankly, he didn't have much of a clue what she meant, but finally he had the fish, flapping on the end of his line, clear of the water.

Jumping to her feet and bracing herself against his shoulder, Kit scooped the net beneath the fish and presented it to him. 'Your first fish!'

He leapt to his feet. His first—

'A bream! Congratulations, Alex.' With that she leaned forward and planted a kiss on his cheek.

He promptly felt ten feet tall. He leant in and kissed her full on the mouth.

She kissed him back.

They drew away and stared at each other. Her eyes were golden with sunshine and fun. Her lips…

The all-consuming need that had been building in him for the last fortnight broke through his control. He had to have more! Before he could think the better of it, he grasped her chin in his free hand and slanted his mouth fully over hers.

She tasted of salt and choc-chip cookies and some memory from his past that he couldn't quite grasp.

His tongue traced the inside of her bottom lip, revelling in her velvet warmth. Maybe if he kissed her deeper, longer, more thoroughly, he'd remember that memory and—

Her tongue shyly stroked his and all conscious thought fled as their kisses deepened. Her hand fisted in his shirt to draw him closer. His fingers slanted around the curve of her scalp, sliding through the silk of her hair to angle her mouth so he could explore every exquisite millimetre of her delectable lips.

Four months! He'd ached for this for four months.

It was worth the wait.

For a moment he thought it might just be worth anything.

Finally, with a gasp, she dragged her mouth from his, rested her forehead against his cheek, her chest rising and falling as if she'd just run a race.

'Alex, you've got to warn a woman if you're going to kiss her like that.'

He was breathing so hard he couldn't speak.

'At least make sure she has two hands free to hold onto you.'

She was still holding the net full of fish. He took the net from her. 'Sorry, I got carried away by the moment.'

No, he wasn't. He wasn't the least bit sorry.

She stared up at him then, a frown in her eyes. 'I'm not sure we should be doing that.'

He blinked. He wanted to do a whole lot more than—

Hell! He snapped away from her.

Kit sighed and sat again. 'Don't fall off the rock, Alex. The current is fierce and I don't feel like diving in and saving you.'

When he sat back beside her she expertly unhooked the fish and popped it in the bucket. 'Okay, next lesson—how to bait the hook.'

He took his cue from her. She didn't want to talk about that kiss and he was damn sure he didn't want to either. It didn't mean anything. It *couldn't* mean anything.

They caught two bream apiece. Even given that kiss, the confusion it sent hurtling through him, Alex couldn't remember the last time he'd had so much fun. 'I have to hand it to you, Kit. This fishing gig was a good idea.'

He grinned when she said, 'I won't say I told you so.' They sat in companionable silence, their lines dangling in the water and the breeze playing across their faces. They swung their feet and breathed the invigorating salt tang that seasoned the air and listened to the cries of the seagulls. 'You know, I always dreamed that my dad would take me fishing like this.'

He glanced at her out of the corner of his eye. She hadn't mentioned her father before. 'He didn't?'

She snorted. 'He didn't know one end of a fishing rod from the other.'

Neither had he before today.

'When I told my grandma about that little dream, she took me fishing herself.'

'On this rock?' He couldn't get enough of her stories about her childhood.

She pointed back along the way they'd come. 'We dropped hand lines further along that way in the channel. A much safer spot for a child.'

'And?' He didn't know what he was waiting for. He rubbed the back of his neck. Would his child dream that one day its father would take it fishing too?

The thought unnerved him.

'And we didn't catch a thing, but we had the best time.' She laughed, the memory obviously a good one. 'Eventually my grandma and I graduated to this rock.' She patted it.

He stretched his neck first one way then the other. Kit's child would have her for its mother. It wouldn't miss out on anything. It wouldn't want for anything.

Except a father.

'Your childhood sounds idyllic. You were close to your family?' He wanted her surrounded by family who would look out for her, support her.

'My family is my mother and grandmother. I adore them both.'

His heart started to pound. 'And your father?'

A shadow passed over her face. He immediately regretted darkening her day. 'I'm sorry, I shouldn't have asked. It's none of my business.'

'No,' she said slowly. 'I think you should know about my father, Alex. It might help you understand where I'm coming from.'

He didn't need to know about her past to know that she was wonderful now. But he was happy to listen to anything she wanted to tell him.

'My parents never married. Their relationship was over long before I was born and my mother had me without any support from him.'

'You and your mum were happy?'

'Oh, yes, but when I started school and saw the other children with their daddies, I wanted one too. I started asking Mum a lot of questions, pestering her about my dad until she finally promised to track him down for me.'

He could imagine the younger Kit with her golden hair and her golden skin and her golden eyes. And her yearning. He swallowed. 'And?'

'And finally she did. I was so happy. He took me swimming and for ice cream. I got to introduce him to Caro and Denise and Alice and all my other friends.'

'And then?'

She shrugged. 'I saw him off and on until I was fifteen. He'd show up three or four times a year with a belated Christmas present, take me out for my birthday, that kind of thing.'

She fiddled with her fishing rod, resettled her hat on her head. Alex didn't move.

'I was a bit slow on the uptake. It took me a while to realize he didn't actually enjoy hanging out with me.'

Bile burned the back of his throat. 'Kit, I'm sorry. I—'

She waved his sympathy away. 'You know, I could've

accepted it if he'd made all those visits out of a sense of responsibility or duty, but…I caught Mum paying him.'

He frowned. He wanted her to turn and look at him, but her gaze remained on the swirling water below.

'My mother had been paying him, bribing him, to play father to me.'

Her voice was strangely impassive and it took a moment for the import of her words to hit him. When they did his hands threatened to snap his fishing rod in two. He'd have preferred to wrap them around her father's throat. The hide of the man!

'I never saw him again. I was pretty angry with my mother for a long time too.' She paused, pursed her lips. 'But now, with a baby of my own on the way, I understand my mother's actions so much more.' She glanced at him and then glanced away again. 'You see, Alex, I want my baby to have everything good in this world and that includes a father.'

Her words chilled him to the very centre of his being. 'Kit, I—'

'I know what you told me, Alex. I know you said you would not be a father to our baby.'

Our baby. He closed his eyes. It wasn't that he wouldn't, but that he *couldn't*.

'I would love to change your mind about that.'

'I—'

'No, just listen to what I have to say. I'm not asking you to respond. I just want you to hear what I have to say. Okay?'

His heart dropped to his knees. He managed a heavy nod.

'I know what it's like to yearn for a father with your whole being until everything else shrinks in importance.

Knowing how important it was to me, do you think I would purposely and consciously ever deny that to my child?'

She turned then and her golden eyes met his. 'I couldn't do it, Alex. I could never do what Jacqueline did. I could never deny my child its father.'

He closed his eyes, tried to block out all her goldenness and the spell she was threatening to weave about him.

'Like I said,' she continued, 'I'm not asking you to respond to any of this. It's just…'

He opened his eyes. He couldn't help it.

'The thing is, Alex, if you're using that as an excuse to avoid fatherhood then you're going to have to come up with another one because that one doesn't exist.'

A hole opened up inside his chest. 'I'm sorry your father did that to you, Kit. You can rest assured that I would never do that to your child.'

'No,' she whispered. 'You mean to hurt it in an entirely different way. At least I met my father and had a chance to know him and find out who he was. Even if he did disappoint me, at least it stopped me from building unrealistic fantasies around him.'

Was that what their child would do?

'Anyway—' Kit shook herself '—enough of all that for one day. Wanna learn how to clean and scale a fish?'

He tried to match her tone. 'How could I resist an offer like that?'

Her laugh could no longer lighten his heart. Her father's absence had left a hole in Kit's life, had left an indelible impression there that nothing could erase. Alex hadn't meant to do harm to anyone. But his actions had harmed Kit, and they would harm her unborn child's.

His child.

He dragged a hand down his face.

'So you're squeamish, huh?'

He pulled his hand away to find her attempting to demonstrate the correct way to gut a fish.

She cocked an eyebrow. 'Not going to throw up, are you?' Her half-grin robbed the words of their sting.

He wanted to lay himself at her feet and beg her to forgive him. For everything.

He didn't. Instead, he took all of the fish from her hands and, following her instructions, cleaned each and every one of them. It was the least he could do.

'Excellent.' She took the last fish, bundled up their things and made to leave their rock. 'I'll cook dinner tonight.'

'Hey, hold on a moment. You can't cook.' He took the net and the bucket from her hand and handed her the lightweight rod instead.

Her eyes danced. 'I said I *don't* cook. That doesn't mean I can't cook. And I can certainly do fish on the barbecue, jacket potatoes and a tossed salad.'

His mouth watered.

They walked back the length of the breakwater. Kit hummed, but Alex's mind churned. And then Kit halted mid-hum, and just stopped to stare.

At a mother and her baby swimming—floating—together in the shallows of the Rock Pool. A pre-toddler-sized baby. A little girl if the pink bathers and sunhat were anything to go by.

A little girl. Alex's thoughts tumbled to a halt. He couldn't drag his eyes from that baby. A great aching hole cracked open inside him.

'Cute, huh?' Kit whispered.

Yes!

Confusion, fear, desire all whipped through him. Kit's father had only visited Kit a few times a year. It had been enough for her until she'd discovered his betrayal. Could

Alex manage that kind of minimal contact—three or four visits a year?

He'd thought his staying away would be best for this child. Now he wasn't so sure. Kit's story had shaken him, left him stranded in uncertain territory with the ground shifting beneath his feet.

'Did you find out?' The question scraped out of his throat, unbidden. He hadn't meant to ask it. He hadn't known he'd wanted to ask it.

'Did I find out what?'

She continued to stare at the baby. Her face had gone soft, her lips curved upwards and her eyes shone. His heart pounded against the walls of his ribs. 'Did you find out the sex of the baby?'

She turned and smiled. 'No. I want it to be a surprise. But if you'd like to know I'm sure the doctor would tell you.'

Her smile, her words, they took his breath away. Perhaps she meant it. Perhaps she would let him be part of her baby's life.

He stared at the mother and baby in the shallows below and his arms started to ache with the longing for a child's weight. Three or four times a year, it wasn't much to ask. He remembered the smell of a baby. The newly washed, baby-powdered and slightly milky smell. The softness of a baby's skin. The surprising strength when a tiny hand gripped a finger.

Three or four times a year...

He scratched a hand back through his hair and then, without another word, he swung away and strode off towards the car.

CHAPTER NINE

'THE barbecue is ready to go.'

Kit's breath hitched, but she refused to turn from the bench where she tossed the salad. Alex—freshly showered—was making her heart beat just a little too hard. That was why she'd sent him outside to clean the barbecue plate.

'Is it lit?'

'Yes, ma'am.'

Her lips twitched at his mock subservience. She doubted Alex had a subservient bone in his body.

Nice body, though.

Oh, stop it!

She finished tossing the salad and wished her pulse would settle as easily. She tried to force her mind to mundane matters. Cooking, dinner, food.

Her mind refused. It wanted to dwell on Alex. On the breadth of his shoulders, the strength of his thighs. Thighs she'd had ample opportunity to examine when they'd been sitting on the breakwater.

She tried to resist glancing around at him. And failed. He met her gaze, moistened his lips. She wanted to groan. She wanted to reach up and wipe the tempting shine away.

That kiss on the breakwater…

Momentary lapse of concentration, her foot! It had been heaven.

And she'd love a repeat performance.

Her gaze zeroed in on those lips—lean, firm and magical. Alex cleared his throat. 'What can I do now?'

His voice came out hoarse. She wrenched her gaze away. Cooking, dinner, food, that was what she needed to concentrate on.

Food…um—she'd seasoned the fish with butter, lemon juice and fresh herbs before wrapping them in foil. They'd take no time at all to cook.

Dinner…um—she glanced at the stove. Jacket potatoes were nearly done. Salad was tossed.

Cooking…um—she lifted the platter of fish.

'You can get out of my way, for starters, because this master chef needs room to move.'

With a bow, Alex held the door open for her. Her heart galloped at the grin he sent her, flip-flopped and then galloped again. She did her best to ignore it. 'Could you bring that plate of corncobs with you?' She sent up a prayer of thanks that her voice actually worked.

After arranging the food on the barbecue, she glanced around her garden. The light was pink and gold and promised to last for another hour yet. A light breeze made the very top of the banksia sway every now and again. 'How about we eat out here?'

'A picnic?'

She wondered when Alex had last been on a picnic. She'd bet it was a long time ago. 'Freshly caught fish tastes better eaten out of doors.' Besides, he had sanded her two Cape Cod chairs and accompanying table and had painted them a crisp, clean white. They were crying out to be used.

'Tell me the first word that comes to your mind when I say "fishing"?'

She wanted Alex to relax this evening. She wanted him to have fun. And then she wanted to talk.

'Rocks,' he returned.

She had an immediate image of his legs dangling over her rock on the breakwater earlier. Strong thighs and—

'Mountains,' she returned.

'Himalayas.'

Good, no sexy images accompanied that word. She turned the fish. And in the same spirit… 'Yaks.'

'Yaks?'

Laughter burst out of him and Kit refused to question the way her shoulders lightened. 'Yeah, you know, big woolly animals with horns.' At least she thought they had horns.

'I know what a yak is.' His grin when it came was sudden and blinding. 'But in four steps we've jumped from fishing to yaks?'

Kit had to grin back. She physically couldn't help it. Besides, grinning wasn't against the rules. 'I'm trying to keep baby brain at bay. Caro has warned me that as soon as the baby is born, my brain will turn to mush. I thought word association games and the daily crossword might help counter its onset.'

'Right, smart move. Okay, here's one—picnic.'

'Ants.'

They both promptly stared down at the ground. 'No ants,' Kit finally said. 'C'mon, let's get this picnic on the road. The fish is nearly done.'

Ten minutes later they were settled in the chairs, plates balanced on knees, eating fish, potatoes, barbecued corn-cobs drenched in butter and salad.

'Heck, Kit, for someone who won't cook you've done a damn fine job.'

Kit licked butter from her fingers. 'I have, haven't I?'

But when she realized Alex followed the way her tongue caught the trickle of butter from the back of her hand, saw the way his eyes darkened, her stomach clenched. She grabbed a serviette and wiped her fingers instead. She left the rest of her corn untouched on her plate. Alex wrenched his gaze back to his plate.

The memory of their kiss burned between them.

That kiss, what did it mean? Alex hadn't planned on fatherhood, but it had found him anyway. He hadn't planned on any kind of romantic relationship either, but...

She refused to finish that thought.

She shifted on her chair. Could she blame pregnancy hormones for the way her heart crashed about in her chest whenever she locked eyes with Alex?

Her lips twisted as she speared a slice of cucumber. Not a chance. That was due to hormones she'd had long before she'd ever fallen pregnant.

'The fishing this afternoon, Kit, it was fun.'

'Yeah.' She smiled. 'I have so many great memories of sitting on my rock—fishing, dreaming, hanging out there with my friends or my mum and grandma. It reminds me of summer holidays and endless afternoons and laughter and all good things.'

He stopped eating to stare at her. 'I'm honoured you shared it with me.'

Regardless of what happened, she knew this afternoon would always be precious to her. And what she'd just said to Alex, all of that was true. 'Do you have a place like my rock?'

He cut into a potato, but he didn't eat it. 'No,' he finally said.

His face didn't shutter closed. She took that as a good sign. 'What did you like doing with your parents when you were young?' She swallowed as a different question occurred to her. 'Are your parents still alive?'

'They died when I was twelve. Car accident.'

There was no mistaking the closing up of his face now. Her heart burned. Her fingers shook and she had to lay her cutlery down. 'I'm sorry,' she whispered. 'That must've been awful.'

'Not your fault, Kit.'

His words, his half-shrug…the fact he ate a piece of fish—fish she'd cooked for him—gave her the courage to continue. 'Who did you live with afterwards?'

'My grandfather. He was as rich as Croesus and as bitter as battery acid.'

Uttered in a flat tone—fact with no emotion. Kit abandoned the rest of her food. 'That's when you moved to Vaucluse?'

He nodded.

The exclusive address hadn't shielded him from life's harsher realities. She could sense that much.

'He'd disowned my mother when she married my father. Apparently a motor mechanic wasn't good enough for the daughter of one of Australia's leading politicians.'

She shuddered. Alex's grandfather sounded controlling and vengeful. It wasn't the kind of home she'd ever want her child being sent to. 'If he disowned your mother, why did he take you in?'

'The papers got hold of the story, and to him appearances were everything.' His lips twisted into the mockery of a smile that made a chill creep up her arms. 'He had to at least be seen doing the right thing.' He threw off his smile with a shrug. 'I'd have been better off in a foster home.'

This was the man who'd raised Alex throughout his teenage years? More pieces of the puzzle fell into place. Kit wasn't prepared for the surge of anger that shot through her on Alex's behalf, though. The people who should've looked out for him, loved him—his grandfather, his ex-wife—they'd betrayed him utterly.

She didn't blame him for guarding his heart.

Her chest ached; her eyes ached. Did he have to keep guarding it against their baby, though?

'I left when I was sixteen. I found work as a builder's labourer.'

And he'd built an empire on his own. But that empire of his, it wouldn't have made up for all he'd lost when his parents died. With an effort, she swallowed back the lump in her throat. She was glad he'd given her a glimpse into his past, but she wanted tonight to be about happy memories. 'When they were alive, what did you like to do with your mum and dad?'

Enough light filtered into her garden for her to see that her question stumped him. She had a feeling that Alex had shut himself off from his past to protect himself from all the bad memories, but in the process he'd shut out all the good memories too.

'I…'

She could see that he struggled. 'Did your dad like to kick a ball around the garden with you? Did your mum make the best birthday cakes?'

One corner of his mouth kicked up. 'Mum couldn't bake to save her life.' He sat higher in his chair and grinned. It made him look younger, wiped all the cares from his face for a moment. It stole her breath. 'We used to play this strange cricket game with a tennis racquet and a ball.'

'We used to play that game on the beach!' She clapped her hands, absurdly pleased at this point of connection. 'We called it French cricket. Though I don't know how French it was.'

'On the weekends Dad would tinker with the car and he'd let me help. He taught me all the names of the tools.'

She could imagine a younger version of Alex—dark-haired and scrawny—handing his father tools, studying engine components in that serious, steady way of his. If they had a son, would he look like Alex? Share his mannerisms?

'Mum's favourite song was by the Bay City Rollers and she'd sing it all the time. Sometimes Dad and I would join in and…' he stilled with his fork halfway to his mouth '…we'd end up on the ground laughing. Mum would tickle me.' His grin suddenly widened. 'And Dad would always say that we were in for an early night.' He glanced at Kit, his eyes dancing. 'I now know what *that* was all about.'

'They sound like fun.' An ache stretched through her chest. 'They sound as if they loved each other very much.'

'I think they did.'

Don't go fooling yourself into thinking you can get that kind of happy ever after with Alex. If it weren't for the fact that she was pregnant, Alex would've left two weeks ago.

Without a backward glance.

He still might yet.

The only happy ever after she could hope for was Alex realizing that he could be a good father, that he would be there for her child. *Their* child.

'I did have a place!' He swung to her. 'A place like your rock. It was a tree in the back garden—a huge tree!'

She could tell he was talking about his garden in the western suburbs and not the one in Vaucluse.

'There was a particular branch I always sat on. It was the best place. Mum would bring me out drinks and biscuits. You're right, Kit, food out of doors does taste better.' He set his now empty plate on the table and glanced around her garden. 'You know, I like the idea of having a garden.'

Her breath caught. Enough to give up his penthouse apartment with its harbour views? She crossed her fingers. 'All kids should have a garden.' She tried to keep her voice casual, which was nearly impossible when this all mattered so much.

'Yeah.' Physically he was present, but she had a feeling he was a million miles away.

'Alex?'

'Hmm?'

'If you decided that you did want to be an active, involved father, what are the kinds of things you'd like to do with your child? Hypothetically speaking, of course.' She added the last in a rush. She didn't want to scare him off. She didn't want him clamming up again. She just wanted to plant the idea firmly—very firmly—into his mind.

'I...' He dragged a hand back through his hair, shrugged. 'The fishing this afternoon was fun.'

'Nuh-uh, I bags the fishing. You come up with your own activities, buster.'

He chuckled but she heard the strain behind it. He swung to her. 'Kit, I've by no means decided—'

'I know.' She refused let him finish, wouldn't let him talk himself out of the thought of becoming a father. She touched his arm. 'But will you promise me to at least consider the possibility? Just to...think about it?'

'Kit, I—'

He broke off and dragged a hand back through his hair. 'I'll think about it. But I'm not making any promises.'

'Thank you.'

He rose and took her now empty plate. 'Would you like some more?'

She shook her head.

'I'll get started on the dishes then.'

Kit watched him take their plates inside, her hand resting across her stomach, her fingers crossed.

Three days later Alex wasn't any closer to knowing if he could manage the kind of involvement Kit wanted from him.

Whenever he thought of that baby girl at the Rock Pool, though, a surge of longing cracked his chest wide open. Longing that had grown into a persistent ache.

He didn't know what it meant. He'd discounted children and family for ever.

But Kit was carrying *his* child. Could he just walk away?

He swallowed, remembering the first moment Chad had been placed in his arms and—

His mind shied away from the memory. Thinking about Chad, he couldn't do it. It hurt too much. Thinking about Chad made him want to throw his head back and howl.

He rolled his shoulders, shoved his thoughts aside. He hadn't signed up for any of this!

When he half-turned from the house to seize the crowbar Kit appeared at the very edge of his peripheral vision, sitting in her Cape Cod chair. She'd gone still, her fingers no longer flying across the keyboard of her laptop and suddenly he realized she'd ceased working to watch him. He swallowed and forced himself back to face the house. He pretended not to have noticed, told himself it didn't matter, pretended it didn't affect him.

Impossible! All the muscles in the lower half of his body bunched and hardened. Her gaze had the physical presence of a warm caress, like a soft finger tracing willing flesh.

He gritted his teeth and ordered himself to focus on the job at hand. Several weatherboards on her cottage needed replacing before he could paint. With crowbar primed, he started prising one off, steadily working his way along its length.

He'd wanted to refit the bathroom before he'd moved to the outside of Kit's house, but the hardware store was still awaiting delivery on the shower unit he'd ordered. The supplier was out of stock. He grimaced. He'd have to hide that particular bill from Kit when it arrived. The unit had cost a bomb and Kit would have a pink fit if she ever found out.

He set his jaw. The unit was top-of-the-line, non-slip, non-breakable glass, and easy-clean. The fibreglass base and interior meant no grouting. Kit had heaved a sigh of gratitude when he'd mentioned that particular fact. He figured she'd be busy enough with the baby when it came without adding a high-maintenance bathroom to her list of chores.

He wondered if she'd let him hire her a housekeeper or a cleaner.

She won't need a cleaner if you're around to help her.

If...?

The nails, rusted into the timber frame of the house, screeched as he worked the crowbar. Finally the weatherboard came free and he sidestepped it as it clattered to the ground.

If only he could sidestep other issues as easily.

From behind, he heard Kit's quick intake of breath. He glanced over his shoulder to find her gaze glued to his butt. She licked her lips, her eyes dark. She leant forward. He went hot, tight and rigid as rock.

He and Kit, they had chemistry. Maybe...

Her gaze lifted with a slowness and thoroughness that had him biting back an oath and fighting the desire to stride over there, drag her mouth up to his and have—

'Oh!'

He blinked. Kit stared at him, her cheeks a deep, dark pink. She swallowed convulsively and then jammed her canvas hat onto her head.

He swore. He tried to loosen his grip on the crowbar. Hanging out with Kit like this—it was murder! For Pete's sake, why had she taken to working outside anyway?

She'd said it was to enjoy the sun. He'd told her that she just enjoyed watching him slave away. His teeth ground together. He'd been joking.

It didn't feel like a joke any more.

He wiped his brow on his sleeve and let loose with another curse—low so she wouldn't hear it. Who was he kidding? He couldn't stay here in Tuncurry permanently. Kit deserved something more than he could ever offer. If he stayed here she would never get it.

What about the baby?

Could he...?

Yes!

His lips thinned. Probably not. He knew Kit was getting her hopes up—hopes that he would be some kind of father to her baby, a better father than hers had been. The thought of dashing those hopes made him want to throw up.

He swallowed back the bile. No throwing up.

No hiding from the facts either. Darkness threatened the edges of his consciousness. He let it in to swamp his soul, smother whatever hopes he dared to entertain. The man he'd had to become to survive his grandfather's rule was not the kind of man who could make marriage and family work. His brief and disastrous marriage had proved that. His grandfather's tyrannical bitterness had killed something essential in him. Something soft that was necessary to make relationships work. That was all there was to it.

If he made promises to Kit—stayed and tried to build a life with her—eventually she'd come to see him for who he really was.

And then she'd leave him, divorce him…and she'd take his child away.

He had to stay strong. Damage control—that was all he could do now.

'You must be ready for a break, Alex. You've barely stopped working all day.' Ice chinked invitingly in the jug on the table beside her. 'At least have a drink.'

'Just one more board to go,' he grunted, working the crowbar again. Tomorrow, with Frank's help, he'd replace these boards.

That would be one more job done. Kit's house would be one step closer to being ready.

And he'd be one step closer to leaving here.

He didn't turn as he spoke. He needed a few more minutes to find his composure, to make sure when he joined her he could resist the spell she threatened to weave around him.

No matter how hard she hoped and wished, she couldn't make him a better man—the man she needed for her child, the kind of man who could share her life. But the thought of the child growing inside her…

Every day the evidence hit him afresh in the shape of her gently rounded abdomen, her heavy breasts. *Every day.* It worried at him until he felt he had a blister on his soul.

Finally, he turned. Kit smiled, but her hand shook as she poured him a glass of fruit juice. He pressed his lips together hard. At certain moments she could make him believe this life could be his. She could make him forget what it had been like living with his grandfather, make him forget Jacqueline's betrayal.

She could make him forget that his heart had grown as cold and hard as his grandfather's.

It was dangerous forgetting those things.

It was dangerous believing in fairy tales.

He had to focus on what he had explicitly promised her—to get her house fixed. Nothing more.

Against his will, his eyes travelled to her stomach.

How hard would it be to be a part-time father? To see his child three or four times a year and make sure it had everything it needed?

To make sure Kit had what she needed?

He glanced up to find her watching him again. He swallowed and took the glass she held out, moving back a few steps. He didn't sit in the other chair arranged so cosily next to hers. He didn't want her sunshine-fresh scent beating at him. He wanted to keep a grasp on reality. He sure as hell didn't want the torture of being so near and not being allowed to touch her.

Would Kit mind if he did touch her, though?

He backed up another step. Perhaps not, but if he made love to her she'd think he was ready for all this…this domesticity. He didn't feel any readier for it than he had on the first day he'd stalked into her back garden.

That thought almost quelled his raging libido.

If he made love to Kit, she'd expect the works—marriage, kids and everything that went along with it. They couldn't unmake the baby they'd created, but he could prevent himself from compounding the mistake.

He surveyed her over the rim of his glass. When she realized he'd caught her out staring at him again, she sent him an abashed grin. 'I don't get it,' she confessed.

All his muscles were primed for flight. 'Get what?'

'For the eleven months that I worked for you, Alex,

you'd come into the office every day the epitome of the assured businessman…'

He relaxed a fraction. 'And?'

'Look, I understand your roots lie in manual labour, but…'

His gut clenched. 'But?' Jacqueline had hated that about him.

'But I don't understand how you can still be so comfortable and capable and *easy* with this kind of work.'

Her admiration—admiration she didn't even try to hide—made him stand a little taller. He drained his juice and then shrugged. 'It's like riding a bicycle.'

'Believe me, I'd wobble. I'd stay upright, but I'd wobble.'

She made it so easy to laugh.

'Top up?'

She held up the jug and, before he knew what he was about, he found himself ensconced in the other chair, sipping more juice. 'I have had some recent practice,' he found himself confessing. 'In Africa.'

She leaned forward. Her lips twitched. 'Did your cabin fall down or something?'

He tried to warn himself that this was how her enchantments started—teasing, fun, laughter. He promised to bring a halt to it soon and get back to work. 'How much would you laugh if I said yes?'

Her eyes danced. 'I'd bray like a hyena, but…' She suddenly sobered. 'I understand you did some aid work?'

It was hardly a question, more a statement, but he nodded anyway. 'How d'you know?'

'The rumour mill at Hallam's was full of it before I left.'

'I was part of a team that helped to build an orphanage.' When he'd read the brochure he'd hoped that building an orphanage would help him forget Kit. And that it would help allay some of the guilt raging through his soul.

She waved a finger at him. 'You might like to act all hard and self-contained, Alex Hallam, but I have your number, buddy.'

He went to correct her, to tell her he was hard and heart-less and that she'd be wise not to forget it, but before he could get the words out she said, 'You're nothing but a great big mushroom.'

That threw him. 'Mushroom?'

She stared back at him in incomprehension for three beats, and then she chuckled. 'Oops, marshmallow. I meant to say marshmallow. Baby brain, I tell you.'

He grinned. 'Is this where I point out that hyenas don't bray?'

'Of course they do.'

She promptly gave her impression of a braying hyena and Alex almost fell out of his chair laughing. 'That's not a hyena, it's a donkey!'

'No, this is a donkey.'

When she gave her impression of a donkey, he lurched out of his chair to roar at full-stretch on the ground. When he opened his eyes again he found himself staring up at an elderly lady.

Her lips twitched as she stepped over him on still spry feet. 'So kind of you to vacate your chair for me, young man.'

'Hi, Grandma.'

Kit's grandmother! Alex shot to his feet and did his best to dust himself off.

'Alex, this is my grandmother, Patricia Rawlinson.'

'Pleased to meet you, Mrs Rawlinson.'

'It's Patti, dear.'

'Grandma, this is Alex Hallam.'

'Ahh…' Those piercing amber eyes—so like Kit's—turned to him again. 'So you're Alex. I've heard all about you.'

She said it exactly the same way Caro had on his first morning here. The collar of his polo shirt tightened around his throat. Was she going to threaten him with a meat cleaver too?

'I hope you mean to do the right thing by my grand-daughter and great-grandchild.'

'I…um…' All the fun and laughter Kit had created in the garden bare minutes ago fled now. He had a feeling 'doing right' meant more than fixing Kit's house up.

Those amber eyes gleamed and he didn't trust them. He didn't trust them any more than Caro's spitfire green. 'I'd eventually like to see you make an honest woman of my granddaughter.'

'Yeah, right.' Kit snorted. 'The way you let Granddad finally make an honest woman of you on Mum's twenty-first birthday.'

'I did say eventually, dear.'

Kit's grandmother hadn't married Kit's grandfather till…

Both Kit and her grandmother laughed at whatever they saw in his face. 'Relax, Alex,' Kit ordered, her smile wide enough to ease some of the tension in his shoulders. The woman was a witch! 'Grandma's just teasing.' She tossed her grandmother an affectionate grin. 'Behave, Gran.'

'You young ones always want to spoil my fun. Now, Kit, dear, can you explain those extraordinary noises you were making as I came around the side of the house?'

'I was trying to show Alex the difference between a hyena's bray and a donkey's bray.'

'Hyenas don't bray, Kit, dear, they laugh. So, how did you get on?'

'Only Alex can answer that.'

Two sets of identical eyes turned to him for confirmation. His lips finally twitched too. He found himself inclined to warm to Kit's grandmother for knowing the difference between a laugh and a bray. And for having eyes identical to Kit's. 'She got on perfectly.'

'Excellent.'

It struck him that when she'd been a younger woman, Patricia Rawlinson must've been very beautiful. She was still striking now and she had to be at least seventy. Still, his collar remained tight around his neck. Hypothetical walls threatened to close about him. He wanted out of this garden fast. 'I'll…um…go put the jug on.' No doubt they had loads to talk about. He edged towards the back door.

'Hold on a moment, young Alex.'

He almost tripped up a back step. He couldn't remember anyone ever calling him young Alex in his life.

'I'd like to invite you both to a luncheon next weekend.'

Kit groaned. Alex's eyebrow lifted. It wasn't the reaction he'd have expected from her. Images of meat cleavers rose in his mind. Patti might know the difference between brays and laughs, but he'd bet she had a whole lot in common with Caro too.

'What on earth is this one for?' Kit asked. 'And how much will it cost me?'

'This one is for breast cancer, dear. A gold coin donation is all that's required. And I'd appreciate it if you could bring a plate.'

Kit's eyes danced when they glanced at him. 'Alex has been threatening to give me cooking lessons.'

'Oh, darling, if he can cook, why bother learning?'

He'd have laughed if his collar hadn't pulled so tight.

'I'll definitely come to your luncheon. Alex will have

to be a maybe. It'll depend on whether any deliveries are scheduled for that day. We've had a couple of delays.'

His collar promptly loosened. Kit had given him an out.

A new sick kind of nausea filled him then instead. Maybe she didn't want him to go to this luncheon. Why on earth would she? He was going to let her down, wasn't he? Maybe subconsciously she sensed that?

'Can I ask Frank and Doreen along? And Caro?'

Of course she'd like to have her friends there. He rolled his shoulders. Maybe she'd let him tag along too if he helped her bake a cake?

For Pete's sake! It was only a stupid luncheon. What did he want with one of those?

'I saw Frank and Doreen out the front so I've invited them already. Caro and co are always welcome.'

Alex thrust himself through the back door, but not before he heard Patti ask, 'Alex does mean to put your house back together, doesn't he, dear?'

'I believe that's the plan.'

He closed the door and made safe his escape.

That night Alex dreamed he was searching through the endless rooms of that brooding mansion, searching for Chad again, the childish laughter always just out of reach.

And, just like the other times, he jerked awake, drenched in sweat and with Chad's name on his lips.

CHAPTER TEN

Alex dunked his paintbrush into the can of paint and set about slapping it on the neatly sanded, newly primed weatherboards of Kit's cottage. White paint.

One corner of his mouth kicked up. She had chosen white for the main body of the house and blue for the window and door trims. She'd snorted when he'd presented her with an array of colour cards with exotic names like fresh linen, grey gum, desert sand and sage. 'I don't want any of that modern nonsense, Alex. I've always wanted a white house with a blue trim. Ever since I was a little girl. I'm not going to change my mind now.'

And she hadn't.

So he was painting her house white with a blue trim, and found he was enjoying himself.

Next week he'd paint the interior—white ceilings, cream walls. She wanted her house light and bright and airy. It was her house. He'd paint it any colour she wanted.

The new shower unit was due to arrive at the end of the week and then he could get to work on the bathroom. Once that was done, all that would be left was the nursery.

His gut clenched and his hand slowed. That would mean looking at baby stuff with Kit, wouldn't it? He could imagine her face going all soft and misty as she looked at cribs and little blankets and changing tables with colourful mobiles. He dunked his paintbrush in the can of paint again and concentrated on transferring it to the weatherboards. Maybe it wouldn't be so bad. Kit had a way of making just about anything fun.

Besides, all that baby stuff could be ridiculously expensive. He slapped paint on with renewed vigour. He had no intention of letting Kit pick up the tab for that.

Kit. The thought of her had images rising through him. His hand slowed, the paintbrush almost coming to a halt. Last night while he'd cooked dinner—a chore they'd taken in turns since the night of their fish barbecue—she'd laid stretched out full-length on one of the sofas watching TV. She'd reached for the remote on the table behind and the action had stretched her T-shirt tight, giving him an eyeful of her baby bulge—small, but unmistakable. And perfect.

He hadn't been able to look away, even when she'd returned to her former position.

Beneath her shirt she carried his baby.

He'd stumbled back into the kitchen, trying to decipher the emotions tumbling through him.

His first instinct had been denial. He couldn't get emotionally involved with this baby. He'd lost it all once before. He couldn't go through that again. His second thought had been...

Hope?

Alex swiped the sweat from his brow with his forearm and gave up all pretence of painting for the moment. The longer he stayed here with Kit the more it seemed possible that he could do what she wanted of him, be what she wanted—an involved father. The thought made his heart thud against his ribs again, just like it had last night.

He'd started telling himself that this time it would be different. As the child's biological father, he'd have rights.

Besides, Kit had more generosity in her little finger than Jacqueline had in her entire being.

Plans started racing through his mind. He could work in Sydney through the week and then shoot up here to Tuncurry for the weekends.

Better yet, he could relocate here. He set the paintbrush down and rested his hands on his knees, his mind racing even faster. Kit had said the tourism industry was booming. There'd be property development opportunities galore. He could set up an office in Forster that specialised in developing eco-tourist resorts.

And he could be a part of his child's life.

What about Kit?

All his plans slammed to a halt. He swallowed. He couldn't give Kit what she wanted, what she needed.

What happens when she meets someone who can?

Sweat beaded his top lip, gathered at his nape and trickled a path of ice down his back. Eventually Kit would meet someone and fall in love with them. She'd marry. And his child would have a stepfather. He tried to push back the darkness that threatened to swallow him whole. He rubbed a fist across his brow. Kit deserved to find someone, to be happy, but…

What then? What if she relocated to Perth or…or to America?

Why would this time be any different? Why should it all work out for him now?

Because he wanted it to?

A harsh laugh broke from a throat that ached. Grabbing the paintbrush, he forced himself back to work. He'd be a fool to get his hopes up.

The back door slammed, jerking him out from beneath the darkness stealing over him.

'Good to see Kit has you working so hard.'

He glanced down from his position on the scaffolding. Caro. Not holding a meat cleaver. 'Nice to see you too,' he drawled.

Kit emerged from the house with a tea tray. At her side trotted a dark-haired child of about four. A boy.

Alex froze.

He didn't know why the sight of the child rocked him, but it did. To his core. He'd seen other children, of course, since he'd lost Chad, but...

He hadn't talked to one, touched one.

His hand tightened around the paintbrush. Maybe it was the combination of a pregnant Kit and child.

Kit and child.

Kit and—

Chad would be about this child's age now.

The thought slammed into him from nowhere and the strength drained from his legs. He braced a hand against a weatherboard. In the back of his mind he was dimly aware that the board was wet. *Ignore the paint. Keep breathing.*

Paint from his brush dripped onto his trainer. He clenched the paintbrush as if it were his last grip on reality as he tried to push the memories of Chad away, deep down into the unexplored parts of himself where they couldn't torment him.

It didn't work. Questions pounded at him.

Would Chad be the same size and shape as the child at Kit's side? How tall would he be now? Had his hair darkened or grown lighter? The need to see Chad, to hold him, burst the straitjacket he normally kept it bound to, and for a moment darkness swirled all around him.

'Look, Mum, I'm helping Auntie Kit and I got the most important job—carrying the biscuits!'

'Not just any biscuits, but chocolate biscuits,' Caro said with what he guessed must be the appropriate amount of admiration. Thankfully she turned the child towards the outdoor chairs and table. 'And you're allowed to have one just as soon as you set them down.'

'Alex, that looks great.'

Kit's voice, her appreciation, pushed some of the darkness away and helped him breathe again. He did his best to ignore the childish patter behind him.

'Would you like some tea?'

He nodded and finally found his voice. 'I'll be down in a minute.'

She turned to carry the tea tray to the table, and Alex clenched his eyes shut and tried to control his breathing, tried to block the images that rose up to torment him, taunt him, remind him of all he'd lost.

Tonight he'd have that nightmare—the endless rooms in that mansion, the childish laughter always out of reach. Despair threatened his control. Some days he thought it would take his sanity. With every ounce of strength he possessed, he pushed it back, tamped it down. He couldn't lose his mind. He had Kit's house to finish.

He gritted his teeth. The mundane *would* allay the nightmare. He opened his eyes, unclasped the paintbrush from fingers that had started to cramp and did his best to wipe the wet paint from his hand with a rag.

'What are you doing?'

That childish voice came from almost directly beneath him. He stared at the weatherboards. *He could do this.* He'd wrapped his heart in ice once before. He could halt the thaw that Kit had somehow started and put it in deep freeze once again. He would not think about Chad.

He dragged in a breath. He didn't turn around. 'I'm painting your Auntie Kit's house.'

'My name is Davey.'

Another deep breath. 'Mine's Alex.'

'Are you Auntie Kit's boyfriend?'

The voice was even closer now, and the question made Alex blink. In another time, another place, he suspected it would've made him laugh. 'I'm her friend.'

'I'm going to marry her when I grow up.'

He had to hand it to the kid. He had great taste.

'Can I help?'

And then Davey's head appeared and Alex's heart lurched. Davey had climbed up the side of the scaffolding. What if he fell? 'Hold on a minute, Tiger.'

His heart cramped. He'd always called Chad Tiger. *Don't think about Chad!*

Alex forced himself to move. He vaulted to the ground and then seized Davey beneath the armpits to swing him down too. 'Your mum will come after me with a meat cleaver if you—'

He couldn't go on. He froze. Davey's solid weight, his warmth, the trusting way he stared at Alex with dark-fringed eyes that were the same brown as Chad's. All of it was imprinted on his memory. A low moan threatened to burst from his chest. Chad would weigh this much now too. He'd still be chubby-cheeked and chubby-legged like the last time Alex had seen him, held him, but he'd be taller. He'd probably be asking awkward question and—

Who was letting Chad help paint a house or sand a chair or let him hand them tools while they tuned a car?

Pictures of Chad flashed through his mind. Chad running towards him to welcome him home from work, arms outstretched. Chad with his head thrown back, gurgling with laughter as Alex swung him around and around. Chad nestled against Alex's chest, his breathing deep and even as he slept.

Alex started to shake.

'Alex?'

Kit came into view. He barely heard her over the rush in his ears. The cramp in his chest grew until he thought he might crack in two. He wanted to haul this child into his arms and hold him close. He wanted…

He thrust Davey into Kit's arms. 'I…I have to go.'

He lurched around the side of the house. He didn't stop at his car. He kept walking. Chad's name echoed in his heart with every step. At some point Kit's started up in there too.

Kit's heart burned when Alex disappeared around the side of the house. His white-lipped stare, his wild dark eyes, the way his hands had clenched, it had almost made her cry out.

Davey had reminded him of Chad! Oh, why hadn't she thought? She should have realized.

Her mouth went dry. But…Davey wasn't Chad. If Alex reacted this way to a child he wasn't related to, how would he react to his own child?

She swallowed back a sob, not wanting to frighten Davey.

Davey's bottom lip wobbled. 'I only wanted to help. Alex doesn't like me.'

'Of course he does, honey.' She pulled him in close for a hug before moving back towards Caro, unable to meet her friend's eye. 'Alex hasn't been feeling very well lately. I think he might be coming down with something.'

Caro raised an eyebrow, but Kit was grateful she didn't snort.

'Hey there, soldier!' Frank popped his head up over the fence. 'Want to come see the baby birds in the nest on my shed?'

Davey's face lit up. 'Can I, Mum? Can I go over to Uncle Frank's?'

'Okay.' Caro laughed and pointed a mock-threatening finger at Frank. 'But mind you don't feed him more than two biscuits. He's had two already.'

'Aye, aye, Captain!'

Caro contemplated Kit as Davey raced across next door. 'Why are you wasting your time on this man, Kit?'

Was she wasting her time? She folded herself into her chair, hunched down to rest her head against its wooden slats. Nausea and exhaustion pummelled her.

'I mean, you had to see the look on his face when he held Davey. Not even Blind Freddy could've missed that!'

She had. Shock, wonder and then pain—a dark, searing, tear-the-heart-out-of-your-chest pain.

And she'd wanted to help him. In that moment it hadn't mattered if he was going to stay or not. Nobody should be asked to endure that kind of pain on their own.

'Kit, do you really believe Alex can change? Come to terms with fatherhood? Be there for you and the baby?'

Kit moistened her lips and swallowed. 'I know if our positions were reversed, I'd be asking you these self-same questions. Caro, my head knows what you're saying. It's saying the same things.'

'But?'

But her heart was another matter entirely. It hit her then that she'd been so busy trying to reconcile Alex to the idea of fatherhood that she'd forgotten to protect herself. She'd left herself wide open. She'd fallen in love with him again.

If she'd ever fallen out of love with him in the first place.

What a mess!

She forced herself to state facts. 'You know he threw up when I told him I was pregnant. Right there in the azalea bushes.'

'Oh, honey.' Caro leaned across, clasped her hand. 'I'm sorry.'

Kit squeezed it back. 'But he took me to the medical clinic all the same and he looked after me until I was over the kidney infection. He knew he didn't have to stay, but he did and he never made me feel bad about it. Not once.'

'Just as well!'

'His parents died when he was twelve and he went to live with his mean old grandfather. You and me, we both missed our dads, but our childhoods were great.'

Caro shook her head, but she was smiling. 'You are such a soft touch.'

'Every time I've just about given up on him, I find out something that gives me hope again. You know, he hasn't had a proper holiday in nearly five years. He took leave the month before last and spent it doing aid work in Africa, helping to build an orphanage.'

She'd grilled him until he'd told her every single detail about it. She could still remember the way his eyes had shone.

'Not the actions of a man entirely beyond hope,' Caro finally agreed. 'But, honey, I'm so scared you're going to get hurt.'

Kit pulled in a breath. It was too late to go back now. 'I know having him here is a risk, but...' She leant towards her friend. 'There's too much at stake to just give up on him. He'll do what he considers his duty—pay child support and whatnot.' She flattened her hands over her burgeoning stomach and stared at it in wonder and gratitude. 'I want more than that for my baby, Caro. I love it so much already. If anything I do now can help Alex with his issues and embrace fatherhood, then...'

'Then you'll do it.'

'I have to,' she whispered, her throat thickening and her eyes stinging. 'I know I might fail. I know the odds aren't great.' After what she'd just witnessed, they might well be non-existent, but… 'I have to at least try. Otherwise, how will I ever be able to look my child in the eye when it asks me about its daddy?'

Caro didn't say anything for a moment. 'What about what you need, Kit?'

'The baby has to come first.'

'Sure it does, but it doesn't mean you're not allowed to have hopes and dreams for yourself too. You know I'd lay my life down for Davey, but it doesn't stop me hoping my white knight will turn up.'

With all her heart, Kit hoped that would happen for her friend.

'You love him, don't you?'

It was useless trying to hide from the truth. She gave a weary nod. 'I started falling for him the first time I laid eyes on him. If I believed in such things I'd have said we'd known each other in a past life. It just felt that…right.'

And then they'd made love. There had been no going back after that.

'Do you know how he feels about you?'

'I know he likes who I am.' She hesitated. 'I sometimes think he has me up on some stupid pedestal. And I know he's still attracted to me.' Her heart fluttered up into her throat. There was no denying she was attracted to him.

'But something is holding him back?'

'Yes.' Chad.

'Honey, if you can't get to the bottom of it, no one can. If and when you do, he'll be your slave for ever.'

Kit wished she shared her friend's confidence. 'And if I fail, you'll be there to help me pick up the pieces.'

'Just like you've always been there for me.'

'Caro, if Alex can't be my birth partner, will you do it?'

Caro leaned over and hugged her. 'I'd be honoured.'

* * *

Kit found Alex on her rock.

She didn't mean to. She hadn't gone looking for him. She'd just needed to get out of the house. She'd needed the fresh air and spring breeze to blow away the fears and worries crowding her mind.

She'd come here to her rock to remind herself of all the good things she'd still have in her life if Alex did leave. Just the thought of Alex leaving bleached the colour out of all that was good. She swallowed and settled one hand on her stomach. That wasn't true. If Alex left she'd still have her baby, and her baby was a very good thing. An amazing thing.

A miracle.

She'd give thanks for her baby every day.

She stared at the rigid lines of Alex's back and shoulders and clenched her hands. Why was he finding this so hard? Their baby wasn't Chad. Their situation was different. Sure, the prospect of a new baby was scary, but it was joyful and wonderful too. Or it would be if only he'd let it.

She blinked hard. She should leave him be. He obviously wanted privacy. Maybe her rock would help him find a measure of peace. She turned to leave, but he swung around as if some sixth sense had told him she was standing there.

'Oh…' The words dried in her throat as emotion, yearning, her love for him, all swelled up through her. 'I'm sorry,' she finally choked out. 'I didn't know you were here. I didn't mean to disturb you. I'll go.'

'No!' He leapt to his feet. 'This is your spot. *I'll* go.'

His vehemence, his evident desire to put her at her ease and to do what was right, made her smile. 'I'm happy to share. There's room enough for two.' There was room enough for an entire family, but she left that particular thought unsaid.

He shrugged. 'I'm game if you are.'

He moved forward and offered her his hand, helped her clamber down. He let her go again as soon as it was safe, and she immediately missed his sure strength, his warmth. She tried to make do with the sun-warmed rock instead.

She rested back on her hands and lifted her face to the sun. 'Summer is nearly here. I love summer.' When she glanced back at him, she found him staring out to sea. Her heart crashed and ached and burned. Was he wishing himself a million miles away?

Regardless of his sentiments, it couldn't be denied that this stay here at least agreed with him physically. His forearms and calves had grown tanned from the sun. His body, if it were possible, had grown harder and leaner.

She'd love to see him naked.

Oh!

She must've made some betraying noise because he turned to her. She waved a hand in front of her face as if shooing a fly.

'Look, I'm sorry. I know I freaked out back there earlier with Davey.'

That was one way of putting it.

'But all of a sudden he was up on that scaffolding with me and all I could think was, what if he fell? It'd be my fault.'

'No, it wouldn't. Caro and I should've been watching him more closely. I keep forgetting how quick he is.'

When he didn't say anything else, a weight settled in her stomach. She stared at the water flowing in the channel. If she fell in now she had a feeling she'd sink to the very bottom. 'Tell me about Chad.'

Every line of him stiffened. 'Why?'

She lifted one shoulder. 'Because I know that's who Davey reminded you of. He's such a big part of you even though he isn't in your life any more.' Alex didn't say anything. She swallowed. 'How old was he when he started to sleep through the night? Where did he take his first step?'

Alex's hands clenched to fists.

'What was his favourite toy?'

He swung to her, his face twisted. 'Talking about Chad, remembering him, whatever you think, Kit, it doesn't help.'

The hairs on her arms lifted and her heart raced. 'You're not the only one who is scared, you know?' she burst out, unable to keep the wobble from her voice.

He frowned then. 'You're scared?'

If she had the energy, she'd have smiled at his incredulity, if she could just get over the ache flattening her chest and stretching behind her eyes and pounding at her temples first. 'Dammit, Alex! Some days I'm terrified.'

She couldn't bear to look at him any more, knowing the distance that stretched between them. She stared down into the strong current that rippled down the channel as the tide came in, at the clean, clear water. Then blinked when a silver-grey shape lifted out of that water. 'Oh, look!' She pointed at the myriad of fins that surfaced. 'Dolphins.'

In the past it had never mattered what it was that she'd brooded about as she'd sat out here; when the dolphins arrived things never looked so bad.

From the way Alex leaned forward to get a better view, from the way his back unbent and his shoulder unhitched, she figured maybe they had the same effect on him.

'What are you scared about, Kit?'

'That I'll be a terrible mum. That I'll be impatient and yell a lot and that being home with a baby will be so intellectually and mind-bogglingly boring that I'll lose myself and blame the baby.'

'Oh.' The word broke from him softly as if he'd thought her above worrying about such things. As if the thought hadn't occurred to him that such things could worry her. 'I think you'll make a great mum. I don't think you'll get impatient or yell. You never did at work. I know you loved your job, but how much more will you love your baby?'

He had a point.

'As for this baby brain you talk about, you're doing the crossword and playing word games and I know you'll beat it. Maybe you could pick up some part-time work that will give you some down-time from the baby?'

She eyed him uncertainly. 'You don't think it's a mother's role to be with her baby twenty-four seven?'

'Nope.'

She let that idea sink in. 'I'm scared of other stuff too.'

'Like?'

'What if dirty nappies make me puke?'

'Keep a bucket by the changing table.'

That made her laugh. She sobered a moment later. 'I wonder how I'll cope with months of broken sleep. I wonder how I'll cope if I get sick again.'

'You have lots of friends all willing to help you out.'

'I know, but...' She wanted it to be him she shared all those things with—the difficulties and the joys of adjusting to a new baby.

He'd loved a child once. Didn't it mean he could love another one?

'But?'

'I know all those things, but it doesn't make the fear go away. I...I mean, the thought of the labour terrifies me.' She gulped when she realized what she'd said. She hadn't meant to reveal quite so much.

Turbulence raged in those dark eyes of his. 'Then why are you going through it?'

'Because the hope is greater than the fear.'

Something fluttered in her stomach—like a hiccup—only it didn't come from her.

'What is it?' Alex barked when she held herself suddenly stiff, all his energy focused on her. It almost threw her concentration. She loved watching his muscles bunch like that, his eyes narrow in readiness.

'Hold on...' She held up a hand. There! It happened again.

It was the baby!

'Oh, Alex, look!' She grabbed his hand and pressed it to her stomach.

'What am I—?'

She pressed his fingers more firmly to the spot where the hiccup feeling grew. 'Can you feel that?' Wonder filled her.

'What is it?' He frowned. 'Should I take you to the clinic?'

She laughed for the sheer joy of it. 'That's the baby, Alex. That's the baby kicking.'

For a moment she thought he meant to pull his hand away but, almost as if he couldn't help it, his fingers spread across her belly and gently pressed against her, sending darts of warmth shooting through her. 'The baby?' he whispered, almost as if he were afraid of waking it up.

'Uh-huh.' She nodded. 'Isn't it amazing?'

'Yes.' Then he frowned. 'Does it hurt?'

He would've pulled his hand away only she laid her hand on top of it to keep it there, to maintain this tenuous three-way connection—him, her and their baby. 'Not a bit. It feels...wonderful! I've been dying for this moment.' Her grin must stretch all the way across the channel to Forster.

His eyes widened. 'This is the first time?'

She couldn't get the grin off her face. 'The very first time.'

Alex's wonder made him look younger. The grooves either side of his mouth eased, the creases around his eyes relaxed and the darkness in his irises abated, his lips tilted up at the corners, and it all made Kit catch her breath.

Beneath her hand, his hand tensed. She dropped her gaze to stare at their two hands. Neither one of them moved, and in less than a heartbeat desire licked along her veins. She wanted to lift her gaze and memorize every line and feature of his face, the texture of his skin, while she could. Here on her rock. So she could have this memory for ever.

She didn't need to look up to do that, though. His every feature was already branded on her brain. She knew that dark stubble peppered his jaw. Alex needed to shave every day, but he'd skipped that chore this morning, eager to get started on the painting instead. Her palm itched to sample that roughness, her tongue burned to trace it, to taste it… to tease him.

Today he looked more like a disreputable pirate than a civilised businessman and a thrill coursed through her at the danger she sensed simmering just beneath the surface.

Finally obeying the silent command she sensed in him, she lifted her gaze to his. At the edge of his right eyebrow was a tiny nick, as if he'd once had a stitch there. She'd always meant to ask him about it, but her breath came in shallow gulps and her pulse had gone so erratic she didn't trust her voice not to give her away.

His eyes burned dark and hot as they travelled over her, and her soul sang at the possessiveness that transformed his features. No longer afraid of revealing her desire for him, she lowered her gaze to his lips. Need, hunger, thirst all speared into her. Her lips parted. Her eyes searched out his again, pleading with him to sate her need. If she couldn't taste him just one more time she thought she might die.

Something midway between a groan and a growl emerged from his throat. His hand tightened on her stomach. Her hand tightened over his. Yes! Oh, please, yes!

Still Alex held back, his eyes devouring her face as if he was picturing in vivid detail every caress he meant to place there. He didn't lift his hand from her abdomen and it felt like a promise. His fingers splayed, sending darts of need right into the core of her, making her tremble with the intensity of her desire.

His other hand came up to cup her face, his thumb traced the outline of her bottom lip, dipped into the moistness of her mouth, traced her lips again, moved back and forth over them as if to sensitize them to the utmost limit of their endurance before taking her to the next level with his lips and mouth and tongue.

She started to pant, wanted to beg him for his lips, his mouth, his tongue, but still his mouth didn't descend. With a low growl she flicked her tongue across his thumb. He stiffened as if electrified. She drew his thumb into her mouth, circled it with her tongue, suckled it until his eyes darkened to obsidian.

And then finally, slowly, inexorably, his head lowered and her blood started to sing. His body blocked out the sun and, as he moved closer and closer, all she could see was the light reflected in his eyes. His lips touched hers, moved over hers—surely, reverently, thoroughly—her eyes fluttered closed and, as the kiss deepened, light burst behind her eyelids. Every wonderful Christmas, every sun-drenched summer and visiting dolphin, every bright and beautiful thing that had ever existed in her life gained a new vitality in that kiss.

The need and the energy, it took her and Alex and

merged them into a sparkling, flaming oneness until, body and soul, she didn't know where she ended and Alex began. It was the kind of kiss to shape worlds and change lives. It shifted the foundations of her world and all she believed about herself.

The hope is greater than the fear.

For the first time where Alex was concerned, her hope was greater than her fear.

Alex eased away from Kit. He didn't know for how long they'd kissed. He barely knew which way was up. Very slowly he drew his hands away—one from her face, one from her stomach. He tried to stop his legs from jerking in reaction.

'Are you okay?'

Her voice came out soft and husky, as if he'd kissed all her breath away. Served her right for kissing his breath clean away too.

He nodded and cleared his throat. 'And you?'

'Oh, yes.'

She had stars in her eyes! No woman should look at him like that.

An imaginary noose pulled tight around his neck, and yet for a moment all he could see was the shine on her lips and he ached to sample them again.

'I'm…' He cleared his throat again. 'I'm sorry.'

'I'm not.'

'It can't happen again.'

'I'll be holding my breath till it does.'

He closed his eyes. He was in way over his head.

CHAPTER ELEVEN

THE phone rang. Alex stared at it and then down the hall-way towards the bathroom, where he doubted anything could be heard over the blast of Kit's hairdryer.

The phone rang again.

He opened his mouth to holler for Kit. He snapped it closed again. She wouldn't hear him. Or if she did she'd ask him to answer it for her.

He snatched it up, barked, 'Hello?' into the receiver.

He hated answering her phone. There would always be a strategic pause, like now, as the person on the other end of the line—one of the very many of Kit's community of friends—tried to weigh him up by the sound of his voice.

'Hello, I'm hoping to speak with Kit Mercer.'

Female. It wasn't a voice he recognized, but something about it made his shoulders loosen a fraction. 'I'll just get her for you. May I ask who's calling?'

'Candace Woodbury. I'm her mother.'

Kit's mother! His shoulders immediately clenched up twice as tight. 'Uh…right.' He headed down the hallway and knocked on the bathroom door. And then he gulped. He hoped Kit was decent.

'I'm sorry—' that pleasant voice purred down the line '—but I didn't catch your name.'

His teeth ground together for a moment. He unclenched them to mutter, 'Alex Hallam.'

'Ah…you're Alex.'

He grimaced and rolled his shoulders, knocked on the bathroom door again. Louder.

Muffled muttering came from behind it, then it was flung open and Kit stood there in a white terry-towelling robe that stopped short of her knees, her hair fluffed around her face. She literally glowed with that golden light he found almost irresistible. He wanted to reach out and cup her cheek, slip the robe from her shoulders and explore her new lush curves. He wanted to kiss her like he had on the breakwater the other day.

He wanted to please her. Pleasure her.

His jaw clenched. He had to remember all the reasons why that was such a bad idea.

'Is that for me?' she said, all sass and fire as if she was aware of the effect she had on him.

She raised an eyebrow and pointed downwards.

Did he have an erection? He'd done his best to quash—

The air left his lungs in a rush. She was pointing at the phone. He shoved it into her hands. 'It's your mother.' And then he fled.

It didn't prevent him from hearing the start of her conversation. 'Mum, I see you've met Alex. I think you scared him off.' And then the bathroom door closed and he was out in the living room again and could breathe. After a fashion.

Kit's mum hadn't scared him off. He stretched his neck to the right and then to the left. He dropped down onto a sofa. Who was he trying to kid? All of it—Kit's whole life—scared the heck out of him. Everyone here, they had expectations of him. He'd rather deal with the savage cut and thrust of a boardroom coup than Kit's family and friends.

He leant his elbows on his knees and rested his head in his hands. He didn't have a lot of friends to speak of. Loads of acquaintances, but not many friends. He had a couple of mates from his building trade days, another from university and one from school.

He'd been a loner as a kid—his grandfather had made sure of it. In the last two years, since Jacqueline and Chad had gone, he'd shut himself away, had thrown himself into work. It hit him now that he'd neglected those four friends of his. They'd rung, tried to arrange outings. He'd ignored them, cut them off. Kit would never do that to her friends. He lifted his head and steepled his hands beneath his chin. When he returned to Sydney he'd contact each of them and make arrangements to catch up, apologise.

He slumped back against the sofa, his lips twisting. He had more acquaintances, colleagues and associates than he could poke a stick at, but it wasn't like the community that surrounded Kit. To his untrained eye, it looked as if everyone in town had clamoured to welcome her home. From her old school friends, to her mother and grandmother's friends, to neighbours old and new and everyone in between. He hadn't known until he'd come here how important family and friends were to Kit.

She belonged here.

He'd never belonged anywhere.

But then he remembered sitting in a tree, his mother coming out with milk and biscuits, humming her song, and his father waltzing her around the back garden. He'd belonged once.

Could he belong again?

'Ready?'

Alex started. He'd been so lost in thought he hadn't noticed Kit enter the room. The vision of her stole his breath. She wore a loose cotton sundress that fell to just below her knees, leaving her glorious golden calves on display. The dress—indigo-blue dotted with tiny sprigs of white flowers—made the golden highlights in her hair and eyes gleam.

The dress scooped down in a low vee at the neckline, making him swallow. He told himself he was grateful she wore a little khaki three-quarter-sleeve jacket with it. He just knew that beneath that jacket the dress would have those tiny shoestring straps. Straps made for being pushed off glorious golden shoulders. Shoulders made for kissing and—

'Alex?'

High colour stained her cheekbones, but her chin hitched up as he continued to survey her. If he reached for her now she'd let him. They'd make glorious golden love.

And Kit would interpret that as a sign that he meant to stay, that he meant to stay and make a family with her and the baby. She'd give all of herself. She'd have every right to expect the same in return.

It didn't matter how much he hungered to lose himself in her softness, her promise; it didn't matter how much he ached to give her all her heart desired.

The hope is greater than the fear.

He didn't know if that was true for him. And until he'd worked it out, touching Kit and kissing her, that was off limits.

He shot to his feet and swung away.

'Alex?'

He heard the frown in her voice and forced himself to take another step away from her and her heavenly, beguiling scent. 'I was thinking my time might be better spent getting on with the painting than attending a tea party.'

'You made the cake so you have to come. It's the rules.'

'You can pretend you baked it.'

She snorted. 'Everyone who knows me would see through that lie in a millisecond. Anyway, my grandmother is expecting you and the luncheon is for charity. It'll only be for an hour or so. Grit your teeth, smile politely, eat cake and then it'll all be over. Oh, and pack your board shorts. I thought we might drop in for a swim at the ocean baths at Forster on our way home. It's supposed to get hot today.'

The rest of his argument died on his lips. He and Kit swimming together? He wouldn't risk it if it weren't in a public place.

But it was in a public place and it was too much to resist.

The retirement village was on the outskirts of Forster. It only took them ten minutes to drive there and, although they arrived on the dot at midday, the luncheon was already in full swing.

Ostensibly the event was supposed to take place in the community hall, but it had spilled out into the surrounding gardens. Kit dropped a two-dollar coin into the donation box before he could stop her. He pushed a twenty-dollar note through the slot. He'd tried to do it unobtrusively, but her gaze had flicked back at him, mouth open as if she meant to say something. She blinked and then she sent him a smile that warmed him to the soles of his feet.

'That was very generous.'

He shrugged. 'It's for charity.'

'Okay, let's find Grandma. We'll say hello, place the cake in her capable hands, make ourselves up plates of goodies and then find some people to talk to.'

He bit back a sigh. It had all sounded great up until that last bit. He'd rather find a cosy corner and settle down to flirt with her. Finding people to talk to, a crowd, was far more sensible. Safer.

There was still the promise of that swim later. He'd hold onto that while he gritted his teeth and made small talk.

'I've been meaning to say,' Kit said, 'that I like this new casual look of yours.'

He wore a pair of long, loose cargo shorts and a cotton T-shirt. The simple compliment took him off guard. He didn't know what to say. 'Can't paint in a suit,' he finally muttered. 'I'd look a bit stupid.'

Her laugh made him grin. He could do small talk for an hour or so. For Kit. He could do anything she wanted him to.

Can you be the man she needs you to be? Can you be a father for her baby?

He pushed the thought away. He wasn't ready to face those questions and all they implied yet.

Well, then, when?

He rolled his shoulders. Later. When he had her house finished and… He gulped. The house was almost finished. Another week or so and…

Soon. He'd have to answer those questions soon.

'Alex, it's lovely to see you again. I'm so glad you could make it.'

He latched onto the distraction. 'Nice to see you again, Mrs…uh…Patti,' he corrected at her glare.

'Thank you for the cake, dear. Now, head on over to the tables and grab yourselves some food before it's all gone.'

'No chance of that,' Alex said. 'You'll be eating this for a week!'

Patti touched his arm. 'Make sure my granddaughter

has something with lashings of fresh cream. It's good for the baby.'

Fresh cream? He frowned. He'd baked a simple sultana pound cake. He wished now that he'd baked something with lashings of cream, like a strawberry shortcake. Tomorrow he'd make Kit one of those. He liked to watch her eat. He'd like to watch her lick whipped cream from her fingers. He'd like to drop dollops of whipped cream onto her naked body and slowly lick—

Whoa!

He did his best to banish that image as he followed Kit. She pushed an unerring path through the crowd towards laden trestle tables groaning under the weight of luncheon goodies.

She glanced back at him over her shoulder. 'How d'you learn to bake anyway? I thought you said your mum couldn't bake to save her life.'

'I spent a lot of time in the kitchen when I lived at my grandfather's, watching the housekeeper. Some of it obviously rubbed off.'

She started filling two plates with sandwiches, cakes and slices. He scanned the table for something laden with whipped cream. He seized a chocolate éclair and popped it onto one of the plates. 'Your grandmother's orders,' he muttered at her raised eyebrow.

Her laugh made him grin. He couldn't help it. He should be doing his best to keep his distance until he'd worked out how he was going to deal with…everything. When he was with her, though, that resolution flew out of the window. She made it impossible.

'Did you like the housekeeper? Was she kind to you?'

He met her gaze and saw hope there—hope that he hadn't been completely alienated whilst at his grandfather's. He swallowed. 'Yes,' he lied.

He told himself it was only half a lie. The housekeeper had been kind. She'd taught him how to cook and had taken him under her wing. She'd ruffled his hair and wrapped an arm around his shoulders at least once a day—her every caress a treasure to a lonely boy's soul. Until his grand-father had found out about it and she'd been dismissed. After that, Alex had been banished from the kitchen. He hadn't tried making friends with any of the other staff.

'Here.' Kit pressed a laden plate into his hands. 'Follow me.'

He shook off the sombre memory and followed her.

The small talk wasn't the chore he'd dreaded. He found himself in a circle with four of Kit's male friends from school talking renovations and home maintenance. He took mental notes when they discussed the predominantly sandy soil compositions of the area and the best remedies. Kit's lawn could do with some serious TLC.

Eventually, however, the crowd and the chatter grew too much. He eased himself out of the hall and found a quiet spot in the garden, lowered himself to a rock that bordered a flower bed. The sun beat down overhead. Kit was right, the day would be warm, but a nearby tree fern provided filtered shade and kept him cool.

'Hello.'

Alex's gut clenched. He swallowed and turned. Davey stood nearby. He moistened suddenly dry lips. 'Hello,' he croaked back.

The little boy took a step closer and frowned. 'Don't you like me?'

Heck, where had that come from? Then he remembered his abrupt departure earlier in the week when he'd thrust the little kid into Kit's arms and had bolted. He hadn't meant to hurt the little guy's feelings. 'Sure I do.' He held out his still half-full plate as a peace offering. 'Want a cake?'

Davey's eyes brightened in an instant. He raced over and promptly settled himself on Alex's left thigh and helped himself to a cupcake. Alex clenched his jaw at the child's warm weight, the smell of him. He beat back the panic that threatened to rise up and smother him. Panic he couldn't explain. *This little guy—he wasn't Chad!*

Chad. His hand tightened around the plate until he thought it might break as he fought the urge to remove the child from his lap.

Normal. Act normal.

He fought for control, fought to find his voice. 'Comfortable?' he drawled.

Davey nodded, oblivious to Alex's discomfort. 'I'm not supposed to get dirty,' he confided. 'If I sit on the ground I'll get dirty.'

Fair enough. He held the plate out to Davey again once the cupcake was gone. 'I hear the caramel slice is very good.'

Davey ignored him and reached for a piece of coconut ice instead. Alex considered eating the caramel slice himself—to give him something to do with his hands, in an attempt to occupy his mind with something other than the smell and feel of warm child—but he doubted his stomach would deal with food at the moment.

Given the choice, what would Chad have chosen—caramel slice or coconut ice? Grief as raw and hard as it had been two years ago sliced through him now. He set the plate on the ground, aghast at how his hand shook.

'Can I tell you a secret?'

Alex nodded. It was all he was capable of.

'Auntie Kit is having a baby. Did you know?'

'Yes.' The word croaked out of him.

'Well, I heard her and Mum talking and if she has a boy she wants to call him Jacob and Mum thinks that's a great name but there's a Jacob at my pre-school and he picks his nose and…'

The rest of the childish patter was lost to him.

The day darkened. He clenched his fingers into the soil of the garden, held on tight with both hands as the earth turned all the way over. He dragged in a breath and fought to remain upright. He would not be sick!

It came to him then, the answers to the questions he'd so desperately put off answering.

He couldn't do this.

He wanted to get up and run. Who was he trying to kid? He couldn't do any of this. He could not be the father Kit so desperately wanted for her child.

Any child, every child, reminded him of Chad, had memories threatening to burst forth—memories and pain. Davey, here, and…and Kit's baby, would act as constant reminders of his loss, would have panic rising through him…and grief.

Not to mention anger. How could he be a proper father to Kit's child when he couldn't see past Chad?

Ice trickled across his scalp and down his spine. He couldn't. The bottom line was that he couldn't.

Was this how his grandfather had felt when Alex's mother had left? Was that why he hadn't been able to show softness and love to his grandson? The way Alex now knew he couldn't show softness and love to his own child?

It would've been better for all of them—but especially for Kit—if he'd left that first day when she'd told him to. It would've been better for her if she'd never clapped eyes on him.

'…anyway, I think it's a dumb name, don't you?'

Eyes the same colour as Chad's lifted to his. It didn't

make any difference telling himself that ninety per cent of the population had brown eyes. At this moment in time they were the spitting image of the child's he'd loved and lost.

'What would you call a baby boy?'

Chad. He'd chosen Chad.

Davey frowned. 'Are you feeling sick again?'

Alex latched onto the excuse. He didn't know what the *again* was about, but… 'Uh-huh.' He glanced down at the child in his lap, blinked to clear his vision. 'Do you think your mum would give Auntie Kit a lift home?'

Davey nodded.

'Can you tell them that I went home because I was feeling sick?'

Davey nodded and jumped up. He raced off.

With a heart that grew colder with every step, Alex made his way back to the car.

Kit found Alex sitting at the dining table when she let herself into the house. Her heart slowed and relief flooded her. Alex did not look as if he were on his deathbed yet. Davey had exaggerated.

So…something had spooked him? Again? Davey?

She fought the exhaustion that threatened to settle over her. She recalled their kiss at the breakwater. She wasn't ready to give up on Alex yet. He'd make it. He just needed…

More time?

She swallowed. How much longer did she mean to keep making excuses for him?

He's worth fighting for, the voice of her secret self whispered.

He was. Her every instinct told her so. He worked hard,

he tried to do what was right, and when he kissed her she grew wings.

The expression that stretched through his eyes when he lifted his head to meet her gaze had a lump welling in her throat. She couldn't keep this up, not for much longer. At her last doctor's visit, her obstetrician had warned her that her blood pressure was creeping up.

Kit knew why. Alex. Her constant worry whether he would accept their baby into his life. Her constant worry whether he could overcome his demons. It was starting to take its toll. He was worth fighting for, but not at the expense of their baby's health.

Just give him one more week.

For a moment tears made his face blur. She swallowed and blinked hard. She couldn't find a smile and she didn't try. 'I see you've made a miraculous recovery.'

He shook his head. 'I'm sorry, Kit, I can't do this. I can't be what you want me to be. I cannot be a father to your baby.'

Her hands clenched, her stomach tightened. 'You don't need to make a decision about that right now. We can talk about it and—'

'No!'

The word snarled out of him. All the hairs on her arms lifted. The skin at her nape and her temples chilled.

'Every child reminds me of Chad. Every child is a source of pain. Remembering Chad every single day, remembering what it was like to lose him, it will drive me insane, Kit.'

His eyes dropped to her stomach and all she could do was stare at the white lines that slashed deep on either side of his mouth. Lines that spoke of grief and pain beyond her understanding.

'That's why I can't be a father to your child.'

For a moment, everything stilled, hung suspended—him, her, those words with their awful meaning. Then her stomach fell and fell and kept falling. She couldn't move, couldn't speak.

He'd warned her, he'd tried to tell her, he hadn't made her any promises. For the moment, though, it was his pain that touched her and not her own. She forced herself forward, sat in the chair opposite. 'Tell me about Chad,' she pleaded.

The darkness in his eyes didn't abate. He shook his head. 'There's no point.'

She reached out to touch the back of one of his clenched fists. 'There is a point, Alex, it's—'

'I can't!' he burst out, pulling his hand away.

She didn't know how one moved on after they lost a child, where one found the strength to pick up the pieces. Already she'd do anything to protect her baby and it wasn't even born yet. Chad might not be dead, but he'd been removed from Alex's world as surely as if he were.

She swallowed. She might not know what Alex was going through, but she did know that bottling it up would only hurt him more.

'You don't understand, Kit. This life of yours—the same life my parents led—it can never be my life. I don't have the openness of heart for it. I don't have any confidence in its permanence. If I stayed here with you and the baby I would ruin it all. I'm like my grandfather.'

'No, you're not!'

How could he believe that? She searched her mind for something that would prove him wrong. 'Look at how you were with Davey that day you were painting. He brought back memories of Chad, but you weren't unkind to him. What would your grandfather have done—yelled at him and frightened him, that's what.'

Alex shook his head. 'That doesn't change the fact that to survive living in my grandfather's house I had to kill off something in my nature that makes it impossible for me to...to do all this.' He waved a hand to indicate the interior of her house.

'You did it with Jacqueline.'

'If I'd done it successfully, she would never have left!'

For a moment Kit couldn't catch her breath.

Alex slumped. His eyes turned black. 'I will finish the work on your house, Kit. After that, I'll return to Sydney. My solicitors will arrange child support payments.'

Panic launched through her in a series of half-formed phrases and pulsing nausea. She surged to her feet. 'You can't leave just like that, Alex! I'm sorry, more sorry than I can say about Chad, but...' She gripped the air, searching for the words that would make him see sense. Words that would make him stay. 'Don't you see? Our baby deserves a father too.'

Alex rose. He stood wooden and stiff in front of her. He looked like a man who'd been dealt a body blow. 'I'm sorry, Kit.'

She reeled away from him as comprehension cleared the fog and confusion from her mind. Fear settled in its place. She swung back. 'You're doing with Chad what you did with your parents—blocking out every memory, good and bad, in an attempt to block out the pain. You think by avoiding those memories you're protecting yourself, but you're wrong. The same goes for love and family and commitment. Doing your best to avoid those things just means you're going to keep losing and losing.' Couldn't he understand that? Her heart ached and ached for him, and it ached for their unborn child.

She lifted her chin. 'I know you care about me.'

Please, *please*, don't let her be wrong about that.

Colour stained his cheekbones a dark, deep red. Hope washed through her. 'Walking away from all of this…' she lifted her arms out in an attempt to encompass the house, the life they could have here '…can you honestly tell me that's going to be easy?'

'It won't be easy.' His voice was pitched low but she caught every word. 'It won't be gut-wrenchingly impossible either. It won't be tear-your-heart-right-out-of-your-chest bad.'

She understood then the pain he'd suffered in missing his son.

'It will be for me,' she whispered.

Alex nearly caved in then. Kit's admission was a knife to his heart.

He'd never meant to hurt her. He'd do anything to take away her pain, but staying…that was out of the question. It was better to hurt her now than hurt her more later.

He should never have married Jacqueline. He knew that now. He'd worked long hours, driven to provide Jacqui with all the nice things she'd wanted—the big house, the antique furniture. She'd grown bored and restless, though, in all those long hours he'd spent away from her. She'd become lonely.

She hadn't been a bad person. She'd lied to him, and it had been a terrible lie, but she'd been too afraid to tell him the truth. If he'd put as much effort and time into his marriage as he had into making a name for himself in the business world…

But he hadn't. The harsh bitterness he'd suffered at his grandfather's hands had leached into his own soul. He couldn't do family. He didn't know how.

Unbidden, that image of his father waltzing his mother around their back garden rose in his mind.

With a swift shake of his head, he banished it. That was a lost dream. He wouldn't hurt Kit by making the same mistake twice.

Kit gulped. He wanted to pull her into his arms and let her sob the worst of her pain into his shoulder. He hardened his heart. She had her family and her friends. She didn't need him. She would be better off without him.

'You really aren't going to change your mind, are you?' Her voice wobbled but she held his gaze.

He shook his head. 'I'm sorry, Kit, for everything, but I'm not going to change my mind.'

'Then I was wrong,' she said slowly. 'You didn't love me after all. You don't really care about me or the baby. All this—' she gestured to the house '—has simply been a salve for your conscience.'

Her eyes suddenly spat fire. 'Get out, Alex! Just pack your things and get out. It's not our job to make you feel better for leaving.'

She was right. He should never have stayed here. 'I'll book into a hotel. I'll be back in the morning to keep working on the house.' It should only take a couple of days to finish the painting and another week tops to do the bathroom.

'No.'

She didn't yell, but the word echoed in his ears as if she had.

'If you don't mean to hang around for ever then you needn't think you can hang around for another week or two.'

But there was still so much to do! He couldn't leave her house in this state.

'In fact I never want to see you again. End of story,' she added when he opened his mouth.

'But—'

'Do you mean to stay for ever?'

He couldn't!

Kit gathered up her handbag. 'I'm going out. You have two hours. I want you gone by the time I get back.'

'Kit!' He surged forward as she made for the door. 'Will you let me know if you need anything or—?'

'No.' Her face had shuttered closed, all her golden goodness shut off from him. 'If you want to make things as easy as you can for me, you will go and not come back.' She paused at the door. 'Go home, Alex.' And then she walked through it.

His world split apart then and there. He turned and stumbled for the hallway and the spare bedroom.

'Alex?'

He turned to find her framed in the doorway again.

'Knowing all that you know now, would you give up those two years with Chad?'

He stared at her and didn't know how to answer.

'Understand that when you walk away from me and our child, that your answer is yes.'

With that she closed the door. And it was as if the sunshine had been bled out of his life.

CHAPTER TWELVE

WHEN Kit let herself into her house three hours later, she found that Alex hadn't left behind a single item, not one sign that he'd ever stayed here, ever been here.

She'd given him an extra hour to pack up, just in case.

She'd given herself an extra hour, just because.

Sitting on her rock for two hours, she'd stared out at the sea and had tried to make her mind blank. The cries of the seagulls, the shushing of the waves and the sight of the dolphins frolicking in the channel, none of it had been able to make her smile or had succeeded in unhitching the knot that tangled in her chest.

She dropped her handbag to the floor, lowered herself to the nearer of the two sofas, rested her head on its arm. When her watch had told her it was time to go home, she'd found she couldn't. She'd gone to a coffee shop and had sat over a pot of ginger and lemongrass tea. But the smell of coffee and cake and the chattering of the clientele, none of that had lifted her spirits or helped her feel connected again.

And now, back home and in the absence of the banging of hammers and the whirring and buzzing of power tools, the enormity of what she'd done sank in. *She'd sent Alex away.* And although none of his things remained in her house, although his absence was evident in the very stillness of the air, his presence was alive in every corner. His handiwork, evident in the freshly plastered and primed walls, mocked her.

And the deep malt scent of the man… She'd take that to her grave.

With a growl, she flew up and flung open every door and window. She seized a cushion and a throw rug and stormed out into the back garden to huddle down in one of the Cape Cod chairs—that Alex had sanded and painted. The day was warm but she was chilled to the bone. She wrapped the blanket about her and tried to stop her teeth from chattering.

A gulf opened up inside her, too big even for tears. Alex didn't want their baby. 'I'm sorry,' she whispered, rubbing one hand back and forth over her tummy. 'I'm so sorry.'

She closed her eyes and rested her head against the wooden slats behind. The sun still shone but it felt as if night had descended around her. Alex didn't want her. She'd always known that his rejection would hurt. She hadn't known it would devastate her.

She wrapped the blanket about her more tightly, knotted her hands in it as if it were the only thing anchoring her to this world.

Alex didn't leave town, he didn't return to Sydney like Kit had ordered him to. He'd meant to, because he hadn't known what else to do. *Go home, Alex.* Funny, but somewhere in the last few weeks Tuncurry had come to represent home in a way his apartment in Sydney never had.

When he'd reached the sign that said, 'Thank you for visiting our tidy town', he'd slammed on the brakes and pulled over to the verge, rhythmically pounding the palm of his left hand against the steering wheel.

There was still the matter of the shower unit. It still

hadn't arrived. How on earth would Kit be able to pay for it?

He'd turned the car around and had driven back into town, booked into a hotel. Not one of the gorgeous plush ones with glorious ocean or lake views. He didn't deserve one of those. His hotel was spare and spartan. His room was spare and spartan. His view... Who cared? He didn't bother looking out of the window.

Without kicking off even his shoes, he'd fallen back onto the bed to stare up at the ceiling.

Would you give up those two years with Chad?

He fisted his hands in the quilt in an attempt to combat the hollowness, the emptiness...and to give himself something to hold onto.

Alex was waiting for Frank at the Rock Pool before lunch the following Monday.

Frank didn't hesitate when he saw Alex; he trotted right on over and settled himself in the sand beside him. 'Saw your car was gone Saturday afternoon. Noticed it didn't come back Saturday night. Or yesterday. Or this morning.'

Alex was suddenly fiercely glad that Kit had a neighbour who took notice of such things, one who cared for her. It shamed him to think he'd written Frank off as a silly old duffer.

'Kit wanted me to leave. She ordered me to go back to Sydney.'

Shrewd eyes surveyed him. 'You haven't, though.'

'No.'

'You're going to stay and fight for her?'

Alex knew if he lied and said yes that he'd instantly win the older man's support, but he was through with those kinds of lies and half-truths and vain reaching for dreams that could never be. He stared out at the water. 'There isn't any hope for me and Kit, Frank.' The words tasted dry and vile in his mouth.

'Then what are you still doing here?'

'I can't leave her house in that mess. Not when she has a baby on the way.'

'Your baby.'

'Yes.' His baby. The baby he couldn't face. He pushed the thought away. This wasn't what he'd come here to discuss. 'Look, Frank, the short story is that Kit doesn't want to clap eyes on me again so I can't finish the work myself. I need someone capable to oversee the rest of what needs doing.' He hauled in a breath. 'I was hoping that person might be you.'

Frank pursed his lips. 'But I'd have to do it behind Kit's back?'

Alex nodded heavily. He'd known Frank would find the clandestine nature of his plan problematic.

'I don't know, Alex. Kit is a proud woman. She won't accept money or charity from me, and it certainly sounds as if she won't accept it from you.'

'Look, in terms of materials most of the stuff is already there. The paint is in the garden shed and the new bathroom tiles are being stored in the laundry cupboard. I'm not stupid enough to offer to cover the costs of the labour. I know Kit can manage that.'

'So…you just want me to oversee the work, see that they do a good job and don't rip her off?'

Alex nodded and pulled a business card from his pocket. 'The hardware store recommends these guys. Maybe you could point Kit in their direction.'

'That all seems harmless enough.' Those shrewd eyes surveyed him again, narrowed. 'And?'

'There's this damn shower unit I ordered.' Alex flung an arm out. 'It's top of the line, but they wouldn't take my money because they weren't sure if they could get it in. Now it appears they can and a bill will be enclosed upon delivery.'

'Ah…'

Realization dawned in Frank's eyes and Alex could read the denial forming there. 'It's expensive,' he rushed on. And then he named the price.

Frank's jaw dropped. 'You're spending how much on a shower cubicle?'

'It's top of the line—non-slip, safety glass and…and it's easy clean, low maintenance.' He dragged a hand down his face. 'I wanted Kit and the baby to have the best.'

Frank threw his head back then and started to laugh. Alex shifted on the sand and scowled at the water, at his feet…at a seagull that screeched endlessly nearby. 'You have to intercept that bill for me, Frank. Kit would never have chosen that unit and her resources won't stretch to covering it.'

'I'll see what I can do.' Frank chuckled before breaking into a fresh gale of laughter. 'Come on, lad. Let's go for a swim.'

Alex waited at the Rock Pool on Tuesday, but Frank didn't show. He knew Frank's routine was a swim before lunch on Mondays, Wednesdays and Fridays, but he waited there on Tuesday just in case Frank needed him for anything. Even though he'd given the older man his mobile phone number. And the address and phone number of his motel.

Frank showed on Wednesday. He told Alex that when he'd offered to organise for someone to finish the work on her house, Kit had accepted.

It should've taken a load off his mind. He knew this team would do a good job. But, as he and Frank swam, it was all Alex could do to keep afloat.

On Friday, Frank told him the painting should be finished by the close of business that day.

On the following Monday, Frank handed him the bill for the shower unit. 'Arrived on Saturday,' he said gruffly.

Not once did he tell Alex how Kit and the baby were doing—if she was eating well, if her last doctor's visit had gone without a hitch…if she was happy. He ached with the need to know, but he didn't ask. He appreciated all Frank had done and was continuing to do. He would not stretch the older man's loyalties any more than he already had.

'Guess once you pay that—' Frank nodded at the bill '—you can head back to Sydney.'

His words punched Alex in the gut. Leave? But…

'You've achieved what you set out to, Alex. Kit's house is coming along. The bathroom will be finished by the end of the week.'

So soon? Alex stuck out his jaw. 'I'm staying till it's completely finished. In case there are any snags.'

Frank opened his mouth but with a shake of his head he shut it. 'Let's go for a swim.'

'It's all done. Completely finished.'

Alex stared at Frank, a ball of heaviness growing in his chest. It was Friday. 'But…they said they didn't think they'd be finished till tomorrow.'

'They stayed late yesterday to finish up.'

The older man stretched his legs out in front of him. Alex couldn't stretch anything. He ground a fist into the sand.

'It looks grand.'

He was fiercely glad about that. He wanted Kit's house perfect. But finished…?

Was Frank sure? 'So the external painting is…?'

'White with blue trim.'

Just like Kit wanted. 'The guttering is replaced?'

'Tick.'

'The internal painting is all done?'

'It's lovely and fresh inside now.'

'And the bathroom is new and clean and functional?'

'Complete with that fancy shower unit.'

As each item was ticked off the list, Alex's heart grew heavier. He wanted to ask what Kit thought of it. Did she like it? 'What about the nursery?' He latched onto that as a last straw.

'She wants to decorate the nursery herself.'

She'd asked him to help her. His shoulders sagged. She didn't want his help any more. She didn't want to clap eyes on him ever again.

Not that he could blame her.

'So your job here is done.'

'I guess so.' The words emerged slowly, reluctantly. So why didn't it feel done?

'Did you know that Doreen and I lost a child?'

Alex swung around.

'It was a long time ago. Benji—he was nine. The sweetest little kid. Cancer.'

Alex stared. Finally he shook himself. 'Frank, I had no idea.' At least Chad was playing somewhere, happy, with his whole life to look forward to. 'Mate, I'm really sorry.'

Frank nodded. 'That kind of thing, it can tear your life apart, you know?'

He nodded. He knew.

'I'm ashamed to admit it, but I took to drinking for a while.'

Alex's lips twisted. 'They call it self-medication these days.'

Frank snorted. 'That's just rot!'

They both stared out at the golden curve of beach spread

out before them, at the clear water in the Rock Pool with its tiny waves breaking right on the shoreline. So calm, so peaceful, belying the swirl of emotions that slugged through Alex. 'What got you through it?' he finally asked.

'I had Doreen and three other kiddies, all who needed me. When I realized I was letting them down, I…' The older man's voice broke. Alex found his eyes burning. 'I suddenly realized that Benji, if he knew how I was behaving, he would've been ashamed of me.'

Alex raised his knees, rested his elbows on them and dropped his head to his hands. Sand from his hands ground against his forehead but he didn't care. He ached for Frank and for all the other man had been through, but their situations were not the same.

'You going to join me for one last swim, lad?'

Alex nodded and followed Frank down to the water. He grimaced at the term Frank had used—*last swim*. It sounded like a condemned man's last supper. When his feet hit the water he had to admit that it felt that way too. He didn't bother waiting for his body to adjust to the change of temperature. He dived straight in and started slicing through the water, pushing his body harder and faster. No matter how fast he went, his thoughts raced faster.

Kit's house was finished. There was nothing more he could do here. It was time to return to Sydney, or…

Or what? Stay holed up in his hotel room like some damn hideaway?

He kicked his legs harder, pumped his arms faster, did lap after lap along the net of the Rock Pool until eventually he thought his lungs would burst. Halting, he shook the water out of his eyes and dragged an agonised breath into his body. Frank stroked up and down not too far away.

Given Frank and Doreen's unrelenting cheerfulness, the way they were always eager for a chat, Alex would never have guessed that they had met with such tragedy in their lives.

Frank's voice sounded through him. *'I had Doreen and three other kiddies, all who needed me.'*

If his grandfather had taken Frank's attitude when Alex's mother had left home and married against his wishes instead of shoring himself up with bitterness and anger, he'd have gained a son-in-law and a grandchild who'd have loved him unconditionally. Instead, he died with all his wealth, but not a soul at his bedside.

Alex shook his head, turned to rest against the net and stare out towards the channel. He couldn't see Kit's rock from here, but—

He froze.

In his mind he'd just given his grandfather a choice. That same choice was open to him too.

His stomach rolled over and over as if he'd swallowed a gallon of saltwater. In his hurt, his grandfather had turned his back on the people he loved and had cut himself off. Frank had turned towards the people he loved. In providing them with the support and care—the love—that they needed, it had mended his heart.

He glanced at Frank and the message Kit had been trying to impart suddenly hit him. Love made a person stronger, not weaker. He pressed his thumb and forefinger to the bridge of his nose, his mind spinning. Turning away from love was the easy thing to do, but a real man didn't turn away from the people who needed him.

The knowledge poured into him, making him feel fuller and more real than he had in weeks. Than he had in two years.

Memories of Chad pounded through him—Chad, hot and grumpy from teething. Chad, tearing the Christmas wrapping from his presents one Christmas morning. Chad, completely absorbed watching a Labrador puppy. His chest cramped, a groan broke from him, but he didn't push the memories away. He readied himself for crashing waves of grief, but...

The pain didn't get any worse. It didn't take him over, bury him or send him mad. It didn't cover him in despair. And as he followed the memories as they flitted through his mind, he even found himself starting to smile. Chad had been a great little kid. He'd brought laughter and love and tenderness into all the lives he'd touched. Into Alex's life.

The answer to Kit's last question came to him bright and shining and full of promise then. He wouldn't give back a single moment he'd had with Chad. If he'd known that one day Chad would be whisked away from him, he'd have done all he could to have spent more time with him, not less.

He couldn't walk away from Kit and their baby. They needed him. They loved him. Such a gift should be treasured. He should be giving thanks for it every day, not walking away from it. He should be doing everything in his power to make them happy—to make them feel as loved and blessed as he was.

He swore and scrambled for the shore and then swung back to grab Frank. 'Frank, I've gotta go! I'll talk to you later, all right?'

'Rightio, lad.'

Alex turned and bolted for the shore. When he reached the beach he bolted towards the car park, half-falling in the soft sand in his haste. All he had to do now was convince Kit to take a chance on him. Again. He swallowed and hoped he hadn't stretched her love so far that it had snapped.

He hoped she would agree to see him.

* * *

'Kit!' Caro slammed her hands to her hips. 'Get down from there at once! Pregnant women should not climb ladders.'

Kit tried to find a grin, but from the expression on her friend's face it wasn't a very successful one. 'It's only a stepladder. I'm only on the second rung. I'm barely two feet off the ground.' She was trying to attach the wallpaper frieze to the wall. She'd thought decorating the nursery might lift her spirits.

She'd thought wrong.

The wallpaper frieze fluttered to the floor.

Decorating a nursery should be a joyous occasion. She hadn't found much occasion for joy since Alex had left, though.

She pushed the thought away. She'd made a pact with herself to stop thinking about Alex. So she forced herself to grin again at Caro. 'Ooh, look, pregnant woman on a stepladder! Must mean she's going to fall.' She gave a mock wobble, back-pedaling with her arms as if fighting to find her balance.

Caro rolled her eyes. 'In all the movies the woman only falls when the hero storms into the room, so he can catch her in his arms and kiss her.'

'Yeah, well, not going to happen here.' Her so-called hero had roared out of town so fast they hadn't seen him for dust. He hadn't phoned, he hadn't emailed, he hadn't nothing! She bit her lip. She had been pretty adamant, though, and for once it seemed that Alex had listened.

She thrust out her chin. Darn man!

'Jeez, Kit!' A large shape loomed in the doorway and her heart hammered all the way up into her throat. 'What the hell are you doing on a stepladder?'

Alex!

This time her wobble wasn't feigned. She recovered

herself and clambered down before she really did fall. She wouldn't let him catch her.

She couldn't let him touch her.

'What on earth are you doing here?' She wasn't dreaming, was she? She hadn't conjured him up through the sheer force of her longing?

But, as his dark malt scent hit her, she knew she wasn't dreaming. She wanted to cry. She'd just about rid her house of that scent.

'Alex?' She did all she could to make her voice hard and demanding, which was difficult given that she could hardly breathe.

He looked delightfully and deliciously adrift.

No! He wasn't delightfully and deliciously anything.

'Find me a meat cleaver,' Caro muttered.

Decision suddenly stamped itself all over his face. It took her breath away.

'Caro—' his hands descended to her friend's shoulders '—if I can't make this right I'll meat cleaver myself. You have my word on it. But until then—' he propelled Caro out of the door '—I need you to give me and Kit ten.'

'Kit?'

It hurt her to see him. It was wonderful too. 'It's okay.'

Caro shrugged and held her right hand up to her ear as if holding a phone. 'Call me.'

Kit swallowed and nodded. 'I will.'

Caro left before Alex could close the door on her. 'Leave the door open,' Kit said as Alex went to close it.

Shadows chased themselves across his face. 'So you can call for Caro?'

No, so she could breathe! His scent beat at her, making her light-headed. Not that she had any intention of confessing that.

She cursed her weakness for this man. And then had to

swallow at the baby's sudden activity. As if it too sensed Alex in the room and couldn't contain its excitement. The thought sent pain shooting through her heart.

She folded her arms and lifted her chin, stared at his throat. 'What are you doing here, Alex? As you can see, the work on the house is done.' Except for the nursery. And Alex wasn't interested in the nursery.

He wasn't interested in the baby.

He wasn't interested in her.

Finally, she lifted her eyes to his and her heart started to pound as loud and hard as their baby's kicks. The expression in his eyes, it said otherwise—that he *was* interested. Really, truly, seriously interested.

She swallowed, stuck out a hip. She'd been wrong about him before.

A ridiculous shyness, a ludicrous nervousness, made her hands shake and tangled her tongue.

'The house looks great.'

It did.

He suddenly frowned. 'May I have a look at the bathroom?'

She gestured for him to go right ahead. It was easier than saying anything. It provided her with an opportunity to feast her eyes on him as he surveyed the newly appointed bathroom.

'Do you like the shower unit?'

That unglued her tongue. She transferred her gaze from him to it and shook her head. 'It's the ugliest thing I've ever clapped eyes on, Alex.' Its fibreglass starkness seemed at odds with the rest of the room. 'What on earth were you thinking?'

'If it wasn't for that shower unit I wouldn't be here. It's that shower unit that's made me come to my senses.'

She pressed a hand to her forehead. The man had gone mad.

'And you. And Frank.'

She pulled her hand away, narrowed her eyes. Frank had been wonderful these past two weeks—solicitous and caring, offering her practical help but giving her space too when he sensed she needed it. The turncoat! He'd known Alex was here and he hadn't—

'He made me realize that running away from you and our child was the worst thing I could do.'

She promptly lowered the brand new lid of the toilet and sat before she fell. She covered her face with both hands. 'Alex, please don't do this to me. I can't stand it. Me and the baby, we don't want your guilt and your sense of duty and responsibility.' She got that, she really did, but... 'That's not what we need.'

'Tell me what you do need, Kit.'

His voice, its intensity, made her lift her head. 'We need your joy, Alex. We need your joy and your happiness, and we need your love.' She dragged in a breath that made her whole frame shake.

She closed her eyes and counted to three. When she opened them again, Alex was still there. She frowned. 'I know those things are not on offer. I understand that you don't have them to give. But please, don't torture me with consolation prizes. I...I can't stand it.'

He sat on the side of the bathtub so they were eye to eye. 'But what if they are on offer, Kit? What if I tell you I've found my joy, my happiness and my love? What if I tell you I've found all those things?' He reached over and flattened his hand against her baby bump. 'What if I tell you I know those things are here in this room with me? Kit, what if I tell you that you and our baby...'

She blinked. He'd said *our* baby. Not *her* baby or *the* baby but *our* baby!

'...that you are my joy and my happiness and my love?'

She gripped her hands together. The only thing keeping her steady was his hand on her baby bump. 'If you did by some miracle say those things to me, I'd say that you'd have a hard time convincing me of their truth.'

But his eyes, his smile, the light shining in his face and the way his hand curved against her stomach. All those things told her that he spoke the truth.

He leaned towards her. 'Frank told me about Benji.'

Her jaw went slack. That meant Frank trusted Alex. Really trusted him.

'And that's when I realized what you'd been trying to show me all along—that love isn't a weakness, it's a strength. And that's when I could finally answer that last question you asked me.'

He met her gaze—strong and steadfast. 'I would not give up a single moment I had with Chad.'

The truth shone from every inch of his being. Hope lifted through her. She tried to keep it in check while she took in the deeper meaning of his words.

'I don't want to waste a single moment of the time I'm given with you and our child either. It's too precious. I want to treasure it.'

He went down on one knee in front of her. Her hope burst free. 'Alex! You can't propose to me when I'm sitting on a toilet!'

His grin when it came was slow and sexy as all get out. 'Considering I stayed in town because of that darn shower unit, I think the bathroom is the perfect place to propose to you.'

She glanced at the shower unit.

'I'll explain it to you later,' he promised, taking her

hand. 'What I have to say now is much more important, believe me.'

Oh, she did. When he looked at her like that she'd believe anything.

'Kit, what happened with Jacqui and Chad, for a long time I thought that must have been my fault. I figured that if I'd been a better father and husband, they wouldn't have left like that.'

'Oh, Alex.' She cupped his face with her free hand.

'But I've started to realize it doesn't prove I'm either a bad husband or a bad father. I just wasn't the right husband for Jacqui. And, if I'm truly honest, she was never the right wife for me. It took a long time for me to realize that because I was so busy counting all the similarities between my grandfather and me. I thought his coldness and bitterness were part of my genetic make-up too. But my mother wasn't like that.

'There's no reason why I have to be like him either. He had choices too. He made the wrong choices.' His eyes didn't drop from hers, not once. 'I don't have to be like him unless I choose to be. And, Kit—' his grip tightened about her hand '—I'm choosing not to be.'

She still held his face cupped in her hand and she couldn't help herself, she leaned forward and pressed her lips to his.

He kissed her back—gently, wonderingly and with the same love that had splintered her mind when he'd kissed her at the breakwater that day.

He gripped her by the shoulders and pulled back. 'No way! No more of that.'

Her eyes bugged.

He smiled that slow, sexy grin. 'Until you tell me that you'll be my wife.' His expression sobered. 'Kit, I love you more than I ever dreamt it was possible to love another person. I will spend every single moment of every single day making you and our children happy. I swear.'

Her breath hitched. 'Children?'

'I hope so,' he murmured. 'You do want more children, don't you? We'd want brothers and sisters for junior here.'

Through a blur she desperately tried to blink away, she nodded. She wanted children, she wanted the life he'd described. She wanted him. 'I love you, Alex. You, this baby, this bathroom—' she suddenly laughed '—it's all I've ever wanted. Yes, I will marry you!'

With a whoop, Alex swung her up and around and kissed her till she could barely breathe. She wrapped her arms around his neck and kissed him back.

She didn't know how long they stayed like that. She only knew that it was quite some time—a wonderful, magical, I-can't-believe-this-is-happening time. Alex rested his forehead against hers. She swore she could stare into those dark eyes of his for all of time. 'Are you sure this is what you want?' she whispered. This had been such a hard road for him. If he needed more time…

'I've never been surer of anything in my life. I'm only sorry it took me so long to come to my senses. Knowing that I hurt you—'

'Shh.' She reached up to brush the frown from his brow. 'It's the future we look towards now, not the past.'

He seized her hand and pressed a kiss to her palm. 'Kit, I don't have much to offer you. I don't have any family and I've only a few friends…'

She smiled then. 'Alex, I don't think there's another billionaire on the planet who would ever say that they didn't have much to offer.' She took his hand then and pressed a kiss to his palm. 'I have enough friends and family for us both. We'll make our own family. Alex, all I want is your heart.'

'It's yours.'

She went to kiss him again and then stopped, cocked her head to one side. 'Can you hear that?'

'Hear what?' he said, nuzzling the side of her neck.

Mmm. She wrapped her arms around his neck and…

She cocked her head to the side again. 'Someone is singing in the back garden.'

He lifted his head. 'They are?'

She took his hand and led him through the house and all the way out to the back door and then stumbled to a halt as four sets of eyes swung to them—Caro, Frank, Doreen and Davey, who was singing.

'Well?' Caro demanded.

'Speak up, lad,' Frank ordered. 'Do we all get to dance at your wedding?'

Alex's grin threatened to split his face in two. Kit's breath caught. She'd never seen him look so happy. If she'd had any doubts left about his feelings for her, they'd be gone now. He glanced at her and she nodded.

He held his arms out. 'You're looking at the happiest man on the planet. Kit's agreed to marry me.'

Frank popped a bottle of champagne as Caro and Doreen swamped them in hugs.

'Ooh, I shouldn't,' Kit said when Doreen pressed a glass of champagne into her hand.

'Tsk! In my day it was considered healthful to take a glass of beer in the evenings. Never did any of us any harm. A thimbleful won't hurt you any.'

Doreen was right. Her doctor had said the same. A sip or two wouldn't hurt her. It was only right they celebrate the happiest day of her life.

'To Kit and Alex,' Frank boomed, raising his glass. 'Many congratulations!'

They all lifted their glasses—even Davey, who had a champagne flute full of lemonade—and drank.

Kit snagged Caro's arm. 'You will be my bridesmaid, won't you?'

'You bet!' She slanted a grin at Alex. 'The meat cleaver gets them every time.'

He laughed and kissed Caro's cheek. 'Had me shaking in my boots.'

Caro nearly spluttered champagne all over them. 'Liar!'

She sobered a moment later. 'Okay, so when are you going to have the wedding? Before or after the baby is born?'

'After,' Kit said at the same moment Alex said, 'Before.'

Caro grinned. 'Right, so you've discussed it then?'

Kit turned to Alex. 'I thought you might want some time to get used to the idea.'

'This isn't some *idea*, Kit. This is my life—our life.' He reached out and touched her face with sure fingers that made her breath quicken. His thumb trailed a path down to the corner of her mouth. 'I know what I want and that's you and the baby.'

She'd never seen him look more serious in all the time she'd known him. Her chest expanded and she could've sworn the only thing keeping her from floating off into the stratosphere and turning weightless somersaults was his hand on her face, with that maddening thumb brushing back and forth at the corner of her mouth. She reached up and seized it before it tempted her to do something that would make her blush.

'So…' She kept her eyes fixed on his. 'Before the baby, then? We'll get married before the baby is born?'

He nodded, his eyes intent. 'Yes.'

A smile built through her. 'In the first weekend Mum can make it down to give me away.'

'Am I rushing you?' He suddenly frowned. 'Weddings traditionally take a long time to organise, don't they?'

She didn't want him to frown; she wanted him smiling. 'I've never much cared about all the trappings that go along with a wedding. I'd be happy to have the ceremony here in the garden.'

'Won't fit,' Caro said, sipping her champagne.

'Lovey, you'd be better off at the community hall in your grandmother's retirement village. She can organise one of her luncheons for you.'

Kit glanced up at Alex. 'What do you think?'

'Does it mean you're going to marry me sooner rather than later?'

She grinned. 'It does.'

His lips descended to hers. 'Then it sounds perfect to me.'

'Mmm,' she murmured against his lips. *Perfect* was exactly how it sounded.

* * * * *

RODEO DADDY

BY
SORAYA LANE

All the characters in this book have no existence outside the imagination of
the author, and have no relation whatsoever to anyone bearing the same name
or names. They are not even distantly inspired by any individual known or
unknown to the author, and all the incidents are pure invention.

First published in Great Britain 2011
by Mills & Boon, an imprint of Harlequin (UK) Limited,
Eton House, 18-24 Paradise Road, Richmond, Surrey TW9 1SR

© Soraya Lane 2011

ISBN: 978 0 263 88922 2

23-1111

Harlequin (UK) policy is to use papers that are natural, renewable and
recyclable products and made from wood grown in sustainable forests. The
logging and manufacturing processes conform to the legal environmental
regulations of the country of origin.

Printed and bound in Spain
by Blackprint CPI, Barcelona

Dear Reader,

Returning to the place where you grew up can be an important turning point for many people, and that's certainly true for my heroine, Sophie Baxter. But as she comes home her hero, Lark Anderson, moves across the world, far away from his own home, in a bid to start afresh.

In New Zealand, the place where I am so fortunate to live, Sophie and Lark fall in love surrounded by horses and open fields. While they both battle with what has happened to them in the past, their bond makes them confront their issues and forge a new life together.

Horses are a great passion of mine, and I hope you enjoy reading about my gorgeous cowboy and the horses he owns. To me, there is nothing sexier than a man who knows his way around a horse—a man who can communicate with such a large, powerful animal in a kind, understanding way. If that sounds like your kind of hero, then I just know you will love reading this story as much as I enjoyed writing it.

Soraya Lane

Writing romance for Mills & Boon is truly a dream come true for **Soraya Lane**. An avid book reader and writer since her childhood, Soraya describes becoming a published author as "the best job in the world", and hopes to be writing heart-warming, emotional romances for many years to come.

Soraya lives with her own real-life hero on a small farm in New Zealand, surrounded by animals and with an office overlooking a field where their horses graze.

For my wonderful father, Craig.
After years of my begging for a pony as a child, it
got to the point where he couldn't say no any longer,
and I will always be grateful for his generosity in
indulging my love for horses. It is only fitting, then,
that my first cowboy book is for my dad.

CHAPTER ONE

SOPHIE BAXTER tapped her fingers against the steering wheel as she drove carefully down the gravel road. It was almost dark and the road was slippery, the ground turned dangerous and sludgy beneath the tires.

She had forgotten what it was like to drive in the country, especially in bad weather. She'd spent too long cruising along perfect city streets.

Sophie's eyes strained as she peered hard through the windscreen. The snow had given way to a sleet-rain mixture that was making it hard to see.

What on earth—?

She slammed on her brakes as a man's silhouette appeared in front of her, arms waving above his head, urging her to stop.

Her car slid as she swerved to avoid him.

Sophie shut her eyes. No, please no! She gripped the steering wheel, forced her eyes to open again and watched as her car traveled sideways in slow motion, before finally grinding to a halt.

Her heart was pounding hard, beating in her ears, in her throat, everywhere. Then, as her eyes started to focus again, she saw a flash of something dark darting in front of the car.

Could it have been…?

A horse. A horse was loose on the road.

She fumbled for her handbag and pulled out her phone, hand shaking as she dialed the emergency number.

"What is the nature of your emergency? Fire, ambulance or police?"

Sophie caught her breath long enough to listen to the calm tone on the other end of the line. "Police," she said.

There was a moment's silence, before the line clicked again. "Police, how can we assist?"

Sophie let her head loll back on the headrest, trying to calm her still-racing heart. Jeez, she'd almost hit a man, then just about taken out a horse!

"I need to report a horse loose on the road," she told the person on the other end, voice shaking. "There's poor visibility. I almost collided with it and the man attempting to catch it."

She finished giving the operator her location and almost leaped out of her skin at a tap on the window.

Damn it! Her heart was racing all over again. She recognized the figure she'd almost run over.

And he looked mad.

Wet and mad.

She wound down her window, about to apologize, but he didn't give her the chance.

"You going to sit there all day, or are you going to help?"

Sophie recoiled at the sharpness of his words. Even his deep American drawl wasn't enough to distract her. How dare he!

"I could have killed you," she told him, angry now. "What were you doing standing in the middle of the road?"

He scowled at her, hands planted on his hips. "I was trying to stop you from plowing into a horse, *actually*."

If Sophie hadn't been so annoyed with his tone she would have laughed. Seriously, who exactly did he think he was?

The guy was tall, well over six foot, and he was handsome, even if she was loathe to admit it. She could tell that, in spite of the dark, even though she could only just make out his features. His dark hair was plastered to his head, he was soaked through, and he was mad. Hands on hips, brooding kind of mad.

But still, rude was rude. Being handsome was not an excuse.

Sophie watched as he sighed, clearly realizing that she was far from impressed at being told off. He pushed a hand through his hair to stop it from trailing onto his forehead. His shoulders fell.

"I'm sorry, that was rude."

Yep, sure was, but she appreciated the apology.

"What I meant to say was that I'd appreciate your help, if you don't mind getting wet." He gestured at his own body. "Before you came along I almost had her. Now she's loose again."

Sophie sighed. Maybe he wasn't so bad after all. She'd probably given him a hell of a shock almost bowling him over, and a horse on the loose would be stressful for anyone.

"It's okay. I'll help." She rummaged in the back for her waterproof jacket and hauled it on before getting out of the car. "I'm with the local animal shelter, so it's no problem."

The guy looked relieved, a tight smile visible on his face. "Thank you." It made him look less guilty and more of a good guy.

She pulled up the hood on her jacket, braced against the cold. "I've already phoned it in to the police. We'll have help soon."

He groaned. Face-falling-into-his-hands kind of groan.

"This is not my night," he muttered.

She raised an eyebrow in question, before realizing he couldn't see. Why wouldn't he want the police involved? "Is there a problem?"

He shook his head, striding ahead toward the horse. "Let's just try to catch these horses and load them onto my truck, okay?"

At least he was being marginally politer now.

Sophie followed. "How many are we talking about?"

The guy pointed. "Three in that field by the fence there, and the one that's loose."

She looked at the horses. "Why don't we catch the group first, bring them over and start loading them. She might follow."

He stopped. Looked back at her, then started to nod. "Why didn't I think of that?"

Lark Anderson looked over the woman who'd almost run him over and who was now his unlikely savior. He shouldn't have been so rude to her, but she'd sure scared the life from him.

He glanced at her as they walked side by side toward the group of nervous horses, but her features were almost impossible to make out. She was tall, for a woman, and slender. Her outline in the near dark showed a slim woman with long hair in a ponytail, but beyond that it was too hard to see.

"So do you make a habit of working with your horses in the dark?"

She said it with a laugh but it made Lark's skin prickle.

Even so, he wasn't going to bite.

"Not usually, no," he said through gritted teeth. "But then it's not every day a fence is left mangled for a horse to get caught in, either."

She almost came to a stop, looked across at him, then resumed her pace. "Sorry."

He shrugged and tucked his chin against his chest as another icy gust of wind slapped against his cheeks.

"You're not from around here, are you?"

"What gave it away?" he asked. "My weird accent?"

This time she did stop. "Are you always this rude?"

Lark shut his eyes for a heartbeat and sighed, pleased she couldn't see his face properly. "I'm sorry. It's been a long night."

She didn't say anything.

"Let's just say that adjusting to woolen socks and numb toes is harder than you'd think."

She laughed. He was pleased that she was laughing at him

rather than walking away, and he couldn't have blamed her for getting back in her car, blasting on the heat and driving away.

"As opposed to?"

This time Lark laughed. "Would you believe it if I told you a cowboy hat in California?"

He stopped a few feet from one of the horses and held his hand up slightly to tell her to do the same. Lark slowly reached for the horse, slipping a rope around her neck before she could dance sideways away from him. "Whoa, girl, you're okay. It's all right."

"So I take it you're the rodeo rider," she said in a soft voice.

Lark nodded, before realizing she couldn't see him. "Yeah, that's me."

"You have your one secure?" she asked.

He looked over at her, pleased that she'd managed to clip a rope onto the other horse's halter. "Yup, let's get them over to the truck."

Lark whispered to the horse, reaching for the third one as it came closer. He now led two of them, and he wanted to get them out of harm's way as soon as he could. He hated leaving the loose horse out on the road where she could get hurt.

"Back to whether you do this kind of thing in the dark often…"

He laughed this time, shaking off the grump he'd been in since he'd found the horses in such awful conditions.

"Let's just say that I'm not good at tucking up in my own bed at night during a storm, without knowing the animals around me have the same comforts."

"Well, when you put it like that," she said thoughtfully.

Flashing lights interrupted them.

Bloody hell.

He'd hoped to resolve the situation before the police arrived. Hoped to have fled the scene. The last thing he needed was to get in trouble with the law.

Lark continued walking as though he hadn't even noticed

the approaching vehicle, taking the frightened horses over to his truck.

Thankfully they loaded easily enough. Someone must have trained them before they'd been left to their own devices. Just as they'd hoped, the other mare wandered close.

"I'll take her," he told the woman, reaching for the horse and running a hand down the mare's neck to soothe her. "Maybe you could go and stall the police for a moment?"

"Sure thing," she said, almost invisible in the dark now. "You finish up here and I'll let them know what's happening."

Lark stifled another groan. How the hell was he going to talk his way out of this one?

In his younger days, he might have jumped in the truck cab and taken off in hopes of outrunning trouble.

But he was no longer that boy who didn't want to face any consequences. He was a man with responsibilities now.

He managed to secure the other horse, now waiting to join her friends, before loading her and pushing the button to close the ramp at the back of the truck.

"Sir?"

Just in time.

Lark forced his shoulders to relax and turned. Slowly. Feet moving in a half circle to confront the male voice he didn't recognize.

"Sophie here tells me the situation is now under control."

Sophie, huh? He looked at the woman standing beside the officer. He wished he hadn't snapped at her earlier. But being beyond cold, almost getting run over and dealing with the rogue horses had been too much to handle. Especially after the year he'd already had.

What he hadn't been able to notice before was how pretty she was. What he could see of her anyway, now that she was illuminated in the police car's lights. Her hair was caught up in a high ponytail, although he couldn't quite make out what color it was, and she had a wide smile on her face despite the cold.

He felt rude that he hadn't even known her name until now.

"I've finished loading them," he responded, gesturing over his shoulder with his thumb. "I'm sorry for any inconvenience."

The officer switched on his flashlight. Lark could make out a frown on his face as the light danced in a bright arc.

"As an animal owner you have an obligation to keep them under control, to ensure they pose no threat to public safety."

Lark felt his neck hairs bristle at the condescending tone in the man's voice. They weren't even his darn horses!

He should have kept on driving. Ignored the horses. Been realistic enough to admit that they weren't his and that he couldn't save every unloved animal in the world.

But even if he'd known this was how the night would end, he probably still would have tried to help them. It wouldn't have been in him to walk away.

"I'll need to see your license, so I can make a formal report."

"Tim, I really don't think there's a problem here."

Lark didn't move. He wanted to hear what this Sophie had to say, why she was sticking up for him when he'd almost caused her to crash her vehicle. Especially after how rude he'd been.

"It looks like someone vandalized the fence, and one of the horses became stuck in it, so this man was doing his best to get the horse off the road and to safety. Right?"

Lark found himself nodding before he even realized what he was doing. "Yeah, something like that."

The officer clearly wasn't convinced. Yet. "License?" he asked again.

Lark pulled his wallet from his pocket. "Here." He passed the license over.

"International license, Mr. Anderson?"

Lark resisted being smart-mouthed. "Yes."

"Tim, let's deal with this in the morning. It's so cold," said Sophie, her voice soft.

He watched as his unlikely advocate wrapped her arms around her body, despite the thick coat she was bundled in. "I can check on the horses' welfare in the morning and report in to you then. Let's all get out of the cold."

Lark stayed silent. He wasn't about to say something and jeopardize a possible get-out-of-jail-free card.

"You sure?" the officer asked.

Sophie didn't miss a beat. "Yes, positive."

"Well, Mr. Anderson, you'll be hearing from us both tomorrow."

He had no idea what had just happened, or why this Sophie had stuck up for him. But he wasn't going to argue. If she wanted to come see the horses tomorrow he couldn't care less. So long as he could get out of his dripping-wet clothes and into something dry, he would agree to anything.

And so long as she didn't try to tell him what to do when she turned up.

"I'm at…"

Sophie interrupted before he could give her his address. "I think everyone in town knows the farm bought by the famous rodeo cowboy."

The officer had started to walk away, shoulders hunched against the wind.

Lark chuckled. "Small town, huh?"

She paused, arms still wrapped around herself. "I'll come past tomorrow and you can explain everything to me then."

"Thanks for all your help," he said, grateful at least that the night was over.

"You're welcome."

Lark watched her walk off, before springing into action himself, running back to the truck.

He'd almost forgotten about Lucy.

Damn it! So much for trying to be a good dad.

He swung open the door to the cab. "Honey, I'm so…"

Lucy was sitting cross-legged, a big smile on her face. Seeing her like that hit Lark like a swinging punch to the gut.

"It's okay, Dad. Did you get them all?"

He hauled himself up behind the steering wheel, pausing to strip off his shirt and throw it into the back in a ball.

"I got 'em honey. But I'm so sorry for leaving you in here."

She smiled like a child far beyond her years. As though she understood, as though she knew why he'd had to do it.

He felt he was making a hash of this parenting business, but she was so patient with him. Tried so hard, more like the adult than he was.

"Are we going to keep them?"

He nodded. "Yeah, I think so."

He didn't tell her that he was worried about getting into trouble. That he could be arrested or charged with theft if the officer decided to make a fuss over it.

That sometimes you had to ignore your heart and be realistic. Which was exactly what he *hadn't* done here when he'd decided to save the four horses.

Instead he reached for Lucy's hand and gave it a squeeze. He often didn't know what to say to her, how to behave or what to do, but somehow, reaching for her always made things better. It was the only thing he knew how to do.

"I…ah…I love you, Lucy." He forced the words out, even though he found it hard to admit to his feelings. The sentence choked in his throat as if it was impossibly hard to get out, as if it wasn't meant to be said out aloud. "You do know that, right?"

She pulled her seat belt on, smiling over at him. "I know."

He might not be the best father in the world, but he was trying. Hell, was he trying.

One day at a time, he reminded himself, *one day at a time.* No one had ever said this would be easy.

Lark shut the door to the barn and braced himself for the sting of the cold. He tucked his head down and broke into a jog, ignoring the twinge in his back. Every time his right foot thumped down it sent a niggle up his spine.

He clamped his jaw tight and forced his legs to go faster.

He'd neglected Lucy enough already tonight, leaving her sitting in the truck. Even though he felt like a failure sometimes, wondering what to do and if what he did was right, he still liked to be there for her. He figured so long as she knew she wasn't alone, that he loved her, he was at least doing something right.

He kicked off his boots on the back porch and the door slammed loudly with a gust of wind behind him. Lark flicked the switch. The storm had taken the power out in the barn, but so far the house hadn't been affected. Yet.

Lark found Lucy sitting in front of the fire, the open logs burning with a steady blaze and illuminating her light blond hair like a halo around her face. She sat with a book in her lap, legs crossed, eyes down. Exactly where he'd left her.

"Hi, darlin'," he called.

Lucy looked up and gave him a smile that made his heart thud to his toes. He had loved in his life, had had his fair share of women, but the way this little girl made him feel was something else entirely. She made everything that had happened in the past year worth it, even if it hadn't seemed like it at the time.

"How's that book going?"

Lark peeled off his woolen sweater and stood watching her.

"It's good," she told him, tucking her book beneath one crossed knee. "What's for dinner?"

Oh. Dinner. He'd forgotten again.

"Um, how about spaghetti? Or maybe eggs?"

Lucy glanced up at him with a look he hoped wasn't pity.

"What about homemade mini pizzas?"

He swallowed a question mark. The last thing he wanted was to ask a seven-year-old how to make pizza. He knew everything there was to know about horse nutrition, but putting food on the table each night for the pair of them was another matter entirely.

"You know, like with the frozen bases?" she said, grinning at him. "We can put cheese and stuff on them. I can show you."

Lark laughed. What would he do without her?

"You sure you can help me?"

Lucy giggled. "Uh-huh. I do know how to cook, you know."

"Of course you do." He stifled his smile.

Lark sat her on the counter and opened the fridge, looked over his shoulder and waited for her to point out what he needed. How on earth she knew how to put food together he'd never know.

One thing he was grateful for was that though his ex-wife had been worse than him in the kitchen, they'd had a housekeeper to put most of their meals together. Maybe that's who Lucy had watched or helped.

His wife had swanned around, spent money and been thrilled with being a celebrity wife. She might not have been a bad mother, but she sure hadn't been a good one. And she'd been a pretty darn awful wife, too, come to think of it.

But it hurt, like a fist to the belly, thinking about what she'd given up. How she'd cut both of them, not just him, from her life without a backward thought. Culling him was one thing, but how a woman could give up her daughter so easily, so willingly…

Lucy gazed up at him and he gave her a wink. Forced the sadness from his face so she wouldn't ask him what was wrong.

It was just the two of them now. Plus the horses.

"You okay, kid?"

She smiled and nodded.

"You know you can tell me if something's wrong, if there's anything, you know, on your mind."

Argh. That had come out all wrong. She was seven, not seventeen. She acted so much older than her years sometimes that he forgot how little she was.

"There is *one* thing." She said the words slowly, almost cautiously.

Lark put down the knife and turned to face her.

"Okay, shoot."

"Well, there's something I'd *really* like for my birthday."

Drat, her birthday was less than a week away.

"Tell me what it is and I'll see what I can do."

He expected it to be a pile of books, the latest toy...

"I really, *really* want a puppy."

She said the words with so much conviction. A puppy? Well, he liked dogs, that wasn't a problem, but did he need something else to look after? It was hard enough looking after the two of them, the farm and keeping the household chores under control.

"A puppy," he repeated.

Lucy nodded until her head looked as though it would fall off. "Yeah, a *Labrador* puppy."

Hell, she'd clearly given this a lot of thought.

"We'll see," he said, knowing that if she wanted one that badly he was never going to be able to say no.

"Really?"

"Really."

Lucy launched into his arms and planted a wet kiss on his cheek. "You're the best dad ever!"

Lark wondered if his "We'll see" had been misheard as a yes, but he knew one thing for sure. Being the best dad ever was pretty important to him right now, so if the kid wanted a puppy, a puppy it might have to be.

He'd been floundering these past few weeks, trying his best, but wondering if he'd ever figure out how to be a good dad. Especially when he had no one to help him. And having Lucy in his arms felt so good. *Beyond good.*

Sometimes he wondered if he'd ever felt so alone. Then he'd realize how silly it was to think like that, when one look at his daughter told him they'd never be alone so long as they had each other.

CHAPTER TWO

Sophie dropped down a gear as her car snaked up the long driveway and approached the house. She had no idea why her stomach was fluttering and twisting, but it had been like this since she'd left the animal shelter.

She stopped outside the house and looked around. It didn't look as if anyone was home. A wide porch stretched across the front, the board siding in pristine condition, a grapevine curling its way up the main posts at each side of the entrance. A white dusting of snow was still sprinkled over the roof even though the weather had cleared overnight.

It didn't look like the home of a bachelor, but then she wasn't sure any country house would have a distinctive single-guy look.

Sophie had heard a lot about the mysterious rodeo rider who'd moved into town. She laughed to herself as she pushed open her door. She still couldn't believe she'd ended up meeting him last night and hadn't clicked the minute she'd heard his honey-laced American drawl.

Given all the gossip she'd heard about him she should have realized immediately, but then, almost running him over had temporarily scrambled her mind.

The American man with no wife that anyone had seen, who was apparently world-famous for his rodeo-riding, had all the women in town swooning. Behind closed doors anyway.

He'd looked handsome the night before, she wasn't denying that, but she wasn't sure he warranted quite that much of a fuss. Although it had been almost dark…

Sophie ran her hands down her jeans, knotted the scarf hanging around her neck and made for the door. She was about to knock when she spotted a huge barn tucked around the back.

Bingo.

"Hello?" Sophie called out as she walked toward the barn.

Nobody answered. She kept walking.

It was still cold, but the snow had stopped falling overnight, and after the rain they'd had since, almost all the white stuff had washed away, although the wind was still like ice brushing against her face.

"Hello?" Louder this time.

Sophie stopped as she approached the big stable block. Wow. The house might be modest, but the barn sure wasn't. The big double doors were open, pinned back, flanked by a large tree on each side.

It was nothing short of idyllic.

She decided to go in.

Sophie shoved her hands in her pockets, wishing she'd brought gloves. It was pristine, the walkway freshly swept, and…

She wasn't alone.

Sophie stopped. Her boots thudded to a halt and wouldn't move.

Maybe she'd hit her head during her sudden stop.

In the daylight, he lived up to every snippet of hyped-up gossip she'd heard whispered about him.

Oh, my.

He was leaning into a stall, one knee pressed into the timber frame, the other leg spread out behind him. Both his arms were crossed against the top of the door, his chin resting on shirt-clad forearms.

Wow.

Now that she could see him more clearly she realized he had to be at least six foot three, maybe taller if those long jeans-covered legs were anything to go by. His hair was dark and slightly messy, as though he'd just trawled his fingers through it.

And if she wasn't mistaken, he was talking to his horse.

A chestnut nose with a streak of white peeked out from above the stable door, nudging at his shoulder. He laughed at the horse, so softly that she only just heard it.

And then he turned.

Oh.

Dark brown eyes met hers, open and smiling, but his expression disappeared, as if he was embarrassed to have been found talking to the animal.

He cleared his throat and straightened, smiling, but his face was slightly guarded, not the same as it had been before he'd known she was there.

"Hi," he called out. His long legs hardly moved, yet the distance between them closed within a second.

Sophie remembered to smile. It shouldn't have been that hard, given the subject in front of her, but for some reason she was having a tough time remembering even to breathe. Let alone answer back.

"Morning," she replied, trying to keep her voice light and breezy, and feeling anything but.

He held out his hand to her. "We didn't really meet properly last night."

Sophie felt her shoulders relax. "No, we didn't get off to the best of starts."

She took the hand he offered, watching as his palm covered hers, its warmth taking the chill from her own freezing-cold skin.

"I'm Sophie, Sophie Baxter," she said.

"Lark Anderson," he replied, before rubbing her hand with his other palm, his mouth lifting in a smile. "And you have mighty cold fingers."

She felt heat crawl across her skin as she met his gaze. Lark just grinned at her and rubbed both his hands over her one cold paw for a moment.

"I'm sorry about, well, snapping at you like I did last night." He looked embarrassed, as though he wasn't used to apologizing. "I was annoyed and cold, and I shouldn't have taken it out on you."

Sophie tried not to become paralyzed. Something about this guy was making her brain and her body refuse to respond. At least at the same time. Somehow, she'd failed to see, to feel, his presence last night.

Granted, it had been dark, he'd been rude and she'd been freezing cold, but still. How had she missed *this?*

"So, where are the horses?" She looked down the row of stalls.

He stood back, thumbs looped into his jeans, leaning back on his heels. "There's one thing I don't understand," he said, not answering her question.

She tilted her head, unsure what he was getting at.

"When you sweet-talked the officer last night, why did he agree to you checking on the horses?"

"I'm with the local animal shelter, so he would have called one of us in anyway, and I've known him since I was a kid," she told him. "I spoke to him this morning, and he wanted me to report back to him. But..."

He took a step forward. "What?"

"He's on his way here shortly, so I'm hoping you don't have anything to, well, to hide." She had this funny feeling that she hadn't just happened upon a guy trying to load his own horses on a truck. She'd wondered about it all night.

Lark smiled at her. A lazy, out-the-side-of-his-mouth, as-if-he-was-about-to-laugh kind of smile.

"What exactly are you asking me, Sophie?"

She flushed, embarrassed. But she was here to do her job. Not get all red-faced over a man. Not now, not here.

"It's just—" she looked down at the horse with his nose still peeping over the stall, anything to avoid those deep, dark eyes watching her "—I can't quite figure out why you were there at that time of night with your horse truck." She paused, but she'd regained her confidence. This time she looked directly at him when she spoke. "They were *your* horses, right?"

"Nope." Lark walked around her and moved down the barn.

She followed him, rushing to keep up with his long strides. Sophie shook her head, wishing she hadn't become involved. She could see this was going to be one of *those* situations.

"I think you should start from the beginning," she suggested. "Please tell me I'm not involved in some sort of a crime, not after I stuck up for you out there last night."

Sophie had no idea what had happened, or how the new guy in town had ended up with a bunch of horses that didn't belong to him in the worst snap of weather they'd had in years. But it didn't feel right.

Lark stopped and turned to face her. Made her feel like the only person in the world as his chocolate-brown eyes softened. But she didn't miss the cheeky upturn of his mouth.

As her mother would have said, if it looks like trouble and smells like trouble…

"There is a slight problem," he said, "with how they came to be in my possession."

Oh, no. Definitely trouble.

Her role was to make an initial assessment, decide on a course of action. She didn't need to deal with additional problems. Especially not when she could be implicated for aiding him.

Sophie waited for Lark to explain himself.

"I uplifted them from where they were being neglected."

Oh, my.

"You stole them!" She gasped. "And I *helped* you to steal them!"

She glared at him. At least he had the decency to look at his feet, boots scuffing at the ground. But he was still smiling when he looked up. Chastised but not easily beaten.

This was going from bad to worse. And fast. Sophie felt her head starting to spin.

"I don't know if *stole* would be the most accurate word." He gave her another smile, as if it would help to soften the blow. "It was about to start snowing again when I passed them, they were bone-thin, with no shelter or feed, and one was injured badly from the wire being tangled around her leg, so I took my horse truck back and brought them home with me." He paused, serious now. "That's when you found me—and helped me."

Sophie shut her eyes for a brief second and took a deep breath. If she'd been on her own she would have pinched the bridge of her nose.

"Lark, I don't know what you'd call it in America, but I can tell you for sure that here we call that theft." She sighed. "In other words you *did* steal them."

He shook his head, and she could see the stubbornness in his eyes. She had a feeling that no matter what she said to him, he'd disagree until she saw things his way.

He'd swear to her that something was black when her own eyes could see clearly it was blue.

But he didn't argue with her. Instead he placed his hand to the small of her back and propelled her forward, warming her with his touch and giving her no other option but to move.

"I did what I had to do, Sophie." His voice was soft, but she couldn't *not* hear him. "Once you see them in the daylight I think you'll understand."

She shook her head but kept walking anyway. She was here now, and it was her job to assess the situation and figure out what to do. All she had to do was make a call on what course of action needed to be taken.

Sophie swallowed away the word *job* and focused instead on the hand resting against the small of her back. She could have quickened her pace, sped up one step, and his hand would have fallen away, but she liked the distraction.

Any little thing that took her mind off the job she *should* be doing, the career she'd run away from, was worth it. Cases like this kept her busy and stopped her from being sucked back into the past.

Lark let his hand drift from Sophie's back as they reached the gate. He made himself take a step to the side, away from her, so he wasn't crowding her space.

But not before he gave her one last quick, sideways glance. She looked troubled, as if something was on her mind, although it didn't distract from her looks. Looks that were different from what he was used to, but she was pretty nonetheless. She was like a colorful wildflower rather than the over-manicured roses he was normally surrounded by, and it was refreshing. Different in a way that took him pleasantly by surprise.

She had a mane of dark blond, slightly curly hair tied in a high ponytail, falling almost halfway down her back. Her stance was strong, confident, her brows pulled together in concern as she watched the horses.

"Come on, girls!" Lark called out and moved to open the gate.

He beckoned for Sophie to follow.

"Are they all mares?"

Lark nodded. "Yeah, but it gets worse. I'm pretty sure two of them are in foal, and the third one is only young. Maybe a yearling. It's hard to tell because she's so small. I've got the injured one in a stall."

He watched as Sophie's eyes narrowed, her face saying it all as one of the mares turned to face them. The horse's hollow expression and lackluster eyes gave away her life story. Her feet were turned up at the edges, they had been left unattended for so long; her coat was so dull it nearly broke Lark's heart.

"I'm not going to take their blankets off to show you their condition. It's too cold and it took me long enough to get the darn things on them yesterday."

Sophie looked at him then back at the horses. They were standing within a few feet of them now.

"The vet's on his way too, so we'll make sure they're all tended to."

Lark nodded. "And your friend with the law isn't going to be enlightened about what happened, is he?"

He watched her face as it flickered with indecision. Lark could tell she was torn between doing the right thing and turning a blind eye.

"I don't know what I can tell you, Lark," she said, looking from him to the horses. "I can't lie and say they're yours. It's not worth it, and he'll only figure it out anyway. Plus I'd only get into trouble myself."

He crossed his arms over his chest. Trusting a woman didn't come naturally to him anymore, but he was at her mercy. Although he liked the fact that she was conflicted over what to do. "But?"

She twirled a strand of hair between her fingers, as if she was lost in thought. "Let's see what I can do, okay? Sometimes owners of neglected animals surrender them without too much of a fuss, but then again, normally an animal shelter is the one to seize them." Sophie paused, before making her point. "Rather than an individual."

He grimaced. Maybe the smart thing to do would have been to call it in. Let someone else deal with it. But then he'd never been the sort of guy to go home to his own warm bed while animals were left out in the cold. Neglected.

"I appreciate all the help you can give me, Sophie," he told her, lowering his voice, knowing she was on the verge of deciding whether or not to assist him. "I did this for the right reasons, you can see that for yourself."

She sighed. He watched as her face softened, chest rising then falling.

"Can I ask you a question?"

"Sure," she said.

"You still call it theft?"

She gave him a sad smile. "Yeah, it's still theft, but I'm not saying I don't get why you did it."

Lark grinned back at her. "Call me crazy, but I couldn't just leave them. Not with backbones sticking out so much you could hold them like handles, or wormy pregnant bellies that would break any horse lover's heart."

Sophie paused to look back over her shoulder before following him through the gate.

"You know, I thought rodeo riders didn't give a toss about animal welfare."

He shut the gate and stopped, crossing his arms over his chest. That was something he hated—presumptions about the kind of person he was, the kind of animal-owner he was, just because of his profession. His sport. He felt his imaginary hackles rising. "I guess you've never met the right kind of rodeo rider."

Lark could have sworn he saw her blush, but she just smiled and placed her hands on her hips before giving him a business-like nod and squaring her shoulders.

"Seriously, my best horses were treated like royalty," he told her. "They only had to perform eight, maybe nine times a year, and I loved every one of them."

He felt a familiar pang just talking about his past. His former profession. He missed the rodeo circuit the way he'd miss a limb torn from his body. He'd played that scene from his last championship rodeo over and over in his mind as if in doing so he could change what had happened.

Lark looked up as he heard her sigh. "They're here."

He leaned back against the post-and-rail fence as two unfamiliar cars splashed mud up the drive, sneaking a sideways glance at Sophie. She took him by surprise, that was for sure. She wasn't the type of woman he was used to admiring. And he wasn't intending on being attracted to any kind of woman anytime soon.

But then maybe that's why he liked her.

Because the kind of woman he was used to being attracted to, to liking, sure hadn't worked out for him in the past.

Maybe her turning up and nearly running him over had been for the best last night. Without her help, he might be facing a larger problem than he'd bargained for with the local officer. And here was to hoping she still felt like sticking up for him when it came to the crunch.

He groaned, watching the cars approach.

If only he could learn to look the other way and keep driving, he wouldn't end up in this kind of situation.

Thank goodness Lucy was back at school. He didn't want his little girl to see him questioned by police. Not ever.

Sophie fought the urge to look back over her shoulder as she walked down the drive to meet the other men. She could feel Lark's eyes on her back.

Maybe the reports hadn't been false. Lark was easily as interesting as the gossip mill had suggested. Tall, dark, handsome, caring…

The only false report was that he was probably heavy-handed with his animals, given his past career.

She shook her head. No use thinking about him. It must be the cold getting to her. She was not the kind of girl to get all hot under the collar over a guy, although it didn't mean she wasn't allowed to look.

And the way he'd just taken those horses? Okay, so she wasn't going to condone his actions, but the man had guts. He was prepared to end up in a power-load of trouble because he cared too much to keep driving past neglected animals.

That gave him a definite tick in the good-guy stakes.

CHAPTER THREE

"MR. Anderson."

Lark nodded as his name was said.

"To what do I owe this honor?" Lark tried not to sound too condescending. He knew damn well what this visit was about.

He only hoped he wasn't in too deep.

Sophie had looked dubious when he'd told her how he'd come into possession of the horses, but not necessarily judgmental. Even if she had bluntly told him it was theft. But part of him hoped she hadn't changed her mind completely, that she was still on his side.

He wasn't so sure now, but it would sure change *his* mind about the pretty blonde if she turned on him.

The last thing he needed was to jeopardize his role as Lucy's sole caregiver.

Even if he hadn't moved them halfway across the world, he'd still have no one. It was him and his daughter and no one else.

The officer glared at him, gave him a look he didn't like. Sophie smiled.

"Lark, I'm going to take some notes, record what you have to say and keep an account of the animals. And Tim," Sophie paused, "I mean, Officer Brown, wants to interview you."

Sophie smiled at him as the second man emerged from his car.

"That's the vet we work with at the shelter. He's going to assess the horses and give us any assistance we need."

She looked flushed, pink-cheeked from being busy, eyes bright, the kind of woman who didn't mind getting dirt beneath her fingernails or having to work a full day out in the open.

Lark hated that he was drawn to her, attracted to her in some way. But then maybe it was because she was so different from his ex-wife. No hair spray held each strand of hair in check, no caked-on makeup or false eyelashes batting at him. Just a real girl out to do her job.

"So this vet's going to help us?"

"He'll be establishing whether there is a definite case of neglect," stated Officer Brown.

Lark swallowed the words held tight in his throat. The bark he wanted to belt out at this imbecile. It didn't take an expert to declare there was neglect. It was fairly obvious.

"Should I take you to the house or do you want to question me here?" asked Lark, trying to sound friendly and knowing he was failing badly.

Sophie moved closer and nudged him sharply in the side. He bit the inside of his lip.

"Play nice," she whispered.

He swallowed another response, this one more like a growl. But for some reason he didn't want to upset her. Didn't want to annoy her.

"Let's get this over with, then," he muttered.

Lark watched as Sophie gave him a look, the kind of look a woman gives you when she doesn't want to be crossed. He obeyed, happy to oblige, *for now.* Only because he was still hoping he'd been right about her genuinely wanting to help.

But he did react to the look she gave the vet. He watched as Sophie turned, a smile lighting her face as the other man emerged from a dusty four-wheel drive.

It made his back prickle, as if he had spikes covering his spine.

He wasn't usually prone to jealousy, but the smile on Sophie's face was making his chest constrict. For a reason he couldn't identify, the thought of her being fond of the man, heaven forbid intimate with him, was tying him in knots.

Lark took a step back, needing distance from her.

He didn't need to be distracted by her. Not when he was a single father, not when he had to put his daughter first.

He caught Sophie's eye as she looked his way, smiling at him and playing with her ponytail as if she might have been nervous.

Even if she was cute as hell, even if there was something different about her that was starting to appeal to him, women were off his radar. For good.

They had to be.

He cringed.

A deep voice jolted him from his thoughts.

"Come on, Mr. Anderson. Let's see what the situation is here, before I decide whether to arrest you."

Sophie tried to keep her eyes on the horses. It wasn't easy, looking at animals that had been so blatantly neglected, but it was the distraction beside her that was proving to be the problem.

She'd thought about Lark plenty overnight. As the rain had pounded on the roof when she'd first gone to bed, and then as the sun had shone across her face and woken her early this morning.

There was something about him, something she couldn't put her finger on, that had her thinking. Interested almost.

Or not.

Argh. She didn't know, or perhaps just didn't want to admit, that she maybe liked this guy for some reason, even though he was causing her more trouble than he was possibly worth. But she had a soft spot for him after what he'd done.

"So you think it's fair to say that they've been like this a long time?" Officer Brown asked.

Sophie scribbled in her notebook, remembering that she was meant to be taking notes.

"Gee, you think?" Lark muttered.

She threw him a tight smile. She got where he was coming from. Any fool could see the condition the animals were in, but his sarcasm wasn't going to help the situation.

"Lark, do you want to take a walk?" she suggested.

He looked back at her. She could see he was angry by the red flush that was creeping up his neck and the steely fix of his jaw.

She gave him her most pleading look.

"Please?"

He nodded, but not before scowling at the two men standing by the horses.

"We need to let them do their job," she told him in a low voice.

Lark turned thunder-filled eyes toward her. She gulped. Angry Lark looked a whole lot more masculine, more intimidating, than smiling Lark.

"I don't have a problem with the vet trying to do his job," he told her. "Or you."

Sophie reached for Lark's arm, let her hand hover for a heartbeat, then dropped it to cover his shirt-clad skin. The fabric was soft beneath her touch, his body warmth radiating through.

She guessed he was getting hot from frustration.

"Lark, you need to be patient."

He looked in the other direction as they moved, making a grunting noise deep in his throat. But he didn't shrug her hand off, and she didn't volunteer to move it. Instead she increased the pressure, trying to ignore how strong his forearm felt beneath her fingers. Trying to infuse calmness through her touch.

He stopped when she did. Turned his big frame to face her, towering above her, something else she wasn't used to.

"Look, I'm trying to help you out here, but you're not exactly making things easy." She sighed. "If you want me to deal with this, then you need to do your bit, too."

Lark's stance relaxed. She watched as his eyes softened and the hard set of his jaw was replaced by a small smile.

He let out a breath.

"You say you're still going to help me?"

Sophie let go of his arm, suddenly feeling vulnerable maintaining contact with him like that now the moment had passed.

"In case you haven't noticed, that's what I've been trying to do."

The muscles in Lark's face relaxed. He folded his arms over his chest.

"I've been rude again, haven't I?"

Sophie felt the blush hit her cheeks before she could think about hiding it. When she wasn't hiding from her regular life she was a practicing surgeon, confident and strong, but he had her acting like a shy schoolgirl!

"Yeah."

He shook his head, slowly. "Okay, well, I'm sorry again. Maybe next time we meet I can try *not* to do anything I'll need to apologize for."

"Leave it to me, okay? I have a plan."

Lark laughed and turned back toward where they'd come from.

"I'm glad you've got one, because I sure don't."

Sophie was still flustered, but she followed him, trying to keep up with his long, loping strides as they made their way back to the horses.

"I think maybe we need to start over," he told her.

"You haven't been that bad."

"Still, next time I see you I'll be better behaved. So long as I do get to see you again?" he asked.

Sophie nodded, not sure what to say or how to respond.

Had she been single for so long that she'd forgotten how to enjoy casual banter with a man? Something told her that if

that little embarrassment hadn't been flirting, then it was tee-
tering dangerously close to the line.

Or maybe she was completely off and he was only being
friendly.

She admired him from her vantage point, slightly behind
him. He was tall but strong-looking, not lanky, the way she'd
expected a rodeo rider to be. His shoulders were broad, his
hair thick, his jeans snug to his hips.

Sophie hurried to keep up with him. She did *not* want to be
caught checking him out, no matter how good the view was.

He glanced at her and gave her that kindhearted smile she'd
already grown to like, even though she'd only seen it a hand-
ful of times so far.

"Lark, I meant to say that I really admire what you did.
Rescuing these horses," she told him.

His steps slowed. This time a smile turned the corners of
his mouth.

"Even after your big-as-boots talk about my committing
theft earlier?"

She laughed. She couldn't help it. "Granted, I was a bit too
high-and-mighty with my morals."

"A bit?" He gave her a nudge in the side, his elbow gently
prodding her arm.

Sophie tried to fight the flush in her cheeks again, but she
doubted it worked. Her skin still felt burning hot from his attention.

"Okay, a lot too opinionated." She held up her hand, not
letting him interrupt. "But…"

He rolled his eyes. "Why do women always have a 'but'?"

Now she glared at him. "*But* it was still stealing, and you
could still get in serious trouble for it."

"But you think it was heroic, right?"

She sped up again and overtook him, not even prepared to
engage. Heroic?

"Arrogant, perhaps." She threw the words over her shoulder.

Sophie refused to acknowledge his gentle chuckle. He'd gone from endearing to annoying in less than a heartbeat.

But she wasn't going to deny it felt good. A moment of flirting with a handsome man wasn't exactly unenjoyable. And it had sure taken her mind off her troubles.

Lark kept his head down. It was the only way he could deal with being a grown man getting a telling-off.

"It was irresponsible, and I'm not ruling out the possibility of criminal charges…"

"Tim, let's be realistic here," Sophie interrupted.

Lark didn't find it easy, but he kept his mouth shut. Tight. He wasn't used to anyone sticking up for him, especially not a woman.

He'd seriously underestimated her.

Maybe he needed to stop judging people so quickly.

He tried to wipe the grin off his face.

"If he stole these horses, I'm not prepared to turn a blind eye. That sort of behavior isn't acceptable here."

"With all due respect…"

Lark felt a throbbing in his temple, a pounding in his head as Sophie placed a hand firmly on his arm to stop him from continuing.

What was this idiot implying?

"Why don't we compromise here?" she suggested, giving Lark a warning look.

He wanted to growl, to put his hand on her shoulder and order this guy off his property. But he wasn't going to lose his cool, and he didn't want to get all protective over Sophie.

She wasn't his to get protective over.

"What if I agree to come here every day and check on their recovery?"

She what?

"Are you sure?" he blurted.

No. No, that wasn't going to work at all. He'd been a horseman for years. He was *not* going to have someone looking over his shoulder and telling him what to do.

Sophie turned toward him, smiling. Her eyes were kind, soft, as if she genuinely cared, wanted to help.

He tried to smile back, not wanting to alert the officer to there being a problem. He wasn't going to fight this, not right now, but seriously?

"Of course," Sophie assured him.

Lark looked away. Even though the last thing he wanted was to be babysat, he wouldn't mind seeing her again—under different circumstances.

Something about her was pulling him in, drawing him closer to her. But he didn't want to be indebted to anyone, didn't like anyone doing him favors.

He didn't have the strength or desire to become close to another female other than his daughter. Not now, and maybe not ever.

The officer was still standing, not talking, one hand rubbing back and forward across his chin.

"If I agree to this, it will be your responsibility to ensure they are not moved from this property, and that they continue to receive the treatment they require."

Sophie nodded. Lark just looked between them. He couldn't believe this woman was prepared to help him. He was grateful, sure, but this was not what he wanted.

"Will you agree not to press charges?" Sophie asked.

And she was a negotiator, too. Who would have guessed?

Lark resisted the urge to put his arm around her. At least she'd got this goon off his back.

"If we find the owner, and he or she agrees to surrender them…" Lark found himself holding his breath as Officer Brown delivered his verdict. "Then, yes, I'll give my word that charges will not be laid."

"Won't you be looking to charge the *owner?*" Lark felt like a kettle about to boil over. Did this idiot not realize that he wasn't the criminal here?

"You're treading on very thin ice, Mr. Anderson. You should be grateful Sophie's decided to assist."

Lark wanted to snap, to react, but he resisted. Even if it felt like stopping a cat from catching a mouse.

Sure, he was grateful, but...

Sophie walked toward the officer, holding out her hand.

"Deal. I'll come here daily and report back to you."

Lark watched as the deal was sealed, before Sophie turned back to him.

He didn't bother to say goodbye to Officer Brown

"You think you can put up with me for a while?" she asked.

Lark pushed his hands into his jeans pockets. "I don't think you'll be that hard to have around." She wouldn't be, so long as she wasn't going to be looking over his shoulder all the time.

Sophie smiled, playing with her hair. She'd gone from stoic negotiator to sweet, pretty woman all over again.

"Do you want a cup of coffee before you go?" He asked her before he'd even thought it through.

Lucy was at school, so he didn't have to worry about her for another few hours. And besides, he liked to be sure about someone before he introduced them to his little girl.

He and Lucy had both been hurt too often only to get close to another person, trust them and then be let down again. Even if it was someone who was just a friend they'd only see once in a while, he was protective. He couldn't help it.

"Sure, why not?" she replied.

Lark made a gesture with his arm, indicating toward the house.

He could thank her for her help, then persuade her that daily visits to check in on him weren't really necessary.

Or something like that.

CHAPTER FOUR

LARK stood awkwardly in his own kitchen. He placed his hands on the counter for something to do with them.

He liked that Sophie was smiling. He hadn't liked the frown on her face, the downturn of her mouth, when she'd chastised him for his attitude. Or given him *that look* that told him he was treading on thin ice with the vet.

Not that he should care. But he did.

"So, why aren't you still riding broncs in America?"

Lark laughed. "Broncs, eh?"

It felt like a long time since he'd been able to sit and relax, to chat with another adult. Especially a woman. And it was nice. Even if he was reluctant to admit it.

But talking about what he'd left behind was never going to be easy.

"Isn't that what you call those crazy horses over there?"

"My last ride was at the championships in Las Vegas," he told her, making himself go back in time. Wanting to talk about it but at the same time not. "I wouldn't have retired if I hadn't had to, but I was told that one more concussion, another big fall, would be the end of me."

He didn't tell her that the reason he feared for his safety and life was because of his daughter. He wasn't ready to go there yet. Was too protective over Lucy even to want to introduce her to anyone new.

"So you had to walk away from it?"

He nodded sadly. "I was defending my championship titles, and I didn't even leave the ring conscious."

Sophie gave him a big grin. "But you're okay, so that's what matters, right?"

Yeah. More than she could ever know.

"And you? Have you lived here all your life?" he asked her. Lark cocked an eyebrow. He saw her hesitate, watched her almost flinch before she planted a smile on her face to answer him.

"I grew up here, but I've recently returned." She paused, before standing and putting her coffee mug in the sink. "And now I'd best be off, lots more to do today."

Lark thought he'd hit a sore point and wondered why she didn't want to talk about herself. But it wasn't as though he was keen on baring his own soul. Talking about how his career had ended had been hard enough.

"Well, I guess I'll see you tomorrow, then?"

And he guessed that now wasn't the best time to tell her she needn't drop in each day.

Sophie wrapped one arm around herself, trying not to stare at Lark. She was feeling off balance, unsure of herself. Standing here in his kitchen, chatting about why he'd come here, she was so curious she could burst.

Something about the guy had piqued her interest, and she was finding it hard not to show her feelings. The last thing she needed was the complication of getting involved with a man, and she wasn't even sure this particular man was interested.

One minute he looked at her as though he liked what he saw, or at least that's what she hoped she recognized in his eyes, and the next he seemed to back off. Big-time.

"Does the afternoon suit tomorrow?"

Lark gave her a lazy smile as he rinsed out their coffee mugs. "Sure thing."

Sophie returned his smile. It was comfortable being with him, but at the same time it wasn't. There was something she couldn't put her finger on. But she wasn't ready to open up to an almost-stranger and tell him her life story or why she'd come back.

"Thanks again for, you know, helping me out like you did," he said.

She kept walking, not looking over her shoulder at him. Not letting herself.

He was too close for comfort. Especially because she was starting to feel more for him than a stirring of attraction. The last thing she wanted was to become lost in those deep brown eyes.

"Don't worry about walking me out," she told him.

She heard Lark's footfalls stop behind her. She did a half spin on her heels, having the confidence to face him now she knew there was distance stretching between them.

"You'll be okay with the horses until tomorrow, then?"

He leaned on the doorjamb. "Yeah, I'll be just fine."

She wanted an excuse to stay longer, to talk to him, to spend the day in his company. She didn't know why, but something about him was drawing her in, making her want to be with him for as many minutes, hours, as possible.

Still, she had to go. Didn't *want* to be pulled further toward him, when she already felt as if a propeller was trying to blow her straight back to his kitchen for another cup of coffee.

She swallowed.

Or across the veranda and into his arms.

The last thing she needed was to think about those golden, muscled arms or the breadth of his chest.

"So, you're, um, clear about what meds the horses are to be given?"

Lark watched Sophie. She was standing with one hand on her hip, the other shielding her eyes. Her face was serious. Part of him wanted to tease her, play with her, make her pillowy lips turn into a smile. But the other, more sensible side of him? That told him he'd teased enough earlier, before they'd come inside.

Teased enough for a man who had no intention of taking things any further, that was.

And he didn't. No matter how cute she was.

The last thing he wanted was to lead her on.

"You don't need to worry, Sophie," he said, trying his hardest not to mock her. "I've cared for a few horses in my time."

She flushed. Lark fought not to laugh. He hadn't met a grown woman in a long time who actually, genuinely blushed. In California, in the circles he mixed in, the women had been bold and brazen. They knew what they wanted and nothing seemed to embarrass them. Ever.

This girl? She was something else.

He just couldn't put his finger on what the something was, and why he was feeling that it was something he should be interested in.

"I don't mean to belittle you, I'm…"

He shrugged, finishing her sentence. "Doing your job. I know."

Sophie tugged at her ponytail as if she was nervous. "Until tomorrow, then."

She turned to walk back to her car, but not before looking back one last time.

"You sure you're happy to care for them? I mean, to take on the responsibility?"

"Maybe it will give me a better standing with the police. Might keep them off my back for good," he said, hoping he sounded convincing.

She looked sympathetic, mouth pursed. "We'll do our best at the shelter to have the animals surrendered into our care, Lark. I'm sure there won't be a problem."

"All you can do is your best."

She gave him a wave, ponytail swinging from across her shoulder to hang down her back.

"See you tomorrow."

Lark would have watched Sophie go, would have struggled to take his eyes from her, but his phone started bleeping. The sharp ringtone took him by surprise. He fished it out of his pocket, glancing at the screen as Sophie opened the door to her car.

Oh, crap.

His ex-wife.

She only ever called when it had something to do with money, never to ask about Lucy.

He'd gotten over his marriage falling apart pretty quickly once he'd realized that his wife had only ever been there for the money and the fame that came with his world status on the rodeo circuit. Once the parties and endorsement deals were over, so was their marriage.

He looked back down the drive, to where Sophie's car had not long disappeared.

If there was one thing his ex-wife was good at, it was reminding him why he was single.

And right now, he had no intention of changing that. Even for an entirely different woman in an entirely different country.

Even for a sweet-natured, pretty girl named Sophie.

CHAPTER FIVE

LARK grinned at his daughter as she excitedly recounted the tales of her day. He couldn't help it. Just being with her reminded him why everything hard in his life was worth it. Something had changed within him when he'd taken over sole custody of Lucy, and it was for the better. Nothing else seemed to matter quite so much as hanging out with her.

He took his eyes off the road for a split second to catch a glimpse of Lucy again. She had the window half-down, face turned toward the breeze, loose strands of hair whipping around her cheeks.

"So what else happened? Did you learn anything?" he asked her.

She wriggled back to face him. "Of course!"

"What kind of stuff?"

Lucy played with her hair. "I don't know, but we did lots." He chuckled.

"Oh, there was one thing," she said.

Lark raised an eyebrow and glanced over at her. "What was that?"

"I asked my teacher about the Fourth of July, because you know how it's next week? And she said that no one here does anything to celebrate it. Or Thanksgiving."

Of course. He'd forgotten all about it.

"Did she explain to you why it's not celebrated here?"

Lucy nodded. "She said that Christmas is the big celebration here, but that Thanksgiving and the Fourth of July were only important for Americans."

Lark leaned back in his seat, one hand on the wheel. He wasn't quite sure what Lucy was getting at, but he had a feeling she expected him to come up with something.

"If we were back home in California, what would we be doing to celebrate?" he asked her.

Lucy looked thoughtful. She had her bottom lip caught between her teeth. "Um, we'd have fireworks I guess, a barbecue, and we'd all hang out together."

Okay, so he definitely had to do something about the Fourth of July.

"But," she said, "it would be really hot, not freezing cold!"

He laughed. "Well, I can't do much about the weather. I think the hot dogs would freeze on the grill if we tried to have a barbecue out in the snow! And the horses might be frightened by the fireworks."

"Oh." Lucy's face fell. "I guess you're right. Does that mean we won't have Thanksgiving, either?"

Darn, Lark hated to let her down. After the past year of upheaval, he only wanted his precious daughter to be happy in her new home. How would she feel about giving up Thanksgiving and the Fourth of July, which had always been big events back home?

"Hey, maybe we could switch them around a bit?"

Lark had to smother a chuckle at the way Lucy's eyes lit up with hope. She had a child's trusting innocence.

"We could have a log fire and a turkey on the Fourth of July, when it's cold outside, and a barbecue and fireworks in November, when it will be hot again. We'll go to the far paddock, away from the horses, so they won't be scared."

Lucy bounced up and down enthusiastically in her seat. "Cool." Her eyes shone with glee.

Yeah, cool, Lark thought. He struggled enough with day-to-day meals, now he had to figure out a turkey dinner. In July!

"But would it only be the two of us?"

Lark shrugged. "Maybe. Let's see if there's anyone else we want to invite closer to the time."

Lucy sat back in her seat, looking out the window again.

The Fourth of July. Funny, it had been such a big part of his life, traditions like that, for so long, and now it was no more than a distant memory.

"You know, last Fourth of July I had dinner with you then went off to the championships in Las Vegas," he told Lucy.

Only to fall and finish my career forever.

Now he was thinking about doing a dinner from scratch himself, for the two of them. No rodeo, no drama, just their little family of two.

"Are you going to ride rodeo again?"

Lucy had her head on an angle, like a puppy waiting for a command.

"No, honey," he said. "Any riding I do will be at home or with you."

That made her grin. "If I had a *pony* you mean."

"Be patient, miss. All good things come in time."

She rolled her eyes like a teenager before catching his eye and laughing.

It was at that moment that Lark knew exactly where he'd rather be. What life he'd rather be living. Even if he did have to deal with a back that still hurt like hell sometimes. And questions about why Mommy no longer wanted to be in their lives.

Especially in moments like this, when everything felt so easy. So happy. So effortless.

Lark reached out for Lucy's hand, her tiny palm slotting in against his. She hadn't even turned from looking out at the fields whizzing past, but her little hand was warm, feeling out for his the moment he reached for it.

If this wasn't love, he didn't know what was.

Sophie parked her car and walked around the back of Lark's house. She didn't bother knocking on the door. He'd be out with his horses or working the land; there was no chance he'd be inside.

She was looking forward to seeing him. He was different from the men she usually met. The kind of successful guys that were used to women swooning, impressed with them being surgeons or specialists. Besides, most of the men she met these days were already happily married.

Lark was different. For starters, he didn't even know she was a successful pediatric surgeon. As far as he knew, she was a nice local girl who worked at an animal shelter. And she liked that. Sometimes her training intimidated men who weren't in the same kind of career, although she doubted it would faze Lark. But she liked that with him she didn't have to be that woman.

Sophie looked up as she heard the sound of a horse moving across the ground, hooves rhythmically thumping.

Lark was working a horse in a round pen. He was standing in the centre, the horse moving around him. She walked slowly over to the edge of the corral, resting one foot on the bottom rail and leaning against the timber.

Wow.

Lark was impressive to watch. He was tall, especially with a cowboy hat on his head. His posture was relaxed, voice soft as he spoke commands to the beautiful big animal moving gracefully around in circles.

At his command, the horse slowed to a walk and came in toward him. It stopped a few steps away, blowing softly from the nostrils, and Lark reached out a hand to stroke its beautiful chestnut head.

Then he moved toward the horse's shoulder and gracefully vaulted onto its back.

She'd never seen anything like it.

No saddle. No bridle on the horse's head. Nothing.

Just Lark, speaking softly, riding bareback, the horse moving to his commands. He was completely in control despite having no gear on the animal.

"Hi."

Sophie looked around, the soft, high-pitched voice surprising her.

Oh.

A young girl stood not far from her, leaning against the corral, a messy blond pigtail over each shoulder and a shy smile on her face.

"Hi," Sophie said back.

The girl let the fingers of one hand trail along the timber as she walked slowly around the edge of the round pen. It gave Sophie a moment to calm herself, to deal with her thoughts.

Who was this child? And what was she doing here?

"I'm Lucy," the girl said.

Sophie tried not to notice the resemblance to the patient she'd lost before moving back here. The girl who had died on her operating table before she'd taken her extended period of leave.

"Sophie," she said back, wishing the ground would open up and swallow her.

Once upon a time she would have loved nothing more than to chat to a child. Now? It filled her with terror. Because it only reminded her of what she'd lost, and what she now knew she'd never have herself.

"He's a very good rider, isn't he?"

Sophie didn't know what else to say.

Lucy nodded. "Yeah, he's the best."

She looked from the girl to Lark, wishing he'd stop riding and save her from this conversation, or that she could simply disappear back the way she'd come.

"Ah, why are you here on your own, Lucy? Are your parents nearby?"

That made the girl laugh. "I'm here with my dad."

"Where is he?"

Lucy scrunched up her face, squinting into the afternoon sun.

"*He's* my dad."

Sophie looked to where she was pointing. Lark was now trotting around in a big circle, seemingly oblivious to the conversation that was going on.

She looked back at the child.

Surely not? Lark was a…*dad?*

Lucy had moved closer to her, was leaning on the fence beside her, so close they were almost touching.

"Are you okay?"

Sophie made her head nod up and down. She was in shock. Seriously?

"What about your mom?"

The child's face lost its perky smile.

"No, it's just me and dad."

Phew. Even though it was awful this child didn't have a mother here, Sophie would have felt terrible for having flirted with someone else's husband. For having the kind of thoughts she'd had about Lark earlier.

Him having a daughter made things tricky enough. She didn't have the heart or strength to be around a child. Not right now.

"Do you know my dad?"

Sophie tried to encourage her tongue to work properly, her mouth to roll around the words she was trying to form.

"I'm…ah, well." She took a deep breath. "I'm here to help your, ah, *dad* with the horses he rescued the other night."

Lucy grinned up at her. "Oh, yeah, I know who you are."

If she could have made the ground open up and swallow her she would have, instead she leaned against the timber railing, focused on Lark rather than his child.

"I'm going back to the barn now," Lucy announced. "See you later."

Sophie gave her a smile and raised her hand. Speechless.

Because that tiny child had promptly reminded her of what she'd never have.

Sophie swallowed the lump in her throat, forcing the

thoughts away. This was not the time or place to start choking up.

"Hey."

Sophie jumped at Lark's voice.

"Hi," she replied.

He moved the horse closer to her.

"I see you've met Lucy."

Sophie nodded. "Uh-huh."

"Hope she didn't talk your ear off."

Sophie didn't meet his eyes. Couldn't. Because suddenly she had guilt twinging in her belly, twisting her insides, at the thought of being even *mildly* attracted to someone's daddy.

She fought in her mind for something to say, anything other than talking about the child.

"I hope I wasn't interrupting, walking over like that to watch you."

He gave her a lazy smile out one side of his mouth. "Nope."

"You're impressive, I'll give you that."

A lightness lifted her shoulders. She had to ignore his daughter. She was here as a professional, nothing else.

There was nothing wrong with observing, with sharing a laugh with him and checking in on the horses. She just had to leave any romantic notions in her head. Or forget about them altogether.

"It's what I do." He gave her a casual shrug.

"It might be what you do, Lark, but from down here it's pretty impressive."

"Do you want to watch while I finish up with Cougar, or are you in a hurry?"

She looked over her shoulder. Lucy was no where to be seen.

"Cougar?" she asked.

Lark nodded, dropping a hand to rub over the horse's neck. "He's my boy. Came with me all the way from California. I've had him since he was a baby."

That figured. They looked in tune enough to read one another's thoughts.

"Maybe for a few minutes. Then you can take me over to check the others."

Lark indicated with his head toward the entrance of the corral. "Come on in. You can stand in the middle and I'll talk you through what I'm doing, if you're interested?"

Sophie brushed her hands off on her jeans and gave him a quick glance before moving around to the gate. She was interested in watching him, to take her mind off things. Until it wasn't just the two of them anymore and then she'd leave. As soon as his daughter returned she was out of here.

"Sure," she said cautiously.

Lark waited until she was in the corral, standing in the center, then he started moving the horse around her.

She was fascinated. He was so controlled, so gentle in his movements, and the horse was so relaxed beneath him.

It cleared her mind of everything.

He was mesmerizing.

"You see how I'm using my inside leg?" Lark spoke softly, his eyes never leaving the animal.

"What does that mean?"

Lark glanced at her, and then she watched as he applied pressure with the other leg.

"He moves away from my leg, that's how I tell him which direction to go in."

The horse started to trot then, making Sophie turn faster to watch them.

"Now I'm squeezing with my leg to ask him to move faster." They broke into a canter, moving faster yet again. "And now I'll ask him with my body to slow down."

Sophie twirled around to watch them. Fascinated.

Then she saw a grimace flash across Lark's face.

He brought the horse back to a walk. Fast.

Was he in pain? It had only been a burst of something, a

reaction, but she knew pain when she saw it. It was what she dealt with on a daily basis.

"You okay?"

Lark smiled, but she could tell he was bluffing. It didn't hit his eyes.

"Fine. Why wouldn't I be?"

She frowned. "I thought something happened up there."

Lark shrugged off her question as he would a fly landing on his shoulder. "I'm fine. Just an old twinge."

Sophie pursed her lips, desperate to examine him. To run her fingers over the spot that pained him and see if there was something she could do to help, even though it wasn't her area of expertise. But to do so would mean she'd have to explain… And that was not something she wanted to do.

Not right now.

Lark brought Cougar into the center to stand a few paces back from her.

"Are you sure you're okay?" she persisted. "I don't mind taking a look if you're, ah, sore or anything."

He looked at her quizzically, and she could almost hear his question. *What could you do to help?* He looked a little annoyed, although he was trying hard not to let it show.

"Show's over," he said, dismounting, boots hitting the ground with a soft thud.

She wondered if maybe he'd pushed himself too far, if it was something to do with his old injury. He had said a fall had ended his career.

But she was too chicken to ask. She had to try to forget who she was, ignore her medical training and not read so much into every situation.

"Can you do that with any other horses?"

He grinned—that sideways, sloping smile that made his eyes crinkle at the edges. As though he'd forgotten all about what had troubled him earlier.

"It takes time, but most horses can be restarted to respond in the same way." He stroked his horse's neck, fingers gently thrumming back and forward. "Cougar and I have been working together a long time, but for a stallion he's incredibly respectful."

Sophie's fingers were itching to touch the horse's silky chestnut coat herself, but she refrained. Doing so would mean moving closer to Lark, and she didn't need to be any nearer to him.

The look of him alone was enough to send her mind and heart racing, especially after seeing the way he was with his horse. Being around him was exciting, infectious, intoxicating.

And being this close to him all of a sudden made her forget all about the pain she'd seen on his face earlier. Right now he looked happy and...more than a little enticing.

She gulped. She'd also forgotten, for more than a moment, that he had a child.

"Shall we head back in?"

Sophie hoped he couldn't read minds. "After you."

Lark didn't want to look at her. Or want to be with her. Or anything else romantic.

But for some reason his eyes were drawn to Sophie and he was finding it darn hard to pull them away. Even the horse nudging him in the side for attention wasn't helping any.

He couldn't help but see the humor in the situation though. After years of rodeo-riding and putting more than a few noses of those who didn't agree with the sport out of joint, here he was getting friendly with an animal-shelter worker.

Lark laughed to himself. The animal advocate and the cowboy. Not something he'd ever thought could even happen, and now he was tripping over himself to impress her.

"Before, when you asked me about my back, how did you know I was in pain?" He had to ask her, it was bugging him.

Sophie looked guilty. Or maybe he was imagining it.

"Just a hunch." She said each word in a slow, deliberate way. "I thought you looked like something was hurting you."

Huh. He thought he'd done a good job of working through the ache in his back before. He might have pushed himself too far, *again,* but he was doing better than he had been last week. Or the week before that.

"So it's been all quiet on the law-enforcement front today?" Sophie asked him.

"There's been no word from our good friend Officer Brown, if that's what you're thinking."

Sophie looked over at him and smiled. He wondered what she was thinking. Whether she'd thought about him in the same way he'd started to think about her.

Ridiculous, when he hardly knew her, but still. Maybe he was lonely, maybe he was just on the rebound after what his wife had done to him.

Or maybe he actually really liked this girl, which was why he was finding it so hard to tell himself to stay away from her.

"You really care about them, don't you?"

He ran a hand down Cougar's neck as they neared the stable block.

"You mean the ones I rescued?"

Sophie moved her head slowly back and forth, disagreeing with him. "No, I mean all of them." She paused and let him pass, so he could tie Cougar up outside his stall. "The way you are with them tells me you actually love them. I can see it in the way you touch them."

Lark nodded. She was right, he did.

Other men he'd met during his career couldn't have cared less about the horses they rode, or the bulls they climbed aboard, but he'd never been like that.

"The work I did doesn't mean I did it without a conscience."

Sophie gave him a funny look. She pursed her lips then sighed.

"I don't mean to judge, it's only I didn't expect you to be so…"

He chuckled. "So what?"

"Nice, I guess."

That silenced him. If he'd been looking her in the eye when she'd said it he might have even blushed.

Lark didn't know when he'd ever had another human being say something so genuinely kind to him. Out of the blue like that.

He picked up a brush to give Cougar a quick rubdown before putting him back in his stall. Sophie was looking around, hands in her pockets.

As though she was nervous.

"You want to help me?"

She stopped fidgeting. "Ah, sure. But you'll have to show me what to do."

Lark bent and reached for another two brushes, holding them up. "You see this one with the firm bristles? It's a dandy brush."

Sophie moved closer to inspect and Lark didn't move out of her way. He stood still, hoping she'd move closer.

"You use this on the sweat marks."

She reached for the brush, fingers skimming his as she took it from him. Lark kept his eyes on the brush, on her hand. He didn't see if she did the same.

"Like this?"

He raised his gaze as her body moved sideways, watched her run the brush over Cougar's coat.

"Yeah, like that," he said, hearing a gruff note to his voice.

She turned back, eyes on his. This time Lark didn't fight it, didn't look away.

"And that one?"

He held up the other brush, before holding it out to her.

"It's soft," she said, running her fingers across it.

Lark took a step in toward her, this time not scared of the proximity. He wanted to touch her, to see if the thoughts in his head were worthy of tormenting him.

"Lark—"

Lucy's pretty face and windswept blond hair suddenly appeared beside them, and Sophie's voice cut off so instantly it was as if she'd been choked.

He didn't have time to turn and look at Sophie. Lucy was bouncing around, vying for his attention.

"Hey, honey."

She grinned and gave him a wave, before skipping over.

"Whatcha doing?" she asked, eyes focused behind him on Sophie.

Lark turned, surprised to see the frozen look on Sophie's face. The start of a smile was locked on her lips, her eyes were wide, and she wasn't moving.

Weird.

"Lucy, you did introduce yourself before, didn't you?"

His daughter nodded enthusiastically. Sophie still stared.

"Hi," Lucy said politely.

Oh, boy. Sophie's head started to pound all over again, little red spots playing in blotches before her eyes.

Her heart somehow rose to touch her tongue then thudded all the way to her toes.

His pretty blonde and blue-eyed girl stood before her, lips pulled back in the widest smile Sophie had ever seen, eyes dancing.

Waiting for Sophie to talk back to her. Anything other than staring at her as if she had two heads.

It was stupid. So he was a parent? Why was it affecting her so badly?

"I've moved the horses a few fields over if you want to take the truck down to them."

Sophie's mouth was dry.

She needed to check the horses, fast, then leave.

Because she couldn't deal with this. Not now. *This was what she'd run away from.* Having to deal with situations like this.

She couldn't face up to little people. Especially not little ones who were the same age as the child she'd lost on her table. And the child she'd voluntarily dismissed all those years ago.

The child growing in her belly that she'd decided not to keep.

"Sophie?"

She looked up, trying to shake off the stunned expression she knew would be taking over her face.

"Sorry, I…" she took a deep breath. "I think it's time I had a quick look at those horses and then let you two get back to your afternoon."

Lucy was still grinning at her. Lark looked unsure.

Sophie knew she had to snap out of it. Fast.

"Why don't we all jump in the truck and go see the horses?" Lark was speaking to his daughter, too.

Lucy nodded.

No. She did not want to be stuck in a confined space with a child and her father. Especially not this particular father. Being witness to a display of happy families was not what she needed.

"I, ah, should really be off," she started to say, not sure what excuse she could come up with.

Lark frowned slightly, his brows meeting as if he was deep in thought.

"You're not interrupting, if that's what you're worried about."

Sophie shook her head. She tried to make the movement subtle, even though she could easily have shaken the darn thing off.

"Really, Lark, I'll take a quick look at them on my way out then get going."

Lark raised an eyebrow, before giving her a tight smile. "Okay, we'll take a rain check."

She watched as Lark dropped a hand to his daughter's head, giving her fluffy blond hair a ruffle.

Sophie swallowed. Gulped. Almost choking on her own saliva.

How had she gone from feeling so relaxed, so *comfortable* around Lark, to wanting so badly to escape?

But she knew. Goodness, did she know.

Seeing Lark like that with his daughter…it reminded her of what she couldn't have.

She could never have children of her own, and that wasn't something she could ever imagine coming to terms with. Not while her heart was beating could she comprehend a life that wouldn't include a child in her future.

CHAPTER SIX

SOPHIE ran her hands over the horse's coat before standing back. It had taken a lot of guts for her to turn up today. She'd been tempted to try to pass the case over to someone else at the shelter. But she never shirked her responsibilities, and there was something about Lark that kept drawing her back, something that compelled her.

But now that she'd been confronted with his daughter again, she'd decided any future visits would be within school hours.

Avoidance she was good at. Dealing with issues—not so much. She'd held it together enough to keep her composure, now that she'd had time to process the fact that Lark was a dad, but it still wasn't easy.

"You're doing well, Lark."

He leaned back, his shoulders braced by the timber stable framing. "I do know what I'm doing," he said drily.

But Sophie could see the glint of a smile behind his sarcasm.

She looked up when she heard a shuffle and saw Lucy skipping toward them again. Not looking at them, lost in her own world.

Sophie couldn't help but ask about her. For some reason she had to know more about her, even though it hurt. More than she could describe.

"Your little girl, she's about seven or eight?" she asked.

Lark followed her eyes, looking where she looked. "Yeah, about to turn seven."

Sophie took a deep breath, hoping she wasn't asking too much. Wouldn't be seen to be probing.

But she had to know.

"And it's just the two of you, right?"

Lark's face darkened. Like a storm cloud ripening over the planes of his cheeks, his eyes and across his mouth.

"Yes. Just the two of us," he said firmly.

Sophie wished a hole would open up and swallow her. "I'm sorry, I..."

He pushed off from the stable door. "No need to apologize," he told her. "I'm hoping we're better off just the two of us, given what happened back home." He paused. "But that's a story for another day."

Sophie patted the horse's neck again before stepping from the stall.

"I didn't mean to pry—but I wondered if she'd lost her mom."

Sophie loved her own mother, couldn't imagine not having her in her life, but she did know what it was like to have only one parent.

And it made her curious.

Even if she did find it hard looking at the child without feeling a pang for what she'd lost herself.

"Let's just say that Lucy's mother had more important things in her life than being a mom."

What? "Sorry. I thought she must have passed away, not..."

He sighed. "Sometimes I think it might have been easier if she *had* passed away. Well, easier on Lucy anyway."

"She *gave her up?*"

Lark smiled sadly. "Yeah, something like that."

Sophie watched the girl play, getting closer to them now.

She knew only too well what it was like to have a parent walk away. It had happened to her. Not as a little girl, as an older girl, but it had hurt all the same.

But still, she didn't want to get involved here. Even thinking about children was hard for her right now. She didn't have the strength.

"You know, call me naive, but I thought the bond a mother had with her child would run deeper. You know?" he said, his face a combination of anger and sadness. "I thought it would have been too hard to walk away."

Sophie gulped. What would he think if she told him what she'd done? That she'd fallen pregnant and given up her child? Did it matter that she'd regretted it almost every day since? Did that make her decision any more forgivable?

"I'm not trying to make excuses for her, Lark, but she must have had her reasons."

He looked angry now, brows drawn together in a furious line.

"There is no excuse for what she did," he said, voice thunderous. "I don't care that she left me, or that she wanted out of our marriage. But look at that child. *Look,*" he commanded.

Sophie followed his gaze, trying to stop the sting of tears as they threatened at the back of her eyes.

"You tell me how *anyone* could walk away from that child."

His voice was low, soft now. Sophie couldn't look at him. Didn't want to. Because the compassion and love in his words had stirred an emotion in her that she wanted so badly to ignore.

"I'm sorry, Sophie." Lark's voice was still raw. "I didn't mean to get all heavy, it's…"

She waited, blinking away tears before turning to him.

"I love her so much, and I want to do everything I can for her. I only wish I didn't have to try to explain to her why her mother doesn't want to see her anymore."

"I wish I knew what to say, Lark, but I don't," she said. "From what I can see you're a great dad. It's all you can do."

She knew from experience that she was right. That one great parent was better than two unhappy parents.

Lark looked down, scuffed one boot into the sawdust below.

"Coming here was tough, but it was the right thing." His voice was soft as his eyes met hers. "We're going to be okay here. I know it."

Sophie's whole body softened.

She hadn't been wrong in her feelings for Lark. He was a kind man, to horses and obviously to children, too.

It had been something that had always been important to her, always been a quality she'd wished for in a man. But now it was irrelevant. She couldn't have children of her own, would never plan a future and a family with a husband.

And that's why being around Lark and his daughter was tough on her.

Lark swallowed; there was a knot in his throat. He had no idea what it was about this woman, but he'd opened up to her in a way he hadn't in a long while.

He'd only admitted what had happened, hadn't even gone into detail. But since Kate had walked away from him and Lucy, the only person he'd really told, really described the reality to, was his lawyer.

Kate hadn't wanted him or their daughter, and he'd finally said it out loud to another person. She'd dismissed them from her life like unwanted baggage.

And the weird thing was that the look that had crossed Sophie's face, the flicker in her eyes, had made him wonder if on some level she understood.

"Do you have children?"

Sophie looked alarmed. "Me? No."

He had a feeling he'd hit a nerve there.

"I'd better be off now," she told him. "I'm already running behind."

Lark wished he hadn't asked her that question.

He watched as Sophie looked at Lucy, before letting out a shallow sigh and collecting her bag from where she'd dropped it.

He wasn't sure what was going on, what had rattled her, but

he had a feeling it had something to do with Lucy. Or what he'd told her.

It had to.

"So you'll be back tomorrow, then?"

She turned sadness-tinged eyes toward him. "Of course."

"You know, you don't have to keep checking up on me." He wasn't sure if it was the right time to tell her that he didn't want to be babysat, that it was grating him that he had to have a supervisor. Even if she was good company.

"Lark, I gave my word that I would."

He sighed, stretching out against the timber fence. "All I'm trying to say is that I know what I'm doing here. I don't need anyone telling me what to do."

Sophie gave him a happy look, but he felt it might have been forced. "If you want a different supervisor, all you have to do is say."

Lark touched a hand to her back, wanting to guide her out, but she jumped. Alarmed.

Although she did turn, eyes tracing his in a sad arc.

"I don't want another supervisor, Sophie. I'm not used to being babysat." There, he'd said it.

She pursed her lips. "You know what you're doing, I get that. But I'm not going back on my word. And besides, you could still get in big trouble."

Fine. He'd said his piece, he didn't want to argue.

Besides, spending time with her wasn't exactly difficult.

"See you tomorrow, then."

He let his hands fall to his sides as she said goodbye. He wished he was still touching her, that his hand was still covering the bare skin of her arm.

Because he liked her. No matter what he told himself, he did like her. And the feel of her skin against his felt good. Better than good, it felt *right*.

Lucy bounded up beside him, catching the fingers of his right hand and tucking herself against him. It caught him by surprise, made his thoughts switch in an instant from Sophie to his girl.

He loved that Lucy could be so kind and affectionate to him, when sometimes he felt like such a failure. When he struggled to know how to be a great dad.

But he saw that same look cross Sophie's face as he pulled his daughter toward him. That same look he'd seen before.

"Bye, Lucy," she said.

Lark watched Sophie go, his arm still looped around his little girl.

And then he realized what that look was.

It was a look he was sure he'd sported on his own face time and time again of late. And it was a look he'd seen on his daughter's face, too.

Sophie was hurt.

It showed in her eyes, in her smile and in her voice.

Anger bubbled in his throat, through his muscles. Made him feel protective, like a grizzly bear over cubs.

He wanted to know what had hurt her, because if she'd been hurt anything like he had, he knew she would be burning, feeling ripped apart inside.

The weird part was he felt it had something to do with Lucy. That his daughter had upset her. It should have made him want to push Sophie away, because he didn't want to get involved with anyone, and he certainly didn't want to spend time with someone who didn't like children. But then he wasn't sure if that was even the problem.

Lucy tugged on his hand. "Can we go feed the horses now?"

He bent and dropped a kiss to the top of her head. "Sure can, kiddo. Let's go."

CHAPTER SEVEN

SOPHIE was starting to feel as if she'd spent more time at Lark's place than anywhere else lately. Silly, but she was stressing herself out over visiting him too often, even though she was under orders to do so. But he *had* indicated that he didn't like her looking over his shoulder.

She walked around the rear of the barn, almost hoping she wouldn't bump into him at all. After seeing Lucy the other day, the conversation they'd had…she gulped.

Who was she kidding? What she couldn't get out of her head were the tiny pinpricks of excitement that had hovered over her skin when Lark had touched her. The tingle she'd felt when his eyes had looked so deeply into hers that her breath had been stolen away.

Sophie's heart landed in her toes before climbing back up to its rightful place in her chest. That was how she felt every time she'd thought about Lark since yesterday.

But then she'd remember Lucy. And it would leave her empty.

Confused. Unhappy. Lost.

How was it that the one man she was mildly attracted to, the *only* man she'd even considered romantically in far too long, had a child? The one thing she was running from.

Sophie sighed. Part of her wished she hadn't had to come here today. But then she knew, deep down, that she was lying to herself. Not coming here would have made her even more miserable.

She shook away the thoughts that were a constant burden on her body, niggling at her, and leaned on the fence to watch the horses. There was nothing for her to freak out about. She didn't need to let anything happen between her and Lark, and she could just come during school hours if she didn't want to be around his daughter.

The stupid thing was that she wasn't even needed here and they both knew it, but the shelter wanted the logbook filled in every day in accordance with police orders. And she'd volunteered for it, after all.

Sophie hitched one foot up on the rail, and watched the horses she was supposed to be keeping an eye on. The sun was shining today, and Lark had taken their blankets off. Their coats were still pretty lifeless, but already their ribs seemed less obvious and they looked happy enough.

The sound of a throat being cleared made Sophie startle. Anticipation fired heat into her belly, and she felt her skin flush, like warm honey being drizzled over ice cream. Telling herself that Lark meant nothing to her was starting to sound ridiculous, even in her own head.

Sophie turned, and…

"Tim?"

She frowned. What was he doing here?

"That would be Officer Brown to you." He said the words with a smile, but she could see more than a hint of seriousness on his face.

Sophie hadn't called the police, which made her wonder if… Surely he wasn't here to arrest Lark?

She mustered up a smile and walked closer to Tim, prepared to stick up for her new friend.

"What are you doing here?" Sophie asked in her cheeriest voice.

He tipped back his hat slightly. "Checking up on things,"

he said, before looking around. "And with a message for Mr. Anderson."

Sophie's heart started to beat faster again. Surely he wasn't going to press charges?

"Did you manage to track down the owner of these poor horses?" she asked.

Tim gave her a look that said it wasn't her business. But it was. She was here every day sticking to her end of the bargain, so she deserved to know.

"I'd prefer to speak to Anderson in the first instance."

Sophie shook her head, willing Lark to appear. Why was Tim being so formal about the matter? "He might be on the property, but I haven't seen him yet."

Tim walked closer to her, then passed her to look into the field, watching the horses she'd only moments before been looking at herself.

"Sophie, you're not covering anything up here, are you? Sticking up for this guy when you shouldn't be?"

Damn it. Why was everyone so wary of new residents? Just because he hadn't been living here long didn't make Lark any less trustworthy than the locals. It was times like this she preferred her city life.

Sophie tried not to appear too angry. "Look…"

"To what do I owe this pleasure?"

Sophie almost shut her eyes with relief as Lark's deep drawl rang out from behind her.

She watched as Tim turned to assess the cowboy standing to her rear. Lark covered the ground with determination until he stood beside her.

"I've been in touch with the owner of the horses," Tim said, not even looking at Sophie.

The steel-like brace to Lark's stance worried her. He had his hackles up and it didn't look as if he was going to be very good at hiding them, and what they all needed to do right now was stay calm.

"I don't believe for a moment that your intention wasn't to

steal those horses, and I'm not convinced Sophie wasn't involved from the beginning, but you can count yourself lucky that the owner doesn't want to press charges. Which means I'll keep my word on not arresting you for theft."

Now Lark was glowering. Sophie bit her bottom lip. He looked like a stubborn, arrogant cowboy, the type she doubted would back down. Sophie just hoped he'd keep his mouth shut long enough for them to hear the rest of what the cop had to say.

"But you'll be charging him with neglect, right?" asked Lark, his tone even.

Tim took a few steps forward, but Lark kept his arms folded, not budging an inch.

Damn it. He clearly wasn't good at keeping his mouth shut after all.

"You should be counting yourself lucky that you're not going to be spending the night in the cells. You stole his animals, and we're fortunate he's prepared to surrender them and not pursue criminal charges against you."

Sophie moved forward, resisted putting a hand on Lark's arm to calm him and smiled sweetly at the two men.

"The animal shelter can still pursue the case, though, right? I mean, that's what we do."

Lark had anger rippling like bolts of electric energy through his veins. He could feel the tick of annoyance bulging near his cheek, and it took every inch of his willpower not to clench his fists.

Or smack this uptight cop in the face.

He tried to exhale some of his anger. Thinking like that wasn't going to help him. And neither was Sophie stepping in and trying to stick up for him, even if she was only trying to help.

"Look here," said the officer, face burning red with anger. "There's a rumor around town that our newest local has a reputation for being a troublemaker, so don't think you getting away with this means I won't be keeping a careful eye on you. And don't even think about telling me how to do my job, or who I should or should not be arresting."

Lark forced himself to calm down. This guy didn't have a leg to stand on, and he had no intention of even being within a step of trouble again. Well, not if he could help it.

"I can assure you, *Officer,* that I'm not a troublemaker, and I have no intention of being a problem in town or anywhere else for that matter."

Sophie looked on edge, angry.

"Really, Tim, I can't believe you'd listen to idle gossip."

Lark turned to look at Sophie as she spoke the same time the cop did. Only, he was trying to stifle a smile and this Tim guy was looking like thunder warmed up.

"It was nice to see you again, Sophie. Mr. Anderson, I'll be back if I have any formal complaints about your behavior."

Lark stood still, refolded his arms and scowled as the officer walked back around the front of the property and headed for his patrol car.

He only changed his stance when he saw the droop of Sophie's shoulders.

He walked up behind her, crossing the grass to where she'd moved to, and touched her shoulders. One hand on each shoulder blade, fingers curling down slightly onto her upper arms.

"You okay?" His voice came out low, softer than he'd expected.

She only nodded in return.

For a moment he wondered if she'd lean back into him, but she just stood, not moving away, not giving in to his touch.

Lark swallowed. And again.

He didn't want anything to happen, not really, but he wouldn't have pushed her away if it had.

He appreciated her standing up for him, that was all. *Surely that was all?*

"Do you know what that was really about?" he asked.

Sophie moved away from him, then turned around.

"That's why I don't like small towns sometimes."

He laughed, relieved that she was smiling again. "You telling me that's the kind of thing I have to get used to putting up with here?"

She leaned back against the fence. "I hope I didn't make things worse for you. I probably should have kept my mouth shut."

"It's my own fault, not yours, so don't go getting worried about it," he told her. "I'm lucky you stood up for me that night."

He watched as Sophie shut her eyes, rubbed at the bridge of her nose then gave an exhausted sigh. He didn't care about the cop turning up—he could deal with that—but he didn't like seeing her rattled. She still had that slightly unsettled look on her face that she'd had the day before when she'd left.

"You sure you're okay?"

She nodded. "Yeah, I'll be fine."

He was still trying to figure out what had upset her about seeing Lucy—it was slowly gnawing away at him—but he didn't ask her. Wasn't his place to. And he wasn't the kind to pry.

"I'll deal with him if he becomes a problem, Lark. In fact I plan on kicking up a stink if something isn't done about the owner being prosecuted." She gave him a smile, a real one, not like the tight smile she'd forced at the officer before.

Good. He didn't need any trouble, no matter how tempting it would be to have it out with the cop.

"I guess I owe you, then?"

She shook her head, ponytail bouncing back and forth. "Not a chance. You did a good thing here, and besides," she said, her smile suddenly shy, "it wasn't theft if the intention was right, huh?"

Lark grinned. Well, when she said it like that…

"How about a tour of the farm? Since you had to leave in such a hurry yesterday before we got a chance."

Sophie looked panicked for a moment, but he watched as

she carefully composed herself. Something was definitely troubling her. Something bubbling away beneath the surface that he couldn't put his finger on.

But the moment passed, and she tilted her head, eyes smiling at him. "Sure," she said, after only the briefest of hesitations.

"Horseback or truck?"

That made her shake her head, fast. "It's been a while since I've sat astride a horse."

She fell into step beside him. "So you used to ride?" he asked.

"More like I rode the odd pony at a friend's place. I can stay on, but that's about all. Nothing serious."

"I thought with you working at the animal shelter that you…"

She interrupted him. "Are we going to tour the whole farm?"

Lark guessed she was trying to steer clear of talking about herself. Suited him fine, he wasn't going to push it. He wasn't exactly one to open up his soul on his own background.

"There's a track around all the flat ground, but we'll stay clear of the hills. I don't fancy getting out to push if we get stuck at this time of year."

He gestured toward his truck with his thumb, and watched as she moved around to the passenger side.

He was on dangerous territory here and he knew it.

The sensible thing would have been to keep his distance. Instead he'd come up with a way to spend more time with her. He'd figured out how to get her alone, to be in close quarters with her when what he should have done was stay as far away from temptation as possible.

His heart thudded as he realized that she was probably under no obligation to visit him anymore. That she might not be coming over daily now, or even ever again if he didn't ask her to.

And no matter what he told himself, he liked her, even if women were meant to be off his radar. To think that only yes-

SORAYA LANE 71

terday he'd been all high-and-mighty and told her that he didn't want her checking up on him and those darn horses.

Lark watched her as she glanced shyly down at her feet, hiding her hazel-brown eyes. The way she tucked a strand of fallen hair back over her ear.

There was something almost sad about her smile sometimes, as though she was holding something back, but he didn't care.

Lark pulled open the door and got in beside her, inhaling the faint aroma of her perfume as he sat close.

"There's not really that much to see," he told her, almost apologetically.

Sophie leaned back in the seat, turned her head to face him and smiled. The same kind of smile that he thought said she was hiding some sort of sadness.

"It's just nice to be here. Doing something different."

Lark focused on driving. His mouth was starting to feel a little dry.

Because the more time he spent with this girl, the harder it was to convince himself that he should remain celibate.

Sophie wasn't sure if she was comfortable being in the cab with Lark or not. The space felt too intimate, which was stupid. She'd traveled with plenty of people in cars and never felt like this before. But there was something about the man, his presence, that made her jumpy. On edge.

That made her feel as though she needed to wind down the window and let the sting of winter air hit her cheeks, or fling the door open and make a run for it. Just to have space to breathe, to stop thinking about how attracted she was to him.

But she didn't. Couldn't.

Something was telling her she had to stay, that she was meant to be here and that something had pulled her in this direction for a reason.

Even if that did sound stupid.

"What made you move here, of all places?" The question burst from her mouth before she could stop it.

The way Lark's jaw hardened, visible from his side-on profile, told her she should have kept quiet.

"Ah, well, it's a long story."

In other words he would rather jump from the moving vehicle than talk about it.

"Sorry, Lark, I shouldn't have asked."

He shrugged, the tightness in his face disappearing.

"It's okay." He paused.

Sophie wasn't going to make the mistake of asking again. She didn't want to talk about why *she* was here. It had been unfair to spring that on him.

"You must be pretty passionate about your horses though. And it's a great place to set up a horse stud."

That made him smile. He threw a grin her way. "If there's one thing I'm going to do here, it's make a name for myself with sport horses."

She laughed. "As opposed to getting up to mischief and having the locals gossiping about you."

The space between them felt calm again, lighter. As though they were friends taking a relaxing drive on a Sunday afternoon.

"Sophie, I know you don't celebrate the Fourth of July here, or Thanksgiving for that matter, but I was wondering…"

She found herself holding her breath. Wondering what?

He looked almost nervous, even though she could only see his side profile. "Well, it's just I was thinking of doing a Fourth of July celebration, and I thought maybe you'd like to join us."

Sophie knew the sensible answer would have been *no*. But sensible fled her brain when she looked at Lark. She saw the worry lines on his face, indicating it was a big deal to have asked her. And something told her that Lark, somehow, was good for her soul. He made her feel lighter and happier than she had in a long while.

"A Fourth of July celebration? Doesn't that involve red, white and blue flags and a picnic? Might be a little chilly!"

She knew she was stalling for time, but she needed to catch her breath.

He let out a chuckle. "We're switching the Fourth of July and Thanksgiving, so it will really be a Thanksgiving dinner—you know, with a turkey and potatoes. Inside." He wished he'd never asked. Why was he babbling? "I didn't want Lucy to miss out on our traditions from back home."

"Dinner. With the two of you?"

He threw a smile her way. "Yeah."

But it wasn't simply dinner with Lark. It would be dinner with his daughter too, and she wasn't sure she was up for that. Would it be healing or detrimental to her?

Lark seemed to sense her hesitation.

"I could be wrong here, but did Lucy say something to upset you? Was she rude when you first met her? Because I thought her manners were pretty good, but I could be wrong."

Sophie shook her head, fiercely. So he had noticed.

"Heavens, no, she seemed like a sweet child."

He kept his eyes on where they were driving. "It was just…"

She needed to nip this in the bud before he asked too many questions. Before he went where she didn't want to go.

"She reminded me of someone else, that's all. It took me by surprise."

Silence stretched between them. She hadn't exactly lied, but then she hadn't been entirely honest, either. She couldn't talk to him about the child she'd lost professionally, or the one she'd lost privately.

"So what do you say about our Thanksgiving-cum-Fourth-of-July dinner?"

Sophie was torn between wanting to make up an excuse and giving in to what she wished she could cope with. Was it stupid to feel upset about his daughter? About letting her own emotions, her personal issues, stop her from enjoying an evening in the company of a man she was attracted to?

"I'd love to." She made herself push out the words, impossible as it felt. She couldn't punish herself forever, and it meant a lot that he'd asked her.

His face relaxed. "Great. I'm sure Lucy would like some extra company. It can't be that exciting hanging out with her dad all the time."

"You seem to be doing a great job, Lark. Don't be too hard on yourself."

If there was one thing she did admire, it was a parent stepping up.

"I'm hoping so."

They both sat in silence for a heartbeat that seemed to last an age. Sophie squirmed in her seat. She needed to change the subject.

"I don't know much about Thanksgiving, come to think about it," Sophie admitted, attempting to change the subject away from parenting. "I know you eat turkey meat, and that's about it."

Lark laughed. The noise so sudden that it took her by surprise. "You know what?"

She tried not to laugh back at him. The look on his face so comical as he slowed the truck and stopped. Mood lightened.

Sophie shook her head. "What?"

"I don't really know anything about Thanksgiving dinner either, because I'm usually just the one eating it."

"At least you know *something* about it."

"Just bring yourself on the fourth and I'll do my best to show you a traditional Thanksgiving dinner. In July." Then in a softer voice, "Lucy is desperate for a proper feast, and I'll be darned if I'm not going to try."

It was as if claws had tightened their grip around Sophie's throat. *He* might not know it, but *she* knew he was a great parent. She could tell simply from the way he spoke, from the way he wanted so desperately to be there for his daughter.

"What do you want me to bring?"

"Just yourself."

The way Lark looked at her, his eyes flickering over hers

for less time than it took for her heart to somehow thud to her toes, made her think that maybe he had just asked her on a date, rather than a regular family dinner. And she'd said yes without quite realizing.

He bent closer, a fraction, and she thought he was going to kiss her. That he was moving closer for a reason. But he stopped, didn't move any more.

She wished her eyes weren't locked on his lips, looking over the fullness of them, wondering what they'd feel like on hers.

He cleared his throat, pulled back slightly.

Made her feel as though a gust of antarctic air had blown between them, chilling the burning heat that had been there only a moment before.

"Why are we stopping?" Sophie half choked out the words to change the subject, to get her mind off bringing "just herself" to dinner.

Lark opened his door then leaned back in toward her, a cheeky smile on his face.

"This is the best view of the land," he said, winking before getting out. "From lower ground, anyway."

Oh, my. Maybe she'd gotten herself in a little too deep here. The man was having a serious effect on her, even if he was someone's father and should be completely off-limits.

Sophie opened her own door and stepped out, desperate to inhale fresh country air and fill her lungs with it.

Wow.

"You know what? I grew up here, Lark, and somewhere along the way I forgot how beautiful it was."

She'd been so busy fluttering inside about the man beside her, and talking a dime to the dozen to him, that she'd failed to notice exactly where they'd been heading. She wouldn't have wanted to miss this for the world.

"If it wasn't still so wet I'd take you higher, but it's pretty nice here."

"Nice? It's incredible." Sophie sighed and leaned against the vehicle.

Neither of them said a word. Lark was propped against the front of the truck, and even his big frame couldn't distract her from the surroundings. Fields stretched out as far as she could see, houses were dotted here and there and the land was full of horses and cattle. Everything looked so green at this time of year, not dry and parched as it would be in summer.

"You talk about this place as though you spent a long time away."

Sophie froze before regaining her composure. She hadn't meant to have this conversation.

"I've, ah, not long been back here," she said, hoping the words didn't sound too stumbled. "I went away for university and to work, but now it's just nice to be home again."

She watched as he looked out over his land. "I can see why you wanted to come back."

Phew. She didn't want to get into specifics. To have to tell him that she'd left to make a difference, to become a success-ful pediatric surgeon. That she'd succeeded but then not been able to deal with the joint blows of losing a little person on the table and coming to terms with her own loss. Of finding out that no amount of loving children could ever help her, be-cause she'd never be a mother herself.

She stifled a sob that was burning to escape her throat, and forced it back down.

"I saw this place advertised on the internet, and bought it before I'd even been to see it."

Sophie was pleased he hadn't noticed her pain, wanted to keep talking about him to take the heat off her. "Had you ever even been here before?"

"To Queenstown?" he asked, raising an eyebrow and look-ing back at her. "Yeah, a long time ago. I was actually born in New Zealand. We left to go back to the States when I was three or four years old when my father's company transferred him again. For some reason it just felt right to come back here."

Words hung unsaid between them. She knew there was probably a lot he wasn't telling her, a lot still unsaid between them, but she found she didn't even want to know. Curious? *Yes.* Nosy? *Desperately.* But until she was ready to share her own reasons for coming back, she wasn't going to pry and try to get him to divulge his.

He surprised her by exhaling a lungful of air and turning to tell her more.

"I'd always dreamed of retiring here one day, but I never guessed I'd only be thirty-five when my career ended." There was what she guessed was a bitter edge to his voice. "And I never thought I'd be a solo dad."

She didn't know what to say. He probably didn't want her to say anything.

"Anyway, being here feels right. Since Lucy's mom doesn't want anything to do with her, in a way I thought it would be easier to have distance from her." He paused. "Does that sound stupid? Trying to protect her, so she doesn't realize that her mom doesn't want to see her? Giving her mom an excuse not to visit her because an ocean divides us?"

Sophie shook her head. Sadly. It wasn't fair and she knew only too well what that felt like.

"So I'm guessing they had this photo on the advertisement?" she asked, looking back out at the view and trying to change the subject. She wasn't ready to open up to Lark. Not yet. Maybe not ever.

"Yeah." Lark turned away from the view to face her. "This, the house, the town—having forty acres to call my own. Everything felt right. I don't know why."

"Have you met many people? Been shown around properly?"

Sophie didn't know why she'd asked. She was hardly the right person to introduce Lark to the locals. Not anymore.

He shrugged. "I've met a few people, but you're the first person I've actually spent any time with."

She sensed he didn't mind that. That he liked being a bit of a loner, even though she was enjoying his company just fine.

"Shall we head back? I'll drive you down past the big field then we can loop back and see the rescue horses."

Sophie followed his lead and walked the few steps back to the truck, opening the door to get in.

"I never asked you how many horses you have here."

Lark stopped, his tall frame making it easy to look at her over the roof.

"I've got my boy Cougar, who I'll be using to launch my breeding program, and a mare that I bought before I left, but I sold all the others back in California."

She noticed a wave of something cross his eyes. Sadness, she guessed. It must have been hard, whatever his reasons, to leave his four-legged friends behind. Not to mention everything else that he'd been through.

"Then there are a couple of mares I picked up locally. But I need to invest some time and money into finding more that will suit the type of sport horses I want to breed."

Sophie lowered herself into the truck when he did. She'd thought it before but she couldn't help thinking it again—it was nice to meet a man who was so passionate about his animals.

Sometimes, especially during her short time back here, she'd started to wonder how humans could be so cruel. How some could see nothing wrong with inflicting pain on defenseless creatures. Maybe that was why she was struggling so hard with her own past.

But Lark? He was the kind of man who restored her faith in humankind.

A big, strong, strapping guy, as manly as they came, yet who wasn't afraid of being seen as softhearted when it came to his horses.

CHAPTER EIGHT

SOPHIE fought the urge to flee, but made herself ignore it. She wanted to leave so badly, but at the same time something within her didn't want to let Lark down. After what he'd told her the other day, the way he'd opened up, she was reluctant to up and leave.

Even if being around Lucy was like torture.

She wasn't sure how she was going to cope with having dinner with the pair of them this weekend, was terrified of playing happy families, but she wanted to try. There was something too magnetic about Lark to turn down dinner with him, even if it was going to test her. Push her boundaries.

Make her confront thoughts she was trying so hard to run from.

But she couldn't run from everything.

"Hi!"

Lucy burst around the corner of the stables and landed almost in front of her. Sophie smiled at the child's enthusiasm. She couldn't *not*.

And in that single moment of exuberant excitement, Sophie felt a twinge of recognition. That look on Lucy's face was why she'd become a surgeon. Why, up until now, she'd dedicated her life to saving the lives of little people.

Even if it had been hard, had pushed her to near breaking, it had been worth it.

She forced thoughts of her old job from her mind, not wanting to go back there yet. Not now.

"Hey."

Lark stepped around the corner a second after his daughter had darted into one of the empty stalls.

"I wasn't expecting you today."

Sophie smiled at Lucy's father. "I'm here to do a final report for our records," she told him. What she didn't say was that she could have done it from the office without visiting again. But she'd wanted one last excuse to turn up without having to be invited. She was going to miss this, seeing him each day. "I hope you don't mind?"

Lark shook his head slowly. As though he was considering her.

"I don't mind at all."

Lucy reappeared from the stall, pigtails flying.

"Is there anything to eat?"

Sophie stifled a laugh, surprising herself that, for a moment, she felt so relaxed around a child.

"Snack time, right?"

Lucy grinned. "Yup."

"You want to join us?" Lark asked.

She wasn't sure if she was up to spending the afternoon with the pair of them, and she did have to get going...

"Sophie?"

She snapped out of it. "I'd best be off, but I'll walk around the front with you now I'm done here."

Lucy ran ahead and Sophie fell into step beside Lark. Something about being beside him felt right, relaxed and comfortable.

"She seems to be doing okay."

Lark tilted his head, looking at her as they walked. "By okay you mean not a complete train wreck?"

His smile caught her off guard. She couldn't help but return it, even though Lucy was the last thing she wanted to discuss.

"I had a parent leave when I was a thirteen," she told him, not wanting to make the moment somber but feeling as though she had to help him. Give him at least a bit of guidance. "I, well, I guess I know what she's going through, in a way. I mean, I was old enough to grasp why he left, but it didn't make it any easier."

Lark's face went blank, then the corners of his mouth dropped.

"Your father?"

Sophie found it hard to push the words out. She didn't often talk about her father's indiscretions. Hardly talked about him at all, come to think of it.

"My dad left my mom for another woman," she told him. "His secretary, just to be a complete cliché. And my mom was left with nothing. Two kids to look after, the house with the white picket fence, but no husband, no job, nothing other than the memory of once having had the perfect family." She tried to keep the bitterness from creeping into her voice, but didn't succeed.

"I'm sorry."

She shrugged. "We were probably better off without him, but it sure didn't feel like it at the time."

"Ditto here," he said. "I hope I did the right thing, but you never know. Maybe Lucy will grow up to resent me taking her away, but all I know is that her mother has washed her hands of her, so all I can do is my best. I'll never understand her, but maybe that's a good thing."

Sophie could have cried. Hearing a father talk like that, it was, well, special. So beyond her experience to hear a dad take complete responsibility.

"She seems fine, Lark. If she's smiling every day then I don't think you have anything to worry about. One good parent is better than two average ones."

That was something she knew from experience.

They walked around the house in silence. Lucy stood on the porch waiting.

Sophie had to look away.

Just seeing that pretty, shining little face reminded her of what she'd lost. The child she should have been able to save, the child that could be waiting for her with open arms on her own porch. And the child she'd now never have.

Sophie gulped, swallowed away the emotion that was starting to pool in her throat. It crept up on her like this, took her by surprise and wrapped around her like a fist clenched around her throat.

Lark's phone ringing took her by surprise. She watched as he fished it out of his jeans pocket.

He looked at the screen, before apologizing and taking the call. "Sorry."

Sophie watched as he answered then walked a few steps away.

"You want to come inside and play?"

She turned slowly on the spot and saw Lucy standing closer to her now. One arm was curled around the veranda post, and she was leaning out as far as she could without falling.

"Ah, no, I should probably get going."

Lucy's smile deflated. "Okay."

Sophie was uncomfortable. She looked back over her shoulder at Lark. He had the phone in his hand now, call over.

"Everything all right?" she asked.

She noticed the hard line of his jaw. "Yeah. I've been trying to buy a horse for a while, and now that they've decided to sell I've suddenly got competition."

"Oh."

He shoved the phone back in his pocket. "They told me I could go look at her now and have first option, but I don't want to drag Lucy out again. She's been doing enough of that these past few weeks."

The words fled Sophie's mouth before she could retract them. "Do you want me to stay with her?"

She regretted them instantly. Hoped he'd say no.

"Would you?"

She kept her voice bright. "Of course."

"Well, if you're sure," he said, a smile spreading across his face. "I could be there and back in an hour or so."

"Go," she said, trying to sound confident, yet too scared even to turn and look at Lucy. "I'm happy to help out. We'll be fine."

"Lucy?" Lark turned to ask his daughter. "That sound okay to you?"

Sophie forced herself to turn toward the child. Raised her eyes.

"Does that mean you'll come and play now?"

"Sure," she said, waving Lark off. "But why don't we play outside? You can show me around all your hiding places."

Lucy shrugged as though she didn't mind what they did. "Can I show you my tree house?"

Sophie watched as Lark turned before walking fast into the house, presumably to get his keys. He mouthed *thank you* before disappearing.

She jumped as a tiny hand found hers. Sophie looked down, knowing it was stupid to be scared of the little girl tugging gently on her hand to hurry her along.

But she was. This was scarier to her than a pack of wild dogs snapping at her heels.

She hoped Lark didn't take too long.

Sophie climbed up the ladder behind Lucy, wondering how on earth she was going to fit in the little wooden house nestled up the tree.

She squeezed through the gap and found Lucy perched, legs crossed, waiting for her. There was more room than she'd expected.

"Wow." The view was incredible. "You can see out over all the fields."

Lucy looked proud, happiness beaming across her face. "Dad made it for me. It's my own house."

Sophie laughed. "Yeah, I guess it is your own house."

They sat there, both staring out at the view, as if they were on holiday and looking out at the ocean. Both were lost in thought. Sophie wondered what such a small girl could be thinking about.

She didn't have to wonder for long.

"Sophie, do you know why my mom didn't come here with us?"

Oh, heavens.

"I don't know your mom, honey."

Lucy sighed, sadness crossing her face, making her eyes and lips turn down at the sides. As if she didn't feel loved.

"What I mean is that I don't know your mom, but I do know your dad," Sophie corrected, scrambling to think of what to say. Of how to help her.

Pain shot through her, told her that she wasn't ready to have this kind of conversation. To get too close to Lucy.

But at the same time she knew she needed to say *something* to help the child.

"Sometimes, well, sometimes parents can't stay together because they don't make each other happy anymore."

Lucy's eyebrows rose. "Is that why Mom doesn't call me? Because I don't make her happy anymore?"

"Oh, honey, no!" Sophie shuffled closer to Lucy, put an arm around her without thinking. Comforting her as she would have done to one of her patients.

She gulped at the softness of the child against her, the sweet smell of her fluffy blond hair.

"Just because your mom and dad don't want to be together anymore doesn't mean they don't both love you. But sometimes it's okay to have only one parent." Lucy's big blue eyes looking up at her touched Sophie's soul, reached within her and tugged at her heart. "I know, because that's what happened to me."

"It did?"

Sophie knew she'd said the right thing. Lucy's voice was curious, amazed even.

"Yeah," she said, leaning and drawing Lucy back with her. "When I was a kid, a bit older than you, my dad moved away and I only had my mom."

Lucy nestled into her, tucked her warm little body against Sophie's.

She wondered if it were possible for her heart to break any more than it had already in the past few months, but it was—because being with Lucy, talking to her and being in her company, was reminding her of what she missed so much.

She'd become a doctor, a surgeon, because she wanted to help people and do something important with her life. And she'd specialized in pediatrics because she loved children and knew she could be the kind of doctor who'd connect with them.

Sophie swallowed and pressed her eyes tight shut, willing the hot, sharp burn of tears to go away. The inferno in her throat, the emotion surging through her told her it was never going to get any better. That somehow she was being punished for what had happened in her past.

"It's okay to miss your mom, but you have a dad who loves you so much, and that makes you the luckiest girl in the world."

"You want to go see the horses again?"

Sophie looked down at Lucy, pleased that she looked happy now. That she was ready to change the subject.

"Yeah, why not?"

Lucy pulled away and made for the ladder, disappearing from sight.

Sophie sat for a moment, knees drawn up close to her chin.

This was why she'd been scared when she'd found out Lark was a dad, after being so attracted to him.

Because this was the life she wanted so badly, and she was only being reminded of what she couldn't have.

"You coming?" Lucy called out from below.

Sophie shuffled to the ladder and wriggled her way back down.

She already knew she liked Lark. What scared her was how quickly she could like his little girl, too.

And that was starting to sound and feel like dangerous territory.

Territory that she wasn't even remotely ready to consider.

CHAPTER NINE

LARK jumped from the car and ran up to the front door. He'd only been gone a little over an hour, had made his decision to buy the beautifully bred mare immediately, but he still felt bad.

"Lucy?"

He walked through the house, not hearing anything, then he saw them sitting outside and sipping from mugs. He opened the door and went out.

"You must be freezing out here," he said.

Sophie and Lucy both looked up as though surprised to see him standing there.

"Hot chocolate." Sophie raised her mug. "Lucy said she hates being stuck inside."

The sun was peeking over the mountain, but the wind was still icy. Lucy grinned at him over her mug.

"I'm sorry I took so long. I should have just taken Lucy with me."

Sophie shook her head. "We were fine, Lark." She paused. He watched the way she considered Lucy, the way she sighed. "I enjoyed it."

Lark looked at her, really looked at her, and found he couldn't break the gaze. Her eyes spoke of sadness and kindness, and he saw a tenderness in the way she watched Lucy that startled him.

"I'd better go."

He wished she'd stay.

"I'll see you tomorrow night though, won't I?"

She stood, casting a last glance at his daughter before rubbing her hands over her jeans and moving away.

"Of course."

He reached out to her, wanting to touch her, needing to make a connection with her.

"Thanks, Sophie. I really appreciate you helping me out here."

She looked startled, froze as his fingers skimmed hers when he withdrew his hand. But she didn't look angry.

Sophie looked as confused as he felt inside.

Lark clamped his jaw down again so hard he felt a pulse tick near his temple. He had to, to take his mind off what watching her was doing to him. What *touching* her had done to him.

He'd vowed to put his role as father first, to do nothing to compromise his relationship with Lucy.

And even thinking of being romantic with another woman was off-limits. It had to be. For now anyway.

So why was his heart still beating that bit too fast, and why was his hand clammy where he'd touched her?

And why was he looking at Sophie standing beside Lucy and thinking it looked so right?

Sophie's hands started to shake as she drove away. She felt a pull back to where she'd come from, back toward Lark, but she wasn't going to let herself be drawn in. Couldn't.

Not now. And probably not ever.

He was a father, and she didn't want to be around his daughter. Even if she did love children more than anything in the world. Because she couldn't face being hurt again.

Lark scared her, terrified her as much as he appealed to her. Because she could see that if she fell for that honey-laced drawl and those dark brown eyes, she could get completely lost. Like a car with no GPS, she'd veer in the wrong direction, lose herself head over heels, then have her heart broken into a million tiny pieces. Not to mention how hard it would be for her to get close to his daughter when she still had guilt riding heavy on her shoulders.

Which was precisely why she had to avoid anything happening between them. Keep it fun at a little flirting, if anything. Try to remember who she usually was back in her normal life. What she had to deal with in her real world. She couldn't get involved with him or Lucy.

Her problem was that something within her, some tiny niggle, kept telling her that he would be an equally fantastic lover, too. The kind of man she'd once imagined a future with.

And that, given the chance, deep down, she'd love to be close to a child like Lucy. To be there for her, give her the mother figure she so desperately craved.

She wondered if that would fill not only the void in Lucy's heart, but the one in hers, too.

Sophie's phone bleeped.

Saved by the bell. Phew. She'd had enough of *those* types of thoughts for the day. For the week, even.

"Hello?" She answered her hands-free phone.

"Sophie, it's your mother. Are you free?"

She smiled, hearing that voice through the earpiece. Good, her mother could distract her.

"I've a house call to make, then I will be."

"Why don't we have a coffee?"

That sounded perfect. Just what she needed.

"I can be at the café in an hour and a half."

Her mother hung up and Sophie turned up the radio. So long as her mom hadn't heard any gossip about her spending time with Lark from some gasbag locals, coffee would be the perfect distraction.

Funny, she thought. She'd come back home to distract herself from work and her own life problems, and now she was here she was needing distraction from a certain tall, dark and handsome cowboy. Not to mention his equally intriguing daughter.

She sighed and let her head loll deeper back into the headrest.

If only that cowboy wasn't quite so handsome, maybe she'd be able to refocus on why she was here.

But so long as she had tomorrow night to think about, there was little chance of dealing with anything else. At least for now.

"Now, I've heard a few rumors about you spending time with our resident cowboy."

Sophie wanted to drop her forehead to the table and thump it hard, over and over. She'd forgotten how fast word could travel around these parts. But seriously, how had her mother heard she'd been at Lark's place? Especially when it was only for work?

Instead of acting like a dramatic child, Sophie raised her coffee cup, took a slow sip, then looked her mother directly in the eye.

"I've been visiting his place a bit for work. Reporting on some horses he has in his care."

Her mother gave her a smile that said she wasn't convinced.

"Don't tell me he's mistreating his horses? Honestly, it's the last thing we need here."

Sophie tried her hardest not to show a hint of emotion, of anything, as she answered. "He's a good horseman. He's helping the shelter out with some neglected horses, that's all."

"And somehow you managed to wangle the job of checking in on our newest eligible bachelor?"

Her mother laughed. Sophie gritted her teeth and tried to take another gulp of coffee. *Do not engage,* she chanted internally. Sometimes she wondered if mothers were secretly like lions or some other predator. They got a hint of blood, or in this case juicy gossip about their offspring, and they didn't back down until they'd completed the kill.

"I'm hardly on the lookout, Mom. And even if I was, I doubt I'm his type."

Now her mother was smiling—the cat-who'd-gotten-the-cream kind of smiling. "So I take it that he's every bit as handsome as the local ladies have been saying?"

Sophie only shrugged in response.

"And from your lack of conversation, I'd say he's gotten under your skin."

Argh. Seriously?

"Mother, I'm almost thirty-two years old, not eighteen, and he has *not* gotten under my skin. He's just a nice man I happen to be assigned to checking in on." She paused, glared at her mother. "That's *all*."

"No need to get shirty with me. I'm just curious. Not often we have a young single man like that move into town."

Sophie sighed, probably a bit too dramatically. "I'm sorry, I've just got a lot on my mind. I didn't mean to get snappy."

She received a pat on the hand in reply. "I'm being nosy, so I probably deserved it," her mother said, her eyes suddenly gentle, telling Sophie the teasing was over. "But I don't want to hear you say you're not his type." She held up a finger when Sophie went to interrupt. "You're a highly successful surgeon and you're beautiful. I'm sure he'd be more than interested if you were sweet on him."

Sophie decided not to comment. The problem was, she *did* like Lark. He was handsome, kind and engaging. She had no idea whether his flirting was him being a tease or whether he was interested, but the timing was way off for her.

But he was a dad. She had to keep reminding herself of that. And that put him off-limits. The last thing she needed was to spend too much time with his daughter, to expose herself to what she'd never have. What she wanted so badly, when it wasn't ever going to be within her grasp.

Besides, she was only here for a while. She had a career to return to, a house that she needed to move back into in Auckland. In the near future she was going to have to slip back into doctor mode and take up residence at Starship

Children's Hospital again. Go back to the life she'd temporarily run away from.

And deep down, she didn't think Lark would be all that interested in her, not long-term. Aside from the fact that she would be living a two-hour plane ride away, he struck her as the kind of guy who'd put down roots and would want a brood of children running through his house.

And that wasn't in her future.

"You sure you're okay, hon?"

Sophie looked back at her mother and forced a smile. "Yeah, I'm fine. Just a lot to think about."

"Maybe you need to stop helping out so much at the shelter and spend more time relaxing. We could do a few day spas or something."

That sounded good. Better than good. She liked to keep herself busy.

"Sounds like a plan."

"Maybe we should do dinner and a movie tomorrow night, then book a spa for one day next week?"

Hmm. Any night but tomorrow. "I'm actually having dinner with a friend tomorrow night, so we might have to take a rain check on that," she told her. "But yes to the spa."

"Anyone I know?"

"Ah, probably not. You want another coffee?"

Sophie waved the waiter over and ordered two more lattes. The last thing she needed was her mother asking her any more questions about her dinner date tomorrow evening.

She was already tying herself in knots over going. Over being with both Lark and Lucy, like part of their little family.

Argh.

The worst thing was she'd started to really like him, couldn't deny it…until she'd met his daughter.

A part of her hoped he had asked her over because he liked her as more than a friend. And another part of her hoped that something might happen. Even if it was only for fun.

As nice as it was spending time with her mother again and

not having to deal with the pressures of work while she took a sabbatical, spending time with Lark had been like a mini holiday in itself.

Sophie's phone rang.

It was the second time her mobile had saved her today. First from loneliness earlier, now from a further grilling from her mother.

"Hello."

She recognized the voice on the other end straightaway. Her colleague from the shelter, and she could tell something was wrong.

"Sophie, we weren't sure whether to say anything earlier, because you're not used to dealing with this sort of thing like we are, but today we're having to put some of the animals down, the ones that haven't found homes yet. We've got so many more animals coming in, and we can't cope with any more."

Sophie fiddled with her spoon, tapping it in agitation against the cup. Her stomach had started to swirl. She felt sick.

"You're right, I'm queasy just thinking about it."

There was silence for a beat down the other end.

"What I'm phoning to tell you is that we're putting the golden puppy down this afternoon, the one you're always saying you're so fond of. The little ones are usually the first to go to new homes, especially purebreds, but times are hard at the moment and adoptions are down. We can only keep them so long."

Sophie shut her eyes. Oh, God.

She was going to be sick. Actually sick.

She pushed back her chair to stand, looked out at the street full of people.

"I'll take him."

There was silence again. "You need to think this through carefully. We can hold off for a couple days if you're serious and need more time. You don't want to make a decision like this without thinking it through properly."

As if she had a choice. There were things in life she regretted, and looking back and knowing that "thinking it through properly" would mean the end of a beautiful little puppy's life was not something else she needed on her conscience. Sure, he was only one puppy of hundreds that were put down each year across the country, but still. She'd bonded with him from her first day there.

"No, I'll take him. Is it okay if I come past later today? I'll need to get supplies and stuff first."

When she hung up the phone, she wondered what on earth she'd done. But it felt like the right thing.

Now she just had to break the news to her mother that she had another houseguest.

CHAPTER TEN

Lᴀʀᴋ threw another log on the fire and stood for a moment, watching it hiss and spit. He loved the warmth from a real fire, the way it sent such dry heat through the air and filled a room with a sweet smell that was so hard to describe.

"Whatcha doing, Dad?"

He looked up as his daughter spoke. Lark had thought Lucy was sound asleep in bed. Instead she stood in the doorway, hair mussed up and half out of its ponytail, warm pajamas buttoned up, woolen socks on her feet.

"You should be in bed, miss."

He wasn't so good at telling her off, or insisting she do something, but he was getting better. It was a fine line between being a good father and treading on eggshells in case he upset her. She'd been through a lot, but he had to trust himself and her more.

Lucy was strong, like him.

"I can't sleep."

He walked the few steps back to the sofa and dropped down, picking up the recipe book he'd discarded and patting the spot beside him.

"Come here, rascal."

She scampered over to him, landing on the sofa with a light thud and tucking in under his arm.

Lark dropped a kiss to her head and pulled her close.

"You do realize I should send you straight back to bed, don't you?"

Her answer was to wriggle in tighter, as though she never wanted him to let go.

Lark sighed and pulled the recipe book back onto his lap, leaving his other arm around her. It hurt his back sitting like that, but he wasn't going to moan. He'd suffer all night if it meant his little girl felt safe and loved. And nothing beat having her close like that.

Made him feel loved, too.

He pushed away the thoughts of what he'd left behind. Sometimes he missed it, rodeo-riding for a living, having his name called over the loudspeaker, winning the title belts. The thrill of doing what he loved.

Having a beautiful woman on his arm, proud to be his wife.

He tried not to snarl. Forced his lip not to curl.

Lark hated that Kate had fooled him the way she had. That he'd thought his wife was in love with him, that there was more to their marriage than materialism.

How wrong he'd been.

But he'd never change the past for the world. Would never wish not to have met Kate, or not to have married her.

Because, as bad as the divorce had been, as unsettling as it had been, they'd made a beautiful daughter and he never wanted to let her go. She made everything right, was worth fighting for, and he couldn't imagine a life without her. Not now.

"So what are you doing?" Lucy mumbled again from her spot beside him.

Lark laughed. Just a chuckle, but she sure drew him from his thoughts.

He flicked the book back to the page he'd had it on. A beautiful golden, stuffed turkey was displayed. Surrounded by sides of candied yams, mashed potato and corn on the cob.

Precisely what he'd like to replicate, yet somehow he already knew it was beyond his capabilities.

"I'm trying to teach myself how to cook a turkey."

"Oh." She wriggled forward so she could lean on his knee and look at the book. "Why can't we just buy one all done like that?"

Lark flipped the book shut and ruffled her head. Why hadn't he thought of that? Surely there was someone around who could help him out, somewhere that sold that sort of thing?

Although it wasn't as though anybody else in town would be celebrating the occasion—even Americans wouldn't be cooking their turkeys for another four months at least! Still, it was worth trying…

"Who taught you to be so darn smart, huh?"

Lucy shrugged and looked up at him, her big eyes melting his heart. "You did."

Lark shook his head, wondering how she always seemed to say the right thing.

"To bed, young lady!" he demanded, standing up as she squirreled away. "It's way past lights out."

Lucy shrieked as he chased her.

"To bed!"

By the time he reached her room, pretending to be a monster as she giggled from beneath her blankets, he wondered why he ever even bothered thinking about what he'd once had. Why he wasted the brain power.

He had a beautiful little girl, a new home and horses out in the fields. And he was starting to feel that he was getting the hang of things on his own.

Just because it was only the two of them, it didn't give him a reason to feel sorry for himself. Not ever.

He was luckier than most and it was time he realized it.

"Daddy, can you read me a story?"

Lark fell onto the bed beside her and folded the top blanket back a little. She didn't often ask him to read to her anymore because she had little books of her own she could devour.

But he loved to be asked.

"Just one chapter, okay?"

She fell back against the pillows and sighed. "Okay."

He had a feeling she'd be asleep before he even finished the first page.

Lark arrived home with a bouncing child beside him and a chicken that smelled like heaven on the floor near her feet. Thank goodness he'd managed to get a precooked one!

"Just don't stomp on that bird!"

He doubted Lucy had heard him; she was out the door and racing up the steps to the house the moment the car stopped. Lark retrieved the chicken, plus a few other bags, and headed on in.

The chicken was going to be served at room temperature—it was already cooked to perfection—but he was in charge of the potatoes and some other vegetables, plus heating up the gravy. It didn't sound like too much, but then he wasn't exactly a whiz in the kitchen.

And he needed to have a bit more of a tidy-up. He kept the place as clean as he could, but he wasn't exactly used to having company over.

So long as there were no other distractions aside from racing out to feed the horses, he'd be fine.

And so long as our guest shows up. Something told him that she wasn't entirely comfortable at the prospect of spending the evening here with them.

He hated to admit that he was hoping more than anything else that she would show.

"When's dinner, Daddy?"

Lark groaned.

"It's only four o'clock," he called back. "Dinner's a while off but you can have a snack now."

Lucy wandered into the kitchen as he started unloading the groceries.

"When's she coming?"

Lucy looked thoughtful, climbing up onto the counter to watch him while he sorted through the bags.

"Sophie?"

"Yeah," she said, kicking her heels on the cupboards.

He ignored it. Her mother would have told her off for banging, but so long as she was happy sitting there yapping to him, he wasn't going to be too hard on her. Her being happy was all he cared about.

"I told her to come by after six, I think," he told her.

"And did you ask anyone else for dinner?"

Lark stopped what he was doing and looked at her. He placed his hands one on either side of her and leaned in so they were touching foreheads.

"Lucy Anderson, are you trying to tell me something?"

She giggled, but she didn't move. Instead she pressed her forehead closer so that their noses touched. "No."

"Like that you have a boyfriend you wanted me to ask over?"

"No!" she squealed this time, wriggling so much he grabbed her and held her in place.

"Are you sure?"

He tried not to laugh too hard. They hadn't goofed around like this, joked, in what felt like forever.

Maybe he wasn't doing as badly in the dad stakes as he'd thought.

Lucy rolled her eyes. "I'm too young to have a boyfriend, Dad."

"Well, if you're sure…"

Lucy angled her head and watched him again. More intently.

"Does this mean Sophie is *your* girlfriend?"

Oh, heavens, no. He hadn't meant to give her that idea. Not at all.

"No, darlin', Sophie's just a friend. Remember I told you she worked with animals? And that she was helping me with those horses we picked up when it was snowing?"

She seemed content with his answer, jumping down from the counter and landing with a thud.

Lark laughed and refocused on what he was doing. Time

was definitely getting away from him, and at this rate they'd be ordering pizza for dinner. Or eating the chicken on its own.

By the time he turned around Lucy was already gone, her attention diverted elsewhere.

No matter how much he was looking forward to an evening in Sophie's company, he still wasn't convinced that asking her over had been the wise thing to do. Was it tempting fate? And should he even allow himself to be attracted to her when he couldn't offer her anything more than an evening or two of fun? He didn't know if he'd ever want a full-on relationship with a woman again.

Not after the way his marriage had worked out.

Sophie might be a different kind of woman, but it didn't matter. He'd been hurt badly enough to last him a lifetime. Been betrayed one time too many.

Now if he could just get his horses fed, a bottle of decent red wine open and warming in front of the fire and dinner on the table, he'd be able to relax.

Sophie sat in her car outside Lark's house. She liked how familiar she'd become with his place, as though her car could find its way here on autopilot.

Sophie could imagine how beautiful it would be here in spring—foals kicking up their heels as they hurtled around beside their mothers, the fields lush with long green grass.

Part of her, deep inside, longed still to be here when the weather changed and winter made way for a warmer climate. When Queenstown was less of a tourist town once the ski fields had shut for the season and it just felt more like her regular old hometown again.

She sighed. The kind of deep, expressive sigh that would have made anyone around her stop to ask what was wrong.

Sometimes she wondered if she should have just taken what had happened all those years ago as fate. Perhaps falling pregnant then had been a sign that her destiny was to be a mother.

That she was supposed to stay here in Queenstown instead of setting her sights on the biggest city and the biggest hospital.

But there was no point thinking like that. Because she *hadn't* had the baby, and, at the time, coming back home single and pregnant hadn't even seemed like an option.

Keeping her pregnancy and her choices to herself was the one thing she didn't regret. It was knowledge better held inside her, not burdening anyone else. But then, maybe that was her being selfish.

Sophie banished thoughts of her past as she prepared to go inside. It was already dark, but the porch was filled with an eerie series of lights, illuminating the exterior of the home. The curtains were pulled, so she couldn't see in, but when she opened her door she could smell the telltale aroma of smoke in the air—logs and pinecones burning in a roaring fire.

She could picture Lark waiting for her, glass of wine in his hand perhaps, warming his feet in front of the fire.

Sophie found herself smiling.

Maybe tonight had been a great idea after all. If it kept her tucked away from the thoughts that kept haunting her, it had to be good. She needed to compose herself, deal with the fact that he had a little daughter whose company she could also enjoy. That was why she'd chosen her vocation, why she worked in pediatrics—because she loved children. No matter what happened, or what her mistakes had been, no one could ever take that away from her.

She reached for the bottle of wine she'd brought, then thought better of it, grabbing her new puppy instead. He'd just woken up from a deep slumber on the passenger seat, and she put him firmly under her arm.

She could come back for the wine. Without a leash for the pup, which she'd accidentally left behind, she didn't want to risk him running off in the dark. Even if he was a touch too big and heavy to carry.

Sophie lugged him to the door, holding him at an awkward angle so she could knock, and hoping it was okay that she'd brought him. There was noise from inside, a few thumps, then the door swung back.

"Hi!"

Sophie's heart beat hard. This wasn't going to be as easy as she'd talked herself into thinking it would.

Lark's pretty, blonde and blue-eyed girl stood with one hand still on the door handle. She was grinning up at Sophie, lips pulled back in the widest smile Sophie had ever seen, eyes dancing.

Then happiness turned to uberexcitement when she spotted the puppy.

"Oooh! What's his name? Is he for me?"

Sophie managed to catch her breath, to function. "Ah, he doesn't have a name yet. I just picked him up today."

"Did Daddy buy him for me?" Lucy asked, petting the puppy over and over until he became so excited and wriggly that Sophie could barely hold him. "I love him already!" The dog licked frantically at her face.

Sophie's heart plummeted again. She seriously needed to get a grip. She was usually the first person to start chatting with a kid, and now she was all awkward and tongue-tied.

Instead of being her usual confident self, Sophie found that her mouth was as dry as though it was full of cotton wool at the dentist's office.

"May I come in?"

"Dad's in the kitchen," said Lucy, rolling her eyes. "Still."

Sophie wanted to turn and go back to the car, but her arm was almost dead from holding the darn dog, he was so heavy.

"Lucy?" Lark's clear, deep voice rang out down the hall.

Sophie looked up as he appeared, a tea towel slung over his shoulder, watching from the other end of the hall.

"Honey, what's our guest doing standing on the porch in the cold?"

She couldn't take her eyes off him. He was so handsome, so gorgeous in jeans, bare feet and a T-shirt.

Her pulse raced.

But he was a *dad*.

He had a *daughter*.

A daughter she'd fleetingly, the other day, imagined herself caring for. Getting close to.

And that was suddenly harder to deal with than she'd thought.

The desire to run came back, and if it hadn't been for the puppy finally breaking free from her arms and careering off down the hallway, child in pursuit, she would have fled and never looked back.

Lark watched a streak of golden dog race down his hallway followed by his own golden streak of a daughter. He looked back at Sophie, who looked as if she'd seen a ghost. That worried look was all over her face again.

He took the tea towel from his shoulder and walked down to greet her, to bring her in out of the cold and to close the front door behind her. He'd had the fire going for hours now, but the chill from outside was starting to fill the house.

"Happy Thanksgiving!" He tried to sound as jovial as possible, concerned by the still-frozen look on her face.

Lark even stopped to drop a kiss to her cheek in welcome. She remained motionless, turning slowly only when he moved past her to shut the door.

"Ah, bottle of wine. In the car. Sorry, I was going back out to get it."

He walked past her, tried to ignore the fact she wasn't sounding quite as articulate as usual.

"I've got wine ready and waiting, so let's save either of us chancing frostbite by going out in that, shall we?"

She smiled. He hoped he was making progress.

"My only concern is that we have an extra guest for dinner and I've only set the table for three."

He watched as she swallowed. Seemed to be breathing kind of heavily. Didn't laugh at his joke about the dog.

"Today didn't turn out quite as planned," she said.

He raised an eyebrow, taking her arm at the same time to propel her down the hall toward the kitchen.

"I got a puppy."

"So I saw."

"Is it okay that I brought him? I mean, I know it was kind of rude to just let him go like that, but he wriggled and ran off with Lucy."

Lark decided to ignore her shy, almost shell-shocked behavior. Didn't want to fluster her even more than she obviously was. He turned and moved down the hall, pleased that she'd followed him into the kitchen, where, he had to admit, it smelled pretty good.

He looked into the living room and watched as Lucy wriggled around on her back, the puppy licking frantically at her face, alternating between diving toward her head or leaping on top of her chest.

"I think they've made friends."

Sophie took the glass of wine he handed her, held it still as he took his own and let the dark red pinot noir swish delicately around the glass.

"I'm pleased she likes dogs," said Sophie, her voice low. Quieter than usual. "I never thought to ask before I brought him in."

Lark held his glass up to clink against Sophie's, then indulged in a sip.

"Unfortunately, Lucy has a desperate need to add to our family by the purchase of a puppy." He threw Sophie a look over his wineglass. "I'm thinking either you're both in on some kind of a conspiracy—" he poked a thumb toward the two playing "—or this is actually the universe telling me she deserves the Lab she's been asking for."

Lark laughed, surprised that Sophie didn't find it anywhere near as funny as he did. Something was definitely up with her.

"Lark, are you sure you want me here for dinner? I mean for your *family* Thanksgiving dinner?"

Was that all she was worried about?

"I wouldn't have asked you if I wasn't sure," he said softly. "And I have a feeling Lucy likes you. *Especially* now that you've brought a puppy around."

Sophie seemed to relax slightly, but he could still see the tension in her shoulders. She looked beautiful though. Hair waving over her shoulders, a snug sweater hugging her curves, skinny jeans silhouetting her long legs.

She looked *darn* good. Maybe he should have dressed up more himself.

He took another sip of wine then turned back to his cooking. Surprisingly, he hadn't seemed to mess anything up yet, and the less he thought about his attractive guest, the more likely it was to stay that way.

He was almost glad Lucy was here. It meant nothing could happen.

But…he almost wished they were alone, just so he could see what *might* happen…

Sophie was fighting the urge to chug back her wine just to block out the too-happy scene before her. It was like a movie, a happy family movie, and she was watching from the shadows.

She should never have put herself in this position.

Sophie leaned back in her seat, not even trying to drag her eyes away now. Lark was attempting to get his daughter to the table, but she was too busy playing with the puppy. They were both laughing. The puppy was grunting with pleasure, trying to jump up high enough to catch his play-friend, who was now being hefted into the air by her father.

Her sexy, tousled, intoxicating father.

Sophie groaned again and hoped no one heard her.

She did not need to be attracted to a handsome daddy.

Didn't need to be reminded of the happy little family scene she'd never have for herself.

A shiver raced across her skin, leaving the tiny hairs on her arms standing on end. She could feel them, even through her sweater.

"I think she wore the puppy out."

Lark's voice snapped her out of her trance. She looked up to see the puppy stretching, yawning, then tucking his little head down against the carpet to sleep.

Lucy, on the other hand, didn't look tired at all. Her face was flushed from playing, smile fixed, eyes shining.

"Go wash up for dinner," Lark told his daughter, before turning to face Sophie. "I'm going to kill you," he said in a lower voice, at the same time as he topped up her glass. "She just asked me if we could talk you into keeping him for ourselves."

Sophie bit her lip. The puppy would be better off here. Another reminder of how different her life was from Lark's.

"He'd probably like living here with you guys more than being in town with me, to be completely honest."

Lark groaned.

Sophie turned.

Oops. She might have answered a little too loudly. Lucy was standing behind them.

"Does that mean we can have him?" she asked.

Lark nodded at the table, indicating for her to sit down, as he carried in the huge chicken.

"No, it means Sophie was just thinking aloud. Right?"

"Right. I mean…"

The girl was looking her in the eye. Pleading with her, even though she wasn't saying a word.

"It's my birthday soon," Lucy told her, bouncing over to the table. "I asked Dad for a puppy. One just like yours."

Sophie watched as Lucy angled her seat so she could watch her new friend, even though he was still motionless, sleeping.

"He's sooo cute!"

A wave of happiness took her by surprise. She felt wrong being part of their intimate family dinner, but she had to admit the girl was delightful.

If it hadn't been now, in the company of a man she was far too attracted to, after all that had happened over the past few months and with so much playing on her mind, she would have enjoyed Lucy's company. She would have *loved* her company. She liked children and they generally liked her.

Only this time, the child in question—and the father setting the chicken on the table—felt a little too close to home.

As she watched them, the way Lark looked at his daughter and she sat to attention, she decided that they could have the puppy. She'd agreed to take the dog on a whim, to save him, and she was glad she had. But compared to the kind of life he could have here, with a farm to explore, a child to adventure with and someone around all day to hang out with, she'd be selfish to decide anything else.

"I'm not sure how this will taste, but fingers crossed."

"It'll be great, Dad."

Sophie nodded in agreement. "It looks fantastic."

"Dig in. Maybe you could serve the vegetables?"

He stood to carve the bird and Sophie helped herself to potatoes and yams and plenty of other things, trying to ignore the pang she felt at putting smaller portions on Lucy's plate, too. Talk about final nails in the coffin, she thought miserably. Every bit of tonight reminded her of what she'd never do for her own daughter.

She caught Lark's eye as he motioned for her to hold up her plate.

And she wished, wished so hard, that this was real. That she was the wife. The mother.

That this scene was one that was making her happy, instead of making her feel as though her heart had been ripped out and replaced by a weak, limp substitute.

She looked down before he could catch a glimpse of the tears shining in her eyes.

CHAPTER ELEVEN

LARK was still convinced that something was wrong with Sophie, but he wasn't going to make a big deal out of it. There was something there, something that he couldn't quite put his finger on, and she couldn't seem to meet his gaze.

The trouble was, even though she had been quiet since she'd arrived, he liked her. Seriously liked her. Nothing had changed there.

And it was unsettling him. Big-time.

He'd promised himself, had just thought it was a given, that he wasn't going to get involved with another woman again. But it was as if the universe was telling him otherwise, refusing to let him fight the pull he was feeling toward this woman sitting opposite him at the table.

"Please tell me it's good?"

Lucy grinned at him, all elbows as she cut through her food.

"The chicken is brilliant," praised Sophie.

"Turkey," he corrected, throwing her a wink when Lucy wasn't looking. Turkey had been impossible to find, but free-range chicken that *looked* like turkey had been easy.

She smiled back—the sweet, soft smile he'd been waiting for all night. The one she usually gave him, but that had been absent since she'd arrived tonight.

"Turkey," she repeated.

"And now I have to confess that it's the only part of the meal I can't take credit for."

She laughed. It made him smile.

"The deli in town, right?"

He raised both hands. "Guilty as charged."

"Well, you did a great job on everything else."

That made him laugh, pleased to see the happy expression on Lucy's face, too. Her main source of happiness might be stemming from the snoring pup in the other room, but she was happy and that was all that mattered. It was why he'd decided to do this dinner in the first place.

"So, if I'm completely honest, all I did were the vegetables. The, ah, *bird,*" he said, giving Sophie a look, "was from the deli, along with the stuffing and gravy, although I did have to heat that up." When he heard her laugh he kept going, happy that she was loosening up, being more like her usual self, the self he'd gotten to know over the past week or so. "The cranberry sauce was also store-bought, but in the end, I thought if we wanted actually to enjoy eating, that was the best option."

"Mommy used to buy everything, anyway," said Lucy, her attention still on the puppy.

Lark grimaced. "Yeah, she did."

Sophie looked up, seemed to throw him a question mark.

"But Mommy's back in California," he said, feeling he couldn't let that particular question hang over the table for too long. "And maybe she'll come for a holiday one day, huh?"

Lucy beamed at him. "Yeah. Maybe."

"We talked about this the other day, Lark," Sophie said, her voice low. "I told Lucy that I was just like her. It's pretty special having one parent to look after you."

Lark could have jumped up and kissed her. It was exactly what Lucy needed to hear. And he did, too.

Now he knew why they'd both been so relaxed the other day. Lucy must have opened up to Sophie. It made him smile harder than he had in a long while.

He was pleased Sophie didn't think it was too weird—a father with sole custody of his daughter living on the other side of the world to the child's mother. *He'd never have moved her here if he hadn't thought it was the best thing for her.*

A sadness passed over Sophie's face that he couldn't miss. It was the way she looked at Lucy, as though she saw something in his daughter that made her sad. Unhappy.

Lark had a feeling that even if he had hoped something could happen between Sophie and him after Lucy was tucked up in bed, Sophie wasn't feeling quite the same way he was tonight. Something had changed, was bothering her, and he had no idea what it was. It was as if there was a distance between them.

All he knew was that he didn't like it. It was as if she had a guard up, a wall she'd built to keep him at arm's length.

Lucy's wriggling caught his eye.

"May I leave the table now?" she asked.

Sophie wanted to leave. She never should have come in the first place. Everything about tonight was wrong.

She might have been older than Lucy when her own father had left, but she felt a pang of compassion, of deep-set pain for the girl. When her father had walked out, gone off with someone half his age and left her mother with next to nothing, she'd known the pain of a parent's betrayal. And this little girl had a mother who'd given up interest in her.

It made her sick.

But it also made her realize, very clearly, that she shouldn't be here. This child did not need another woman in her life who wasn't going to be around for long, and she wasn't about to become "another woman" to Lark anyway. Maybe, just maybe, she'd have been tempted into a temporary love affair, something fun and casual for a short burst of time, but not now.

Even if she wanted so desperately to be there for Lucy.

Even if, deep down, she wished she could be the child's mother. To care for her and love her as she deserved to be loved by a mother.

"Lucy, why don't you go play with the puppy again?" Lark suggested.

Lucy jumped from her seat as though there was a rocket stowed beneath it, charging back into the adjoining room. Sophie watched as the puppy stretched, sleepy-eyed, until he realized his friend was back to play with him. Then he leaped up, eager as she was, lapping at her face.

"He might need to go outside, since he's just woken up," Sophie said, moving to stand.

Lark reached over and halted her with his touch, the backs of his fingers brushing her arm. It stopped her dead, made her heart hammer, wishing he hadn't connected with her bare skin.

"Lucy, grab the horse rope at the back door and clip it onto his collar. You can take him outside for his toilet stop."

"Are you sure?" Sophie asked. It might have been her chance to slip away early. She *needed* to get away. Needed an excuse.

Lark's hand fell away from her forearm, but not before his eyes met hers. Something unsaid passed between them, something Sophie didn't want to acknowledge.

She remembered that look. Knew it only too well from the other day in his truck. When he'd watched her, looked at her, leaned in and almost kissed her.

She'd known it had meant something then, and now there was no doubt left in her mind that she hadn't been imagining it. Only now she wasn't sure if she wanted it. Or whether she *should* want it.

Sophie bit the inside of her mouth as a shudder trawled its way with slow intensity down her back, tingling across her shoulders.

When every bone, muscle and fiber in her body screamed at her to want him, to let herself say yes to anything that might, that could happen, why did her mind tell her *no* so firmly? With such determination?

She knew why; she wasn't ready for this. Didn't want to be exposed to Lark's family life, not when she could never grasp it in the future for herself.

But still, his eyes held hers, captured hers. She was like a hopeless fish caught in an expert fisherman's net.

She only hoped she'd be better able to escape.

"Sophie, you seem kind of quiet tonight," he said, once the child and dog had disappeared.

His words were kind, softly spoken. Genuine concern shone from his eyes.

"I'm fine," she assured him, knowing full well she was far from fine. "I'm, well, tired I guess."

He nodded, a thoughtful expression on his face.

"If you say so."

That got her back up. Bristles and all. "What do you mean by that?"

He shrugged, clearly unconcerned by her tone. "You don't seem like your usual self, that's all. Looks to me like something's troubling you, and all I wanted was to make sure that that something wasn't me."

Sophie looked down at her plate, then fiddled with the napkin resting over her knees. "It's not you, Lark. Honestly it's not. I've just got a lot going on right now."

He smiled, but this time it was different, as if he understood.

She relaxed. He wasn't going to pry, she could sense it.

"I know what that's like, believe me."

Since he had an ex back in the States and a daughter to care for, she didn't doubt him.

"Can we just leave it at that?" she asked.

He nodded. "Sure can. But not before I thank you for the other day. Whatever you said to her must have helped."

They watched one another for a moment before he stood up. She didn't know what to say.

"How about another glass of wine, since neither of us want to talk about our problems?"

Sophie shook her head. "I really shouldn't, not when I have to drive back into town."

He placed both hands on the back of his chair and leaned

forward. "You could always stay over, if you don't want to drive."

She couldn't help the burning heat that hit her cheeks at his words. Embarrassed from the intense way he watched her, eyes skimming hers, laughter dancing in their dark depths.

"Sorry—teasing," he said, raising both hands in mock surrender. "But you've only had a small glass. I'm sure you could have a tiny bit more."

Sophie nodded, holding her glass out and trying to regain her confidence. "Just a little more, then," she choked out.

She really had to leave.

And soon.

She stood up to help clear the table while he went back to the kitchen to fill their wineglasses. She was nervous, her hands shaking, enough for her to see them tremble.

She walked the plates into the kitchen, stopping only when she saw Lark watching her. He held both wineglasses, each half-full, and he was leaning back against the counter.

His dark, chocolate eyes were somehow smiling at her, teasing her, making her belly flip hard, over and over again.

Sophie looked down, moved past him, put the plates down. She suddenly felt claustrophobic, didn't know where to look, what to do, where to go.

"Sophie." He said her name in that casual drawl of his, as though the word itself was laced with sweetness.

Her legs turned to liquid.

Make that, dripping in buttery sweetness.

She turned half her body, too scared to face him front-on.

She watched as he put both glasses down and slowly crossed the space between them. Sophie tried not to hold her breath, but she couldn't do anything else.

"There's something I've been wanting to do," he said, his tone low. Soft yet strong.

Sophie watched him. She couldn't do anything *but* watch him.

He leaned toward her. She knew she should move away,

should take the step backward that told him she needed space between them. That she didn't want whatever it was that he'd been wanting to do. Because it was wrong.

But she couldn't.

Not after so many days of thinking about him. Of seeing him. Of *wanting* him.

Lark raised his hand to her chin, two fingers curling gently against her skin, cupping her face to tilt her head back. She didn't even try to resist. Couldn't.

He shuffled closer, just his body, so close to her that she could feel the heat from him.

"Sophie," he said, before dipping his head low, crushing his lips to hers with such tenderness that she barely felt the touch at all.

Hardly felt the pressure of it, but felt the warmth of him everywhere. She sighed into his mouth, wanting so hard to pull away and yet desperate to melt against him, press her body into his and never let go.

Lark's hand moved from her chin to touch her cheek, the softest press of his palm against her, his lips moving more firmly against hers.

Then it was over.

He pulled away so abruptly she was left openmouthed and breathless. Empty. Alone. Standing in his kitchen, wondering what had happened and where that had even come from.

"Lucy's back inside," he said, voice gruff.

Sophie raised a hand to her mouth, touched her lips.

Then looked up at Lark. His eyes were soft, tender, the look on his face so gentle that it had the potential to make her heart melt.

And then Lucy appeared, all red-faced and happy-looking.

Thank goodness he'd heard her come in and she hadn't walked in on them.

"He's been to the toilet," his daughter announced proudly.

Sophie nodded. Lark put his arm around his daughter's

shoulders and squeezed. "Good work. Maybe you *are* almost ready for a puppy, huh?"

Lucy let out a delighted squeal.

It was too much for Sophie.

The kiss, Lark, his daughter…just being here was more than she could cope with. She should have left before it got to this point. Before it became too much.

"Thanks for a lovely dinner," she said, hoping her voice sounded stronger than it felt. "It's been great but I really have to go."

Lark looked at her, confusion on his face, eyebrows knotted. Lucy only looked, not saying anything.

"Are you sure? We haven't even had dessert yet."

She ignored the hurt she sensed in his voice. The confusion.

But she had to go. Had no other option but to leave. Right now.

"It's only ice cream, but…"

"I'm sorry," she said, before scooping up the puppy and trying her hardest to smile at Lucy.

"Will you bring him back to play?"

"Sure," she answered, prepared to say anything so long as it meant she could escape. "Thanks for entertaining him tonight."

"Sam," Lucy called out as Sophie headed toward the door.

She stopped, looked back, watched as Lark left his daughter's side to follow her.

"I'd call him Sam," Lucy said.

Sophie continued toward the door.

When she got there, Lark stopped her, walking in front of her so his frame filled the doorway.

"What's happening here?" he asked, his face worried, drawn.

She refused to look at him.

"I'm sorry, Lark, truly I am."

Then she pushed past him and walked out, sucking in deep

gulps of freezing-cold air as she hurried to her car. She dumped the puppy in the passenger seat and moved around to the other herself.

She wanted to, but she never looked back.

She just drove away as tears filled her eyes, burning the back of her throat, and she fought not to let them fall. Didn't allow herself to give in to them.

He was just a man.

With a daughter. With a *Lucy*.

He didn't mean anything to her, and that's why she had to walk away. Before she got sucked into something that she *couldn't* walk away from.

Before she experienced more of what she could never have herself.

Before she started to yearn for his daughter, too. Because even though she'd tried so hard to keep her distance, she'd fallen for his little girl, as well.

Sophie sobbed then, one big gulp of tears.

She reached for the puppy, one hand steady on the wheel, the other caressing his fur.

Then she fought the emotion in her throat again, refusing to acknowledge it—let alone let it out.

CHAPTER TWELVE

THREE days later, Lark was steaming. Furious. The more he thought about Sophie, the wilder he became with himself.

He'd thought she was different and yet she'd run out on him. Just like his wife had.

He'd pledged to himself to remain single, and what had he done the moment a pretty, charming woman had crossed his path? Almost become involved, that's what.

Lark smiled as a very happy Lucy walked past on her new pony, Cleo.

"Best present in the world?" he asked.

She grinned. "Best ever."

The pair had bonded immediately, from the moment he'd taken her out to the field, blindfolded, to meet her horse. And now she was already having her second ride of the day. Thank goodness the pony was obliging.

"I love her," Lucy told him as she circled past. "She's the best."

He laughed, almost forgetting his woman troubles. "I can see that."

She seemed to have forgotten about the puppy today, for now anyway, although she'd talked about Sam nonstop since Sophie had visited that night.

The night she'd walked out on them and not been in touch since.

"Can I go faster?"

He watched as Lucy came past again. "Sure, ask her to trot. Squeeze your legs lightly and sit up nice and tall."

"I do know how to ride, Dad," she told him, although she was still grinning.

Lark laughed at her; he couldn't do anything else. He probably wouldn't have listened to his own father either, had he been trying to tell him what to do, and she was naturally gifted. She did know what she was doing.

"Come on, then, show me how it's done."

And she did, expertly moving into a trot and riding Cleo out in a big circle.

It was what he needed, to watch her having fun like that. Took his mind off the woman who was still managing to cause him an itch beneath his skin.

She'd been no better than his ex. He'd made a bad judgment call. And he certainly shouldn't have ever introduced her to Lucy or brought her into his home.

Maybe he was a bad judge of character when it came to women. Maybe it was a wake-up call telling him to remain single.

Either way, whatever the case, he needed to forget about her and focus on his role as a father to Lucy. That was all that mattered and he'd temporarily lost sight of the fact that he didn't need a woman in his life.

He didn't need Sophie and he wasn't going to spend any more time thinking about her. Or how she'd walked out.

Even if stopping his mind from thinking about her was like trying to keep a fish alive out of water.

Sophie was taking time out from her time-out. She'd called in sick again to the animal shelter. Not that she had to—her role was purely voluntary and they seemed surprised every time she turned up, they had so few volunteers. But after what had happened the other night…

She still shuddered thinking about how it had ended.

The puppy curled up beside her, tighter, snuggled on the sofa and into her blanket. It was silly, but every time she pressed her face or hand into his fur, she thought of little Lucy. Of her smiling face, of the way she'd so genuinely loved the puppy from the moment she'd set eyes upon him.

And wanted to call him Sam, she reminded herself.

Or the way the girl's father had looked as she'd fled from his house so rudely.

She closed her eyes again, trying to block out the image of his hurt-filled expression, the confusion on his face—followed by what she was sure was a flash of anger.

She couldn't blame him though. He'd put so much effort into the evening, preparing a lovely meal and then…

Another thing she didn't want to think about.

The kiss.

The spine-numbing, lip-tingling kiss that she hadn't been able to forget no matter how hard she tried.

The way his mouth had felt against hers, the look in his eyes before he'd bent and closed the distance between them. And the kindness, the gentleness of his face as he'd pulled away.

Sophie sighed.

She didn't know what he'd wanted from her, what he might have expected. And maybe he didn't, either. But she wasn't ready for whatever might have transpired.

She was here to spend some time on her own, find herself again and deal with her past. With the nightmares that continued to plague her. With the realities she had to face before moving on and taking up her position as a surgeon again. Before slotting into her old life.

There was no way she was ready for a relationship.

And what if something deeper had developed between her and Lark? What then?

She'd have to complicate things by admitting to Lark that she couldn't ever have children. That he'd never have any more kids to add to his brood. Never be able to give Lucy a brother or sister in the future if they stayed together.

And something within her, something she couldn't ignore,

knew that Lark had introduced her to his daughter for a reason. He'd wanted her to know, to show her his life, and she couldn't deal with it. She wasn't ready for confronting that kind of situation.

She owed Lark an apology, but for now she was going to avoid him.

No one liked an ostrich with its head buried in the sand, but it was what she had to do right now.

Tomorrow she was going to pick herself up, shake herself off and deal with life again.

There was a local horse show on and she could go and watch that. Eat hot dogs and chips, guzzle some fizzy drinks, pretend that she had nothing better in the world to be doing. The more junk food the better, just for one day.

Then she was going to suck up the courage to apologize to Lark.

She snuggled back into the sofa, eyes shut, smiling as her puppy snored away beside her, oblivious to her troubles.

He was the only family she had on her radar now, as good as it was going to get for her, so she'd better get used to it and enjoy him.

No wallowing over happy families. Or men she wouldn't appeal to. Or what she couldn't have.

She had a better life than many, and it was time she dealt with it and moved on.

Sophie stood on the sidelines, picking at a plate of hot fries, and watched the horses circling. She loved watching them jump, especially the ponies with their pint-size riders.

One came past her now, a pretty pinto pony with black-and-white markings. Its rider had a braid flying out behind her, but no number on her back. Sophie guessed she must be here to practice, not compete.

She stepped back, smiling as the little rider went past. And then…

Her smile turned to a gasp as a large horse came careering

past, too fast, clipping the tiny pony on the side as they thundered out of control.

The pony tried its hardest, but it stumbled sideways, sending its rider tumbling.

Ouch.

Sophie moved fast, dropping her fries, running to the rider's assistance. The girl had fallen hard, the pony treading on her as it tripped before righting itself.

She was there within an instant, at the girl's side.

"It's okay, sweetheart, I'm a doctor," she said, placing a hand on the girl's chest to keep her lying down flat. "You're going to be just fine."

The child looked up at her. And it was only then that Sophie recognized the blue eyes, now fast filling with tears.

"Lucy?" she asked.

The little head nodded. Sophie's heart started beating that bit too fast.

The stakes had just been raised.

Any child was important, but this one was Lark's precious daughter.

"I'm going to check your head first, make sure you haven't hurt your neck or back, then I'll move you."

"I want my daddy," she whimpered.

"I'm here."

Sophie didn't look up, kept her focus on Lucy, even as the deep, strong voice belonging to Lark joined her.

Lark knelt beside her, one hand on his daughter's chest, as if to calm her, the other holding her hand.

"Where's Cleo?" Lucy cried.

He bent over and pressed a kiss to her hand. "She's fine. Someone's looking after her."

"She didn't mean it, Dad. It wasn't her fault."

Sophie looked up then, met his gaze. She'd seen what happened herself, and Lucy was right. The pony *had* tried her hardest.

"Would you mind telling me what you're doing?" Lark's

question was said in a low voice, but there was no denying the fury in his gaze.

She recoiled, scared of being so close to him. But she had a job to do, and she wasn't going to let her feelings for Lark affect her assessment of the situation.

Lucy had taken a bad tumble.

"Sophie?" he questioned her again.

"I'm a doctor, Lark. She's in good hands."

If Lark was surprised he didn't say anything.

At least he seemed to believe her.

Sophie gently eased off Lucy's helmet, felt her over carefully, then moved on to her arms. She knew straightaway that one was broken.

"Aaarghh," Lucy moaned. "It hurts so bad."

Sophie looked up at Lark, focused now, no longer worried about any looks he may or may not be giving her.

"We need to get her to the hospital. This arm is broken, and I want her X-rayed straightaway."

"Can I lift her?"

Sophie locked eyes with him. Saw that right now he didn't care what had passed between them. All he cared about was his little girl and making sure she was okay.

"You lift her, carefully, and I'll support her arm," she instructed. "I'd prefer to ice it, or not move her at all, but we don't have a choice."

He lifted his daughter so gently it was as though he was lifting a broken, shattered doll and trying not to lose even the tiniest of pieces.

"I've got an ice pack in a cooler in the truck," he said, before dropping a kiss to his daughter's head, his lips touching her hair. "I always have one on hand for the horses."

Sophie nodded, but before Lark could even see her movement Lucy was sobbing again.

"Honey, where does it hurt? Tell me."

Lark's voice was desperate, a crack in his throat.

"I don't want to leave without Cleo," she cried. "Put her in the truck, *please*."

Lark looked at Sophie. She looked back at him.

"Taking a few minutes to get her pony isn't going to matter," she assured him, siding with Lucy if only because of the look on her face. "Let's get her back to the truck, you grab Cleo, then we can go."

Lark didn't look happy about the situation, but he didn't argue. She doubted he ever would when it came to his daughter.

They'd been at the hospital for more than three hours. Lark was exhausted, drained from the worry, and now he was starting to panic over the snow that had begun to fall outside. He was most worried about his daughter, but he had to get Cleo out of the truck and get home to check the other horses, too.

If he didn't go soon, he was concerned the road might be too dangerous to navigate. Especially once it was dark. But at the same time he wasn't going to leave his girl.

Lark walked back down the corridor, tasteless cup of coffee in his hand, and almost ran smack-bang into Sophie.

"Hey," she said.

He held up a spare coffee he'd poured. "Didn't know how you like it, but I went with white and one sugar."

She took the cup from him and blew on the hot liquid.

"She doing okay?" he asked.

Sophie sipped then reached out a hand to touch him. Her hand trailing down his arm, squeezing, then letting go.

He wished he didn't like it so much, but he did. He was still annoyed with her, but mostly he was grateful she'd been on hand to help. Even if he was confused.

She sure had a lot of explaining to do.

"Lucy fell asleep the moment you walked out the door," said Sophie, turning back to the room she'd come from so he could look in the tiny window.

"She looks so small, lying there like that," he said. "So—I don't know, vulnerable."

The pink cast covering his daughter's lower arm made him cringe.

Lark swallowed another sip of coffee to get rid of the lump of emotion straining to be released. He cleared his throat.

"You know, it wasn't the pony's fault," Sophie said to him. "I saw the whole thing happen. The other rider was an adult and she really should be held accountable."

"I shouldn't have let her ride there," he said, still seeing his little girl lying on the ground, worrying that she'd done herself a serious injury. "She was so desperate to take the pony down there, to ride her, and I couldn't say no to her. Can't ever seem to say no."

"I'm not going to tell you to stop beating yourself up over this, because I know you can't not be a father," Sophie said to him, taking a step back. "But she's going to be fine, and I think the best thing you can do is follow the doctor's orders, leave her here until morning and then take her home."

That was the last thing Lark wanted to do. He'd rather sleep by her side and not let her spend a moment alone.

But he did have to get back home. Maybe he could go to the farm, do what he had to do, then be at the hospital before she woke up again...

"There will be a nurse assigned to her. Because of her age she won't be left alone once she's awake. They'll call you straightaway if anything changes."

He still wasn't sure.

"I don't want her to think I've abandoned her," he admitted, feeling that chunk of emotion rise up in his throat again.

Sophie didn't say anything, she just looked at him.

And something told him that part of her, whatever it might be, understood what he was trying to say.

"She knows you love her," Sophie told him, her head down, voice so soft he could hardly hear her. "Lucy knows she's the most important thing in your life. She's not going to think you've left her."

Lark knew Sophie was right. Deep down he knew, but walking away from his daughter was still hard.

"And she'll probably sleep until morning anyway. They gave her pain relief and it's best if she's under observation for the night. It was a decent fall."

"I know," he said, looking through the window one last time. "I know it was."

He walked past Sophie to go in to Lucy. If he was going to leave her, he wanted at least to kiss her goodbye first.

Before he opened the door, he turned back to Sophie.

"I really appreciate what you did today."

She shook her head, one arm wrapped around her body, the other still holding her now-empty cup.

"It's what I do."

He frowned. He couldn't help it. "Yeah, about that," he said, staring at her, hard. "I think you have some explaining to do."

She looked embarrassed, but she didn't look away, maintained eye contact with him. This was a different Sophie to the one he was used to. This woman wasn't as shy, she was more confident. There was something more courageous, stronger, about her.

"I'm a doctor, Lark. I'm taking some time off, but that's what I do for a living."

He sighed. "You doing anything tonight?"

She looked wary. "Why?"

"Because I'm about to go out into the snow and head for home, and since you don't have a car here I think you should come with me and explain on the way."

She gulped. He saw the movement.

"Okay?" he asked.

She flushed slightly, the confident doctor starting to disappear.

"Okay," she muttered.

He didn't give her a chance to change her mind. Instead he

walked into Lucy's room and hoped Sophie hadn't bolted the moment he turned away.

His back ached, more than ever, as it always did when he was stressed or tired. But he ignored it.

He had more important things to think about than his back. Or the fall. Or dealing with this alone.

All that mattered was Lucy.

CHAPTER THIRTEEN

SOPHIE was nervous. She didn't want to spend any more time with Lark, but she hadn't had the heart to turn him down. Not when he was clearly so upset, so devastated about what had happened to Lucy.

And she did have some explaining to do. Maybe she didn't necessarily owe it to him, but he'd been nothing but kind to her, and she hadn't exactly been truthful.

She watched him through the window, almost turned away because she felt as if she was intruding somehow on a private moment between father and daughter. But she couldn't *not* look. Her eyes drank their fill of the handsome man bent over his child, lips whispering across her forehead, hand caressing her hand, before he turned away.

He saw her, his eyes locked on hers as he stood to walk from the room.

"I don't feel right leaving her," he said, voice gruff.

"I know."

She doubted she did know. Couldn't really know, since she wasn't a parent, but the anguish on his face said it all.

"Let's go," he said, looking into the room one last time before pulling on his jacket and turning away.

Sophie followed him, staying a distance away, careful not to walk too close. Not to brush against him. After seeing him again, all she knew was that she had feelings for him that she had no choice but to ignore.

"Will the pony be okay?"

Lark kept walking, but slowed his pace slightly. "Yeah, she'll be fine. Tired, but fine."

They didn't say anything else until Lark pushed open the double doors at the exit to the hospital.

"Jeez, it's freezing out here!"

He grabbed hold of her hand, tucking it against his and pulling her toward the truck. "Don't slip."

Snow fell lightly down on her head, skimming her nose, touching her cheeks. She had a sweater and jeans on, not enough to keep her warm, but they were moving fast.

She tried to ignore Lark's palm against hers, the strength of his hold, but it wasn't easy. He never looked at her, only took her to the truck, unlocking her door before making his way around to the driver's side.

She jumped in; he landed beside her. It wasn't like the other day in his truck, when they'd been so close, but it was still intimate. There was still the sense that they were breathing the same air, that they were alone together, that...

"So you're a doctor."

He said it as a statement. His voice was flat.

Sophie wriggled a little away from him, all too aware of what she had to tell him. What she had to admit. Her whole life story.

"I'm only here on holiday," she said, looking out the window into the darkness to avoid Lark. "Kind of an extended sabbatical from my job." She laughed, a low noise in her throat that escaped before she could stop it. "Actually a sabbatical from my life, if I'm really honest."

Lark didn't say anything for a while. She was pleased. The snow was still falling, heavier now, and he had the wipers on fast as he peered out the window intently.

"Going back to the part where you're a doctor..." he said, a hint of sarcasm in his voice.

She sighed.

May as well just get it all out there on the table.

"I'm actually a surgeon," she said, glancing at him this time. Wanting to see his reaction.

"A surgeon," he repeated, his voice giving none of his feelings away.

His expression didn't change; he was still focused on the road. She was pleased they weren't sitting facing one another. At least she didn't have to look into his eyes as she spoke. She could avoid seeing what he thought of what she was saying.

"I live in Auckland mostly, about two hours away by plane," she told him. "Usually my life consists of working as a pediatric surgeon at Starship Children's Hospital. I spend my day wearing a white coat, talking to parents and other doctors about treatment options, and trying to save little people from all sorts of problems."

"I see."

If he was particularly shocked he didn't show it.

"I should have told you, but I'm taking some time off from that life right now. I didn't want to be that person while I was here."

He briefly glanced at her, but his eyes quickly refocused on the road.

"You don't have to explain."

But she did. He wanted to know and she felt she had to tell him.

"I didn't mean to lie to you, Lark," she told him truthfully. "I just needed to escape that life while I was back here. I wanted to be a different person for a while, so I could think and reflect about what I'd run away from. There are things I couldn't deal with, and it was time for me to take a break."

He stayed silent.

"I'm helping out at the animal shelter on a volunteer basis, and I don't have to be back at my real job for a few more months."

"So you're hiding out here and running away from something," he said.

"I wouldn't say running away exactly."

"I'm not judging you, Sophie. I've run away from my own problems too, so you're not exactly alone there," Lark told her.

"Maybe you're right. Maybe I am running," she admitted, "but I don't want to run. I want to figure things out, and it seemed like a good idea at the time to come back here. To come home."

He laughed, a small chuckle that caught her by surprise.

"You've run *back* home and I've run away from home," he told her. "We might have different reasons, but in the end we've both hidden from our problems."

She leaned back in the seat, actually pleased she'd opened up to him, told him what she'd done and why she was here. Or at least part of it.

"Maybe we haven't hidden from our problems, Lark. Maybe we were simply smart enough to offer ourselves a fresh start." She paused. "You've left something behind that clearly wasn't working for you, and you've started over."

"I still ran," he said, "but I'm pleased I did. It was the right thing for me, for Lucy, too. But you? I have a feeling you're not so sure about your decision."

Sophie looked out the window again, hardly able to see anything. The ground was covered in white and the snow was still falling.

"I should have stayed and dealt with my problems, but instead I came back here, thinking, somehow, that it would make everything right. That I'd have some time out and be ready to go back to how things were," she told him.

She recognized the motion as the truck pulled into Lark's driveway, the start of the incline.

In a way she was relieved they were back at his place, but then that also meant she was going to be alone with him. In his house. Without his daughter as an excuse.

The home ahead looked dark, there were no lights on. His roof was covered in white; it was all she could really make out.

"How about I give you the keys so you can head in and open

up? I'll drive around the side, take Cleo off and feed the other horses."

She nodded her agreement, holding out her palm for the keys as he idled outside the house.

"There's firewood in the basket if you want to light the fire, get the house warm, and help yourself to anything you need. A sweater, just whatever," he said, his voice slightly gruff. "You know, because you look a little cold."

Sophie took the keys, hopped out of the truck and walked in the light made by his headlights. She carefully trod up the steps to the door, turned the key and let herself in, fumbling for the light switch.

It was cold in the house, but not as cold as it was outside.

Sophie stood in the hallway, the door shut behind her, as the truck lights disappeared and dipped around to the side of the house.

She couldn't help but think about the last time she'd been here. How nice the night could have been, but how badly it had ended because of her.

Now she was alone in his home, about to start a fire and boil some water for a coffee. To look through his fridge and try to find something that she could make into dinner, since neither of them had eaten since goodness only knew when.

In a way it seemed too intimate, being in his house like this. Although something about it also seemed…special.

She wasn't sure which was worse, but right now she needed to get the house warm. Pull the curtains and try to remember how to start a fire, rather than just push a button for a gas one to ignite.

Sophie walked through to the living room first and closed the curtains in there, but not before she peeked outside again. The snow had started to fall fast and heavy, and she had a feeling it was only going to get worse. They often had snow here, but this was worse than usual. Especially this early in the season.

She hoped Lark had a radio so they could tune in and see

what the local weather report was, because something told her the roads were probably close to being shut now, if they weren't already.

She gulped.

Which would mean she could be stuck here, alone, with Lark all night.

Until morning.

Lark made his way slowly across the yard to the house. He would usually go in the back door, but he'd locked it and he doubted Sophie would hear him if he knocked.

The weather had taken a turn for the worse. The only consolation was that it was still snowing, so the air felt almost still. It was when the wind picked up and the rain started pelting down with fury that it was terrible.

He pulled off his boots at the front door and let himself in. Strangely, it didn't feel like his home tonight. He could hear the television going, not loud but enough of a hum for him to detect. There were lights on throughout the house, and he could smell something cooking.

It was like arriving home to the kind of domestic scene he'd always expected he'd have. His wife had been beautiful, and they'd had plenty of seemingly good years together before everything had started to unravel, but arriving home had never felt like this.

The only thing missing was Lucy, but he didn't want to think too much about her. It would only send him hightailing it back to the hospital, and the last thing either of them needed was him driving in this weather. Besides, they'd told him rather forcefully to stay away.

He walked into the kitchen.

And stopped.

Sophie had let her hair down to fall around her shoulders, and her head was bent. She was busy chopping something on the counter.

He was still angry with her. Even though she'd helped him with Lucy today.

He was still annoyed at how she'd left the other night. Out of sorts about the fact that he'd thought he'd connected with her, that there was something between them, and he hadn't known about her, not truly, at all.

But seeing her like this, in his kitchen?

Lark gulped.

She was something else.

He listened to her hum as she kept her hands busy, turning to the stove then back to the counter again.

And then she looked up.

Light brown—hazel—eyes met his, her expression widening as she realized he was standing there.

"Lark! You gave me a fright."

He crossed the room. "Sorry, I was just admiring the view."

She blushed. Bright, tomato-sauce red.

"I mean…" he stammered. That had come out all wrong. "Well, you look great, but I meant I was admiring seeing someone else in my kitchen. Arriving inside to find a meal under way and the house warm isn't something I'm used to anymore."

He watched as her shoulders visibly relaxed.

"It's only an omelet, and I'm not convinced the fire is going that well," she told him.

Lark went over to check it. "Doesn't look bad to me, and it's still a heap warmer in here than it is outside."

He opened the door on the large fireplace and threw in another log before poking the fire vigorously then closing the door.

"I didn't know if you had a radio, but I managed to catch the end of the news on the television when I first came in," she said, standing over a pan filled with an almost-golden omelet.

"Roads closed?"

She grimaced. "Yeah. They're saying it's the worst storm in the area for almost twenty years."

"Typical."

She turned to look over her shoulder at him. Lark had to resist walking up behind her and placing his hands there, covering her shoulders and upper arms. Connecting with her.

"What's typical?" she asked.

"That when I decide to move here the weather packs in."

Sophie reached for the plate she had beside the stove and expertly flipped the omelet onto it.

"You've got to admit that it's pretty beautiful though," she said, followed by a sigh. "If you're tucked up inside with a fire, a glass of wine and good company, then it's not half-bad."

He walked toward her, unburdening her of the plate.

Was she referring to him as good company or just making a statement in general?

"Is this mine?"

Sophie glanced at him, eyes partially hidden by her lashes.

God, she was beautiful.

All the anger, annoyance, he'd felt toward her earlier simply disappeared over one look. One connection.

What he'd felt for her before she ran out on him the other night had been real. No matter how much he didn't want to become involved or told himself she wasn't for him.

There was something between them and they both knew it.

"I, ah, didn't know what you'd want in yours, so I just worked with what I could find."

They were still looking at one another, but Sophie kept glancing away. He couldn't have cared less what was in the omelet. What he liked was the fact that she'd made it for him, and that she was standing in front of him right now.

"I'll like it," he said.

"There's tomatoes, onions, cheese…"

Lark put the plate down on the counter. He didn't take his eyes off her.

She looked frightened, as though she didn't know what to do, but she didn't move away.

He leaned past her, turned off the gas on the stove and then stood before her, arms hanging at his sides.

"I don't care what's in the damn omelet, Sophie."

She tilted her face back up toward him.

"You don't?"

He shook his head, the smallest movement from side to side.

"All I care about is why you walked out on me the other night. Why you ran like that."

There. He'd said it. Gotten it off his chest.

He needed to know, damn it!

"I don't know what to say to you," she said.

Lark could see she was being honest. He doubted, now that he was standing before her and looking into her eyes, that she'd easily lie or deceive anyone.

His ex-wife had started to make him think that all women behaved a certain way, but what he could see in Sophie's eyes told him that maybe he'd been right about her from the start.

"Tell me the truth, Sophie," he told her. "I need to know why you walked out."

She looked as though she was going to cry.

Lark had the overwhelming urge to open his arms to her, to fold her against him and hold her. He felt that was what she needed, but he wasn't sure *what* to do. Whether that was the right thing, what it would mean to her if he did it.

"Sometimes it's the truth that hurts the most," she said, her voice low.

Her face was tilted down, shoulders slumped slightly, but he wasn't having it. He did reach for her then, knew it was the right thing to do, drew her into his arms.

She hesitated for a beat, seemed unsure, before taking the final step toward him, falling against him. Tenderly at first, and then deeper into his embrace as he folded his arms around her.

Lark had thought he'd feel uncomfortable, holding her like that, but it seemed the most natural thing in the world. He let his lips fall to the top of her head, not kissing her but allowing them to sit there, inhaling the smell of her. Enjoying the feel of her slim, womanly body in his arms. Touching him, length to length.

He didn't want to ask, but he felt he had to. Needed to know, even if the answer wasn't the one he hoped it would be.

"Was it because of Lucy? The reason you walked out?" he said, the words low, lips hardly raised from her head.

Lark was holding his breath. He wanted the answer to be no, wished it to be.

She didn't say anything, only nodded.

His body stiffened, even though he tried hard to stop it from doing so. She hadn't said why, there was still so much left unsaid, but Lucy was his everything. He could compromise, he wasn't set in his ways, but Lucy was the one thing he'd never change. He would never compromise her happiness for the sake of anything. Maybe it was because she'd gone through something similar to his daughter. Or maybe it was something else.

Sophie didn't look up at him and didn't say anything else. She turned back to the stove, flicked the gas and stirred her egg mixture to pour into the pan.

Lark didn't know what to do, what to say, all over again. So he collected his plate and moved to sit at the table.

He could see she needed a moment to compose herself, and he was starving hungry. Maybe eating something would help him deal with whatever it was she was about to say.

It had been a long day, he was tired and he didn't want to say anything he would regret later. Not when she hadn't had a chance to explain herself.

He focused on his food, then changed his mind, unable to ignore the beautiful woman in his kitchen. While he ate he watched her, the way she moved, body elegant and fluid. Then she placed her own omelet on a plate and faced him again.

She was clearly unsure of what to do.

"Come and join me."

Sophie looked hesitant but she did as he'd suggested. She

walked slowly, put her plate down on the table and sat across from him.

"I hope you're good at board games," he said, trying to kill the tense atmosphere.

Sophie finished her mouthful then smiled, hesitantly. "You think we'll be stuck for a while?"

"Yeah, I'd say."

She went back to her food, eating each mouthful slowly, as though she didn't want to have to sit and talk, happy to do something to avoid chatting.

Just as he was about to get up, to go and look out the window or try to tune in the radio, Sophie put her knife and fork down.

She sighed. A deep, belly-filled exhale of breath that made him stop, compelled him to sit back in his seat.

"Lark, it's not because I don't like Lucy," she told him. "She's a gorgeous child and you should be proud of her. I had a great time with her the other day."

"But?" he asked, eyes trained on her.

"Why does there always have to be a *but,* right?"

Yeah. His life sometimes felt as if it had been changed by a series of *buts.*

"You've got your reasons, Sophie. You don't have to tell me."

She looked almost tearful. Clearly it was hard talking about whatever it was that was troubling her.

"I work with children every day," she explained. "Well, back in my usual life."

He nodded, happy to listen so long as she was comfortable talking.

"Before I decided to take a break, I had a hard time. I'm used to losing patients, it's part and parcel of the job, but a little girl I'd known for years as she came in and out of hospital, well, she died on my table."

Lark could see the genuine pain in her eyes, wished he didn't have to see how much talking about this hurt her. But at the same time he wanted to hear. Wanted to know her background, what troubled her, so he could understand her.

"Telling her parents, when they loved her so much and had fought for her for so long, was dreadful. I've done it so many times before, had to be the bearer of bad news, but this one hit me hard." She paused. "She was the same age as your Lucy."

Lark waited.

"She was four years old when I first met her as a perky little kid, and the last time I saw her she was a cancer-ridden seven-year-old."

"I'm so sorry, Sophie."

He should never have been so hard on her. So judgmental.

"Her name was Rose and I don't think I'll ever forget her."

Lark didn't know what to do, other than look away to give Sophie the privacy to brush away her tears.

He swallowed. Thought of how his own little girl had looked in that big hospital bed when he'd left her there earlier.

She was only in with a broken arm; he couldn't even imagine what it would be like to see her battle a serious illness. To have to have major surgery.

"And that's why you found it hard being with Lucy the other night?" he asked. "Being close to her like that?"

Sophie raised her eyes and her shoulders.

"It wasn't only that though, Lark."

He thought about walking around to her side of the table, reaching across to touch her, to comfort her, but he didn't. He didn't know what to do.

Now there was a waterfall of tears in her eyes that neither he nor she could ignore. Sophie wiped them away. Lark willed his heart to stop beating so hard from watching her pain.

"A long time ago—seven years—before I knew better, I terminated a pregnancy."

He didn't think she would continue, but after a deep breath, she did.

"I was able to forget about it for a long time, but after..."

Lark didn't know what to say. What to think. How to feel.

Sophie caught her breath.

"Everything just caught up to me, and suddenly those seven years seemed like seven weeks or seven days. It felt like only yesterday that I'd made that horrible decision. And if there is anything I could change about my life, it would be that. I'd give up everything else if it meant I could be a mother."

He wasn't going to judge her—decisions like that had to be made by women in difficult situations every day—but it was still hard to hear. Hard to know how to respond.

And he knew firsthand how rewarding it was to be a parent. A life without being a father, without Lucy, wasn't something he could even comprehend.

"In the last couple of years I've had some, ah, female health problems, and in the end I had to have a hysterectomy. A few months ago," she said, the words coming out so fast it almost sounded as if she was relieved to have told him. "I'll never, ever have the chance to be a parent, and I'll never forgive myself."

There was nothing he could say. She wasn't crying, although tears were still shining in her eyes. Emotion had leaked steadily through her voice, made her crack, but she was keeping herself together. In check.

And he felt heartless.

Not because he didn't feel for her now. But because of what he'd thought, what he'd *presumed* the other night. He'd lumped her into the same category as his ex-wife, thought that she was shallow and callous, when in fact she'd been battling something greater than he could ever have imagined.

"Sophie, I don't know what to say," he said, being as honest as he could.

She gave him a sad smile. "There's nothing you *can* say, Lark. That's the problem. There's nothing anyone can do. I'm living with a decision I made, and there were consequences I wasn't prepared for."

"But you can't blame yourself. You obviously had your reasons at the time."

She raised her eyes. "I was twenty-four years old, and the med student in me said that it was only a fetus. That it wasn't a *child* yet, and that it would be better off without me as a mother. That I shouldn't give up my own dreams or bring a child into the world without a father." She laughed, almost hysterically, to herself. "And now I have to live with that decision forever."

Lark stood up, walked around the table, placed a hand on her shoulder. She didn't shrug it away, but he had a feeling she wasn't ready to be comforted. That whatever she was feeling was hard enough to talk about, let alone to connect with someone else over.

"I wish I'd known, Sophie," he said, taking both their plates into the kitchen to give her some breathing space. "I'm so protective over Lucy sometimes that I don't think beyond my own needs."

She turned her chair around, facing him as he rinsed the dishes.

"What do you mean?"

He let the hot water run over the plates before he answered. He hadn't been this honest with another human being since... he couldn't remember when. But she'd opened up to him, talked about something that must have been difficult to get off her chest. He owed her the same. Or maybe he didn't *owe* her. He just felt it was the right time to say something, to be real with her, too.

"Back in California, I was on the rodeo circuit all season," he explained. "I would tour for months, I won plenty of championships, and I ended up with the classic trophy wife."

He watched her face, saw she seemed interested.

"I don't mean to put my ex down, at the time she was everything I'd dreamed of in a woman. Beautiful, outgoing and always the life of the party." He paused, trying not to get sucked back into the memories of their marriage becoming a train wreck. "We had Lucy, everything seemed perfect, and we had more money than we needed and a great lifestyle. But it wasn't until I had the fall that ended my career that the cracks in our marriage really became apparent."

Sophie stood up and walked back into the kitchen. She leaned against the counter, listening to him, making him feel better about talking. Knowing that she wanted to hear.

"What happened?"

Lark shut the dishwasher and braced his frame against the cabinetry.

"As soon as I wasn't famous, once all the attention about my injury died down, Kate became disinterested. Didn't care how heartbroken I was at giving up what I loved. She liked being the celebrity wife, and all I wanted was to settle down on a ranch and try to enjoy my retirement. Spend time with her and Lucy. I'd made more than enough money for us to be comfortable forever and just enjoy being a family."

"But she didn't want that?"

He tried not to sneer at the thought of Kate wanting anything like that.

"She liked to spend money and party with the right people," he told Sophie. "Lucy and I were suddenly a burden, and I filed for divorce. I was going to take her to court for joint custody, but she gave her daughter up like an unwanted puppy, and now she's already engaged to be married to some other poor guy."

"Lark, I'm so sorry. That's terrible."

He shook his head, perhaps too fiercely. Could feel the fire in his eyes. "No, it's life. I should never have married her. But you know what? If I hadn't, I wouldn't have Lucy, and she means everything to me."

He regretted the forcefulness of his words when he saw a flash of pain cross Sophie's face. Knew now that she'd do anything to have her own little Lucy.

"So I worry about her getting close to another person. I keep her away from harm's reach at all times and protect her, don't like the idea of anyone new coming into her life that could make her feel unsettled or hurt her."

Sophie sighed. "And I walked out on you, after you let me in."

"Yeah," he agreed, his voice low. "Yeah, you did. But she was so darn excited about the puppy I don't think she even realized how strange your exit was."

Sophie looked uncomfortable again, as though she wasn't sure what to do.

"Speaking of the puppy, where is he?"

She looked more relaxed, pleased the subject had changed. "He's with my mom for the day," she told him. "And speaking of that, I really should phone and tell her…"

A sudden noise startled Lark, followed by the lights in the house shutting off and the television shuddering to a halt.

The house was suddenly pitch-black, a deathly dark blanket descending upon the room, over the entire interior.

Heavens!

He felt a hand in his.

Sophie must have moved fast.

"What happened?" she whispered, her hand hovering against his forearm.

"Snow must have taken the power out," he said, trying to think logically about what he should do yet distracted by the soft touch of the woman beside him.

"Oh."

He laughed. "I guess that puts an end to the hot shower I was about to offer you."

Sophie tucked tighter against him as a soft bang echoed outside.

"What was that?"

He turned his body half toward her, letting his arm tuck against her back, drawing her slightly against him. He shouldn't have touched her, but she'd initiated it and now he couldn't help himself. Not the way he was feeling right now. Protective in a way, conscious of what she'd been through and how thoroughly she'd listened to him. The way they'd both opened up to one another.

"Everything's magnified because there's no noise inside now," he said. "It's just the weather raging outside."

"Do you have a generator?" she asked, not moving away even as he went to take a step.

It really was pitch-black. He could make out her outline but little else.

"No," he replied, pleased she couldn't see his grimace. It was something he'd meant to look into and had completely forgotten about. "But I do have flashlights and candles handy."

She leaned into him and followed him as he walked.

"Well, that's a start, I guess."

"At least we've eaten. Rustling up something cold might have been harder."

Sophie laughed, but didn't let go of him. It was comforting, having her near.

Lark was about to offer her a sweater, go upstairs and find warmer clothes for them both, but then… He didn't want to stop thinking about Lucy, to stop worrying about her, but was it so bad that he also wanted to think about Sophie? That he wanted to show her that she meant something to him? That she didn't have to be miserable, suffering because of her decisions forever.

"There is another way we could get warm without power."

"How?"

"Our outdoor bath."

He tried not to laugh as her hold on him turned to a grip for a second. Then she let go.

Even if she turned him down, at least he'd taken her mind off the power outage. And his mind off the fact that he'd had to leave his little girl for the night, and there was nothing he could do about it until morning.

"An outdoor bath?" Sophie didn't know what to say.

If tonight could get any stranger, it just had.

She'd never talked to anyone as candidly as she had to Lark. Didn't know how that emotion, those feelings, had spiraled from her mouth as though she'd been holding them close, desperate to spill them.

"It's on the edge of the garden, over the fence in the field," he told her, still standing near even though she'd let go. "I can light the fire and have it steaming-hot pretty quick."

She hoped Lark couldn't hear the way her heart was thudding. Sophie tried to play it cool, not wanting to let on that she was terrified of being alone with him, in the dark, outside. Let alone in a bath.

"You can light it even in the snow?"

Lark's hand found hers, his skin connecting to hers.

"I have a small propane tank out there. One flick of the switch and the fire beneath the bath ignites."

She could imagine how nice it would be. The cool air surrounding them, snow falling and a steaming-hot bath out in the open. It sounded…idyllic. And it would take her mind off everything that was troubling her.

But was she brave enough?

"I don't think I'm up for skinny-dipping." *Ever.*

Lark laughed, but not in a way that belittled her or made fun of her. She relaxed before he even answered.

"Well, I don't think you'll fit anything of Lucy's, and I don't have any women's bathing suits in my wardrobe, but I'm thinking you could either get in before me so I can't see anything, or you could wear your underwear."

She blushed. Even in the dark, she could feel the heat in her cheeks and was pleased he couldn't see her face.

"You won't leave me out there in the pitch-black, or try to scare me, will you?"

"Scared of the dark?" he asked.

She laughed. It sounded scaredy-cat even to her ears. Like a high-pitched bell being tinkled.

"A little."

Then he moved his fingers and she realized they were still palm to palm.

She hated that it felt so good, that she didn't want him to let go.

Hated and loved it at the same time.

"So what do you say?"

She was about to say no, but something made her say otherwise. Something compelled her to disagree with the rational part of her brain.

"Okay."

"Okay?" he questioned her.

"Just don't let go of my hand."

He didn't reply, simply held her hand more firmly, fingers linking with her own.

"Let's get the flashlights and go."

Sophie leaned against the fence post, chanting inside her own head. He'd left her. But then he hadn't really had a choice and she didn't want to go marching off after him. He'd wanted to quickly check on the stabled horses, and she was left watching the water slowly heat up.

The snow was still falling, only lightly now, but still it left a blanket of white in its wake. She'd heard the odd whinny of a horse from the stables, had listened to something rustle far too close and was now shivering, even though she was tucked up in Lark's big jacket.

"Just me," he called.

She shone the light toward his voice, jumping as something rustled nearby.

"I'm not thinking this was such a great idea."

He chuckled and reached for her.

They stood there, close but not touching. She wished they were. His body against hers made her feel that nothing could happen to her, that she'd be safe.

It was a feeling she wasn't used to, not having ever let a man close enough before. She'd always been so determined to be independent and stand on her own two feet.

Right now though, there was something nice about feeling she could depend on Lark, even if it was just for the evening.

He bent down—she could see because she kept the light trained on him—checking the fire. It glowed red with a bluish tinge, more magical when she flicked off the light and watched it in the dark. The big old cast-iron bath was near a water trough, a freshwater pipe feeding into it.

"I'll leave it going on low, but it should be warm enough to get in," he told her.

She kept watching, nervous all over again about getting in, even if she did have to admit that there was something special about a hot bath in the snow.

"Where do we put our clothes?"

"I'll turn around while you strip off, then stow your things in the tree here." He turned his own flashlight on and showed her the hidden cubby within the tree. "Promise I won't look."

She felt to make sure the water was hot enough, then took off her clothes and tapped Lark on the shoulder, passing them to him. She slipped into the piping-hot water, not caring whether it might be too warm for fear of him seeing her. She was still wearing her bra and panties, but she didn't want him shining the light her way and getting an eyeful.

She should have turned her own head away once he'd put her clothes in the tree, but she didn't. Instead, Sophie slid deep into the bath, savoring the hot water on her skin in contrast to the icy air still hitting her cheeks.

And she watched.

Even in the dark her eyes had started to adjust, so while she couldn't see a lot, she could make out Lark's outline. The silhouette of his body, the height of him.

She wondered for a moment if he'd go bare, but looked away before she could find out.

She shouldn't even be thinking like that, no matter how tempting he was. Even if she had explained herself to him, drained herself emotionally by telling him what she'd done in her past, it still didn't mean anything could happen between them.

"I would have lit candles but I doubt they'd last a minute."

Sophie turned back toward his voice, breath catching in her throat as she looked at him standing before her.

Candles she did not need. In fact, nothing else could make this feel even more romantic than it already did.

He eased himself into the water. She could make out his smile as he leaned back opposite her. Their legs touched, brushed, but there was no room to move away so she left hers still, even though they quivered against his in the hot water, made her feel flushed all over, her skin heating even more than it was already.

Lark was watching her—she could feel his eyes on her before she could make them out.

"I told you it was good out here."

Yeah, it was definitely good. "So strange having such a warm body and such a cold face."

They sat there, motionless and silent. Sophie didn't know where to look or what to say. In a way it felt too intimate being here with Lark. And on the other hand, it seemed absolutely right.

Fingers brushed hers. The gentlest of touches.

It almost took her breath away.

Lark was still watching her, waiting for her to react. She didn't do anything, *couldn't,* to start with. But then she wiggled one finger back, then another.

He took her palm, lightly, tugging her toward him.

"Sophie."

The word was only a whisper, but she couldn't ignore it. It was the only word said against a background of dead silence, of wilderness surrounding them.

Somehow she let him draw her closer. As far forward as he could move her within the confines of the bath.

"Turn around," he ordered, voice low.

She wriggled, shoulders coming out of the water, conscious that he might see her wet lace bra.

He pulled her back toward him, so her body was cupped against his. Lark didn't touch her with his hands now, instead he let his arms rest on the rim of the bath, but his legs were on either side of hers, and her back was against his torso.

She knew what he was doing. He was waiting for her to make a move, for her to decide whether she was relaxed enough, ready to be that intimate.

She wasn't, but she did it anyway. Pressed back into him, her skin against his beneath the water, letting her head fall back, to nestle into the space against his chest and beneath his collarbone.

Sophie had sunk lower in the water, and it made her fit against him just right.

They still hadn't said anything to one another, but the silence felt comfortable. As if it would be wrong to break the moment, the feeling that a spell had been cast over them, by saying anything.

Lark's arms slowly moved from the edge of the bath, his hands sliding into the water and landing on her thighs. Gently, so gently. One moved up her torso, landing on her stomach, the other stayed on her leg.

Sophie leaned back farther into him, her head on the side. And then Lark's lips found her skin. His mouth touched her neck, the side of it that was above the water.

A shudder traced through every inch of her body, but she was powerless to move away. Didn't want him to stop.

Ever.

His lips caressed her skin, softly worked their way down her neck and over her shoulder. His fingers were now gliding against her, tickling and teasing her.

"Lark," she said, not knowing why but feeling she had to slow things down.

"Mmm," he murmured against her skin.

"Lark, I think…"

"Don't think," he whispered.

She pulled away, enough so that his mouth fell away from her.

"Are you sure? I mean, you've just come out of a marriage, I've got, well…"

"Sophie?"

She sighed. "Yes."

"Shut up and kiss me."

She gulped. "But…"

Lark wasn't standing for her chatter, for her trying to distract him with her reasons why they shouldn't.

He turned her again in the bath, made her face him this time, moving forward so that her legs could wrap around his torso.

Sophie felt that they were moving too fast, becoming too intimate, even though she wanted it so badly. He held her there before doing anything, arms looped about her, holding her, making her feel secure.

And then he leaned forward, bent his head, took her lips so softly that they were barely touching.

All reason, all argument, fled her mind. She lost herself to the way he felt pressed to her, the hardness of his body in contrast to the silky caress of the water.

Her shoulders were bare, exposed to the cold around them, but she didn't care. Couldn't feel anything other than Lark's lips on hers, especially as they became more insistent, more urgent.

He pulled away only enough to whisper, "Any more arguments?"

Sophie shook her head. It was the only response she was capable of.

"Good."

This time Lark dropped a single kiss to her lips before working his way down her neck, tracing her collarbone, lips dipping almost into the water before moving up the other side of her neck. Then back to her lips, taking her mouth in a kiss that left her feeling drained, incapable of anything other than moving her mouth in time against his.

If he didn't have such a tight hold on her, she might have slipped beneath the water.

Instead, she lost herself to his touch and started to explore. Felt the hard muscles of his back, the strength of his broad shoulders. Reveled in how male and masculine he felt.

"What do you say we head inside?" he asked her, lips whispering across her skin.

She shook her head, suddenly feeling braver than she had earlier.

"No."

"No?"

She pushed him back against the edge of the bath, hands to his chest, moving her legs so she was straddling him, knees planted on either side of him in the deep bath.

CHAPTER FOURTEEN

LARK almost slipped beneath the water he was so surprised. He looked up at Sophie above him, her eyes a level higher than his as she sat on top of him. Her arms were draped across his shoulders, her thighs against his, wrapped around the outside of his legs.

He let out a deep, shuddering breath.

Wow.

When he'd suggested a bath, he hadn't let his mind wander this far. Or at least not *this* far.

He'd kissed her thinking he was pushing his luck, thinking she'd probably shove him away. But there was something about being out here in the dark, with the freezing-cold weather surrounding them, tucked in their own little slice of warm heaven…

This was what he wanted—to keep his mind on Sophie and nothing else. He didn't want to think about his little girl when there was nothing he could do to help her. But this, this was what he wanted.

What he wanted right now was Sophie.

He let her push his head back with one hand, didn't resist as she took control and kissed him. As she set the pace.

Even if he'd wanted to he couldn't have stopped her. Her body fit so snugly to his, her breasts—covered by her soaking-wet bra—skimming against his chest.

"Lark, I'm sorry for walking out on you the other night," she whispered into his neck.

The other night? He couldn't have cared less. He just wanted her lips on his again. Her lips anywhere so long as they were touching *him* somewhere.

He didn't want to be a bad father, would have walked away from even *this* if he'd been able to be at the hospital, but he didn't want to feel guilty for being with Sophie. Not when there was nothing he could do for Lucy until morning.

"You're forgiven," he told her, realizing she was waiting for him to answer.

She took up on his mouth again, before pressing light, feathery kisses to his forehead, then his eyelids, then his nose.

He groaned deep in his throat, wanting to stay submissive beneath her yet finding it so hard. He was desperate to grab her and pin her down with his weight. To explore her body, to touch her, rather than let her have her wicked way with him.

They both had their underwear on, but he couldn't imagine feeling closer to her. It was as if they were bare, skin to skin, their bodies made to fit.

"Kiss me," she ordered, hovering her mouth above his once more.

He didn't need to be asked twice. Lark pushed his arms from the water, taking hold of her face, one hand tangled in her hair, tugging her forward. She landed harder against his chest, her entire body over his, as he took control of her mouth and kissed her over and over again until they were both breathless.

"Sophie," he managed to croak, pulling away from her to speak.

She looked up at him with lazy eyes, a hooded expression on her face. His eyes had adjusted enough now to see well, and he enjoyed her happy, lazy expression.

"Yeah?" she mumbled.

"I think we should go inside."

He didn't say what he wanted. That it was time to drag her to his bed. But she knew what he meant.

He watched as her eyes widened, then softened.

"Okay."

Lark gave her a gentle kiss, rubbing his lips softly against hers, before lifting her and pushing her to the other end of the bath. He got out, ignoring the freezing blast of cold on his hot, wet feet, and raced to the nearby tree. It was only a few feet away but the cold was almost unbearable. He slipped his feet into his boots, grabbed one of the oversize towels he'd brought out, and tucked another towel and her shoes beneath his arm.

He passed them to her, turning his back as she wrapped herself, giving her a moment to emerge from the water as he retrieved their clothes then turned off the gas.

Sophie was wrapped tightly in the towel, and he flicked on his flashlight to light the way.

"Quick, before you get frostbite."

She didn't need any encouragement, trotting along quickly beside him.

Lark moved fast too, but not from the cold. He couldn't have cared if the temperature dropped even lower. All he wanted was to get her inside and pay her back for all that teasing in the bath.

Sophie's entire body was shaking. Her teeth were chattering, the tiny hairs on her arms standing on end, her face burning from the sting of icy air.

She hurried inside when Lark opened the door for her, rushing into the living room after she kicked off her shoes and making for the fire.

It was still burning, embers glowing red, but it needed attention to get it roaring back to life again.

Lark was by her side within an instant, towel now secured around his middle, bending to throw more logs on. She admired his muscular frame as he moved, drinking in the sight of his tanned, golden skin. The pull and release of his shoulder and bicep muscles.

She looked away before he could turn and catch her.

"Are you still cold?" he asked, finished with tending the fire.

Sophie shook her head. The light from the fire made them visible to one another, but the way the fire started to lick up the fresh timber made shadows dance.

He stood up anyway, reaching for the thick throw at the end of the sofa and putting it beside her.

"Here, this will keep you warm."

His voice was low, deep and sexy. She doubted she'd ever tire of that almost-lazy cowboy drawl.

Sophie shuffled closer to him. To wrap herself in the throw would mean ditching the damp towel, and she wasn't sure if she was ready to do that.

She gasped as Lark took charge, moving on his knees toward her and slowly slipping the towel from her shoulders, exposing them, before forcing the towel down lower until it was sitting at her waist.

Then he took hold of her body, hands on her bare skin, and pressed her gently down onto the throw.

Sophie let him, nervous, but at the same time exhilarated. Wanting his hands on her, desperate for his touch.

She forgot about her soaking-wet underwear and relaxed beneath his touch. Lark took her hands and pinned them above her head in his one big hand, the other resting on her belly, where his lips soon followed. He traced a path up her skin, skimming across her breasts as they rose and fell in rapid succession, inching his way up her chest and neck, until his body covered hers and he kissed her full on the mouth.

"I'm starting to like power-outs," he whispered.

Sophie sighed, lost to his touch. "Me, too," she said back.

Lark feathered his kisses across her face, down her shoulder and arm, stopping at her wrist.

"I want you, Sophie."

She mumbled something even *she* couldn't understand, not sure what to say to him.

"Just say yes," he whispered against her skin.

"Yes," she said on a bubble of air, exhaling deeply.

Lark refocused on her mouth, kissing away any doubt she might have felt. His fingers skimmed her bra strap before slowly slipping it away.

Sophie sighed. Again.

For a girl who was usually scared of the dark, she was coping remarkably well.

Tomorrow, they could deal with reality—the fact that they were both worried about Lucy, going back to the hospital.

But tonight? Tonight she wasn't going to feel guilty about being pleasured in a way she'd never experienced before.

CHAPTER FIFTEEN

Sophie woke to something tickling her face and the hard frame of a man pressed tightly against her back.

She opened one eye to peek and saw that it was only the faux-fur throw that was touching her cheek before shutting both eyes tight again and willing herself to go back to sleep.

There was time to panic later. Right now, she wanted to enjoy the feel of Lark against her, the way his still-naked body felt against hers, the warmth of his skin, the strength of his arm curled around her protectively even in slumber.

Last night had been…she didn't even know how to explain it. One moment they'd been talking over dinner, discussing things she'd never talked about with anyone, and then they were bare and making love in front of the fire.

Wow.

Sophie turned, knowing sleep wouldn't find her again, not now she was awake and analyzing the night before. She wriggled slowly, turning to face Lark, his arm still around her.

She watched him sleep. The way his lips were parted, dark lashes touching his cheeks. His hair was messy and disheveled, stubble lined his jaw. Her fingers itched to touch, to run along his face and tug through his hair. But she stayed as still as possible, not wanting the moment to end. Or a new moment to begin.

"You're staring."

She jumped in his arms. "Lark!"

His eyes opened in a lazy kind of way. "I could feel you watching me."

She tucked against him, face to his chest, not wanting to brave his eyes yet. "You scared me."

He chuckled, clearing his throat and removing his arm from around her to rub his eyes.

Sophie felt bare all of a sudden. Cold from not having his skin against hers, she wished she could tuck her body against his and snuggle for the rest of the day. Forget everything and stay here with Lark.

She sighed. If only.

"You sound like you've got the world resting on your shoulders."

Sophie wriggled against him again, pleased when he opened his arms back up and enveloped her. "I was thinking that it would be so much easier if we could stay like this for at least today."

"Agreed, if I didn't have horses to feed." He grinned. "And then a little girl to retrieve."

She nodded, refusing to think about anything other than Lark right now. She pressed her lips to his chest, not meaning to tease him but realizing she was by his groan.

"And just like that I've forgotten all about the horses."

Sophie pulled away so that her chest left his. "Don't let me make your animals go hungry."

He tugged her back, his lips finding hers, locking their mouths. She happily gave in to his kiss, enjoying the relaxing way he touched her, how comfortable she felt with him.

A knock echoed out loud and clear through the house.

"Please tell me that wasn't someone knocking at the door."

Lark kissed her one last time before sitting up.

"Who on earth would be here in the snow at this time of morning?" he asked.

Sophie grabbed the blanket and wrapped it around herself, shyly watching as Lark stood up, naked, to search for his clothes.

"Lucky we had the fire going all night—everything's pretty dry."

She averted her eyes as he bent to pull on his things.

"Shall I stay here?"

He nodded and moved down the hall, still doing up his jeans.

"Wrap up and stay here," he called over his shoulder.

She did as he said, suddenly very self-conscious about the fact she was sitting with nothing other than a blanket around her. Her clothes were strewn around the room, but she wasn't brave enough to attempt to get dressed in case the person at the door saw her.

Muffled voices echoed down the hall, but she couldn't hear what was being said. Only that it was another man.

Lark appeared within minutes, looking handsome as ever.

"Local farmer," he said, bracing himself in the doorway. "He's clearing snow away from driveways with his tractor, but he said the road's pretty dangerous from here into town still. They're advising everyone to stay home."

"Lucy," she said, yesterday's events playing back through her head. "Will you manage to get to her?"

Lark looked distant, as though he was focused on something other than her or the conversation they were having. "Yeah, I'll get there. Might take me a while but if I can't drive I'll ride a horse in and bring her home."

Sophie knew she'd lost him now. There was no chance of snuggling back up under the blanket and forgetting the day away.

"So you're going out to feed your horses?"

"Yeah," he said, looking back at her and crossing the room, his eyes searching hers out as though he'd been momentarily distracted and was now connected again. "Want to come?"

She smiled up at him, pleased to be included. "Can we drink coffee first?"

He bent to kiss her before retrieving her clothes and putting them beside her. "I'll make an exception this once," he told her. "You get dressed. I'll find a warm coat for you and get coffee started."

Sounded good to her.

Lark's head was full of too many thoughts. He was stressing about Lucy being at the hospital for so long, guilty about the night he'd spent while she'd been alone. But he would never have left her if he'd been allowed to stay, and it was still too early for her to be discharged. It wasn't that he wanted to leave Sophie— heavens only knew he'd stay curled up with her in his arms for days on end if he could—but he had to bring Lucy home. She'd hate being there alone, wondering where he was. He already felt guilty enough about leaving her there for the night.

And he had to do the rounds outside, check that the horses had fared okay through the night and give them all more hay.

He turned from pouring coffee as Sophie cleared her throat behind him. She looked beautiful, as she always did, but the gentle flush in her cheeks and the shine in her eyes made his heart race even more than usual.

Last night had been…incredible. Completely unexpected.

He dropped the spoon into the cup he'd been about to stir and walked toward her, stopping only when he reached her to press a kiss to her forehead, then her lips. He drew her into his body, wrapping his arms around her.

"Hey," he said.

She nestled tighter into him.

"I'm sorry we couldn't stay like that for longer."

He felt her nod against him. "Me, too," she mumbled.

"Promise I'll make it up to you, okay?"

He didn't know how, but he was sure there were plenty of ways he could.

"Coffee?"

Sophie stepped back. "White, one sugar."

He squeezed her hand before going back to pour her a cup. "Coming right up."

* * *

They walked their coffees out the back door with them, sipping at the piping-hot liquid as they strolled.

"At least it's not snowing anymore."

Lark led the way, walking a step ahead of her. "You sure you're warm enough?"

"I'm fine, stop worrying about me."

He walked into the stable before her and she couldn't help but laugh at the neighing that ensued when he called out "Good morning."

"They know who Dad is, right?"

He glanced back over his shoulder, grinning. "Sure do."

Lark marched down toward the first stall, stopping to talk to the horse she recognized from the other day, Cougar. Then he moved on, calling out as he went and emerging from an open stall with an armful of hay. She stood and watched as he went back and forth between the stalls, each time with hay.

"You all right waiting while I muck out their stables?"

She spied a large empty bucket, upturned it and sat down. "Sure am."

Sophie finished her coffee as she watched him work and listened to him talk to the horses.

"Do you think they know what you're saying?" she called out.

Lark's head appeared over the door. "Maybe not, but they're very good at pretending."

She thought of her own animal then, the little puppy. Sam, as Lucy had named him.

Just being here with Lark made her think about giving him the dog all over again.

"You know the puppy?" she asked.

"Yeah," Lark called out.

"Were you serious about getting a dog for Lucy?"

He appeared again, this time pushing a barrow full of sawdust and horse manure. "Why, you thinking of giving yours away for sure?"

Lark stood, leaning against the stable door and stroking his horse when he stuck his head out to see what was going on.

"I am actually."

"Why? He seemed like a nice pup."

"He is, but I can't offer him the sort of life that you and Lucy can," she explained. "If he stays with me, I have to take him back to the city with me when I go back, and I work such long hours. It's not really fair."

A darkness crossed Lark's face, made his eyes change, but he didn't say anything. He just stood, watching her as though he was waiting for her to say something else.

"So what do you say?" she asked.

He shrugged. "I'd say that the last thing I need is something else to look after right now, but Lucy is desperate and we probably both know that I'm inclined to say yes to her. Over something like this, anyway."

She was sad at the thought of giving Sam up, but thinking about the way the dog had played with Lark's daughter and the farm he'd have to run around on, told her it was the right thing.

"So you'll take him?"

He walked back down the row of stalls and went into another, calling out as he moved. "If you're absolutely sure, but I think you should take your time. You know, deciding."

She stood up and followed. "I've had enough time to think about it."

She watched him move around the stall, careful not to disturb the horse as he worked. It didn't take him long.

"You want to know what I think?" he asked.

Maybe. Maybe not.

But she was curious about what he was going to say.

"Shoot."

He pushed out the barrow again. "I think, from what you told me last night, that you're not sure about anything right now. Am I right?"

Sophie bit down on her lower lip. What she wasn't sure

about was having this conversation with him, or with anyone for that matter.

"I think you're unhappy with your life in general, and you're at a crossroads of sorts. Like I was," he said. "You don't really want to go back to your job, but you feel you have to, and you're not happy here, either. You don't feel like you fit in anywhere right now, and your guilt is eating at you from the inside."

She swallowed, more than once, trying to ignore what he was saying. Her eyes were starting to burn as if she was about to cry, but she wouldn't let herself. She was too strong to break down like that in front of him.

"So am I right?"

She wasn't going to admit that he was anything close to right, even if he was.

"What is it you suggest I do, then, since you claim to know me so well?" she asked, hearing the frostiness of her own voice.

He looked hesitant, uncertain about the blunt way she'd replied.

"I was wondering if maybe you want to be back here, at home in Queenstown, but you don't know what you'd do here. Don't want to give up the life and job you've worked so hard for," he said. "Maybe you should open up a practice here, explore another field as a doctor."

"Give up surgery?" she asked, incredulous.

Lark let his shoulders rise then fall. She wanted to curse at him, yell at him and tell him to mind his own bloody business. But she didn't want to show him that he'd hit a nerve, or have an argument. Not when he was so close to the truth.

The thing was, it had crossed her mind, but she wasn't ever going to give up surgery. Couldn't. She owed it to herself not to, and she sure wasn't going to do it because a man suggested it.

But at the same time, spending time with Lucy had made her think that maybe she couldn't *not* have children in her life. As hard as it was, she'd be lost without the smiling little faces she'd become so accustomed to seeing each day in her job. To the good she could do.

Even if there was pain to deal with, baggage that came with what she'd been through and what had happened to her in the past.

"You know what? What do I know," Lark said, surprising her, reaching out to touch her arm before moving off to finish his work. "All I can say is that it would be nice if you were around, you know, permanently."

She went back to sit on the bucket.

Him wanting her around was exactly what she'd been afraid of.

Lark rode down the snow-covered road at a slow, steady walk. If he'd waited another few hours, he might have been able to use the car, but he doubted it. And the local farmer might have come back for him, but he didn't have time to wait around. He'd waved goodbye to Sophie, saddled up Cougar and headed for town.

The horse had a blanket folded over his rump to keep him warm, and he had extra-warm clothes for Lucy tucked in a bag. They'd make a sight arriving at the hospital, but he didn't care. He wanted his girl up in the saddle in front of him, then tucked up in her own bed.

Then he'd be happy.

Make that, he was already happy. This was simply the final piece of the puzzle.

He couldn't believe how wrong he'd been, judging Sophie like that. She was exactly the kind of woman he'd originally thought her to be. More deeply troubled than he could have imagined, but still genuine. Kind.

The type of woman he wished he'd met years ago.

He'd never believed for a moment that he could find a woman he might one day want to bring into Lucy's life permanently. And now maybe he had.

The only problem was that she'd be leaving.

He wished she'd decide to stay, but it seemed unlikely. Although he wasn't averse to seeing how things worked out long-distance before they figured something out…

Lark stopped himself. That was getting *way* ahead.

They'd only just spent the night together. Only known each other how long? He needed to slow things down, remember what his priorities were. Take this nice and steady.

So why was he feeling that he'd finally met his soul mate and had to do anything to make the relationship work?

She was on the verge of hyperventilating.

Sophie paced back and forth, eyes on the window, feeling trapped. She needed to get out of here. Didn't want to be here still when Lark returned, even though she'd kissed him good-bye and told him she'd wait.

Last night had been incredible, magical, but she was starting to panic. She needed space, because suddenly she could see her life before her, see the mistakes she'd already made and the ones she could so easily make now—if she didn't do the right thing.

Her own mother had given everything up for a man, and it was something Sophie had always said she wouldn't do. She'd never give up her dreams for a man. Or for anyone else for that matter.

And it wasn't that Lark had asked her to do it for him, but she knew he wanted her to stay. He'd said as much. Suggested she give up her life, walk away from what she'd worked so hard to achieve to move back here.

At least her mother had had a family. She had given up her own dreams of becoming a veterinary surgeon, had married young, then had children. But that was the missing piece of the puzzle for Sophie.

If she gave everything up for a man, she still couldn't have a family of her own. Would Lark really want her in his life, long-term, as anything more than a fling, if she couldn't have his children when he clearly loved being a dad so much?

When her father had walked out on her mother, at least her mother had had *something*. She could hold her head high, and no matter what, she could look at her children and be proud of her role as a mother.

Sophie only had her career. It was too important to her to give it up.

So why was she thinking that what Lark had suggested wasn't so ridiculous after all?

And why was she thinking that having a child like Lucy in her life might make up for not being able to love a child of her own?

A noise made her look up, stop pacing.

The farmer was back.

She ran to the door and threw it open. "Hi."

He tipped his hat and climbed down from the tractor cab. "You still okay here?" he called out.

She smiled and walked out. "You're not heading near town, are you?"

He gave her a wink. "Close enough. I can give you a ride most of the way."

Sophie smiled and gave him a thumbs-up before running back inside, grabbing a pair of wellies and closing the door behind her.

She knew Lark would be upset to find her gone, but she had to go. She couldn't stay here and feel suffocated any longer.

She had to go.

Sophie hated that she was always running from Lark, but she couldn't stop herself.

She couldn't torture herself by thinking that she could ever mean anything to Lucy. Not as more than a fun babysitter.

She would never be her mother, just like she'd never be a mother to her own children.

There was no point pretending otherwise and breaking her heart all over again in the process.

CHAPTER SIXTEEN

Lark opened the door and carried Lucy inside.

"I can walk," Lucy said, giggling as he held her tighter.

"You might be able to walk but I want to carry you."

Even if it did hurt his back a touch, he didn't care.

She wriggled, but not hard. If he'd really believed she wanted to be put down he would have done so, but she seemed pretty happy tucked in his arms.

He was about to call out, to see where Sophie was, but something felt off to him. He'd been gone for a few hours—surely she would have been waiting for them, listening out. And he couldn't hear any noise in the house.

The silence annoyed him.

He'd expected to come home to a woman in his house. To a smile and a kiss, to open arms even, and instead all he was hearing was silence.

Anger started to gnaw its way through his gut, but he forced it away. He had Lucy back home and that was what mattered right now.

"Can I go to my room?"

He dropped her gently to her feet. "Sure thing, kiddo. You hungry?"

"Nah," she said, bouncing off down the hallway.

"Careful of that arm!"

She ignored him, or pretended to anyway.

"I'm going to go put Cougar back in his stable. I'll be back in soon, okay?"

"Yep!" she hollered back.

He went to the back door, pulled on his boots and went to retrieve the horse he'd left tethered to the post.

Lark didn't have to look around to know Sophie wasn't here. There was no sign of her and he could just *feel* that she'd gone.

He wanted to give her the benefit of the doubt, but after she'd run out on him last time? He had a feeling the same thing had happened again.

Lark forced himself to smile as he approached his horse, not wanting the animal to think he was angry with him.

Inside he simmered with a rage that was hard to ignore, a burning flare of pain that told him what an idiot he'd been.

He'd given her a second chance, acknowledged that he'd been wrong to judge her when she'd fled the other night. But if she'd run out on him again, he didn't know if he could be quite so forgiving. He was starting to see a pattern and he didn't like it.

Even if she had been through hell and back recently, there was no excuse for walking out like that.

Lark led the horse to the stable, wanting to get the job over with so he could pummel his fist into something and curse before joining his daughter back inside.

He'd thought last night had meant something. That even though Sophie might not be hanging around for good, that they had something. Something real. Something he had doubted he'd ever find.

Something he hadn't even known he'd been yearning for.

How wrong he'd been.

"Sam!"

Sophie called out to the puppy, trying her hardest to sound perky. It wasn't easy, but she'd learned enough since she'd been helping at the shelter to know that dogs responded best to upbeat and happy.

"Come. Sam, *come*," she commanded.

The puppy continued to run laps around her, tongue and ears flapping in the wind.

Sophie was starting to realize that she wasn't particularly skilled in the art of animal-training.

She winced as her phone rang again. She checked the caller identification.

Lark.

Again.

He'd already called once before, and she'd ignored it. And she was about to do the same again. She couldn't face talking to him. Didn't know what to say.

She wished she hadn't run out, yet she knew it had been the only option she had.

Except for maybe staying to confront him. Admitting that the night before had probably been a mistake. Telling him that she wasn't prepared to change her life for him. Or for any man.

Sophie groaned and dropped to the ground, lying flat-out on the still-damp grass. She no longer cared.

"Argh!"

She raised her hands to shield her face as a pink tongue swept back and forth across her skin.

"Sam!"

She managed to push herself up into a sitting position, the puppy clambering all over her and trying to sit on her knee.

"So that's all I had to do to get you to come, huh?"

The dog wagged his tail some more and tried to lick her face again.

"I do love you, mister, but I still think you'd be better off on a farm."

He cocked his head to the side, looking at her with what she could only imagine was a curious expression on his face.

"I know, all you want to do is play, right?"

Sophie reached for her phone, switched it off, then got up to find the ball they'd been playing with earlier.

Anything to take her mind off the man she couldn't stop moping over.

Lark dropped Lucy off at school and started the drive back to the farm. He'd almost kept her home, but she'd put her hand on her hip and told him it was only a broken arm, and he'd had to agree.

He couldn't shield her from everything, not forever. Even if that did mean she was going to gather some bumps and bruises, be hurt every now and again. She was a kid, and he had to deal with it.

He gripped the wheel a little tighter as he thought about what else he wasn't dealing with particularly well.

Sophie.

She was driving him mad. Or it was more that her absence was driving him mad.

It had been two days since the snowstorm. Two long days since she'd walked out on him. Again.

He'd called her a few times, trying to ignore his anger and telling himself that he was only attempting to make contact to check she was all right. That she'd gotten home okay.

Then he'd called her the last time wanting to give her a piece of his mind.

He was pleased she hadn't answered *that* call.

But each time he'd tried then failed to get hold of her, he'd known she was avoiding him. That she didn't want to hear from him. And although he hated to admit it, knowing she had run out on him hurt.

Like hell.

Lark pulled up the driveway, traveling slowly, and drove his truck around the side so he could unload some supplies into the barn.

He looked up as he hefted a sack of grain, eyes skimming the old bath on the edge of the field.

Lark looked away.

But then he saw the rescue horses he'd been caring for.

And he realized what he had to do.

If he wanted an explanation, wanted to talk to her and find out what the hell had happened and what was going on, he only had to use the horses as a ploy.

She cared too much not to come if she thought something had happened to them. If she thought something was wrong.

It might be a dirty trick, but then her running out on him hadn't been exactly aboveboard, either.

He picked up his mobile and called the animal shelter.

Two could play at this game.

The last thing Sophie wanted was to explain to her work colleagues why she was avoiding Lark.

"So you need me to go now?"

Elisabeth frowned slightly, as though she didn't mean to but couldn't help it.

"I can go myself if it's a problem," she said. "It's up to you, but Mr. Anderson did sound rather concerned."

Sophie wasn't sure what to do. On the one hand she had every right to refuse. She was only volunteering, whereas Elisabeth was a paid employee.

She dug her nails into the soft skin of her arm.

Now she was starting to be a complete bitch just thinking like that. She was the one who'd offered to volunteer here. If she had to face up to Lark, then face up she would.

"Sophie?"

She shook herself out of her mood. "Of course, I'm sorry," she said. "I've just got a lot on my mind, not concentrating properly."

"Only if you're sure?"

She gave Elisabeth a beamer of a smile and collected her

bag. "I'm fine, honestly. I'll give you a call later and let you know what the situation is."

Sophie didn't even let herself think about where she was going or what she was going to have to confront. The horses were the priority here. Her personal issues with Lark were irrelevant—she simply had to remain professional and hold her head high.

Even if she did still feel guilty about what she'd done.

Again.

Lark had no idea why he was so tied up in knots over Sophie, why she had gotten under his skin and wouldn't go away. No matter how much he'd tried to tell himself over the past few days that she wasn't right for him, that he wasn't ready for a new, serious relationship, he knew it was a lie.

She had some explaining to do, sure. But there was something special between them. Something he couldn't ignore no matter how furious she made him, and he wanted to know the real her. Know why she'd run out on him, *again*.

He ran his fingers over the timber fence, waiting for her to arrive.

What he wanted right now was to hear her out—if she was prepared to talk.

Maybe he was thinking too deeply into the situation. Maybe she just wasn't interested and had run because she regretted the night they'd spent together.

But then maybe she felt the same way he did.

A man could only hope.

CHAPTER SEVENTEEN

As she walked toward Lark, Sophie felt as if there was a troop of butterflies in her stomach, all caught in a cage and trying to escape. Her palms were sweaty, her mouth was dry and all she wanted to do was run.

But this time she wasn't going to. Wouldn't. Because she'd come here as a professional, to do a job, and she owed it to Lark to face up to him. Ignoring his calls had been gutless, even if she hadn't known what to say to him.

She was here now and she was going to act like the grown-up, professional woman that she was.

Sophie made herself smile as she approached him. He was leaning against the post-and-rail fencing, one foot hitched behind him, elbows resting.

As though he didn't have a care in the world.

Except, the glint in his eyes told her otherwise.

"Hi," she called.

Lark raised his head slightly, looking straight at her. "Hi."

She rubbed one hand over her jeans—nervous—and the other gripped her notepad tightly.

"I was told you had a problem here? That something was wrong with one of the…"

Lark stood up straight and walked toward her.

"You won't be needing this," he said, removing the pad from her hand and tucking it into his back pocket.

What? "Lark, the horses? I…"

"This way."

He pressed a hand to the small of her back and forced her to walk forward.

"I really don't have time for this," she grumbled, wondering what he was up to.

"Make time," he said, his voice telling her he was deadly serious about whatever it was he was up to.

She didn't argue with him. Didn't have the strength to.

Or maybe she didn't want to.

"Can you at least tell me what we're doing?"

He pointed toward the stable block. She squinted, straining to see inside.

"What?"

Then she realized. There were two horses saddled up. Waiting. The call in about the horses had been no more than a trick to get her here.

"Oh, no…"

He pressed harder on her back. "Oh, yes."

Sophie tried to stop walking, but he pushed her forward.

"We're going for a ride. No arguments."

"Lark, I can't. I'm sorry, but I can't," her voice was little more than a whisper.

He reached his arm around her waist then, forcing her to spin. To face him.

"You owe me an hour, Sophie," he said, eyes and voice intense. "One hour to explain yourself, and to let me explain myself to you."

She gulped. Tried to focus on the rise and fall of her chest, of her breathing. "No."

He lifted her chin, placed his fingers beneath it to make her look up.

"Is it that you regret what we did? Was it you wishing we'd never spent the night together?" he asked. "Was that why you left? Or is it something else?"

Sophie shook her head. She didn't want to go there.

Lark smiled at her, his face as soft and tender as when he'd held her that night in his arms. When they'd made love.

"Tell me," he said.

This time he didn't touch her back; instead, he took her hand, and she didn't have the heart to pull away.

Because as much as she didn't want to admit it, feeling his hand in hers felt so right.

It always had.

Lark reached for the quiet mare he'd saddled up for Sophie.

"Give me your leg and I'll help you up."

He almost laughed at the serious expression on her face, but he stopped himself. He'd expected more of a fight, but she was being surprisingly obliging.

"Are you sure?"

He beckoned her forward with his hand. "She's quiet as a lamb and you've got good sturdy boots on. You'll be fine." He paused. "And if I wasn't sure I wouldn't be putting you up there."

She looked pained, as if she wanted to say no but couldn't.

"Fine," she grumbled.

Lark bent, held out his hand. She placed her knee in it.

"Like this, right?" she asked.

"Yep, on the count of three."

He was impressed by how easily she sprang up into the saddle, landing with only the softest of thuds.

Lark passed her the reins. "I can keep a rope attached to you, if you want, but she should happily walk along beside me."

Sophie patted the horse on the neck. "Take it just in case."

He turned around to the horse he'd saddled for himself, placed his foot in the stirrup and mounted.

"Let's go."

They rode in silence, walking, for a while. Lark wanted to give Sophie time to think. To be in the saddle, beside him, so he could try to gauge what to say, what to ask her.

He smiled. He hadn't realized that he'd finally stopped pining for rodeo-riding. Stopped thinking about what could have been. He was happy here, and he was thankful at least to still be in a saddle at all.

"Lark, I know I'm going to sound like a broken record, but I am sorry about walking out on you again. Truly I am."

He looked over at her. Watched her face, saw real pain there.

He would do anything to take that ache away. To be there for her.

If she'd only stop running.

"I need to know why, Sophie. Why you left, why you wouldn't answer my phone calls. Why I had to pretend the horses were in trouble before you'd come back to me."

He could see tears welling in her eyes, but he had to ask her. Had to make her give him the answers he needed to hear.

"Sophie, please. I need to know." He could hear how gruff his own voice was, hoped she could tell how much he needed her to be real with him.

"Lark, I don't know what to say to you."

"Just tell me, Sophie. If you didn't regret what happened between us, tell me what it was."

She looked away. He let her. Didn't ask her anything else. Didn't tell her to look at him.

Lark simply waited.

It could never work between them.

She smiled sadly, her eyes damp.

"What do you want from me, Lark? Why are we here?"

He had thought that much would be obvious.

"We're here because I want to know why you walked out on me." He paused. "Because I thought there was something between us, that we could *be* something. And right now you can't even let me in."

He pulled back on the reins lightly, asking his horse to stop. Sophie's mount stopped when his did. He nudged his horse in the side to make him walk closer, so he was beside Sophie.

Lark placed a hand on her thigh, looked into her eyes. "I know you feel it, too."

A large tear plopped down her cheek. He reached to wipe it away, let his finger linger there.

"You don't want me, Lark. Trust me."

He shook his head. "You're wrong," he said, in a voice no louder than a whisper.

She glanced away then back again. "I can't have children, Lark, and that means we won't ever be right for one another, okay?" She shook her head, as if it might rid her body of the guilt and tears. "I did it because I didn't want what happened to my mother to happen to me, or to my child." She gulped back air. "It was one night, one mistaken night, and that means I'll never have a pretty nursery and a crib for my baby, or a happy little family."

Lark forced his fists to soften. "Who says that has to define you, Sophie? Tell me why you can't be happy without that?"

"I can't deal with what you have here, Lark. Your daughter, the fact you obviously love children…"

He waited for her to finish her sentence. She didn't.

"Do you think it bothers me that you can't have children?"

Her eyes looked as though they'd sprung a leak. Tears started to trickle down her cheeks and onto her nose.

"Don't you?"

He jumped from his horse then, landed heavily on the ground.

"Come here," he ordered, reaching for her and helping her to dismount, too.

She landed beside him, her face distraught.

Lark opened his arms and drew her against him, his lips falling to her head. Then he bent, to look into her eyes, to kiss her cheeks, her nose, her forehead. And then her lips.

"I already have a daughter, Sophie. And even if I didn't, that's not what's important here. It's you I want."

He felt pain. Physical, heart-wrenching pain as she took the time to compose herself.

"I've seen the way you are with her, Lark. Why would you want to be with a woman who can't ever give you any more?"

He sighed. "You're who I care about, not some hypothetical children I *might* want in the future."

"But don't you want more children?"

He took a few steps back, turned away. Looked out over his land.

Too late he realized that it was a mistake. That he shouldn't have paused, should have answered her straightaway, because the look on her face showed a broken woman.

"Sophie…"

She shook her head fiercely. "I need to go, Lark. *Please.*"

"Sophie, I didn't mean…"

He'd mucked that up without even meaning to.

She wouldn't meet his eyes. "Take me back."

Lark bent to take her foot, to lift her back into the saddle. He didn't know what else to do.

"Sophie, come back tomorrow," he said, hand still resting on her leg, wanting her to look at him. "I don't care if you can't have children. I don't care what you've done in your past. I just want to give us a chance."

She turned sad eyes toward him, eyes still filled with tears.

"If you're ready to trust me, come back here tomorrow afternoon." He paused. "I'll be waiting."

He could have said what he wanted to say then and there, but there was someone else he had to talk to first. Someone else whose opinion mattered as much as his own.

Until then, he had to keep his mouth shut.

CHAPTER EIGHTEEN

LARK'S heart started to beat so hard he thought it might explode from his chest. She was here. She'd actually come.

He'd hoped. He'd wished. And at times he'd been sure.

But for the past hour or so, he'd thought he'd been wrong.

"Daddy!" Lucy ran around the corner, cheeks flushed bright red. "She's here."

"I know."

He smiled at his daughter, pleased that she was so excited. He'd risked breaking her little heart this morning by letting her get involved, but he felt strongly enough about Sophie to want to make this right. To want to give them a chance.

Sophie rounded the corner and he couldn't help the smile that hit his face. Surely if she'd come, it meant she felt the same way he did. Or at least he hoped.

"You came," he said, his voice laced with gruff emotion.

She looked as though she'd been crying.

"Sophie?"

He pulled her into him, feeling her reluctance but holding her tight anyway. It only took a second for her to wrap her arms around him, sobbing softly as she pressed against his shoulder. His lips fell to her head, he inhaled her sweet fragrance.

Lark wanted so badly to hold her, but he pushed her back, looked into her eyes, hand on her chin.

"Lark…"

He held up one finger to touch her lips. "Shhh."

She didn't make a noise.

"Sophie, a few weeks ago I would have told you I didn't want a relationship again, ever," he told her, voice low. "I thought I'd never want to be close to a woman again. That I'd never be able to trust someone enough ever to let them in, to let them close to me or to Lucy."

She watched him back, eyes shining with emotion.

"And then I met you," he whispered, reaching for her hands, holding them tight in his. "I met you and you changed my mind, just like that."

Her head moved from side to side. "But…"

Lark shook his head, not letting her interrupt.

"I love children, Sophie, but if being with you means that's not in our future, then I don't care."

He could see in her eyes that maybe, just maybe, she was starting to believe him.

Lark closed his eyes for a moment, before pulling Sophie forward. Pulling her against his chest and tipping her head back, going to kiss her then stopping before their lips met.

"Marry me," he whispered, his voice barely audible.

His heart leaped as Sophie looked back at him, wide-eyed. "What?"

"Marry me," he repeated, his voice stronger, more assertive now. "Marry me, Sophie. Promise me you won't walk out again. *Marry me.* Be my wife and be the stepmom to Lucy I know you'd love to be."

She stepped back, her face frozen in an expression he couldn't fathom.

"No."

He grabbed her hand, pulled her back in toward him.

"No?" he asked.

"Lark, you can't just ask me to marry you! I don't even live here permanently. We don't know enough about one another. We…"

"Sophie, I knew from the moment I met you that you were different. If I wasn't sure, I wouldn't have asked you."

She kept shaking her head, but she didn't resist when he kissed her. Her lips moved against his willingly, even though she'd said no to his question.

"Tell me why you won't say yes?"

Her lips were plump, full from being kissed. She didn't pull away from him, but she still hadn't said yes.

"I have a job in Auckland. I'm not just going to give that up because you want to get married. Even if I would consider moving back here, well, I'm not going to be pressured into anything."

He gave her some breathing space. So that was the problem.

"My mother gave up everything to marry my father, Lark. I'm not prepared to do the same."

"I like that you have a career," he said. "We can be together while you're here, figure something out when you have to go back. I've had the relationship that looked perfect on paper, Sophie. If we have to bend the rules a little to make things work between us, then so be it."

Sophie placed her hand on his chest, moved him back, then stood there. Palm still resting on him.

"What if I did move back here for good? What if I did it because I wanted to, not because you suggested it?"

Sophie's head felt like a spinning top. She couldn't think, could barely breathe.

And all she *could* think was that he'd asked her to marry him.

Lark Anderson, the handsome cowboy she'd liked from the moment she'd met him, had asked her to marry him. And now he was trying to talk her into it.

Her heart beat faster. Pounded.

Could I really become part of this beautiful little family and be a mother to Lark's gorgeous child?

"Have you asked Lucy?" she heard herself ask, not wanting to get her hopes up.

Worry clouded her brain like storm clouds before rain.

She couldn't believe she was even discussing this. She should have done what she was good at, what she'd already done to him before, and run. Run like the wind.

But something was keeping her here. Not allowing her to leave. Stopping her from saying no again.

Because she did want to be with Lark. Couldn't believe that he'd worn his heart on his sleeve and told her how he felt, that he was offering her the chance to be a mother. To be stepmom to his precious girl.

"You might not be able to have children of your own, Sophie, but you'll make an excellent stepmom," he paused. "And a beautiful, wonderful wife."

She could have cried. But she didn't let herself. Wouldn't.

Was he serious? How could he feel that way about her when she'd been so rude? So careless with his heart by walking out on him after the night they'd spent together?

"Marry me, Sophie?" he asked again.

"Why?" Her voice was a whisper, a choke now.

She watched as his Adam's apple bobbed. As he swallowed hard.

"Because I think I love you."

He looked so vulnerable, as though he'd been stripped bare of his soul.

She laughed, just a little. She couldn't help it.

It was then that she let herself admit the truth, too.

"I think I love you, too," she whispered.

And she did. She'd known it for sure after the night they'd spent together out under the stars.

He took her face in both his hands, pressed the softest of kisses to her lips.

"I'm not moving because you want me to," she protested, her lips struggling to move away from his.

Lark gave her one of his lazy grins. "I don't care where we live, or what we do, I just want to be with you. And no more running, okay?"

Sophie giggled. "No more running," she agreed.

"Promise?"

"I promise."

Sophie sighed into Lark's mouth as he kissed her, his lips moving against hers. When he pulled away, she couldn't take her eyes off him.

"For the record, I'd already decided not to renew my contract at the hospital."

He raised an eyebrow, eyes trained on hers. "Yeah?"

"I love what I do, Lark, but I need to figure something else out. It's not the right place for me anymore."

"Whatever you decide, I'll be here for you."

She wrapped her arms around his neck. "I know."

"Did she say yes?"

Sophie jumped back as Lucy's excited, high-pitched voice sounded out behind them. Lark swiftly pulled her back to him, arm woven around her waist.

"What do you say about Sam coming to live with us, too?" Lark asked.

Lucy's eyes lit up. "Sam the puppy?"

He laughed. "Yeah, Sam the puppy."

"Cool!"

Lark dropped a kiss to Sophie's head. She felt her face flush, not sure why she was embarrassed, nervous, about him telling his daughter.

"Are you going to be my stepmom, Sophie?"

She laughed, happier than she'd ever been. "I'd love to be, Lucy. More than you could ever imagine, so long as you'll have me."

"So I'll get a dog *and* a stepmom, right?" she asked her father.

Sophie laughed with Lark as he swung his daughter around before placing her on the ground.

"A stepmom and a dog," he repeated.

Sophie bent down to look Lucy in the eye, wanting to be on her level.

"I know it must be hard being without your mom, but I do know what it feels like, Lucy. And I promise I won't leave you."

She watched Lucy reach for her father's hand. He squeezed it and then reached a hand out to Sophie, to draw her up to her feet.

"What do you say we welcome Sophie to the family with a big old hug?"

Lucy giggled, seeming unsure what to say. Or do.

"Then am I allowed to have my first ride again?"

Sophie and Lark laughed together.

"Yeah, you can ride Cleo again," he told her, before giving her a stern look. "If Doctor Sophie says you can with a cast still on your arm."

Sophie closed her eyes against tears as Lucy wrapped her arms around their waists and hugged them both tightly.

"Of course you can, hon. Of course you can."

Somehow, without knowing why or how she deserved it, Sophie had become part of a family. The kind of family she'd thought she would never have.

Maybe she'd been wrong. Maybe she wasn't being punished for the decisions she'd made, for what she'd done in the past.

Maybe, just maybe, having children of her own hadn't been her destiny.

The family she'd hoped for for so long had been ready-made and waiting for her. And even if it did mean a change of life-style, doing something different, she knew in her heart that she would have made the change anyway.

She wasn't doing it because a man had told her to. She wasn't doing it for someone else, to allow someone else to fulfill their dreams and put hers on the back burner.

Marrying Lark would give her the man of *her* dreams, the daughter and lifestyle of *her* dreams, and allow her to figure out what her own career dream was. When she was ready.

"Happy?" Lark asked her.

She smiled up at him. "More than you could ever imagine," she said.

"Oh, you'd be surprised," he said with a laugh.

Then he kissed her, his lips feathering over hers in a motion that threatened to take her breath away.

Again.

EPILOGUE

SOPHIE arrived home exhausted, but she still managed a smile as she pulled up the driveway. It was funny how the long drive into the property had once filled her stomach with butterflies, made her nervous, when now it made her want to drive faster to walk in the door as quick as she could.

But she didn't even bother going up the steps and putting her key in the door. She knew exactly where to find her family, and it wasn't inside. Not at this time of day and with the sun still shining.

"Lark!" she called.

She needn't have bothered. She saw them before they could have even heard her. Lark was sitting astride his horse, one hand on his knee, the other loosely holding the reins. Lucy was circling around him, fast, hurtling over a series of jumps as he called out instructions and encouragement.

Sophie walked over to them, stopping only to pat a bursting-with-excitement Sam.

"Hey, you," she said, dropping to her knees to give her dog a cuddle. "You been hanging out with your dad all day?"

She grinned at the dog, loving the way his tail wagged so rapidly, tongue lolling out the side of his mouth as he gave her a big canine smile.

"Hey, beautiful."

Sophie rose at Lark's call. He still made her blush, made her skin hot and a tingle form at the base of her spine. Even after a whole year of being with him, looking into her husband's eyes after a long day at work always made her smile.

"You two having fun?"

He nodded his head in Lucy's direction. "Seems she's better than her dad already."

Sophie walked closer to him, hand falling on his leg as she rose on tiptoes to kiss him as he bent.

"Mmm," she murmured.

"How was work?"

"Exhausting, but good at the same time."

It had been a long time since she'd worked in general practice, but the change was good. After fulfilling her contract and working out her last few months until they'd been able to find a replacement surgeon, she'd moved back to open her own practice.

And even though her fingers missed the feel of the scalpel and the environment in the hospital, she was *happy* here with her patients, with her business, with her life.

She looked up at Lark, who had his eyes trained on Lucy again.

But more than being satisfied with her work, she was in love. She'd gone from believing she could never have a family to being welcomed wholeheartedly into one.

She now had a husband *and* a daughter.

And she couldn't have imagined a happier life for herself if she'd tried.

"What do you say we go for a ride?"

"Now?" she asked.

Lark reached down and ran a finger across her cheek.

"Yes, *now,* unless you have something better in mind?"

Sophie laughed at the lazy way he watched her, the faint lines around his eyes and mouth creasing as he tried his hardest not to laugh back at her.

"Oh, there are plenty better things I could imagine doing," she whispered, "but for now a horseback ride will have to do."

Lark winked at her and Sophie slapped him on the thigh.

"Don't tease me, Mrs. Anderson."

"Or what?"

He winked at her. "Just you wait and see."

* * * * *

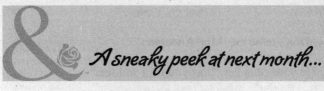

A sneaky peek at next month...

Cherish™

ROMANCE TO MELT THE HEART EVERY TIME

My wish list for next month's titles...

In stores from 18th November 2011:

☐ Firefighter Under the Mistletoe – Melissa McClone

& A Marine for Christmas – Beth Andrews

☐ Unwrapping the Playboy – Marie Ferrarella

& The Playboy's Gift – Teresa Carpenter

☐ Christmas in Cold Creek – RaeAnne Thayne

In stores from 2nd December 2011:

☐ Expecting the Boss's Baby – Christine Rimmer

& Twins Under His Tree – Karen Rose Smith

☐ Snowbound with Her Hero – Rebecca Winters

Available at WHSmith, Tesco, Asda, Eason, Amazon and Apple

Just can't wait?

Visit us Online

You can buy our books online a month before they hit the shops! **www.millsandboon.co.uk**

1111/23

MILLS & BOON® Book Club

2 Free Books!

Get your free books now at
www.millsandboon.co.uk/freebookoffer

Or fill in the form below and post it back to us

THE MILLS & BOON® BOOK CLUB™—HERE'S HOW IT WORKS: Accepting your free books places you under no obligation to buy anything. You may keep the books and return the despatch note marked 'Cancel'. If we do not hear from you, about a month later we'll send you 5 brand-new stories from the Cherish™ series, including two 2-in-1 books priced at £5.30 each, and a single book priced at £3.30. There is no extra charge for post and packaging. You may cancel at any time, otherwise we will send you 5 stories a month which you may purchase or return to us—the choice is yours. *Terms and prices subject to change without notice. Offer valid in UK only. Applicants must be 18 or over. Offer expires 28th February 2012. **For full terms and conditions, please go to www.millsandboon.co.uk/termsandconditions**

Mrs/Miss/Ms/Mr (please circle)
_____

First Name
_____

Surname
_____

Address
_____

_____

_____ Postcode _____

E-mail
_____

Send this completed page to: Mills & Boon Book Club, Free Book Offer, FREEPOST NAT 10298, Richmond, Surrey, TW9 1BR

Find out more at
www.millsandboon.co.uk/freebookoffer

Visit us Online

0611/S1ZEE

Have Your Say

You've just finished your book.
So what did you think?

We'd love to hear your thoughts on our
'Have your say' online panel
www.millsandboon.co.uk/haveyoursay

- Easy to use
- Short questionnaire
- Chance to win Mills & Boon® goodies

Visit us Online

Tell us what you thought of this book now at
www.millsandboon.co.uk/haveyoursay

YOUR_SAY